THE TRUTHS WE MAKE

HOUSE OF POE BOOK I

SAMANTHA JON

CONTENTS

To anyone who's ever felt the thin slice of rejection.
Who's had to choose between what's right for who they want to be
and who they've always been.
Who's never really fit in but wanted to be fiercely loved anyway.
Gold or steel, don't let yourself be handcuffed to a past
that doesn't allow you to reach for your future happiness.
And for Jess, who I was terrified might burn the world down if she wasn't
included.

CONTENT WARNINGS

I went back and forth on if or where I should put trigger or content warnings for this book. Surely, anyone interested in something inspired by the life of Edgar Allan Poe would know there are a lot of dark undertones. But I never want to gatekeep or assume or judge someone who's interested in reading anything, ever.

For those of you who'd like to be surprised, turn the page.

If you'd like to see the content warnings before reading, they are located in the back of this book.

GLASS HOUSE

WEDNESDAY, PRESENT

THE SLEEK, CHARCOAL TOWN car streaks through the rain-splattered roads. Drizzle pelts the window so that all I see are the shadows of a suburb beyond its pane. This neighborhood never felt like home to me, with its French doors and wrap-around parapets. Too rich for the likes of me and mine. Luck, the only reason my mother and I found ourselves a small live-in opportunity on a property that needed a governess. Luck, that the property's family didn't pry too closely into our past and welcomed a single mother into the fold. And luck, even if it was bad luck, that the family just happened to be the Poes.

I loved the Poe boys before we ever moved to the elegant streets of Weston. Even at seven, with my knobby knees and flat brown hair, my little heart understood what it meant to be special. And I knew Oliver and Paxton Poe were the closest I would ever come to it.

They were flames burning hot and wild against a blackened sky, and my soul felt rested being warmed by their opulence. Seeing them weave themselves in and out of my days had given me a hope that, while frayed at the edges, had never felt worn thin.

Until, one day, every thread snapped clean.

"The storm has flooded the main gate, so we'll have to go in through the service entry, Miss Pierce," the driver, Tad, calls back, eyeing me through the rearview.

I press on a polite smile and nod. I should say something. He's been shooting me worried looks ever since he picked me up from the airport, no doubt searching for the girl he knew, waiting for her incessant questions and prodding nature. I should ask about his kids or his brother, Mike, who had surgery on his bad back last year, just as Mother told me to do. I should tell him about my promotion at the library last month, and the guy I've been dating for six, and how my mother recovered from her last cancer scare with only a few more battle wounds this time around. But I can't bring myself to say a single word, my sealed lips a barrier between my life and the memories that threaten to overtake it.

The back gate pieces itself into view in front of us through the rain. The old iron swings in at the last possible second and the deep red brick lining the drive creates a knot in my throat big enough to choke on. I blink and behind my lids, I can see a hundred pictures from my past clamoring for my present.

The leaning tree where my palms were skinned so badly, I was sure they would never heal as Paxton dared me to slide down its trunk face first. Or the short A-frame rooftop that sits off to the left, and the way you can climb onto it from the second-story closet window—if you're brave enough to try. Or the small kitchen entry, a single-paned door with a cracked jam from two stupid kids carving their names a little too hard into it, only getting the O and the E before being swatted away by Mrs. Brunskey.

The kitchen door in question lashes out as we turn into the circular drive as we come to rest beside it. Tad puts the car in park, hurrying out his door to open mine. I beat him to it. My flat black riding boots crunch the rocks beneath them and for five glorious seconds, the rain soaks me before an umbrella can block their chill. The dripping ends of my now nonexistent curls plaster my neck, and my mascara paints tears underneath my eyes and down my cheeks, but it was worth it. I needed the icy reminder that I'm not asleep and this is no dream.

Tad's eyes question me, concern lining his brow. I imagine he sees this house swallowing me whole again, but is at a loss on how to stop it. Instead, he holds out his arm, which I take, and glides me forward under the cover of his umbrella, up to the door. A woman, not much older than me, with a white half-apron tied around her waist, waits for me. Her hair is slicked tightly into a bun, pulling her grey eyes into a headache I recognize. She's newer to the house, the lack of a braid her tell. You can only take the constraint of the rules in this home for so long until you start looking for loopholes. I should know. I've broken more rules the Poes have set than anyone.

My hand brushes against letters, catching on a newer 'P' scratched in just like the others, as I take my first steps inside. I feel Tad's arm slip away as he hesitates. Of course he won't follow me here. The burn of fear at walking into this alone grips my heart, but I let him go, anyway.

"Your bags will be delivered to your room, Miss Pierce. Everyone should be waiting in the Nest when you're ready," Tad says behind me, his pity evident, making my cheeks heat and stain.

"Would you like something to go before you head back into Boston, Tad? You've been at it all morning and I know your blood sugar runs low." The woman's voice is a starting pistol in this silent room.

It spurs me forward without a single glance back. It's rude and unlike the girl I want to be, *that I am now*, so I can only hope I'll be forgiven. Even if I'm not, I don't care. Not enough to stop. Not anymore. Not when I'm back here. None of this will matter by the end of the week when I'm on my flight home.

I walk through the chef's kitchen, under an archway that leads into the hall. Dark ravens and murky grey walls follow me. If I take a right, I'll be on my way to the formal room, christened the Nest, streaked with less pleasant gloom and more sorrow, right where I'm expected. Instead, I go left, climbing the wooden stairs. Instinctively, I skip every third one as I spiral up, knowing the creaks they'll give if I don't, alerting the room above someone is on their way.

Muscle memory is the damnedest thing. I have no reason to hide my entrance. As every letter I've received on every holiday and birthday since I left has said, Dellbrook will always be my home. My room still sits, second door on the left, the same as it always has. My mother is back home in New York, not within shouting distance. But all my nights sneaking in and out of this same staircase overtakes my common sense. My feet rush faster than my nerves want, but twenty-seven-year-old Evangeline Pierce isn't in control anymore. Right here, right now, I am just sixteen-year-old Eve, with a bed that will be checked in ten and a dress caked in mud from the yard.

The stairs end in narrow walls lined with doors, each bearing a name of a story written long ago, by a man steeped in strange. *Eleonora. Black Cat.*

Ligeia. I pass them all, unwilling to get caught up in the nostalgia of my room, or the ones like it, just yet. Pictures of the staff throughout the years smile out at me in black and white, my own childish face catching my eyes every few steps, giving a historic feel to our modern life. I ignore them, too, as best I can, heading instead for the open room at the back.

A living room sits before me under an open rafter arch. The pale wood gleams from a fresh coat of stain that the lights pick up. I can just smell the overwhelming Pine Sol scent. A sectional sits on an antique rug, faded between brown and red, with a purple ink stain a few inches from its center. It cradles itself around an old wooden coffee table, the large screen TV it's facing, out of time from the rest. I avoid it all as I make my way to the glass doors and out onto the iron-wrought deck.

It's slick from the rain that now blows sideways onto my face. I let it whip into my cheeks and hair, closing my eyes against its wrath. I think about crying. Letting it all out here where they cannot see. Where there is no proof. Before I have to say words I don't mean and placate people with stories I'd rather forget. The afternoon is growing dark and I'm running out of time to hide.

Illness could take us at any moment, too, Evangeline. If you've learned anything from the Poes, my darling, let it be that we all must face our demons before it does, my mother said when I told her I didn't want to come, her recovery keeping her at home. I hated myself for the envy I felt at her excuse, my guilt allowing her words to be true. Forcing me to promise to stay for the week and wallow in the pain of my past. And now was as good a time as any to face them.

My hands twist against the metal of the handrail in one last act of resistance, focusing on the burn of its curves in my palm. Hair lashes against my lips as I release it and spin, tendrils sticking to my gloss as I do. I freeze in the doorway, unable to breathe, let alone move another step.

In front of me, in the shadow of the hall, a dark suit leans. His feet are kicked out, his body spreading the width of the hallway. Thick black boots, wildly out of place from his trousers, are tossed casually across each other. His hands are in his pockets, shoulders slumped heavily against the wall as if he's holding the entire weight of history on them. Damp jet-black hair curls around his ears, his eyebrows, his chin. Messy, just like the smirk I know he must be forcing himself to give. His eyes give no quarter, let no secrets slip, and yet I remember everything I need to when he looks at me. Or rather, what I need to forget.

There is one truth that is universally acknowledged. One lesson the past has tried to teach over and over again. Only the cursed fall in love with a Poe.

I know my voice is cracking before I can even break my silence—before his name reaches my lips—which is so perfect, it makes me want to laugh. Or cry.

"Oliver."

ENDLESS SKY

"**E**VANGELINE! YOU'RE WRINKLING IT!" Momma swats my hands away, my fist full of dress falling open, releasing the fabric in waves.

The gravel in front of us makes my feet sweat, the crushed particles of rock weeping from the humidity. It stretches forever, making my hands itch to hike my dress back up, freeing my legs from the fabric that's already clinging from the moisture. Only the fear of sitting back in the car, cooked vinyl digging into skin, has me leaving the hem where it is. Momma's hands brush down the polyester.

"At least it's not so bad, I s'ppose," she sighs. "Now c'mon. The faster we climb this road, and the nicer you seem, the better chance these fine people will let us sit in their air conditioning for a bit."

I want to run up the sloping hill, to the door, at the thought.

We've never had air conditioning before. Not in our car. Nor in our home when we had one. *Home is where your heart settles*, is what Momma always says when she's reminding me not to ask about the small one-bedroom cottage back in Carolina. I never have the courage to tell her it feels like my heart never settles when we're driving winding roads and sleeping in parking lots.

We make it to the back steps, a grey metal door standing between us and the chill I know is in there. Momma grabs my hand, cupping my fingers. She looks down at me from the corner of her eye, her back still straight as a pin, and murmurs, "Remember what I said. Only speak if spoken to. Mind your words. Give only what you must."

She doesn't want me rambling away our secrets or letting something slip through my crooked little teeth. I know because that's exactly what she said on our panicked drive over. I zip my lips with a key that, while invisible, feels heavy. She only closes her eyes, then takes a small step forward to rap her knuckles on the door.

A maid answers, white apron tied around the paunch of her middle, mouth crooked into a frown.

"We don't allow solicitors here," she says, already closing the door on us.

Momma steps forward, a look of panic taking over her face, as she reaches toward the screen door.

"Actually, there was a posting in the paper. You're looking for a governess?" Momma holds up the newspaper in question. Her voice is calmer than her eyes but even those ease, too, when the maid nods her head and opens back up the door. She gestures for us to come in and wait by the door as she escapes down a dark hallway. Only three steps in the cool breeze and the stick of humidity is already disappearing from my cheeks. My lips tip up, despite Momma squeezing my hand too tight.

The house feels ancient, older even than the movies Momma makes me watch sometimes. Out of focus from the rest of us in the 21st century and stuck somewhere before computers and electricity. Time still ticks by, even when the oddities here don't, and all I want is for it is to slow some more. The pools of sweat that were trapped behind my knees have dried, and I want to live without the rub of slick grit as long as I can. Too soon, a man comes to the door. He's squat, a mustache curling at the end of his mouth. He wears black like a starless night. All except for the white gloves that he intertwines in front of him.

"This way, please. Mrs. Poe will see you in the Nest," he drawls like molasses is sticking his tongue to his teeth, sounding an awful lot like home.

Momma pulls at my hand, directing me to walk behind her. The man stops abruptly, causing me to step into Momma's heels. Her shoulders stiffen, but she does not snap as she normally would. I hurry to give her space, while the man's beady eyes watch me.

"Does she need supervision?" he asks.

I know Momma wants to say I do. She worries about the questions I'll ask. Or the things I'll snoop through. She mourns my curiosity, saying it's the worst thing I took from my daddy, and she prays every night that I'll give it back. But her mouth still creases, eyes filled with doubt, as she shakes her head, *no*. The man smiles as if this is the right answer. Or as if he wants us to fail.

"Very well. She can stay here in the kitchen until your interview is complete. Bea will watch for her when she returns."

He turns to leave, Momma hesitating only long enough to give my hand a squeeze, a glare her final warning. *Stay*, it says. And I want to obey. I stand in the kitchen for what feels like forever. The clock ticks on and my heel taps in rhythm. No one comes to check on me. I think I may hear the hum of voices or the creaking of stairs, but neither is loud enough to be sure. The fear of the heat dissipates until I hardly remember consequence at all. I twist my hands in my dress, trying to contain their wandering nature. I can't.

My feet are moving toward the counters before I realize it. The black marble is slick as I run my dirty fingernails from it to the steel of appliances: a sink, a fridge, a dishwasher. I'm about to open a drawer to snoop when I hear the tiniest scuffle of feet. Spinning, I hide my hands behind me to look as if I am innocent.

He stands in the shifting light of the afternoon, black hair wisping down his cheeks like feathers on a wing. He's pale, glowing like the moon, skin striking out from the black of his clothes. Everyone here must be made for darkness. He isn't much older than me, if at all. There isn't a scar or a mark to be found, making mine burn in embarrassment at being seen. He steps toward me, hands held out as if I'm a wild thing in need of calming. I smile.

"Hello," I say softly, cutting him off out of fear of his accusations being heard by the adults. "What's your name?"

He shakes his head, a smirk barely lifting his lips, his trepidation dissolving. His body is so still as he watches me before he answers.

"Do names really matter, you think? Madeline says they do. That they hold the whole of our history in them. That they deserve to be respected." He sighs as if he's lived the full life of an adult instead of the half-measures of a child.

"What do you think?" I hear myself ask, somehow knowing he needs me to.

At that, he smiles fully, voice full of mirth. "I'm still deciding."

As I'm about to ask again for the boy's name, fast steps approach. A taller boy, hair cut short but black as the first, barrels into the space between us. He slams to a stop, hands on his knees as he pants. He swivels his face between us, delighted to find us here. His smile could crack a window with its sharpness as his gaze lands on me. Like a whip, he lashes out, slapping his hand into the chest of the other boy before hightailing it outside.

We look at each other. The boy's smile fades, and he sighs, resigned. He drags his feet to me and the sweat that had dried pools again. When we're face to face, toe to dirty toe, I can see the light green swirl of his eyes, like the tide pools of the coast. He reaches out and swats at my bare arm, leaving the sting of skin on skin. My fingers wrap around the space, appalled.

"Sorry. It's rules of engagement," he shrugs. "You, mystery girl, are it."

I take several seconds of standing there to process what he's said before I slap back at him. He lets me, not moving an inch, just rolling his eyes.

"You can't tag back. You'll have to find Paxton," he says slowly walking backward, toward the hall.

"And what if I can't find him?" I huff.

He shrugs his shoulder before turning his back to me. "Then you've failed, and you'll be it forever."

With that ominous deliverance, he walks off. Alone in the kitchen once more, I look between the hallway and the open door beside me. There are two options: let these boys think they've beaten me, or chase after Paxton and hope Momma doesn't come back too soon. My feet move before I know what I'm doing, the heat and humidity of the outdoors slapping into me like a bucket of warm water. I pump my legs as fast as they go, unsure of where I'm headed, but knowing I can't fall much further behind if I have any chance of catching up.

By the time I find him, he's hanging upside down from the tree we passed on our way up the drive. Its massive branches stretch and sag, as if to defy any rules nature may have for its growth. His arms swing, cheeks bursting red. I run and jump, hoping to slap an exposed hand, before he pulls them across his chest, just out of reach. My eyes squeeze in a curse Momma would ground me into next year for if she heard. He just laughs.

"You couldn't think it would be *that* easy, could you?" He swings himself upright and a part of me wishes he'd overshoot, catapulting himself to the ground with me. He doesn't.

"You can't stay up there all day," I huff, knowing full well I can't stay here all day either. Every second that ticks by brings me closer to Momma finding me gone. The devilish smile he's giving me tells me he knows that.

"In the name of good fair play, I'll give you a way to win, although I'd like it recognized that I could..." He doesn't get to finish.

Momma likes to think there's a lot I got from my daddy, but my tenacity and dislike of being told anything by anyone? That I got from her. And there is no way on this green earth that I'm going to let this stuck-up rich boy beat me. Or worse—let me win. I know I'm in for a whoppin' the second my hands grip the bark. My dress is already snagging, and I can feel the rough textures of the tree daring my skin to break. But just like the boy, I don't let it win.

I race up the footholds I can find and hang on for dear life to the ones I don't. I get to the branch before Paxton remembers to move and now, he's only got two choices: be tagged, or jump. My tongue peeks past my lips in happiness as I crawl on my belly toward him, the justice of exceeding his expectations filling my tummy with butterflies and the dangerous feeling that I can do anything. What I don't expect is that same feeling being reflected at me by Paxton.

Before the yell can leave my mouth, he jumps. I scurry forward, my hands flailing to catch any part of him, but I miss. There's another branch to the side of the one I'm on, large and dipping, bending to the ground like a slide. He grabs onto it, hoisting himself up, then scoots his butt down until his feet plant to the grass. His laughter echoes through the leaves. Anger rises from my toes to the tips of my ears, making the humid day scorching. I expect him to run away again. Instead, he looks up at me, smiling.

"What's your name?" he yells.

I stay silent, unwilling to be friendly through my disappointment and rage. I shuffle backward.

"You can't go that way. It'll take you forever and you'll tear your pretty dress. You'll have to follow what I just did or jump from there. Tell me your name and I'll stay right here so you can tag me when you get here. *I dare you.*"

He's calm, the laughter gone. I don't want to take his offer, but I'm already playing with fire. If I go back to Momma with my dress anymore ruined, she'll send me off to boarding school, away from the only person I have left—her. I can't have that. He's also said the three words that demand I partake. A dare can never be ignored. Still, if my pride needs to be swallowed, I'm at least going to ask for enough to wash it down.

"Fine. I tell you my name and you are it." I think about it for another moment before adding, "AND you have to tell my momma you forced me to play."

He thinks it over, finger dramatically rubbing his chin, before he snaps them together.

"You have a deal!" he says triumphantly.

I sigh, big and exaggerated, like I'm losing a limb instead of a game. Honestly, I think they feel the same.

"MynameisEve." I rush the words together, embarrassed to have said them. "Now, how do I get down?"

He makes no move to help me.

"Eve. That starts with an E?" he asks instead.

My eyes roll. "Yeah. How else would you spell it? Now get me down!"

He shakes his head. "That wasn't part of the deal. You saw me do it. Surely, you can figure it out."

The branch creaks below me as my hand fists around it. That little snake. Just as I'm about to let out every curse word I've ever heard, the other boy walks up beside his brother, somehow looking both irritated and bored.

"What are you doing, Paxton? You know Madeline doesn't like when we torment guests," the boy says.

My nose scrunches at the second mention of Madeline, wondering if she's a nanny or their momma, unused to either possibility.

"Oliver! I was wondering when you would join us. *Eve* was just about to find her way down the slide," Paxton replies.

Oliver looks between Paxton and me for several moments. He must come to some conclusion, a clue I'm still missing, as he steps between me and the branch I'm supposed to jump to. He scowls once at his brother before giving me his attention.

"OK Eve, I'm going to need you to stand on the branch, knees bent, hands still on it for balance. You're not scared of heights, are you?" he asks.

I want to tell him, *maybe*, that I've never tested it before today, and that lying here looking down now is making me queasy. But I can't say it. Not with Paxton still smirking at me. Instead, I shake my head, *no*, and move into the position he's told me to. The branch sways only a little, the motion of it sticking in my throat.

"Now, Eve, this is the scary part. I am going to need you to jump. But not just a little jump, I need you to commit to the jump. Really push. I'm going to stand between the branches so that if you fall, I'll catch you, but to make it over there, you'll need to want it. You can do it."

I nod. Even though I don't know if I can. Their legs are so much longer than mine and these worn-down dress shoes don't want to stay put. But I can't let Paxton win and I can't let the grown-ups see me up here, like this, which they will if someone has to come get me down. I move my feet into what I hope is a better position.

"On my count," Paxton yells.

"ONE!" I take a deep breath, hold it.

"TWO!" I release it, unwilling to let him boss me around, and jump with as much force and power as my body holds.

I'm flying, weightless. My hands and legs flail, but I feel like I could live in the sky for the rest of my life. The light ease of being suspended, given a single focus that doesn't allow me to worry or feel anything more than this. At this moment, I know I want to be a star when I grow up, to hang in the sky for eternity. Maybe I, too, am made for darkness. I want the night to take over this cruel summer day and for the star dusted heavens to hold me in place.

The curved branch comes at me fast and I slam into it, stomach first. All the air rushes out of me and taking a breath is impossible. Still, I hold on. I wrestle the rough surface in my palms, desperate to pull my little body up. By some miracle, I do, my face sloping down, staring at the sweet, sweet grass below.

"Perfect! Now, slide, Eve!" Oliver yells as he comes into view below me, arms stretched out wide.

So, I do. I slide. Without adjusting myself. Without questioning his directions or the possibility of hitting the ground face-first. Without considering the scars the bark tearing up my hands and wrists might leave. All I think about is the boy who didn't question my fearlessness and made me part of the sky, waiting at the bottom to catch me.

LOVELORN SEA

"Eve," Oliver sighs, eyes closing like he's finally found salvation. "You look different." He pauses, slivers of green flashing open. "But not."

He's drunk. I can smell the spicy florals of it from here. I shouldn't be surprised, but the sting of it still makes my skin itch to pull his face into my hands as he breathes whisky onto my cheeks and ask him what's wrong, even if I already know. I let the anger I've been cramming under my broken heart seep out enough to stop me from doing something we both regret.

"You know what I mean," he offers like a truce, hand hanging out between us, his shoulder kissing his tilted chin in a shrug.

He isn't used to this long silence from me. I can see it in the shift of his feet and prodding his words. Of course, I know what he means. I see it in him too—his cells have aged, but every single one of them is still wholly Oliver, even if they have shifted. I would recognize them anywhere, even when they're different. I've spoken Poe since I was seven years old; even if I hadn't, every part of me has always understood. I was hoping time away from here could heal that, but apparently, you cannot cure your nature. You cannot outrun your truths.

Small trails of rain slick down my skin and I focus on not wiping them away instead of on the curve of Oliver's mouth. *I've made a mistake.* I shouldn't be here. I am not ready to be here. But death doesn't bend to our plans. It doesn't make space for words like *ready* and *healed*. It doesn't care that I'm here. The rituals of death are for the living, making me unsure what I'm even doing when these people might as well be dead to me, too.

"You look like you're about to run, Eve." He sings my name like a sad song I can't help but want to hear on repeat. "If you do, can I come with you?"

Eight simple words and yet they sound like a sonnet from his lips. Eight words and I desperately want to say yes. I want to pool into a puddle at his feet and let him drag me into whatever adventure he's seeking next. I want to hear every bit of poetry I know he is dying to spill. Eight simple words and I can almost forget myself. Almost.

But eight words don't erase eight years.

They don't erase the leaving. Or the distance. They don't erase mistakes and stolen kisses and broken promises. All they do is dig the grave deeper, and for once, loving a Poe to death doesn't hold any appeal.

I realize that somehow, I've moved closer to him. Right now, I can see the missed button of his Konkikyou blue dress shirt and the dirt marring the top of his boot. Instead of slowing down or changing direction, I push forward, determined to pass him, and make my way to the Nest. Oliver changes tactics, snaking his pointer and thumb around my wrist in a hold that is both easily broken and impossible to escape. My whole-body freezes in time.

After what feels like an eternity, my eyes dart to his. He's already staring. Waiting. Patient as a poet and just as beautiful as I remember. I can't break my silence, for the words that'll spill out once the dam is broken will be vengeful and wild. Desperate and tattered. Love and war. So, to keep things locked safely away, I quirk my brow, leveling him with my gaze as I do.

He reads my moods like a favorite novel he's picked up once again. I watch the creases in his face dip and shift, fluttering from excitement to worry. The small callous on his middle finger from too many sleepless nights holding a pen drifts across my wrist, causing an involuntary shiver. His eyebrows shift in acknowledgment as he does it one more time, for good measure, before releasing me.

"You can't stay silent all week, Darkness. Eventually, you'll need to speak to me with more than just your looks. Although," he looks me up and down slowly, "I don't mind looking at you either. Maybe we bring back poetry speak?"

He's trying to lure me in with familiarity. His nickname for me honey dripped. Wanting me to give in and play his games while he's too drunk to remember the consequences that'll rain down no matter if we win or lose. Poetry speak was a favorite of both of ours. It drove Paxton mad with his inability to keep up, which I suppose was part of the fun. The draw is too overwhelming, the timing of it too perfect to resist. Thousands of quotes flash through my head before I land on the perfect one.

"There is a stubbornness about me that never can bear to be frightened at the will of others. My courage always rises at every attempt to intimidate me." The words drop into the room like a whisper, pieces falling down long stretches of vowels and rolls of my tongue.

Oliver just tsks softly, stepping closer. "Pride. Prejudice. How fitting. Though Austen is hardly poetry, Eve. Have you lost your edge?"

My face swells, cheeks tinting pink with every minuscule lean closer to me he gives. A light sparks to life in his eyes, a piece of our past igniting the draw our bodies can't help but feel. I let myself reach for him, my fingers pulling down the seam of his jacket, trailing his chest. I struggle not to think about it bare, as my gaze follows down, desperate to not let the past pull me under. Before I reach the crest of his belt, I release him, tilting my chin up, and softening my lips as if for a kiss.

"Anything can become a poem if tasted on the lips of a poet… Isn't that what you said to me?" *The night you made me a poem when you still believed you could be more than just a Poe.* I don't say the last part. I don't need to. We both know what came next. I step back, further into the hall, retreating from this game we're playing. "Besides, for as doom and gloom, as macabre as you can be, you and I both know the lovesick fool beneath your clothes. Austen has just as much space on your poetry shelves as Edgar."

It's a knife I can feel slipping between his ribs, reminding him of the years between us, and no matter how I want to pretend, the feeling of it exhilarates me. A tiny sliver of the pain he's caused me, I can give back. Proof that I'm no longer just the girl he left behind. But when I look up and see the strife slackening his cheeks, my heart squeezes. I work to ignore the guilt, turn my back on his dejection, and walk down the staircase instead.

He follows.

Angry moths tear through my stomach, battering against my ribs and up into my throat. Eight years ago, he would have let me go. Avoided me. Run into his room and scribbled his notes. Eight years ago, he would have made sure his absence was felt and that we both paid the price for my words. And that's why, eight years ago, I never would have said it. It seems we've both changed.

The echo of his steps surrounds me, the creaks and groans filling the space as neither of us bothers to skip them. My foot barely touches the bottom rung before I realize he is towering above me, stopped mid-way down. I glance back for only a second before deciding to leave him behind. If he's changed his mind about following me, that doesn't change the fact that I need to go to the Nest. I've delayed it too long as it is.

"Evangeline, wait," he pleads.

I don't. I keep moving. He has no choice but to clomp down the stairs and follow me if he wants to tell me whatever it is he's now desperate to share. He probably has an apology on the tip of his tongue. Or an accusation he's been clinging to for years. There are a million things he could want to say, and there's not even one I want to hear. Before I can reach the end of the hall, where just beyond I hear the gathering that's waiting for me, he calls out.

"He didn't just die."

His words stop me cold, chills racing up my spine, every hair on my body standing on end. They echo in the emptiness of this house. Of my spine, and my resolve. He comes to a stop right above my shoulder, his breath causing my hair to brush wildly against my neck. He eases it from the hollow of my ear. Goosebumps break across my skins as he leans down to whisper a secret, one I beg him to keep to himself.

"I think someone killed Paxton."

A choke thunders from my lips. He's baiting me. Saying things he thinks will prove some theory he has, some fear he's let grow, by making me react to the news. He must be. *If Paxton was murdered, why wasn't it in the papers? How would Oliver know when everyone else thinks he was sick? Why wouldn't Madeline be turning over every stone to find the killer instead of serving cocktails in the Nest before his funeral?*

At that last thought, I pause. I'm not sure Madeline would demand justice for the oldest son. Not with her chosen namesake still alive and well, wearing the family name better than any before him. *She could be holding the information for a more opportune time, waiting on the precipice of greatness to share it.* Another piece of factoid to add to the history books or stoke the flames of fame when notoriety runs low. No one ever pegged Madeline Poe as mother of the year.

Still, someone would do something, right?

My teeth gnaw at my inner cheek, an anxious ritual that has left me with the taste of copper more than once. Technically, Oliver is doing something. He's here. He's drunk. And he's following behind me, telling me things neither one of us wants to discuss, Paxton, just one of the many walls that have been built between us. Even in my suspicion of his accusation, I cannot write him off. I turn to see him, chest lifting, up and down, in defiance of the stillness.

"Why?" I ask.

He knows I'm asking more than one question: *why me, why now, why us? Why did you leave? Why should I care? Why do you say these things that will only hurt us both?*

He only answers the last.

"Because he told me so." He looks around cautiously, the dim bass of conversation beyond the walls bringing us back to reality. "I can tell you everything after, but I needed you to know."

So, I'd stay. So, I wouldn't dart from this room the second my past caught up to me. So, he can keep me close until he chooses to set me free. The familiar chains of curiosity wrap around me. He knows I would live within these walls until my dying breath, if only to follow the breadcrumbs he's laid down. Disgust and hate coil through me. I hate that I'm so predictable. Hate that he knows it.

"Fine," I spit. "But I am only here for the week. Whether or not you give me answers, I'm gone on Sunday night."

My words are firmer than my actual resolve. I beg them to hold in the depths of Oliver's hesitation over the years that are lost between us. I need him to forget the girl he knew and replace her with my performance now. He nods, passing by me without a single trace of contact, and I'm left unsure if I've won or not.

DEAD NIGHTS

T HE NEST IS AS rich as I left it. Saturated silk fabrics adorn every seat, their black sheen only obstructed by the elaborate gold stitching fitting for any 19th-century style home. Bookcases surround the perimeter while rich mahogany tables are scattered between the couches and chairs, lending the space to set a drink or grab a book for a quick read in their dark corners. Madeline would have you believe it all inherited from Edgar himself, but history tells us the only fortune left by him was his name.

Chances are, everything here was custom made, orchestrated to fit the depiction popularity made of a man long since dead. A weight every member of this family has passed from shoulder to shoulder. No matter the generation of the heir, the expectations of history never changed. Trinkets of the Poe family were handed down to bolster the reputation that came with it, such as royalty did with their crowns. Except these items were meant to drown you in more than just power. They were meant to burrow into your feelings under the guise of unrequited love. Of death. Of *murder*.

Fitting, we would all meet here to say our first intimate goodbyes to the lost son. The performative nature of the whole thing makes my stomach turn. But as much as all of this is the exact opposite of everything Paxton was, I knew he would have loved it. When you've lived with your legacy being passed over you in life, it's only natural to hope it'll finally be given with your goodbyes.

Cocktail tables and candlelit centerpieces cluttered the center of the room, forcing the crowd of mourners to be shoved together. Few small groups stray from the throng to huddle in the shadowed corners, whispering amongst their own. My feet step onto the ornamental red rug that holds the main mingling area of the room, and silence descends and my presence is acknowledged.

"Evangeline. It's so good of you to come," Madeline Poe, in her spiked black heels, tight black dress, and ornate black veil, drifts to me. The matriarch of the family only by her marriage to Alexander, although you would never know she wasn't born for this. She grabs both my cheeks in her delicate hands, kissing each before releasing me.

Her eyes are sharp, flashing from silver to blue, the same as Paxton's. She looks me up and down, her neck and shoulders bending out of sync, a posture that no ordinary woman would care to hold for a moment, let alone a lifetime, as she undoubtedly has. Stick a needle-thin cigarette holder between her fingers and you would believe she was simply posing for a photo with the way her hips push forward and her back curves into a 'C'. I cringe at just the thought of how her bones must wish to snap.

In our closeness, I can see the drag of her lips and the creasing of her skin that mourns even when she cannot. A lover of death who's supposed to smile in the face of her son being taken by its cruelty. She may not openly show it, but she hates this. *Or me seeing her vulnerable.* A slice of sympathy brushes my heart like a paper cut.

"Hi, Madeline. It's good to see you again. I am so sorry it's under these circumstances." I squeeze her hand, which has somehow fallen into mine.

We're both being cold and polite. Even though we're broken. That's what Poe women do. They never have the luxury of falling down rabbit holes or getting lost in temporary insanity. Only the men, with weaker hearts and flowery words, get the privilege. We all have expectations to uphold, and it's what she demands of me. What she always has. And tonight, in this room full of unwanted memories, I'm more than happy to don the mask for her.

She nods her appreciation before guiding me further into the room, displaying me to those within.

"Most of you are well acquainted with our dear Evangeline." She tilts her chin to her husband, Alexander, who winks back at us with a cautious smile.

"But for those of you who are not, please know that she is family. She will be afforded the same grace you bestow on us, as she has also lost a great deal."

My breath catches at the public display. Never has she so openly claimed me, and my guard immediately shoots up. While this is a private gathering, these are not all friends. Apparently, the political balance of wealth asks you to sleep with knives, even at a wake. Madeline has just made a strategic move to let everyone know that I'm in play, an ally in their games, and that Paxton and I shared a great bond. There are many things I mourned when I left this family. This is not one of them.

My belief in Oliver's accusations strengthens. I vow to remember this isn't a normal family with coincidences and meaningless threats. Everything here has a purpose. The hairs on my arms rise in trepidation. Not that this game is unusual, but that this is allowed to happen now and that I'm being herded into the fold is. Oliver's words play over in my head, and I can't help my mind from wandering. *Is the murderer here? What is Madeline hiding? Whose side am I on?* Before I can let my curiosity run any further, I feel Alexander Poe's arms wrap around me.

"I am so glad you decided to come. I was worried after we didn't receive your RSVP…" he whispers down to me.

All I can do is nod my head in acknowledgment. He has the exact opposite effect on me than his wife, making me melt into him. If there is one Poe I have always been sure of, it is Alexander. His hug warms pieces of me that have been numb for years. Pieces I didn't realize needed to be thawed. I beg my tears to hold back under the weight of his familiarity, the only father I've ever considered *good*. The only man who hasn't tried to break me with his love.

"You have grown into a beautiful lady, Evangeline. You must find me once this is done and tell me all about your adventures," he whispers so softly no one else can hear.

He carefully pulls away, and I can breathe again. My eyes stay dry, at least for now, and I cannot send up enough thank-you prayers for their obedience. He sends me off into the crowd with a nod. I take small steps deeper into the Nest, eyes focused on a dim nook in the back corner where I can hide. The room begins to move and swell, an ocean confined only by the wood and paint covering these walls. Hands are thrust into mine, names from those I don't already know thrown without caution or intent to be remembered.

I am adrift until a hand I know as well as my own grasps mine in its warm embrace. The sweet smell of maple dashed with espresso fills my nose, giving me gooseflesh in anticipation, as Oliver bends down to my cheek. He kisses me once, the public greeting I can only imagine every gossip in here has been holding their breath over. I haven't been heard from in years, and they all know the swiftness and secrecy of our falling out can only mean scandal, no matter how Madeline tried to spin it.

Their eyes burn into us from all corners, whispers waiting to dissect every shift my face makes. Not for the first time, I wonder what Oliver and Paxton have told them in my absence. Did they stick to Madeline's lie that I was not accepted into Harvard with the boys? That I could only live on their coattails so long? I school my irritation, my hurt, my memories. Here in this den of snakes, I cannot be angry with the past. Or with Oliver.

I lean into his lips, the shock of them on my skin enough to break me, but I hide away the pieces as we step apart. The slick of my teeth being cooled tells me I must be smiling. Oliver doesn't return it, but no one would expect him to. If the rumors are true, the writer of heartbreak doesn't smile often anymore.

His eyes roam over my face, falling back to lock in with my own. *Is he forgetting the past too? Is this how the world starts anew?* His voice comes out firm, not loud, but commanding all the same. He wants us to be heard.

"The wind drifts you back. I feel complete now that you're here, and yet so many pieces are still missing, with Paxton gone. I wish we had reunited under different stars. Still, death is not the end—for any of us—but especially for Paxton. We will lay his name, and his secrets, bare, so as to mourn him properly."

I can't control myself from glancing around at the faces that are eyeing us, wondering if Oliver's veiled words are a threat to someone in this room or if they're a promise of retribution meant just for us. Oliver and Paxton Poe could not have been more different, but they loved each other fiercely. If Paxton was murdered, Oliver would not rest until he believed justice had been served. *That, or revenge.*

Pinpricks spread through my limbs. Not trusting myself to speak, I find Oliver's hand and tangle my fingers in his, giving a light squeeze. Even though his picture on the jackets of his books I sort at the library does little to me after all these years, being together in the flesh again is electric. His eyes shine brighter, the ghost of a grin threatening to split his drawn features, but doesn't. *It's just for the watchers.*

I tell myself half-truths that even I can't fully believe.

Apparently, Oliver doesn't either. He seizes my change in demeanor, sweeping our hands into the crook of his arm, never loosening his grip.

"Eve," he breathes, a plea I know all too well. "I would like to introduce you to a few new friends."

He says the word friends as if they are thorns and the word new as if it is painful. I nod, allowing him to guide me away from his parents, who are whispering to the Hortons, who live six houses down. We make our way through a few more people whose smiles are razors, as I pass, making me quirk an eyebrow at their display. Whispers and smiles are weaponized, like heartbeats to the guilty. I make sure to show them I have no shame to hide.

When I'm sure I can take no more of being a spectacle, we stop in front of the literary classics bookcase. Their shelves are meticulously cataloged to contain all the '*necessary knowledge of the greats before us*', as Madeline has told me many times before. The worn spine of *Crime and Punishment* nestled almost lovingly against *Othello* catches me, and I can't help but wonder if it's an omen.

One man looking to be around my age stands in a dark grey suit, absorbed by a woman, at least ten years my senior, who is all but whispering a story to him. Her features are sharp, demanding, showing the calculation of someone who's been around the board enough to know how to play the game. Everything about her is obstinate, except for her size, which looks as if a strong wind might break her.

The man beside her, however, is a boulder, average in height, but not in the width of his shoulders or in the trunks he calls legs. The closer I get, the more I realize how mundane he seems. All but his eyes. One, ice blue as an ocean cap. The other, murky brown as the mud in a pond.

When we approach, the conversation stops, both turning to us, faces stiff, as if we are intruding on something private. The man holds out his hand in greeting.

"Oliver," he says as their palms clasp, skin slapping at the force.

"Hey, Issac. Thank you for coming. I wanted to introduce someone very close to both Pax and I." He gestures his head towards me. "This is Evangeline Pierce. She's lived with us since childhood. The final letter in the Poe name."

The old misnomer guts me, but I work to keep my face passive as Issac looks between us, a violent grin lighting his face.

"Eve! It is so nice to meet you. Pax spoke of you often. It's almost as if I already know you."

His hand is outstretched, but Oliver doesn't to let my arm go. I'm unable to pull from him without making a scene, leaving me no choice but to use my left hand. Issac takes it, paying no mind to the awkwardness. Instead of shaking it, as I expect, he leans down and presses a light kiss to its top. Oliver squeezes me tighter.

"Lovely to meet you," he whispers, eyes lingering on mine. A jolt of fear goes through me, intuition telling me to tread carefully. He lets me go and turns to the woman. "No doubt you noticed the resemblance, but in case not, this is my dear cousin, Emily Monroe."

I hadn't noticed the similarities until he'd said something, but now they sit, striking their familiar ties. She doesn't move to greet me, instead she hardly tilts her chin in acknowledgment. Thankfully, Oliver's voice interrupts the silence.

"Issac and my brother were working together on a project to bring the decomposition of dead bodies into becoming living plants to the mainstream. They were working on ways to allow for permitting so families could bury their loved ones on their own properties." Oliver produces a slick smile, one he reserves for the social climbers and press, as he moves tighter to me. "They were also working on several other cost-effective solutions for people to honor their dead without going bankrupt, from what I understand. You see, the Langleys own practically every morgue in this and the surrounding three states."

"Yeah, and there is no one better to go into a morbid, yet necessary, business with than a Poe," Issac says as he claps Oliver on the back.

The boys dig into where the project left off, what patents are left, the contracts that need to be found and filed, and what will happen now with Paxton gone. I have trouble focusing on anything more than the brush of Oliver's fingers at my hip and the way they tap out a rhythm of music I once knew. Somehow the conversation leads into jests of which family is more comfortable with death. As Oliver's fingers still, leaving only their unyielding pressure on my skin, I look for a distraction and let my focus drift to Emily.

I'm startled to find she's already staring at Oliver's hand on me, a sneer pressed on her lips. She doesn't shy from me when our eyes meet. Instead, they roll to show how unsatisfactory I am to her. How little she fears my judgement. Before I can determine their characters, or find potentially deadly flaws, I'm being pulled away, back into the chattering swarths, by Oliver.

We glide to the other side of the room, closest to the door, unaccosted, and huddle close to each other in the corner. Oliver blocks me from the view of the other guests. If anyone were to look over, it would appear we may be up to more than just talking with the way our bodies fill in the space between us as if they were born to it. *Maybe they were, once.* The moths in my stomach rise at the thought.

"Most of the people here could have had something to do with Paxton's death." Oliver's eyes bore into me. "But those two have the most motive and opportunity. The Langley's have gotten themselves into some serious troubles over the years. Their reputation has taken a nasty hit, which is why I assume they wanted to work on such noble pursuits. And they haven't always been friends of the family. Alexander and Madeline despise them. Not to mention that Issac hates Paxton like the jealous fool he is," Oliver whispers.

"What about Emily?" I ask, curious about the woman who smiles with her brutish cousin, and has a clear contempt of me. Oliver, lost in his own thoughts, doesn't seem to hear me. I grab his forearm. "Oliver. What about Emily? You said *both* of them."

His eyes lose their glaze as he comes back to me, his stare transfixed on my hand that's still holding him. "Emily..." he starts, "she's in love with him. *Was* in love. With Paxton."

He struggles to swallow, more to the story than he's giving, almost as if he fears what he must say next.

"Why would she want to kill him, then?" I ask, never seeing the trap.

Oliver looks up at me, resolve hardening his panic. The drunken, romantic fool has fled and in his place is the man I remember leaving behind. My legs twitch in anticipation, begging me to run, my mind catching up too slowly to what my body already knows comes next.

"I thought it would be obvious. Paxton didn't give her the time of day. For all I know, he never really talked to the woman. He gave *no one* a second thought that I'm aware of." His words are cool as his eyes dance around my face, searching, my gut coiling before he delivers the blow we'll both feel.

"Not after you." He flexes and releases his hand, pumping it like a heartbeat, a tick I thought he left behind long ago. "Please, excuse me. There are a few other people I must speak with."

"Oliver. Wait," I whisper, tears of frustration and guilt threatening to fall, no matter how much I demand them to heel, knowing he's too far to hear me anymore.

SPLINTERED WOOD

SPRING, 17 YEARS BEFORE

THE DAY IS GETTING late; the sun shedding pinks and blues across the sky as it makes its final descent. It's the first bit of weather that has felt like spring, making the injustices I faced at school this afternoon even more abhorrent. I should have known better than to have lingered. I have no one to blame but myself.

For the first few months at my new school, I went unnoticed. It took all summer for Madeline to convince Momma to let them pay for private school, telling her it was a necessity of the job. *How would it look to have a young girl growing up in their home without a proper education*, they'd say. It was a perk. A *benefit*. To whom, I wasn't sure. I hadn't wanted to go. Starting over with new people was never something I'd been good at. But once it was decided, I had little choice in the matter. And I stayed quiet enough... until I didn't.

Oliver insisted I bring the raven skull to class for my family project. I didn't have much else to show, since I didn't have anyone but Momma and the Poes. He had told me it would make me friends. That no one would question it and it would confirm I was one of them.

It didn't. It only encouraged the nickname *Eve Reaper*, giggled as I passed. Rumors that I killed and cleaned the skull myself, all in a desperate attempt to be tied to a family that I would never be part of. To be more than I was. They laughed at my questions. Stole my lunch and snacks. Anything to torment me, the killer of birds.

But I couldn't tattle. *Wouldn't.* I knew how to endure, so I did. All of their cruelty was invisible, after all. I had a home where glass didn't break unexpectedly, and love wasn't given in bruises. I had nothing to prove to my stuck up classmates. Not when I had a safe place. It made it easy to tuck away the insults the moment I ran up the drive.

It did, that is, until today.

I knew I needed to get on the bus. Knew I couldn't walk home alone. But I was so damn excited about my science fair project, and it just needed a little more time to be perfect. I couldn't let inspiration slink away from me while I had it. So, I stayed. And so did they.

Now I could feel the bruises along the backs of my legs from being kicked stabbed into by the edge of the tree trunk I was sitting on. The curled branches hiding me from the view of the house. I couldn't go in or someone would ask me what had happened. And I couldn't stay out here much longer, the lingering dusk desperate to sweep me in for the night. The boys could only hold them off so long before someone came looking for me.

A branch rustles and I look to find Oliver stepping through the trees, Paxton hot on his heels. *Time's up.*

"Your mother sent us to find you," Paxton says as he stumbles into Oliver's stopped form. "What are you doing? You make a better door than a window, Ol," he laughs, slapping at him.

But Oliver doesn't move. He's dead set on my left cheek, face scrunched and turning red from the strain. Paxton catches sight of what has his brother in thrall. He runs to my side, fists curled into hammers next to me before he loosens one and brushes it across the forming bruise, gently cupping my cheek.

"What happened, Eve?" he asks, deadly as a secret.

I know I can't tell them the truth, but I can't lie either. Not to them. I sit, unable to look at their waiting faces.

"Who? *Who* did it?" Oliver interrupts, crouching down beside us.

I shake my head and it spins a bit from the pain. Even if they can guess what happened, I'll never tell them names. That would be disastrous for us all, causing problems I'd never be able to break out of. They can't be my guardians when I'm alone at school. They can't feel responsible for the cruelty of others. No, I have to deal with this myself somehow.

"It... it's fine. It's my fault, really. Can we just forget it?" I stutter, hands fiddling wildly.

Oliver stares, hands opening and closing on the grass, and I think I have him. He wants me to tell him everything, but knows that time is needed before I will. Which he'll never get if he pushes now. Paxton doesn't care what I say. He refuses to relinquish his protection, regardless of my heart. He's tugging me up by the hand, our palms rough together. I try not to cry out when my leg bruises drag on the stump.

"No. Your face is turning *purple,* Evangeline. This is unacceptable. Madeline will not stand for this. *Who did it?*" he spits.

Paxton's fury is a sight to behold. A golden boy in every aspect as he stands in the dying sun. He's the top of his class. First string in both football and baseball. He's the king of their all-boys private school, but never a bully to anyone less than a bully. The only place he can't quite live up to expectations is in this house—where none of us can—and I hate that I'm adding to his feeling of helplessness.

Still, he would *never* understand why I'm being picked on. Why anyone wouldn't accept who I am when his family has welcomed me into their home. In this moment, all he knows is one of his own has been hurt, and so he sheds all the polite words and uninhibited laughter. He exchanges it for the darkness the Poes are all known for, except, for him, passion easily shifts to justified rage and back. From a boy to a young man in a blink.

"Paxton, that hurts," I whine, more with needing him to stop than actual pain.

Just as I expected, he lets go. My brain pounds as I try to find the perfect thing to say to keep him from running to Madeline and my momma. We all stand there staring at each other, Paxton fuming, Oliver lost in thought, and me scrambling, desperate for something to make this go away.

"Well," Paxton says, exasperated, "are you coming?"

"No. Paxton, please don't do this! It won't help. All that'll happen is I'll be a tattletale and then I'll have to spend the rest of school knowing they're just waiting for a chance to get back at me," I beg.

Oliver takes me by the shoulder, his slender arms warm from the faded sun. Tears fall down my cheeks from the fear of having to explain, of being put on display and having to live my humiliation all over again. Paxton looks between us, disgusted.

"You can't coddle her out of this, Oli. If we let this be, the next time might be a broken bone or worse. As clever as she is, Eve isn't cruel enough to outsmart a group of delinquent rich kids from ganging up on her. And the school is more than useless unless Alexander or Madeline steps in. We can't just *let* this happen," he puffs out each word, begging his brother to take his side.

Oliver waves him away. "Go, Pax. Talk to them. Eve and I will be in soon."

"Fine," he huffs. "Both of you are acting like babies and I expected better. Madeline will expect better." He turns to me, "Eve, you're a Poe and Poes are *revered* for their *choice* to be outcasts. They're not supposed to be forced into it and ridiculed. What good is this stupid name if not to stop stuff like this from happening? Use it to your advantage."

Paxton says the last in a tone punctuated with antipathy before he stomps off and Oliver and I are left to the porch lights switching on.

"But I'm not. Not really. Not at all," I whisper, self-conscious and ashamed.

"Not what?" Oliver asks, curious.

"Not a Poe. I'm a Pierce. I'm a guest of the Poe house, a worker. I go to a private school at the grace of your family, but not because I earned it. I lucked into all of this, and they know it. I'm not an outcast... I'm a nobody." The tears start fresh at speaking the truth that's haunted me since we moved in.

The boys have never made me feel less, but Momma and the rest of the world never let me forget it. She said we are blessed to not have the burden of wealth and legacy. That I needed to remember what a real family was like, and that it would destroy me if I let it. That all we needed was each other and I shouldn't wish to be part of the Poes, because one day I would want to leave Dellbrook. That one day, being banished to the sidelines wouldn't be enough anymore and I could never be in their spotlight.

They couldn't know our secrets. Of the people we come from, who we run from, or the trouble they would try to bring. Couldn't fathom our past. The fists and screams and the family who would make excuses for both. Family who wanted to trap us in the cycle. They would never understand. And no matter whether the handcuffs were iron or gold, I should never want to be bound to others again. It was better to *know* them than to *be* one of them.

Yet, all I wanted was to be accepted. So when a glimmer of possibility peeked out, I tested it. And when I tried to show that I, too, was a Poe to my classmates, as Oliver had encouraged, they made sure to beat me back to my proper position in life. I could *want* to be a Poe, could want for their attention and affection, but they'd never accept me thinking I *belonged* with them. That I was *equal* to them. I wasn't. And now, more than ever, I understand that. I would never forget it again.

"Eve…" he says.

"No, Oliver. I'm not and that's ok. I need to accept it. I'm just me. It's always going to be just *me*."

He's quiet. The only sounds are my traitorous sniffles. I can't look at him, but I feel his warm hand land on mine.

"Eve, I need to show you something. Come on," he says, pulling me to the kitchen door.

I let him tug me through and up the spiraling stairs to the staff's quarters. He passes the rooms and instead opens the closet that's tucked at the very end of the house. He drags me in and closes the door. My tears are all but dried, my curiosity fierce and overpowering. Oliver slides the tiny closet window up and throws his leg over its ledge. I watch as he disappears to the other side, face barely peeking back at me.

"Are you coming?" he asks, a small grin pulling on his cheeks.

I hurry to follow. My leggings are not much of a barrier between the sill and my bruised skin, but I make it, and realize where we are. I laugh, surprise and thrill pushing the sound out of me. The yard weaves out beneath us, the higher rooflines of the rest of the house rising behind us.

"Don't tell anyone this is here. Even Paxton doesn't know. And I'd like to keep it that way, got it?" His serious face looks at me, waiting for a response and I nod, locking the imaginary key across my lips along with the laughter.

He grabs the imaginary key I've tossed and pats it into his heart before his head bobbles back, satisfied. Reaching down, he grabs a black leather book that's tucked under the eave. He kicks his legs out in front of him to sit, and I follow suit, close enough to read from the light we left on in the closet. The book opens to a page that has large ravens scratched along its edges, a title bolded at the top that says, *What's in a Name?*

"Do you remember the first day you came to Dellbrook?" he asks.

"Of course. How could I forget the first time you two tried to kill me?" I quip.

He doesn't laugh as I want him to, but a small smile still plays at his lips.

"Madeline had just given us another history lesson on our family, and I was so tired of being called a Poe before Oliver. It seems like everything I have ever wanted is only allowed to come second to being called a Poe. *You want to play soccer, Oliver—how will that look to your ancestors? Oh, you're writing again, Oliver—you can thank your great grandfather for that!*" His voice takes on the stern clip of Madeline before he drops back into his Oliver tone.

"It's exhausting. Paxton and I were complaining about it all day. And then you showed up, and it didn't feel so bad anymore." His smile grows larger. "You see, Edgar believed fate wasn't something we had to beg for. That it would show up and just be. Madeline said we're too young to understand that, but I think Paxton and I both understood that day."

He points to the page, and I see the list of our names scratched down the middle.

Paxton.
Oliver.
Evangeline.

Each beginning letter is bolded, showing an acrostic poem. I search the page, finding more jumbles of the words, Madeline and Alexander, both added to change it up.

A Poem
Poem

But the biggest, boldest one was just the three of us:

POE.

"See, Eve. Me and Pax can't be Poes without you. When I showed Madeline, she said that Edgar would have loved it. You cannot be more Poe than that."

His eyes gleam a little as he waits for me to react. I take my time memorizing the page and let Oliver's words sink in. I throw my arms out over Oliver and squeeze, hugging him tightly to me even though it hurts.

"Thank you," I whisper, meaning it.

I don't know if I feel any more like a Poe than I did before this afternoon, but suddenly I don't feel so alone. I may not know where I belong, but as long as Oliver does, it feels like enough.

"You're welcome." He pulls away, cheeks tinting pink as he looks at me. "Now, go to your room and we'll talk to the parents to figure this out before going to Isabel. No doubt Paxton has already gone on the warpath. You'd think he was mayor instead of thirteen with the way he insists on being the boss."

I laugh despite my nerves. I know Paxton has already taken charge. There's little I can do to stop the fallout, but knowing they'll be on my side, the three of us, has me feeling less fragile about the outcome, at least.

We crawl back into the house and Oliver leaves me with a small wave goodbye. I can contain my curiosity for an entire fifteen minutes before I have to know what's going on downstairs.

I sneak down, planting myself in front of the entry to the Nest. Alexander paces feet from me as both boys stand to the side. Madeline sits in a wing-back chair placed in the farthest corner from me, making me lean further in to even see. I slide back out of view, careful not to be seen, and just listen.

"You did right, Paxton, to come to us," Alexander says, pride evident. "We'll have to tell Isabel about what happened with her daughter, but I'd like to have a solution before we worry her."

"I couldn't agree more, dear," Madeline coos. "Those terrible little hooligans need to be punished, and their parents should be warned. We made a promise to Isabel and Eve that she would receive a great education, and she cannot very well do that if they are laying hands on her. It's disgusting."

"We'll go to the school first thing tomorrow and talk to the dean. As well as get a list of her classmates so we can call their parents. It'll be resolved, my love, I promise," Alexander pronounces.

"Father, before you do that, Oliver and I have another idea," Paxton interrupts. "We'd like to be transferred to Kingsley. The school allows for both our grades, and I'll be moving on to high school next year anyway, so now would be the perfect time for a change. We've been talking about how Advent Prep has taken us as far as it can."

The room is silent. I worry my bottom lip with my teeth, shredding my skin with them. Alexander and Madeline will never let them change. The Advent is the top boys' school in the nation and the Poes have been sending their boys there for at least the last four generations, if not longer. There's no way they'd let them flout tradition for me.

"And you both feel strongly about this?" Alexander asks, his voice more serious than I'd ever heard it.

"Yes sir," both Oliver and Paxton say in unison.

"Very well. I have no objections to young men following their hearts. I'll let you decide, Madeline. Whatever you believe is best," Alexander says.

The click of heels echoes through the room and to my ears. I cannot help but move further into the doorway to glimpse what is happening. Madeline stands tall over both boys, her gaze lingering down on them as her shoulders bend back, making her seem a giantess.

"You're sure?" she asks, voice stern and even. "You are giving up a piece of tradition, of your legacy, to go to a school with less education. You are showing your hearts for a girl that may very well resent it. You're both putting yourselves at the mercy of these social circles, and even your presence may not change anything for Eve, other than she'll come to rely on your friendship, even if that friendship is all it'll ever be and isn't guaranteed. Is that the responsibility you are ready to shoulder? The decision you think you are old enough to make?"

Neither boy speaks, a single nod their only reply. She bends down to their eye level, then looks between them, drifting her head from one side to the other. She straightens, a deep sigh leaving her as she does. Her heels click as she sits back down in her chair.

"Fine. You may transfer. But, Paxton, I demand a sacrifice in return. As the oldest son, this is your burden to bear. You'll begin piano again..."

"Madeline," Paxton interrupts, the whine of his age thick in his words. My heart still skips when they call their mother by her name, feeling as if a scolding will happen any moment. And with his tone, I worry the name will only solidify her demand. Even if, to them, it is normal.

I know how long Paxton worked to stop the lessons, how he hated every moment sitting on that bench. But Alexander played. And his father before him. The Poe legacy rested in creative endeavors. In the heart of words and song and art. Their trust, inherited wealth, and wives allowed them to never need to dirty their hands with business or practicalities. In fact, it was frowned upon. After all, Edgar himself had said that the pursuit of beauty was the most intense happiness and if you couldn't find it in one artistic medium, you had to try the next. Making it mandatory that both boys learn this instrument, among other things, no matter that Paxton struggled with it.

My heart squeezes knowing that he'll never make the sacrifice. I would never expect him to. It doesn't mean that the small amount of relief their plan had brought me is dashed and I'm left riddled with anxiety of what my tomorrows look like until graduation.

"What if I take up another extracurricular? I know there is something..." Oliver tries, desperate to make this work, more than likely coming to the same conclusion I have that Paxton will never agree.

"No," Madeline says with no room for barter. "Paxton will do this, or you will all continue as you have, and Evangeline will be dealt with our way. I can understand..."

"I'll do it," Paxton's voice is soft when he interrupts and I'm unsure if I've heard him or if I've just made it up.

"What was that?" Madeline asks.

"I said, I will do it," he says louder, voice turning to steel. "Piano will be reinstated twice a week, and Oliver and I will go to Kingsley with Eve. We will remain at the same school with her until each of our respective graduations."

Paxton is very precise with his bargain, knowing that if he slips even a little, she will take a loophole just to teach him a lesson. Silence follows his demand. Madeline's frown only deepens, proving that Paxton's agreement was not what she wanted, even if she'll never say as much.

"Good. We have a deal. But, boys, a word of advice," she shakes her head, "no, rather a plea from your mother. You may love this girl, both of you, but I beg you to remember to always, always, love each other more. You are family, and in loyalty, blood is the toughest binder. Understood?"

Oliver throws his hand across Paxton's shoulder, a look of pride and awe lighting his face. Paxton turns so they can look at one another. Slowly, his mouth curves into a victorious smile matching Oliver's. As if they alone have just beaten the heavens themselves, and in my hiding spot in the darkened crook of the door, I cannot help but mirror them.

SLEEPING GIANTS

WEDNESDAY, PRESENT

I 'VE ONLY JUST MADE it to the foyer before the same maid who fussed over Tad earlier comes bolting toward me.

"Miss Pierce, you have a phone call," she says, the care she held in her voice for the driver gone.

I stare at her, unable to put together the words so they make sense through all the thoughts I have fighting for my attention in my head.

"I'm sorry? Did you answer my cellphone?" I ask, perplexed and irritated at the thought.

To her credit, she treats me as dumb as I sound without being outright rude. A trait all house staff of the wealthy learn.

"No, Miss Pierce. You have a phone call on the landline. It's your mother. You can take the call in either the office or the kitchen."

She's waiting for me to catch on, hands wringing in front of her, eyes darting toward the kitchen. It's obvious that she wants to get back to more important matters instead of serving the likes of me. The Poes are one of few who still believe in corded landlines, otherwise I'm sure she would have happily brought the phone to me, instead of doing this dance.

"Oh! That makes sense," I say, feeling sheepish. "I'll take it in the office. Thank you."

"I'll get it transferred. Do you need to be seen where to go?" she asks, voice pitched in suspicion.

We both know I don't. I've lived in this house almost as long as the boys. I know every nook and cranny that Dellbrook has tried to hide. But her question isn't about directions, it's about status. It's about whether or not I'm worthy. In the kitchen, she can watch me. She can listen and gossip about all she hears, tell her friends I am just like her after all. I can only imagine how it rips at her pride when I'm treated as a guest instead of as an ex-employee. How it would rip at mine. I pull the thread that connects my spine, snapping it into place, frustrated that no matter where I go, I fit in with no one.

"No. I know the way. You're dismissed," I say, cold.

I hate the way my words reflect every kid that ever bullied me in school. Hate that I can hear Madeline in every vowel. But I don't take them back. I know I'm taking more out on her than I should, but if I'm going to survive a week amongst this crowd, I need to leave my upbringing at the door and take hold of the mask the Poes have provided me.

Her nose flares in enmity, but she does as I've deemed, the scuff of her shoes echoing as she leaves. I release the strings holding my chin up and my shoulders down, breathing easier as each vertebra of my spine sinks back into my well-known bow. Guilt sinks like a stone in my stomach, but I don't have time to succumb.

Oliver's words of Paxton's death, *of his murder,* ring in my ear. I can't help but shift through what I think I know. Mother told me Paxton had died of illness. Natural causes he hid from us all. But Oliver has never been one to cry wolf. Sure, he lengthened and exaggerated his emotions, but always grew them on seeds of truth. He wouldn't be trapping me here unless he believed Paxton was murdered. And if he is asking me for help, this might be the closure our hearts both need to heal. Whether I believe him fully. I try to outrun my thoughts, hurrying my steps to Alexander's small writing closet, jokingly referred to as the office.

I reach a tar-colored bookshelf that could be easily passed by if only you do not know it for the doorway it is. It is an open secret that to get in you must look for a faded blue book amongst the swell of spines, obvious in its purpose, if you only read the title, *The Mysterious Key*. I still smile as I grab it now and the soft mechanical whir of the hinges pop loose. Alexander may not be the most strategic of the Poe family, but he held whimsy close all the same.

Inside is like I never left—a converted walk-in coat closet, bigger than the draped off corner that was my childhood bedroom before we fled here. The dark grey walls close in, leaving only enough space for a few people to gather around the massive desk and chair that sits center stage. Both are filled with papers and notebooks and literature, spilling out past their worn wood. Ink dots every surface like dew, which I know from experience is best to consider still wet.

A tall gold stick stands apart, making it easy for me to find the classic 1919 telephone in the mess. I move to the desk and lean down, resting my weight on my wrist on its paper filled top. I pick the phone up in my hands, flustered by the weight and inconvenience of its use, and hold the earpiece up so I can hear.

"Mother? Can you hear me?" I ask, speaking into the cone which functions as a microphone and always makes me feel silly using it.

Static breaks, and then I can hear her voice. "Evangeline? You sound far away. Don't tell me you're in that hoarder lair Alexander refuses to let be cleaned."

I smile, remembering the pleading my mother had done to have this room tidied or boarded up. She would often complain to me, in the confidence of our rooms, that she worried he'd be lost forever here, suffering the fate of heavy toppled over literature. *What a death that would be.*

"Well, I wouldn't have to be here if you would've just called my cell," I reply.

I set down the transmitter so that my fingers can rustle through pages, allowing me to glance at the newer poems and short stories Alexander has been working on.

"I have been calling your cell! You didn't answer. You haven't called or texted to let me know you made it. I was worried," she guilts.

"Liar. I know that the minute I got out of Tad's car, he called you. And I haven't picked up because I've been busy. I told you I would call you right after my scheduled call with Roger. You know... you know how this house gets," my words catch, trying to mask how I'm feeling with how she expects me to.

There is less prodding that way. I couldn't take another lecture about using this to move on. Or worse, have her worry over Oliver and me.

"Anyway. I made it. I'm fine. We're having drinks at the wake before the funeral tomorrow," I say to appease her.

She pauses, letting the line cut in and out.

"And you're still coming back on Sunday?" she asks.

She's worried she'll lose me to them. If I'm being honest with myself, her fear is well founded. Every second I'm here, I can feel the memories trying to pull me back from my resolve. My curiosity damning my heart to be pulled under once again. I steel my mind against the softening of my soul for this place. *And its people.*

She plows ahead at my silence. "Hold tight your heart, Evangeline Pierce. Love is what traps us all. Remember what happened last time."

Last time I was a child who believed in dark-haired boys that loved fiercely enough to take on the world. And I wasn't that little girl anymore, even if my heart wanted me to be. Coastal green eyes drunk on love and whisky flash into my thoughts, and I wiffle them away in embarrassment for my pride.

Before I'm able to respond, the bookshelf door creaks open and my eyes dart to it. Madeline's striking frame walks in. Her eyes pin me, cascading from the phone in my hand to the notebook I have open in front of me.

"Eve? Are you there? Have I lost you?" my mother asks, voice getting louder.

The ambiguity, I think.

"No, Mother. You haven't. I have to go. I promise I'll call later. Bye," I say, the words tumbling out in a rush.

I don't let her respond. I just hang up the phone and set it back in place, where I found it. There's no coincidence Madeline has sought me out here. She rarely seeks the company of anyone in private without cause, and that she has, makes all the hairs on my body stand on end. *Maybe she knows about Paxton.* I push the thought aside. Even if she did, she wouldn't share her thoughts with someone who was only family adjacent on the matter.

"It really is good to see you," she says, gliding into the room. "I thought, well, your mother led me to believe that getting you here would be an impossibility. I'm glad to see she was wrong, much as I'm sure her ego was wounded. And her nerves, I'm sure. But Paxton wants you here. We all do."

Her words should feel like a balm to my wounds. Instead, they're like cheese in a trap.

"I... regardless of what happened, I couldn't miss this. You all know I consider you family," I say, hoping it's enough of the truth to be sincere but not enough to have overstepped the tenuous truce we seem to have. After all, she declared it first in a room full of people. Reassurance was something Madeline craved, even if she would never ask for it outright.

"I'm so glad you think so, Evangeline."

She pauses her words as well as her body, right next to me. I feel her weighing my worth in a way she's done every day since I was a child. Some days, I would be elated to find that I had passed whatever test she'd internally laid. Most, I swam in the thick, ropey swamp of her disappointment.

"You know, I always wanted a daughter," she continues, still eyeing me. "Not, of course, before my sons, but after. We tried with no luck. And then your mother came to me with you."

She stops just short of calling me *like her own*. She wouldn't dare. Her stature would never steep low enough. All she can allow herself to do is allude to the sentiment. To let me know, in the little slices of love she can spare, that I matter despite her reservations. Even if her love hurts more than heals.

Her fingers lift to flick a piece of hair from my cheek. A few frizzy strands that are out of place after the rain. Her lips tip down, but she doesn't say a thing about her disapproval of it. She doesn't need to. I can see the judgment and how my appearance doesn't suit what she expects me to be, especially in front of her casual acquaintances. I hold back any excuses I may have, knowing my interruption is unwelcome. I can feel the crescendo of her story climbing to its point with furor.

"It's unfortunate, the falling out between you and Oliver." Her words split and slice at the boundaries I've built. We've never talked about this before, and I don't want to now.

Still, she continues, "Truthfully, it should've never gotten that far to begin with. I knew to step in and stop whatever silly crushes were being harbored. I knew they could never be born. Could you imagine the rumors?" she scoffs as she looks at me for agreement. I stand stone still, saying nothing, which she accepts. "Still, I thought my sons would know better. Would do better," she sighs. "But they didn't. It's my fault for not interfering. For that, I am sorry."

My eyes widen at her apology. It's backwards and laced with pity instead of empathy, but that she's given one to me at all makes my heart pound with suspicion.

"As *family*, though, I'd like to ask something of you while you're here..." she says, words innocent enough.

But I know the intent. I know how she twists and curls things into what she wants. I know the crushing grip she can have on the world when she chooses. She rounds the desk to sit at its head, leaning back so her face remains in shadows. A trick to show the power she wields, and even though I know better, my spine still tingles at the haunting of it.

"I'm sure Oliver has already told you of his suspicions. More than likely roped you into some plan. He's never been one to leave well enough alone, as you well know." Her thin fingers spread across a stray paper hesitantly, before her eyes narrow and they sit firmly on the desk again. "But you're smarter than that. I *am* looking into all his concerns. The business dealings with that wretched family and his erratic behavior before his death. But more than that, I am also mourning my *son*. To do that, I cannot have you both playing as if you are William Legrand."

She moves just the slightest bit closer to me, voice inching down in volume with intimacy. "And I think we *both* remember what happened the last time you two got close." She eyes me with pity before righting herself back to full control. "Do we have an understanding?"

Her words sting with their truth, causing my hackles to rise and my brow to bend. She wants me to agree to let this go. She doesn't want us to dig holes in her perfect little morbid story. But most of all, she wants me to stay away from Oliver. My blood wasn't good enough eight years ago, and it has become none less tainted since. She doesn't want whatever tore us apart to be repaired and knows that if I refuse him this, it never could be.

What she doesn't realize, but should, is that her warning only removes the indecisiveness I've had to stay. It hardens my need to defy her. Even if I don't have the fortitude nor the courage to tell her there's no fixing the bond that's been broken between us. That by me helping Oliver, it'll only tear us further apart, Paxton a bomb waiting to go off, solidifying exactly what she wants. I don't tell her that my curiosity, just as my loyalty, would never allow me to leave well enough alone, either.

Still, I have seen no one deny Madeline a request, who didn't come to regret it. So, I don't.

"I understand," I say.

It isn't a lie or a promise. Just an acknowledgement of her words. But she doesn't see it that way, and that is all that matters in this room. She stands from the chair and comes to pass next to me, turning only when we're shoulder to shoulder.

"Good," she says. "I would suggest you get settled. You're looking a bit tired, and we have a long week ahead."

She exits the room, leaving the bookshelf open, a cue that I should follow. Still, I linger, listening to the quiet cadence of her heels disappearing. I turn to look at the last line on a page scrawled in Oliver's handwriting at the front of the desk, struck by his ability to be present, even in the smallest moments, with his words.

And like a sliver, she burrows
deeper into the abyss
where not even a razors edge
can get her out.

TIDAL SUNSETS

Wednesday, Present

M Y ROOM, ALTHOUGH FAINT, still smells of bergamot and vanilla from the expensive candle I received on my 18th birthday. It sits on the ledge of the thin window opposite my bed, its dark golden glass catching the globed overhead light. My eyes trace the ravens etched around its edges, watching them take flight around its lip. The sound of chimes from my bag sitting next to me on the floor startles me out of my trance. *How long have I been standing here,* I wonder before shuffling through it to find my phone, expecting the voice on the other end.

"Hey, babe," Roger husks out. I can just picture him, wiping his sweaty ash blonde hair from his face as he walks down the street to his second-story apartment from our gym. Even musky with red tipped cheeks, he somehow manages to be handsome. "How are you holding up?"

The look on Oliver's face before I ran out of the Nest flashes through me, making me wish, not for the first time, that I'd never come. Roger doesn't know about Oliver and Paxton, at least not about why I left. Of course, he knows who they are and that I'm here, but one look at his patient face, willing and waiting to listen, I couldn't get into the details of our fallout when I'm still trying to forget it myself.

I'm sure he assumes, even if most of his assumptions are wrong, but he'd never stop me from coming back. No matter how much my silence wounds him. We bonded over our broken families, and he holds that, even broken, they are ours. And whether or not I liked it, this house was my home. These people, mine. I owed them my presence, if not my loyalty.

"I miss my library," I say, and he laughs, as I intend him to.

"I know, baby. If you were anyone else, I'd be worried that the first thing you miss is work." His voice is throaty and playful before turning serious. "But you'll be home soon. And I promise we can spend the first date night back curled up in the stacks. You just got to get through this. Say your goodbyes and I'll be right here to be your first hello."

Roger understands little of my past, only ever learning curated parts I've provided, but he has always known my restlessness and still has given me the space to move. From the first day we met, when I had just started at the university library as a part-time assistant in school, he understood when I needed sunlight and fresh air, or old books and dark corners. When I wanted to be pushed or left alone. His patience is the only thing that allowed me to hope.

Somehow, he knew parts of me I thought were too sporadic and misunderstood. It's why when he asked me out three years into our friendship, I said yes. It felt like the first open and honest relationship of my life, with no axes over our heads. Even when I couldn't spill my secrets. Even if I was still broken and lost, unsure if I still believed in love.

"I don't deserve you," I whisper, fresh tears filling my voice.

"Hey, now. It's ok. Shhh. You deserve everything good in the world, E. Everything. I wish I could be there right now. I can tell how hard this is on you..."

His words of endearment and promises go on, but my attention shifts to the quiet knock, and then my door handle rustling open. I'm quick to wipe clean any sign of homesickness or self-degradation before Oliver walks in, mouth open, ready to say something. My mind scrambles as I cut Roger off.

"Ro, someone just knocked. I've got to go. I'm sorry," my words come out rushed and quiet. Roger ignores it all.

"Ok, babe. I love you," he says at a normal volume, but I can feel the words vibrating through the room.

"Ditto," I croak before I hang up and stare at Oliver's narrowed brows.

He casually moves to the other side of the room, picking up the candle, whose wick is already burned low. I sense the judgments he's harboring. The questions he will never ask because he knows I'll never answer. If only he knew how desperate I once was to give him every secret I held. Maybe there wouldn't be six feet and a lifetime of regret between us. His whole chest expands as his eyes drift closed, head tilting in memory.

"I do admire your ability to seem like you're giving something when in reality you're giving nothing away at all," he says. "It's almost comforting that you're keeping yourself locked away, not allowing just anyone into your heart. I was worried for a moment on the stairs that you'd become an entirely different person."

His eyes still haven't opened, the candle of ravens still butted up against his nose.

I scoff. "I have changed, Oliver. I'll have you know I'm in a very happy, and healthy, relationship with an amazing man who knows what I want."

In this room, this moment, where every piece of me is so entangled with the Poes, every word I speak sounds like a lie that rips at my demand for honesty.

A soft laugh escapes him. "And yet, you cannot say *I love you* back. Or at all, I'd bet. Everyone always thinks they know what you want, Eve. That has never been your issue." He removes the candle from his face to look out the window before continuing. "Your issue is that no one has ever got you to go after what you *really* need. It's that strong spirit and hard head. Always running in the wrong directions simply out of defiance."

Fury rises to my cheeks, blood running hotter and thicker than a tropical storm on the Carolina coast. Tiny fists of determination beat a rhythm through me, telling me to prove him wrong. Begging me to make a point, call Roger back, and say words I'm not sure I mean just to see Oliver's face fall.

"Enough, Oliver. I can't play these games with you anymore tonight. I'm exhausted and, frankly, missing more than just my bed. So, whatever you've come here to say, just say it, or leave," I spit.

He hums, stuck between digging in and letting go. Thankfully, he relents.

"Paxton, somehow, knew what was going to happen. Or at the very least, he feared it. *Prepared* for it. He left me a letter," he reveals.

He's staring at me now, eyes clear, sobering up from his earlier binge.

"Can I see it?" I ask, desperate to start this morbid game, even against my better judgment, knowing I've got a ticket home on Sunday I'm determined not to miss.

"In time. I've hidden the physical copy of it for now. I don't want someone to find it, especially with all these people moving in and out of the house for the next few days. I'm positive there's more I'm not seeing and although I've made copies, well, you know Paxton."

His shoulders shrug and I nod in understanding. For all Paxton's schemes, there could be a thousand clues hidden in the seams of the paper besides his words... or none at all. He was a devil at puzzles, bettering both of us individually. But when Oliver and I worked together, there was little we didn't figure out. Which is exactly why Oliver is here. He *needs* me, regardless of the conflict he may feel. My best guess is that he has already tried to solve this without me.

"How long have you had it?" I ask. A sheepish grin slides into place, and I know I'm right.

"Two weeks. It came in the mail just after he passed," he says.

Bastard. I know I have no right to be angry, but that doesn't stop the heat of it from pooling in my gut, the thick rope of being left out refusing to be cut down by the years we've been apart. He didn't even try to include me until it was obvious he may never solve it on his own. My arrival was simply too much of an opportunity to surpass. *If I had not come, would he have reached out to me at all?*

Fragmented pieces of my heart I had long ago thought dead, fracture some more. No matter how many times I tell myself I am lucky for not being part of this family, for not being *his,* whenever I am confronted with proof, it is like pouring gasoline on a raging fire. It makes me want to cry and scream. Still, my expression does not waver. At least I have learned to control that much. I splay my fingers along the comforter on my bed, then let my legs cross to sit on top of it.

"If you've had it so long, why are you telling me? You must be close to solving it—you've got your top suspects and everything. Surely, you can gather all you need to give to the police and solve the mystery. Madeline will be over the moon to see her Oliver live and breathe the Poe name so wholly *while* bringing justice to your brother. You must be dying with delight at the prospect," I taunt.

The pettiness that sits in my chest like a toddler is beneath the woman I want to be. Still, I can't stop the delight when his brows furrow, and I know he's moments away from admitting he needs me. I may be here out of obligation, defiance, and curiosity, but I would be lying if I didn't say I was also staying to inflict a little pain, especially now that I knew I could. I hide the excitement when he shakes his head, putting the candle down to cross his arms, biceps flexing as he does. A deep sigh escapes him.

"You damn well know that isn't the case," he growls. "Paxton made it so I wouldn't... that I *couldn't* do it alone. I can't even start it without you. Pax made sure I needed you, Eve. Even though it pains us both."

The flirting, sad, drunk Oliver from earlier is gone. A mirage in the wake of our inevitable first meeting after everything. In his stead, the serious, hurt one stands. The one with accusatory eyes. The one who is desperate and hates himself for it. My elation cools with the change in the tide of my fickle heart.

"Oliver, enough. You know I'm going to help." I let the excitement of the puzzle override my pain. Already slipping into old habits I swore to myself I'd outgrown. "What has he done? What's the first clue?" I ask, eager to know the lengths his brother has gone. I hate the way my voice betrays how readily I am to agree. How much I want to chase after the Poe boys, even now. Even when I know better. Thankfully, he sets *us* aside, too.

"The very top of the page is a bible verse. Genesis 2:18, *'Then the Lord God said, It is not good for the man to be alone; I will make him a helper suitable for him.'* Obviously, that's you, Eve. I tried to read through the rest, and I have some notes, but it was clear he put pieces in the clues I'll never be able to find. And it looks like they're all connected in order. He wants us to go on a scavenger hunt. The places are in all the clues in the letters, but each place holds a clue of its own."

He metes out the information in vague bits, unwilling to tip his hand to me in full. *A reassurance I won't try to leave him behind like he's done to me.* Apparently, Oliver doesn't trust me to stay anymore. *Good,* I think. Still, the facts he's laid out still feel flimsy, forcing me to pick at them.

"How did he put together something so elaborate? If he was scared for his life, sure of what was to come, why didn't he tell anyone? Why make it a game?" I ask, astounded.

Not that the letter is unbelievable, just its timing is too perfect. The plan, well laid. But, also, that was the Poes. Dramatic. Elaborate. Meticulous. Especially Pax. He was ready for anything. If Paxton died of natural causes, as

Madeline says, Oliver doesn't believe it. Which means there's enough reason to doubt. Still, I needed to know why.

"Well... I... Maybe he did. Maybe he was interrupted while putting this together for other reasons and changed tactics. Maybe he knew it was coming and didn't know what else to do. We'll never know now, so we just need to focus on what he left behind. On what he can tell us now," Oliver says. Frustration lances through me.

"What do you mean, *maybe he did?* Wouldn't you know? If you want my help, you need to tell me everything," I say. He sighs again, clearly at a loss, knowing the rest of the story must be told regardless of its end.

"Paxton and I haven't spoken outside of pleasantries and the occasional run-in for years. He did start calling more in the last few months, but I ignored them." He hangs his head in shame. "I've been busy with my publishing schedule and tours. And after everything that happened when you left, it just hasn't been the same. I... there was no way to know that *this* was what he needed to talk about." My heart thrums seeing the canyon Oliver's guilt has laid in him.

His eyes dart to me and away, throat bobbing with his hard swallow. "He started leaving a ton of voicemails and texts, each getting more urgent and secretive. I thought he was playing games. He kept talking about business partners, and old friends, and *reunions.* None of it made sense. None of it sounded urgent." He looks away, a small heat lighting up his throat. "The last message he left on my voicemail was that he wanted to talk about *you.*" Oliver's fingers turn the face of his watch, causing a soft *click* to sound over and over as he speaks.

"So, naturally, you ignored it. Makes sense," I snark. I should be sympathetic. *This is your fault too, Eve.* Instead, I let out a little more of my anger.

He stills, staring daggers at me.

"Don't be snide as if I'm the only one acting childish. You *left home.* And you've come back here, pretending to be different when I know the color of your soul, Evangeline Pierce. Paxton could've come to me. He knew where I was, and he knew I would've helped him anyway I could. We've all taken the coward's way out, and everyone was doing just fine with it until now. You don't get to look down on me. Not anymore," he says, his eyes wild and filling with unshed tears.

Guilt claws at the vault of memories I've locked away, begging to be let loose to ravage me. *Not anymore.* His words ring through me. *As if I ever did,*

I answer him inside my head, too gutless to open that wound today. I brick it up behind all the other things I cannot say. Instead, I look away, unable to face my past head on, and change the subject. My sorrow gives way to spite.

"What does Madeline say?" I ask, giving us both a new scapegoat to throw our fury at.

I'm unwilling to let him know Madeline warned me against this very thing not so many moments ago. That she, more than anything else, has welded me to stay. I want to know if Oliver has asked his mother what she thinks, and that it wasn't Madeline poking her nose in where it doesn't belong. Oliver just laughs, a humorless sound coming from his lips.

"He died of natural causes, Oliver. You've got to let it go, darling. Paxton wouldn't want this," his voice is raised in pitch, the long elegance of each vowel being over pronounced as he mimics Madeline. "As if she ever knew what Paxton wanted. But if it doesn't have to do with Alexander's legacy, or the good of the family name, it isn't worth talking about. You know how she is," he finishes, resigned to the truth.

I nod my head in understanding. Madeline had come by her information honestly, it seems. And just as she had warned me off, so too had she warned Oliver. I knew before she had even sought me out she was a long shot, but occasionally, she would surprise me and do something completely out of character. I was hoping this would be one of those times. It wasn't. And if there's no Madeline, then there's no Alexander, so I don't bother asking about their father.

"Okay, well, I'm here. So, you've completed clue one. Now what?" I ask.

Oliver shakes his head. "That wasn't a clue, just a preemptive direction. The first clue can only be solved by you. I'll send you the photo so you can have some time if you need it."

Oliver pulls his phone from his pocket while he's talking to me. I hear the chimes of my text notifications go off, and I'm startled that he has my number. Before the anger of it can take hold, I click into the zoomed-in picture he's sent, seeing only the first stanza in the shot.

> *Do you remember...*
> *There was a cracked pier we were walking on, the entire scene pulled from some forgotten place where no one cares to repair, or clean, or change.*

I breathe in, the air hissing through my teeth. I can feel Oliver's eyes watching, a sharp excitement expanding the walls of the room like a balloon at my recognition. I ignore it, needing to consume the whole thing before jumping to conclusions. Oliver beats me to it, reading the next part aloud for both of us.

> *"Remember, you turned to me, and you asked something the Poes have danced around for decades but needed you to say so plainly. Do you remember? I do."*

Oliver stops. The text runs out. A blank space where my words should be. Of course, Oliver never would have been able to solve this. He wasn't there. A private moment meant just for Paxton and me. Tears fill my eyes, but I leave them unshed. This is a happy memory, all things considered. One I'd buried to hide from the pain of that same day. One of many that reminded me how much I loved Paxton Poe.

I look into Oliver's waiting eyes. He doesn't know what happens next, and it's slicing him open with the need to know and the distinct desire not to. Ripping off scabs can either heal you or kill you. I have the sinking feeling that looking for Paxton's killer will tell us which.

My throat bobs as I try to clear it and croak out the question we both need to hear. "I remember, Pax," I whisper, eyes drifting down. "I had asked, *'Do you think the dying see beauty in the decay? Do you think they see it in themselves?'*"

Oliver's eyebrows dance on his face, trying to put the pieces together. I'm sure he wants to know when and where this happened. He doesn't understand the weight of the memory of the day Paxton and I took that walk. Instead of asking, he continues reading a piece of the letter that he didn't send me.

"That's right, Eve. And then you quietly built them a memorial of broken things; shells, rocks, wood... anything to honor the dying. Go there. Find the beauty."

SINKING CASTLES

I NEVER THOUGHT MY first-time flying would be without my mother. Or in first class. Or to see a family I have always been told I was better off without.

Oliver hums beside me, more vibrations than noise, with one headphone dangling down. The other blasts out the sounds of an action movie that bleeds into the cabin. The seats are couch-like if the couch were more crunchy than soft. Paxton had referred to this as their 'budget airline' in a way that made me feel his disdain, but to me, it was enough to hold my legs in place as we stumbled and bumped into the sky. All I needed was to land safely, which could be where the 'budget' detail might become a problem.

I had known, once, what it was like to fly with the Poe boys beside me. But that was from a tree to six feet down. This... this is something else. Like swimming underwater if the ocean was a metal tin. I don't like how my stomach tosses and the air feels thick with use. But in only a few hours we'll be landing, and I know I'll feel sick for other reasons.

This whole trip was a mistake.

I should never have let Oliver talk me into this. He insisted I come, while he pushed the letter from my grandmother into my chest. He warned of regret. Of closure. Of cutting my roots needlessly as he convinced me to lie to

Momma about me joining the boys at their Spring Break camp. *"We're lucky I even found out about this in time. Madeline and Isabel were sloppy throwing this one out. But you've got us now, Eve. They can't hurt you anymore, no matter what your mother says."* If only he knew the stories as I did.

She didn't talk about my father much. Didn't call his parents grand. It was always *them* and *him*. When she mentioned them, she made sure I knew there was a reason we left. With a stern look and a fixed finger pointing at me, she would say, *if you ever give them a chance to take you back, it'll be the end of any possibility of happiness.* She didn't need to say more. I remembered what the absence of hope felt like before we moved into Dellbrook. Any family left in South Carolina was effectively transformed into my personal boogie men.

And now the Poe boys were pushing me to open the closet door at midnight.

I hunker into my seat and take a cue from Oliver, stuffing my own headphones into my ears and the splitter to zone out for the rest of the flight. It works only partially, the faces of my family taking over the different characters of the movie causing me to play out blurry childhood memories as *'Die Hard'.*

Every gunshot is another pound of a fist; on walls, through plates and countertops. There are no heroes in my story, only screams and the breaking of things we couldn't afford to replace. When the tears softened and the quiet made the room feel stuffed with cotton, the manipulations would start. The *I'm sorrys* and *I love yous.* The excuses from grandparents and friends when they were unlucky enough to bear witness; *you know how he gets.* From Momma, when she was the only one around. Hugs and kisses and promises that it's *just a fight,* and *that's what adults do,* to soothe my fiery face and shaking hands. And then everything would be fine until the next drinking binge came on.

I think Momma would've lived that way forever if his knuckles would've never purpled my skin. But they did. And in the morning, before Grandma and Papa could talk her out of it, we fled. Momma never looked back, even when I struggled against her, afraid to leave behind everyone I'd ever known. Even when I told her it was only an accident. When I vowed I'd be good and that Papa promised he'd take me to the park and how I couldn't remember a bad thing about the only people I'd ever loved.

Sometimes, even now, the memories slip out of focus and I'm not sure it was ever as terrible as I remember, even as I watch it all unfold again on the screen. It feels like a detached drama that I'm trying hard to weigh down for the sake of the story. Lost in my own world of weighing the truth of my past, I hardly notice that we've landed until Paxton's hand rests on my shoulder, startling me from my seat. He notices my disorientation and helps to guide me off the plane.

The boys continue to take charge, leading us away from the gate into the belly of the airport and out into the lingering swell of storm filled air and the waiting town car. I'm not sure why their confidence and capability surprise me. Why I expected them to hesitate and morph into *less* when we landed. Turning into teenagers who feared what came next. Who were insecure and fragile, just like me.

The Poe boys had never been stripped of their ponderosity and it was silly of me to believe that, in the light of day, South Carolina would scare them. They'd already faced their past, embraced it even, and to them this was just my initiation. I've never wanted to be accepted less if it means doing this, and yet it is all I want.

"Are you hungry?" Paxton asks.

His voice slips in between my fear, unbidden. Both sets of boys' eyes stare, worry etched into teenage faces, making them look much older than they should. I know the paralyzing angst I've been inching towards has roared to the surface where none of us can ignore it much longer, but I'm determined to hold on to my charade just a little tighter. *Almost home.* My head shakes.

"I think we should just get on with it. I'm assuming you know where we're going?" I ask.

My voice sounds weird in my own ears. As if I've said these words too many times and they've lost all meaning. If they can hear it too, they ignore it, plowing ahead as we've all silently agreed to do. The car slips through streets once known, into a neighborhood reminiscent but unfamiliar.

A tall house with a peeling white-columned front porch stands in front of us while a black pointy fence pins us in. Black storm shutters flank row after row of windows, mocking the sky to give 'em all it's got. I rally myself to the memory of their shield being battered by the weapon of a windy night. Creeping tendrils of acid crawl up my stomach and into my throat as thoughts slog through my head. *They could've helped us. Could've provided us shelter. Could've made him change. We could've been a family.* Still, my feet move forward, keeping pace with Oliver's shoulders as he moves ahead of me to the door. They lift and fall with each step, the only star in the night sky guiding me.

A whiff of a woman answers, her dishwater hair tidied into a bun. Her sharp nose and thin lips are striking. If it wasn't for the light hazel eyes bordering on amber, the same as my father, and my own, I would share little with the woman in front of me. As little as we look alike, our demeanor is even less. The way she tilts her chin upwards, eyes downcast, at all of us standing in her front door, you'd think we were solicitors begging for money instead of her being the one to summon us here.

"Hi, Diane. Is he here?" I ask, trying to keep my words even instead of laced with all the frustration of a child ripped from her home has.

She scoffs away the name and my tone. "*Diane.* As if you don't share at least a quarter of my DNA... or however it works. We're *family,* and as little as that may mean to your momma, and your new 'city boys' here, it still means something." She stands to the side, gesturing us in. "You can call me grandma and yes, of course, he's here. Where else would a dying man be other than his deathbed, hmm?"

She asks it so casually, each word a slap. A push. A gut punch. *This is what they do, Eve,* my mother's voice reminds me, *they bind you with blood then break you with derision that sounds an awful lot like truth.* The boys don't hesitate as they walk by me, nodding each to Diane, unaffected by the web she's weaving. Or unaware of it. Then their attention is on me and my frozen frame in the doorway. My hands shake and legs wobble as I step inside.

I force myself to still, to find Oliver's eyes instead of the memories I don't have in the pictures and walls of this house. I don't want to dig too deep into what could have been. What they tried to take by force when they threatened to take me from Momma. What never was. I didn't come here to see how they live, or ask about vacations, or decorations, or why they never cared before it was too late. I came because it is Papa's last wish, and who am I to oppose a dying man's wish?

I steady my nerves, and without looking away from Oliver ask, "Can I see him, please?"

Her sigh rocks the room, but she brushes past me anyway, resigned to my behavior. "This way, child," she murmurs.

I look away to see her climbing a pale grey staircase with a worn wooden rail that sits to the side of the foyer. Quickly, I follow her, my first step cushioned by plush carpet. The impracticality of it blinds my eyes, as it is completely white. I float in the idea that this isn't real, moving only in time, and yet, still turning into the first door on the landing and arriving next to a bed where a large man lies.

The light blue sheets are pulled up to his chin, his white-socked feet dangling just off the edge. His breathing is uneven—I count the inhale, as shallow as it is, and wait, panic gripping, before finally he releases the air and starts again. All I can think is, *I've never been this close to death.* His eyes open like a doll, rolling from open to closed a few times before finally settling on me.

"Evangeline, my darling granddaughter," he wheezes.

His hand scoots jaggedly across to me and instinctively I rush to grab it. Regardless of if I really know this man, I cannot let him die reaching for comfort when all I can remember right now is the boom of his laugh and the smell of pine when he rubbed his stubble against my cheeks making me squeal in delight.

"Hi, Papa. I'm here. I made it."

It's all I can think of to say. A sweet sigh escapes him, his body deflating with the effort, and I think it's enough. Before I'm able to say anymore, heavy boots pound up the stairs. Oliver steps to the side of me, Paxton in front, as if to take on whatever danger is coming. But as I hear the calling of *hello, anyone home,* I know they cannot save me from this.

I turn to the door just as a lanky form slides in. Faded brown hair that is bleeding color from its tips hangs in tangles down his chin, hiding his face before his shaking hands can push it back into the crook of his ear. He smiles at me. Then he catches the matching dark heads of the boys at my side and frowns.

"Hey, Ma. You throw a party you forget to tell me about?" he asks as he saunters over to Diane, bending down to kiss her cheek.

Diane shakes her head, swatting him away from her. "You're here, aren't ya? Besides, I didn't know there would be... *so many* people in attendance today. I had just asked for the girl, but you know Isabel. Always wanting to make things difficult."

She eyes Paxton and Oliver. Anger boils up on behalf of my momma. *If only they knew she didn't want me anywhere near here. That the boys who are such difficulties are the only reason I came.* I stay silent, even as my fingers curl into my palms. The man takes me in, turning to acknowledge us.

"Hey, there, Puddin'. Who you got here?" he asks, voice pitched just past friendly.

He moves to lean down to kiss me on the cheek, but I take a step back, releasing my grandfather's hand and stumbling into Oliver. His hands immediately wrap around my waist, firm enough to keep me steady. The whole room stills, the kind of moment just before violence breaks. The kind of moment I've witnessed this man in more times than I care to count. Even if I was young, my body remembers. I step away from Oliver to break the wave before it can build.

"Hey, Dad," I say as I reach to embrace him in a sideways hug—a peace offering he begrudgingly accepts as his arm wraps around my shoulders.

He's lean, his dense, ropey muscles coiled tightly under my arm. I can smell the thickness of tobacco and sweat on his clothes, and the stale whiff of alcohol seeping from his pores. I school my face from showing the fear it brings being next to him. *He doesn't mean it. It was an accident.* The words roll through my mind like a mantra, one I've listened to my whole life. I suck in a breath, then motion to both Oliver and Paxton.

"This is Paxton and Oliver. They're friends. Friends who were kind enough to front the bill on this trip down memory lane." I say, eyes pleading that the boys understand this isn't important to me, only to *him.*

If there is anything my father understands, Momma always said it's taking advantage of every opportunity that is offered. I need him to see the boys as his ally. I wouldn't tell him that Momma worked for the family, or that I was practically one of them. He didn't need to know the details. All he needs is enough to cool his hot temper and remind him that I am his daughter, even if inside I'm not sure if that's true anymore.

His eyes relax as he turns to them, arm still draped around me. "Well, hey boys. Thanks for bringing Puddin' home. Been awhile." His voice is easy, almost kind in a way that would make anyone want to agree. "We can take it from here though, if you've got other places to be."

"Actually, we're right where we need to be," Paxton responds, not falling into the lull. I want to both kiss and slap him for his bravery. Before my dad can light up again, Diane saves us all.

"As a matter of fact, all of you need to be somewhere else. Robert needs his rest. Why don't y'all go down to the diner and catch up for a bit before you come back to visit some more? Then we can talk about what your plans are from there. I do want to discuss the possibility of you coming home for good, young lady," Diane says, eyebrows bent down into the bridge of her nose.

The only response I have would make her reconsider letting me leave this house, so I just nod my head. There's no way I'm coming back here to live. So, even though I think I might puke if I try to eat, anything is better than this bedroom where a dying man lies and where Diane wants to discuss my future. Where I'm sandwiched between my old life and new. I need air. I need space. *I need home.* If only I knew what that meant.

We funnel out, Diane rounding to our side of the room, ushering us as we go. She chatters about local odds and ends to my dad as she does and I can't help but wonder, *how much has he changed?* A small hope flickers to life as we file down the stairs, past framed photos and affordable artwork. By the time we get outside, I've almost forgotten the smell of too warmed skin and stale cologne.

Ahead of us on the walk, Dad lets out a long, low whistle at the site of our waiting chauffeur and SUV. "When you go big, Puddin', you really GO BIG," he calls back to me.

My cheeks tint in embarrassment. I pray the Poe boys won't believe their money is the only quality drawing me in. Fear grips me at the thought that after this trip, they may never look at me the same. It's that fear that has me barking out, *Dad,* a little more sternly than I should. He just shrugs and opens the back door himself, sliding in.

"I'm sorry," I whisper to the boys.

They say nothing as they follow me into the car. We take the five-minute trip to 'Bill's Place'. What you would think would be a cozy little hometown burger joint is just a bar with only enough food items on the menu to keep people drinking. Inside is dark and hazy, remnants of decades spent having cigarettes smoked every minute they were open. The lights are sickly yellow, a few tittering on orange, showing a long bar top, a few cocktail tables with tall chairs, and three pool tables. The floor sticks to my sneakers with every step, ear-splitting squeaks calling out from the feet of our group as we enter.

A few people mill around, but none of them are eating. Dad leads us to an open table and sits, patting the space next to him for me. A bottle dyed blonde with roots halfway down her face sways up, dropping menus for the three of us before turning her smile to my dad.

"Heya, Bobby. You want the usual, doll?" Her mouth smacks on the gum she's probably had in her mouth all day.

Dad smiles back and nods. "Yes, please, Maggie! Make it a double, though. With the rugrats in town, I need a little pick me up."

Her hips swing her back behind the bar and silence descends as we all pretend to look over the options of cheeseburger, nachos, and chicken strips. By the time she comes back, hands full with multiple beers and a dark liquid sloshing in a shot glass she places in front of my dad, I am ready to leave. My skin crawls seeing the familiarity my dad has with this place and the number of drinks he's starting with. My gut is telling me this is a bad idea, but I have little choice at this point but to push on. The shot is up and gone, Dad wiping his mouth, when the silence can hold no longer.

"So, *Bobby*, what do you do?" Paxton asks, only a fraction of his distaste for this place and the people in it clear.

Still, my dad is not amused.

"It's Mr. Hillton to you, son. You may have money, but I am still your elder. Some might say your better, so I'll ask the questions."

"Did you say Hilton? Like the hotels?" Oliver asks, intrigued.

My hand goes up to rub my forehead that burns in my palm.

"I did. But it's two L's son, so don't be too interested. We were the Hilltons, of peanut fame, before our good for nothing great granddaddy sold it off. If he would've just held on, we would have been millionaires! Can you imagine?"

"I cannot," Oliver says, as he stares down the glasses Dad has already emptied.

"What about you two? What do you do? Or better yet, your family? And how do you know my daughter?" he asks with rapid fire interest.

Oliver and Paxton look at each other before looking at me. I want to tell them not to answer, that I still don't think it's safe that he knows. My momma's voice warns me to be careful. Don't let any secrets slip. *You don't want to leave again, do you, Eve?* She asks in my head. Before I can say anything, before they can answer, a call from across the room saves us.

"BOBBY! We got a bet over here to settle!" A man yells.

"Just hold your horses, Ray! I'm coming." He gets up and looks at me as if remembering something important. "C'mon, girl! It's time to learn how to *really* hustle a man out of his money." He grabs my arm and pulls me toward the pool table and who I can only assume is Ray, his questions already forgotten.

Ray is a short, balding man, whose belly protrudes well beyond the tips of his feet. For as portly as he is, he's agile as he throws a pool stick at my dad. Dad's hands are slick, and his eyes are glassy, so it's no surprise when it clatters to the floor.

"RAY! IF YOU THROW ONE MORE POOL STICK, YOU'RE BUY-ING A NEW ONE!" Maggie, the lip-smacking server, calls out.

Ray just chuckles, shaking his head in good humor.

"What you got there? You giving a last-ditch effort on your debts, Bob? Begging the gods for mercy with a good luck charm? C'mere, let me see her," Ray says, laughing.

My dad swings me around to face Ray.

"This here is my daughter, Evie O," he says, smiling proudly.

"Actually, Dad, it's just Eve now," I say, trying to quell the overwhelming need to run from this room and never be around any of these people again.

His face falls, and I want to apologize. For correcting him. For changing. But then Ray whistles, just like Dad did when he saw the car, and I see the dirty parts reflected by him in this place, and I don't feel as sorry.

"Anyway, she came around to see her pop. She's thinking about coming back home, too. Bout time if you ask me. She came here all by herself, all grown up and such. Hell, she'll fit right in around here, too."

My dad looks around the bar and I can just picture his plans for me—I'm waitressing here, serving him and his friends drinks, and when I get paid, he'll take every dollar to spend right back here. It'll be a cycle I'll never break. Momma's words come to me: *once they have you, they'll never let go. Love is a trap, my darling.*

"Well, where in the heck she been hiding? Is she of age? Maybe I'll just take her as payment for your debts. What do you say, sweetheart? You want to go on a date with big daddy Ray and help out yer old man? I promise to treat you real nice," he says, voice slick and sloppy.

Ray gets close to me, his thick fingers grabbing at my chin, the other reaching around to my backside. I can smell the stale taste of beer with every word he breathes into my face. He's laughing, but there's a gleam in his eye telling me this isn't a joke. Not to him. Not if we allow it. My hand flails behind me, begging my father to remove this man's hands from me, but I only catch air. Panic swells as he steps closer, lips pursed and eyes closing as he takes the silence as permission. I'm frozen in disbelief, unsure if the laugh I hear behind me is really my dad.

A hand breaks in, shoving Ray and his putrid lips away. His fingers snap the skin on my chin as he's forced from me. Another hand tugs on my arm, my shoulders, pulling me through the dingy room. Voices, loud and angry, screaming about *that's my property* and *who the fuck do you think you are*? Footsteps following. Hand holding as we run. Then it's just the air conditioning of a town car and the streets speeding away.

The boys are talking to themselves and on their cellphones. Conversations about plane tickets and what we should do now, where we should go, do we tell Isabel. It's all in the background. My dad's laugh and dirty fingers touching my face and backside are all I can focus on. My body feels like his grime has seeped into it, and now I'm tainted by it. My mind runs down the fear of possibility. *What if I'd come alone?* It's too much to think about. My momma was right. She knew. I should have listened. And now, Paxton and Oliver know what I come from. Who I am. They'll never look at me the same. My arms coil around me, trying to hide away the parts I wish they'd never seen.

"Eve? Eve! Did you hear me? Diane just called your cell. Your grandfather passed away..." Oliver is holding my hand, thumb rubbing comforting circles in my palm, his voice drifting from urgent whispers to terrified pleas.

Everything is numb and then the sound of his raspy breath, the feel of his papery thin fingers wrapped around mine, comes into focus and I know I should do *something*. I can't let them see that I've lost all respectability, even if I think I have.

"We have to go back," I say.

I know it makes little sense to stay here, but Diane can't rely on my dad. He's drunk and selfish and furious. *You know what he's like.* And I do. With no one else to blame, will he take it out on his grieving mother? Shouldn't I at least warn her? The boys have already begun disowning me, so I need to hold tight to what I have left. And right now, she's all alone in that house, with only the body of her husband, and no family around to ease the pain. My southern manners demand that I do what's right, even if it's stupid. Even when I'm terrified of what my dad might do if he finds me there.

"Absolutely not," Oliver scoffs, dropping my hand in disbelief. The air between my fingers sears with loneliness. The next cut in a thousand that proves I don't belong. He's angrier than I've ever heard him. On the cusp of destruction and malevolence. And it's all directed at me.

"But…" I start, eager to remind him of why we came, that he insisted I not cut roots needlessly. But there is no give in his fury.

"Evangeline. I said no. I mean no. That family is trash, and we are not dealing with it for one more second. We're going home and we'll forget this place exists."

"Oliver, that's my family," I hesitate on the word, but I can't stop the heartbreaking truth of it. *I can never forget.* That's when I realize he doesn't mean me.

Regardless of the romance the thought of being a Poe brings, I was born a Pierce. A Hillton. Their blood runs through my veins and as ashamed of that as I am, I have to face it, especially now that they know. Now that they can't accept me after this tiny glimpse into my history. It isn't their fault—a family built on legacy can hardly help but weigh my own.

"That's… *That's* your family? You can't be serious, Eve! Your *family* just watched as you were practically molested in the middle of a bar. You want to trust they'll behave just because someone has died? There's no beauty in something this fucked up." He's spitting fire and I can barely make out the words, sure I've misheard a few of them. Paxton must see the pot boiling over.

"Driver, can you pull over here?" Paxton says, breaking up Oliver's tirade.

The driver does as he's asked, finding a turn-out in the road that leads onto what seems to be a forgotten beach. I jump from the car, unable to look at Oliver's judgment any longer. Paxton is hot on my heels before popping his head back in and holding his brother back from following. I turn to see, unable to stop my curiosity.

"Just… give us a minute, Oli. Please," I hear him say, voice muffled by the wind.

"But…" Oliver tries to protest, scooting toward the open door.

"I know. Just a minute," Paxton reasons, face stern, as he shoves Oliver back in the door.

"Fine. But, Pax, you and me? *We're family.*" Oliver says.

I can barely make out the words, but it's enough. Another bolt of guilt and shame goes through me. It hurts to know that Oliver needs to remind Paxton that I'm an outsider. Like I'll corrupt him, too. I walk away from them both, down toward the water. Paxton jogs to catch up, taking up my hand in his.

Tears threaten my eyes as I take in everything that's around us. The jagged bottles of glass and salty rot of shell carcasses the seagulls have unearthed. There's a broken pier that I head for, its wooden spikes standing jagged in the water. My sneaker kicks at a dirty flop of seaweed, revealing the old bones of a mostly eaten fish.

"This place is so broken," I burble. "Fitting, isn't it? Just like my family. Just like *me.*"

My papa is the first I've known to die. First, who's held my hand mere moments before taking his final breath. And I don't even have the right to mourn him, let alone the support. I only remember his pleas for Momma to forgive Daddy. His empty assertions that he would fix it. The truth that I didn't know him at all hits me and I can only hope that he found peace somewhere between when we left and his last exhale. That I wasn't a complete disappointment, even if I feel like it now.

Paxton sighs, "Oli just…" but I don't let him explain it all away. It doesn't matter. I won't be the one to break up his family, too. Instead, I change the subject back to the turmoil that's engulfing me.

"Do you think the dying see beauty in the decay? Do you think they see it in themselves?" I ask, frightened but resigned.

I know the answer, but I want to hear him say it. Want to have him tell me I'm worthy in some way, even when I feel broken. Even when the last pieces of my family tree have been poisoned. Because if he can't, that means I really am a ship at sea with no hope of returning.

WATERY GRAVES

Thursday, Present

Tʜᴇ ꜰᴜɴᴇʀᴀʟ ᴡᴇɴᴛ ᴏꜰꜰ as expected.

Exuberant in its darkness: the black hardwood coffin, with ash grey silk lining, that sat empty in the room. The seven holy men, meant to usher in Paxton to whatever lie in front of him now, garbed in enough wealth to drown them.

Luxurious in its morbidity: the blood-red roses, thorns climbing up every stem, that lined the entire grave and crypt. The ravens that were released, blessed to look over the memory of this generation's first son.

Everything Poe is thought to be. Everything Madeline knew the papers, the followers, the history books, would want to see.

And very little of what Paxton actually was.

The only comfort I found was knowing he'd love finally being accepted by this show. He always worried that they might just disown him altogether when he died. Death was talked about so often in Dellbrook, I never stopped to realize that maybe he knew it'd play out like this. As if some prophet met him in his dreams to devolve secrets better left to gods than men.

Oliver hands me a damp cloth from across the bench seat of the town car we're in, breaking me from exploring the existential-ness of it all. I stare at him, forgetting where I am. He smiles softly, knowing me well enough to pick up the signs of my slip from the moment. He points to his cheeks.

"For the ashes," he whispers, even though it's just us in this car.

Right. With no body to show, Madeline made do by providing a bowl of ashes that each guest could dip their fingers into and spread across their cheeks - a physical show that we all carry Paxton with us. They weren't his actual ashes. I was told those were safely in the family crypt, away from prying hands, but I wasn't sure everyone knew that from the way Annie Murphy pinched some into the locket she was wearing around her neck.

The procession we are in would continue to the house, where we would all commence the necessary glad-handing and posing that the funeral didn't offer the time nor space for until the next event. *Soon enough, it'll be all over,* I remind myself again. The dying ache I've felt since leaving New York has been growing since arriving back in the suburbs, and unsurprisingly, only amplified when in the presence of Oliver. I was beyond ready to shove it back out of sight.

I look over to find him lost in the drab landscape that's flying by his window. His teeth are clenched together, allowing for his jaw muscle to tick from the strain. He isn't quite drunk, but definitely not sober by the glassiness in his eyes. I wonder how long he's been ping-ponging between the two. As far as I knew, he had sworn off the stuff. At least, that was before. Everything had been different then. If I gave his imperfections no other quarter, surely I could for this. For now. His brother just died and if I didn't fear what alcohol would loosen up in me in his presence, I might be drunk, too.

But I wasn't the one predisposed to ruin my life over a drink and had used it as a coping mechanism one too many times as proof of my problem. I should leave it alone but can't. A heart can only change so much.

"How long have you gone?" I ask, not breaking my stare as his head bobs with each dip and turn of the road.

"Mmmm," he hums, pointedly lost without me.

"I said, how long have you gone? Between drinks? Has it only been like this since Pax died?"

He finally turns to me, cheek and jaw still bouncing up and down with tension. I don't look away. I don't move a muscle as I wait. The silence stretches on.

"Too long," he sighs, then turns back to look to the road. "And yet, not long enough."

Riddles and puzzles. Poems and words. He thinks the incompleteness of his answer is sufficient. It isn't, but I won't press like he wants me to. I won't let him know I see through the layers. That I know he wants me to see the jagged darkness he hides from everyone else. I won't build on our past. Instead, I, too, look out my window. Only to realize we're no longer following the procession.

"Where are we going?" I hiss at Oliver.

It's just like him to kidnap me from a funeral. I just pray this isn't some misguided romantic gesture. Or a reckoning for our mistakes.

"South Carolina. You made it clear I only have you until Sunday. Madeline will understand," he says.

Right. I should know better than to think he would give up or move on when the clue led us to another state. Plane tickets are not obstacles in his world. My skin prickles at the destination, knowing my own roots lay near, but I don't let it overshadow that the boys have history there, too.

"You could have told me. I didn't pack for a trip, Oliver. I didn't even bring my cell phone with me. You know, since I assumed we would be only going a couple of blocks." The sour notes in my tone are sharp and they ping against the roof of the car and back with a snap that makes me feel like my mother.

The Eve of before would have loved this. *Did* love this. Sporadic adventures and unimaginable surprises, big or small. The thrill of chasing the unknown. Of feeling needed to solve life's mysteries. I soaked them up. Cooed at their perfection like each was born of brilliance. Now though, my thoughts slip to forgotten clothes and other baggage, both internal and ex, that I need to hold tightly if I'm going to make it through this spine-splintering anxiety that has been eating at me. Oliver looks cross, his derision at this change in me, plain.

"You have a bag in the car. I had Melissa pack anything she thought necessary for a two-day trip from your room. And you can live without your phone for a day or two. Unless you need to call Isabel, or that boyfriend of yours. Ro, was it?" He looks at me as if he's asking a genuine question. I feel myself welling up with both frustration and embarrassment that he's still swimming in my familiar waters. He shrugs his shoulders. "Well, I've got mine if you need one for anything." He looks away, sighs, then can hold the disappointed silence on his face no more. "Did New York wipe your memory, or have you always had this little faith in me?"

His words are a kaleidoscope, causing my mind to shatter into a million different retorts:

If only New York could erase you.

You've known where I've been this whole time? Did you visit? Did you know I was sleeping in the bed of another man?

I had faith in you — I worshiped you until I didn't. You know when everything changed, why are you asking me this?

Melissa touched my things? Did she find the black lace lingerie that I had no business buying, let alone packing, but couldn't stop myself, even knowing Roger was staying behind? Did she tell you about it?

I can't say any of them. My vocals have been robbed by the tightness in my chest and if God had any mercy, he would bless me with a distraction so that Oliver would stop looking at the spot that's coincidentally stinging in my eyes. But his benevolence doesn't extend to wretches like me, and the car stays silent and waiting.

Fine. If he wants to dig graves and dance around the edges as if he will never fall in, I am not above pushing him. My breath pulls in, the perfect Edgar quote welling onto my lips, like an arrow being drawn to shoot. My aim is perfect and with any luck, it'll teach him to stop poking at open wounds.

"Years of love have been forgot, in the hatred of a minute," I say aloud.

Every syllable that floats to his ears brings his frown further down, his brows more drawn, and the pain more evident than before. The last word doesn't even get said before he's back to staring out the window.

We ride along in silence.

Oliver hasn't said a word to me since the car ride. We've taken a flight, ordered a car, and driven to the ocean. Nevertheless, he pretends I no longer exist. We sit in a dusty little pullout on the side of a roadway, staring out onto a neglected beach. Broken pillars and scatters of plastic can just be seen below the pathway's tiny hill. Oliver's hands still cling to the wheel, and I cannot take another second of his cold shoulder.

"I can't believe you remembered this place," I say, words hushed and leaking from the dam of a heart that's too full.

His frown deepens, hands squeezing against the leather of the rental. I know it isn't the best thing for me to say, given our last conversation, but that doesn't mean it isn't true. I'm over being held to a secret standard we never talk about. If we can't heal our past, maybe careless words can make it not hurt so much.

"You'll have to lead from here," he sighs out. "I don't exactly know the rest of the way."

My chest falls. Constricts. Remembers. I open my door and hear Oliver doing the same. Taking slow steps, I lead him into the sand and the graves of rotting tide pools and broken driftwood. I don't know why I start explaining. Maybe it's the smell of salt slipping off the waves, or the sudden chill of déjà vu, but once I start, I find myself unable to stop.

"You know, the moment I'd stepped onto this beach with Paxton was the first time I'd felt like you didn't see me. That I knew, the second I got back in that car, you'd never see me as one of you again." I suck in my breath, a cold shot of ocean stinging my throat. "Not that I ever *felt* like family. Or that other people weren't sure to rub my nose in mud while reminding me I wasn't." The memories feel like pebbles in my veins, my heart desperate to pump them out.

"But before then, I could see you and just know that *you* believed I belonged. And most days, that was enough. Then... then, you got so mad about my actual blood, and you saw what I had every chance of becoming, and I knew you'd never look at me the same. I hated it," I finish, head turning away from Oliver.

My tears well and I can't pull them back anymore as a few slip down to my chin. We're almost to the site from so long ago when I catch on to something new. Large driftwood is driven down into the ocean bed, unable to be unearthed by whoever might try. The hope that Paxton was here, and the overwhelming flood of sadness knowing this was where the first crack in my heart happened, the one that would start its weakening until the moment it was bound to break, was all too much.

Oliver sees the driftwood too, and my somber words get swept away. Eagerness blossoms across his face alongside the sadness that matches mine. I know him well enough to know he wants to say something, but we've both been struggling to find words that don't stab like knives. We're bound to bleed out from good intentions if we don't just stop. I'm grateful this time, that he clenches his fists and moves ahead, allowing me to release the memory without a fight. It's the best thing he can do for me now.

Thankfully, we reach the spot, giving us both a needed distraction. What looked like a pile of garbage from a distance is a memorial, not so unlike the one from many years ago. And yet, so much larger, and more beautiful. A mountain of shells cascades down from the driftwood, smashed pieces filling in as if the mosaic patterns of it all were intentional. Blushes of internal pinks, ivory ridges, and the rare flare of orange and browns burst from the sand like a jagged bed of nails, waiting for an unsuspecting foot.

Oliver and I stand and stare for a moment, taking in the glory of it. The time and precision. The very feeling that Paxton is still here with us. I turn to Oliver.

"Now what?" I ask, a shy smile playing on my lips, tears only a sticky remnant on my skin. For a minute he smiles back—we're just kids again solving a puzzle Pax left for us to find him. *If you can solve it, I'll play with you,* he'd say.

Then reality slaps him, the roll of it rippling across Oliver's face reminding us both that it isn't Paxton we're looking for this time.

He shrugs. "I guess we dig around? Was there anything you did that might be a clue of what we should do next?"

I shake my head. "Not that I remember. The driver came looking for us shortly after it was built, telling us you were *insisting* we leave."

"OK, well, look around. There's got to be another clue."

He doesn't wait for me to respond before he's crouching down, examining the shells. I leave him to it, instead moving toward the large driftwood stuck into the ground. My hand drifts down each piece, the smooth wood barely scratching my palms as I do.

The pieces are cut jagged, but well-worn from a lifetime of rough waters. Just like me. *Just like us.* Like the swell in a storm, I know it's here I could drown. And that means Paxton knew it too. I eye every piece, fingers and nails digging into crevices and marks, looking, until one finger breaks free.

"Eve, look at this. It looks like he left a bunch of mementos in waterproof bags. There are photos of us. And ticket stubs. And... god, I don't even know what all this is. Is that? *He stole my favorite pen. I knew it!* Can you believe it? Eve? Eve!"

I don't stop to look. In fact, I barely hear him knowing that the items must be a distraction. Instead, I focus on the thin sheet of wood that has been glued onto the larger piece with great care. I claw at it frantically to give, determined to know what's underneath. With every flake that comes off, I see spatterings of dark paint and then finally the last of it is gone. I stand before the message. What would look like graffiti to anyone else is to us art.

"Oliver..." I whisper.

He stands, the shells and memories that are zipped in plastic bags, clattering around him as he does. He comes to a halt next to me. Then he laughs as if madness has taken hold and he's excited for the ride.

"I'll go get the shovels," he says before trekking back to the rental for us to exhume the next piece of Paxton's puzzle.

The pads of my fingers glide over the words, each one burning as I do.

`Even in the grave, all is not lost.`

VACANT HEARTS

Thursday, Present

T HE HOTEL IS RUNDOWN but clean. At least it was, before I kicked off muddy shoes and sopping wet leggings onto its shabby carpet. I flop onto the queen bed that smells of stale smoke and lavender detergent, wishing this trip could just be over.

When we reached the bottom of the photos and broken things, all we found was an address, a time, and the word *shame* scrawled along a piece of driftwood. Oliver had looked it up on his phone, his lips turning into a thin line of disapproval. The only thing he'd tell me was that it was a bar, and to be ready in an hour. I fought, demanding to be told *now* where we were going, but he wouldn't relent, shutting his own room door in my face. I stormed in here, determined to find my own way, somehow. That was thirty minutes ago.

All I've come up with is that I need to shower and then run until all of this is so far behind me, I can mistake it for the mirage that it is—nothing more than my hopes masked as a bad dream. But without another plan, there was no doubt Oliver would be here on time, beating down the door, and unwilling to take any excuse to be late. I'd seen him suffer worse than my complaints for a lot less.

So, I stayed, underwear exposed, t-shirt riding up, leaving very little of me covered—a live wire of skin and emotions, to be easily caught on fire or rubbed raw from the strain of trying to burn. I couldn't bring myself to get dressed, or move, for fear that if I did, I would walk myself right to Oliver's room and demand answers for more than just the clue. I was hanging on by a very thin thread that right now couldn't take the strain of being pulled.

I hear a knock at the door, and my heart races, but I don't move. *He's early.*

"Five more minutes," I yell, frustrated.

Really, I just want to irritate him. Make him feel every second that he is forced to stand outside a locked door, wanting in. Or better yet, for me to come out. *How does it feel to want?* I stare at the picture I took while those words grow loud in my head because I want *so much.*

It's from our trip to Salem, the three of us with our arms wound around each other, smiles shining in front of the Nightmare Gallery's sign. It had been our first trip together, the boys insisting I not be left behind. The first time our friendship had faced the challenge of our statuses and gone up against Madeline. The tattered letters I had written to both boys while they were away at Artist's Creation camp when I was twelve. I had missed them more than I thought possible and had written every day. Paxton had kept them all. Even Oliver's. My eyes had stung rereading my clumsy handwriting through the sandy plastic bag.

Even now, thinking about it, I'm having trouble holding myself together. The old me is slipping through the cracks demanding satisfaction any way it comes. But who I am now cannot allow it. Even as I want to run to the door, I refuse my muscles. *It's his own damn fault for being early. He can wait,* I think.

Thankfully, he doesn't disappoint. Several more pounds shock the poor, battered door.

"Eve," he growls through the wood and into my skin. "We have a time limit."

He doesn't need to remind me. I know. Just a few more minutes should do. My nerves will be satiated enough to shove everything back behind the locks and pretend that none of how I feel is real. But he can't even give me that.

It was stupid of me to keep the door unlocked in my hurry to go nowhere. Stupid of me to forget that I had. The handle is turning, and the hinges squeak as it does. I hurl myself from the bed, trying to grasp for anything, embarrassed to be caught in such a state of undress, both emotionally and physically. *Stupid, stupid, stupid,* I scold myself. *You're not strong enough to play this game with him.*

"Oliver! I said give me a minute!" I yell, but it's too late.

I scurry, no longer comfortable with the thought of him seeing me like this. The covers are pinned too tightly to the bed frame to budge. They won't allow me to pull them free to use as coverage, and my bag lay on the other side of the room.

Between it and my exposed self, Oliver finally steps inside. We stare at each other, my shirt still barely holding onto my nipples and my underwear only a scrap over what's left. Oliver's eyes are glued to me. I can only imagine the rasp his breath is taking from the way his jaw is left unhinged. He takes me in as if he's ravenous, pupils blown out and wild within fractions of a second. The fragility of our distance and our resolve to keep it comes sharply into focus.

"I'm not ready," I manage to whisper.

This moment feels like a glass house, our words the stones, and even at a whisper, it shatters. Oliver twists from me, hand coming up to shield his face, rubbing his brows, his cheeks, his lips. Needing to feel skin in all the places, I'm sure his mind roamed. All the memories of where he's touched before, unbearable.

"I know. But we don't have a choice," he sighs. "Five minutes."

And then he walks out. I explode into action, locking the door before ruffling through the suitcase that was packed for me for a pair of pants. My breathing is uneven, heaving in desperate gulps. My skin is electric, but my heart knows I can't think about what just happened. About the way Oliver looked at me. About how I wanted the rough grip of his fingertips on my thighs and wrapped around my hips. The way I remembered the sound of his sighs as they fluttered along the hollow of my throat and how much I ached to hear its echoes again. Guilt washes over me as Roger's hurt face flashes, imagining him knowing where I am now and with who. But its hold is slippery as my mind drifts to thinking about how different this all could've been, *if only*.

Because it isn't.

Paxton. Killer. Beach. Bar. Those are the things I need to focus on. Those are the pieces of the puzzle I'm trying to solve. And if I don't get my butt in gear and Oliver out of my head, we could miss it. I shove the jeans I found on, and then stuff my feet into a pair of sneakers with no socks, desperate to get out of this room and away from the memory of Oliver's eyes on my skin as fast as I can. I open the door where Oliver stands, cheeks and neck red as a firework.

"Ready?" I ask as casually as I can.

He spins, leading us to the car. I follow silently. We're both lost in our own thoughts through the drive, and I hardly notice when we sweep into the parking lot, gravel spitting up as we do. *Bounty Dive Bar* flashes in red neon, every other letter nothing more than a flicker. My gut clenches as I remember another bar like this one, probably a few miles away. A day that could've been like any other but wasn't.

I reach for the handle, only to feel Oliver's warmth engulf the hand he's now holding. A shockwave of relief and want and pain flies through me at his touch, and I look at him, wide eyed and hopeful, in reflex. He's staring at our joined hands, thumb rubbing over mine, soothing jagged pieces of my soul as he does. He's sober, at least enough that his cheeks have lost their ruddy tint and his breath isn't acidic. This is not the flirtatious Oliver of one too many drinks. This is something else. Something serious. Something new.

"I know," he chokes before clearing his throat to start again. "I know we're not in the best place right now, but you need to trust that I'm here for you. Whatever happens in this bar, or with Paxton's letter, I'm always here, Darkness."

My gut clenches, his fingers suddenly like ice against mine. He's holding something back from me. Something more to the letter, or the clues, or this whole damn thing. With Oliver, you never can tell. He holds things so closely, laying pieces down in patterns only he can see. Always believing his way is the right one. The *only* one.

I jerk my hand free and yank open the door, frustrated at being treated like a child and that I now have the undeniable urge to throw a tantrum like one. I am a twenty-seven-year-old research librarian at NYU! I don't need handholding and secrets. I have survived watching my mom beat cancer. Twice. I have skirted through college and lived paycheck to paycheck for years, taking care of us both. And I have watched the person who I loved most in this world rip my heart out as he walked out of my life without turning back. Whatever waited inside this dirty little pub, I could handle.

I wrench open the door to Bounty, not caring if Oliver is following or not. I'd rather he just left me here so I could hop a flight home and leave this mess behind. *But you'd never find out what really happened*, the voice of my curiosity whispers. I let the door slam behind me, hoping to quell my fury, and watch as a handful of eyes turn to me. There are half a dozen people here, most with the glimmer of an early evening drink already come and gone.

There are no bar games. No darts or pool. No karaoke machines. There's a bar top. A tiny stage built only five inches from the ground. There are cocktail tables and tall stools pushed off to the side so a small dance floor can welcome any guests of the band. There are three booths, in different stages of disarray—benches ripped up and dining chairs taking their place. Broken tabletops filled with plywood or said benches. Everything here is broken, then pieced back together to function *just* enough.

I step in, unsure of what I'm looking for. *What could Paxton see in a place like this?* I walk up to the bar and the man behind it smiles at me. He's about my age, surprisingly good-looking in that '*I don't give a fuck*' kind of way. He has tattoos and piercings lining his body, his dermals making the art pop out into 3D. So unlike the men I have known. Have loved. It makes me quick to smile back.

"Hey, what can I get you beautiful?" he asks, voice husky from many nights drinking, probably in this very bar.

"A beer. *Any* beer. I'm not picky," I reply, flushed from the compliment.

He shakes his head. "Didn't get our shipment today. We've rush ordered, but it's mixed or straight only tonight, love. No bottles and the tap's been broken since '93."

"Then she'll have a whisky sour, *friend,*" Oliver's voice pipes in from my shoulder before I feel his hands on my waist in an overprotective manner I haven't felt since high school.

The bartender looks him up and down then goes about making my drink, over pouring. I know I should order water instead and remove Oliver's hands from my hips and scold him for his jealousy. But in the blurred lines between *now* and *then,* it feels nice. Comfortable. I allow the hypocrisy of both the drink and the way my body curls towards him, under the guise of giving myself grace. A girl can only take so much when faced with death and heartbreak. He slides the orange-tinted glass in front of me, plopping in a maraschino cherry as a final ta-da.

"Looks like you needed this more than a beer anyway with a guy like that and the look you're giving." He raps his knuckles twice on the wood. "Let me know if you need another."

And then he's gone, talking to someone at the other end, not even bothering to offer Oliver a drink, which leaves me smiling into mine.

"Rude," Oliver huffs.

"Yes, you are," I can't help but quip. "Now, what do you think we're looking for? I want to find it and get out."

I drag down a large chug of my drink, the whisky burning all the way to my stomach. I'm not much of a drinker. Never have been. When you grow up in a house that's keenly aware of alcoholism, you learn it isn't worth it. Old habits die hard, but I tried not to let it stop me from enjoying one now and then. That Oliver remembered the first drink I liked, makes me take another swallow.

Instead of keeping my gaze on the bright red cherry atop the ice, I look to find Oliver searching around, probably for anything familiar or out of place. This part of the clue doesn't feel familiar enough to me, so I let him guide us. His head swings to the walls, filled with posters and random scraps of paper.

"It might be something up there. It looks like a lot of notes have been left on these walls," he says before moving to one side to look through them.

I follow his lead, walking to the other, toward what's left of the booths, and scour the pieces hung around them. *Cherie and Mac were here and fell in love!* one reads. Dusty memories of nights long past with people who wanted to remember, makes me long for a simpler time. One that never existed, where Oliver and Paxton and I could get lost in a place like this, even just for the night. Seeing the smiling photos makes me think of my 21st birthday and how different it all could have been. Tiny slices of *ifs* and *onlys* make paper maché of my heart.

I move on, trying not to linger in words that aren't meant for me. There's only one I'm hoping to find. All the others only hold regret, and I've had enough of that to last a lifetime. The worn seats crease and creak beneath me as I rest my knees on them to get a closer look.

"Eve," I hear Oliver call.

But I ignore him, too entranced by the cluster of notes and photos I'm looking at. One, in particular, that's almost out of reach. It's there I find a scribble I recognize. A curled word that cannot be mistaken. I step onto the tattered chair and push my face right up to read:

Forgiveness is the fragrance, rare and
sweet, that flowers yield when trampled
on by feet.

My fingers curl around the edge of the paper, eager to pull it down when I feel the heat of someone standing behind me. Before I can turn, I hear the last thing in this world I ever thought I would again.

"Puddin'?"

ANTIQUE PAGES

WATER DROPLETS FLING ONTO the page, blurring words I'm trying to read. I cup my hands around the cover, desperate to keep it dry.

"Paxton! Stop! This is a *first edition*. You cannot waterlog a Neruda first edition!" I squeal, equal parts irritation and elation.

Bringing a book to beach day with the boys was asking for trouble, I knew, but with summer winding down and my first year AP English reading due, I had no other option. I needed to finish in the next week, or I would start already behind. And I couldn't let Madeline and Mom down like that. But I was also a teenager, and the long days winding down called me outside. That, and the two teen boys who wouldn't take no for an answer. They were a bigger force than nature could hope to be.

"Eve! Put the book down. We're at the lake. It's the last week of summer. Madeline cannot expect you to study yourself into the ground before you've even landed on the shore." He throws his hands onto the top of the rolling surface, sending another smattering of water my way.

His eyes snag on someone behind me. "Oliver! Grab her and throw her in here!"

Sun-warmed hands slide into the crook of my arms, and I lurch forward, throwing my book into the safety of the towels.

"Oliver! No! Don't!" The high pitch of my protest causes Paxton to shudder in laughter, his arms and legs pumping through the lake and silt as he jogs into position to help his brother.

Oliver's laugh is changing into the deeper husk of age. His breath sends gooseflesh across my arms as he lowers his voice into a deep whisper I'm only starting to get used to.

"C'mon, Eve. You've hardly hung out with us all summer. Give us just an afternoon and I promise, we'll let you read into the morning," he says.

I sigh, knowing I lost this fight the moment I came down here with them. I stop fighting, letting all my weight go into Oliver's arms. They may have convinced me to play, but I would never make it easy on them. His soft grunt brings a smirk to my lips.

"Paxton! She's gone dead weight! Help me, dammit!" he grumbles.

Pax is already shooting out of the water to grab me. At the last moment, I try to make a dash for it, catching them both by surprise. It's not enough to escape their clamoring hands. Oliver's wrap around my chest and a thrill I barely understand pierces through the fun. I throw my head back and laugh anyway, even as it all comes into sharper focus. Even where hesitancy is creeping in. Paxton blasts through the moment, hauling me up by my hips, taking my feet clean off the ground. They're carrying me now like a giant jump rope as the water laps at their calves.

"Boys! You didn't start the party without us already, did you?" A female voice calls.

I can't turn my head to see who it is, but I know. My stomach sinks as several feet slap their way towards us. Paxton laughs, swinging my legs back and forth.

"Perfect timing, Al! We were just about to christen the waters. You ready?" he asks Oliver.

Oliver responds by matching his swing and my whole body is in motion. My hands flail in a last-ditch effort.

"Wait, guys. No! Don't..."

I don't get to finish my plea. I sail through the air, arms and legs swimming before I even touch the lake. And then I am consumed. The water soaks into me, sucking the last bit of sunshine from my skin. I let myself drift, suspended in the blue, letting the silence and darkness of it put me at ease. Tiny bubbles float out from my lips, up to the surface, before popping. A hand juts down around me, the water beading at its presence, the peace shattered by its grasping.

I find the foot it's attached to and wrap my fingers around its heel, pulling it deeper into the water. The hand reels out of the water and his face plunges in next to mine. Oliver's black curls are weightless, his smile bright and bubbling. He opens his eyes to look at me and we're locked together in the tide. He reaches out, twining our hands together. Time is fathomless. I could stay wrapped in this watery haven forever.

My lungs start to burn and before I can protest, Oliver is hauling me up behind him to the surface. My head pops up just behind his and we are gasping for oxygen, smiling and sputtering, as our feet find purchase.

"Oliver! Can you help me? Matt, June, and Paxton just *left* me to set up the picnic stuff by myself!"

Ally McVie. Who was always destined to end up with Matt Mason but couldn't help loving Oliver Poe. Even when it wasn't accepted. The Poes were a legacy and a powerful family, but the wealthy can still be a bunch of snobs, especially with only daughters.

Ally's parents would never entertain her dating Oliver. He too seeped in the passionate pursuit of creating. Of naming the emotions most are too scared to face, losing himself in death and grief and heartbreak, writing stories some adults couldn't bear. Too entrenched in his family name. In embracing the familiarity of power and pain. Of exploring the world in all its morbidity, regardless of how it looked to those who hid behind pleasantries. And being different scared them.

While the wants and goals change as we grow up, where boys become desirable and dating consumes entire social circles, the rules of popularity and acceptance shift little. Regardless of Oliver's wealth, there were some things money couldn't buy—and that included respectability amongst the closed minded. Which was fine by me, even if that meant Oliver stayed out of reach for us all.

"On my way, Al!" Oliver calls back.

He gives me one more smile, hesitating for only a second when my hand slips from his. He waves me up after him. I know I should go. Be the buffer. More and more, it felt like that's what I'd become for the boys. The chain-link fence to keep them separate from the world. Not that I minded keeping others out, I just wanted to be let in, too.

I slip out of the water after him, dripping from my shorts and bikini top, hat and sunglasses, forgotten somewhere in the towels before I was thrown in. Ally is unpacking a large beach blanket from a backpack filled with bottles and snacks. Oliver jumps in to grab one end of the blanket as they lay it flat. Ally smiles up at him, one of her hundred-watt grins, that makes my stomach sour.

"Thanks, Oli! At least there's one gentleman left in all of Boston!" she giggles.

Oliver's cheeks tint pink as he nods. The silence stretching between them makes me squirm. I shouldn't be here, and by the look on Ally's face when she glances my way, she couldn't agree more.

"I'm just going to go find Paxton..." I point over my shoulder toward the dock where the boys and June are taking turns jumping in.

Oliver snaps his eyes to me, startled. Before I can move past him, he's already jumping into action, shouting over his shoulder to me.

"Race you there, Eve!"

Now it's just me and Ally staring after Oliver's backside. I take a step to follow him when the scoff at my side stops me dead.

"Figures," she spits.

I should stay silent. Nothing good will come of asking what she means. But the itching to know forces the words from my mouth.

"What does?" I ask.

"Him. You. That you say jump, and the Poe boys are already guessing how high you want them. Eventually, they'll learn. They'll drop you like the bad habit you are, Evangaline Pierce." Her eyes gleam, fingers delicately placed on her hip. "You might have them fooled with your innocent, wide-eyed act, but I see right through to your tattered family bones, and no one will want you like you want them. *No one.*" Her hands slide off her hips, satisfied that she's hit home and continues unpacking her bag, as if nothing has happened.

My mouth has gone slack. It's not that I haven't heard the whispers. That my classmates don't talk about the girl riding the coattails of the Poes. That the families who come over to visit don't whisper about the help's daughter. It's that my father's letter the Paxton forced on me just this week is burning a hole in my book's pages, almost an exact match to her words, imploring me to come home. *No one can love you like family, Puddin',* it reads while holding the place of my favorite love poem. An irony that this morning I found hilarious.

Now the humor sinks like stones to my feet.

"Eve! You lost! You know the drill!" Oliver bellows from the edge of the dock.

He's waiting for me, arms crossed, hair still glistening beneath the sun. I turn to find Ally already staring, smiling.

"Go along," she says, waving me away. "What's a flame without their biggest fan?"

I hate her. But I love them. So, I turn and walk away, practicing lifting my lips into a curve until it's almost real by the time I reach them.

"Alright, *loser,* let's hear it! Give us that poetry speak, woman!" Paxton howls.

They're all ears, waiting to see what I'll recite. Hanging on words not yet spoken. My mind is on the letter. On the poison Ally has dumped into my head. I'm too full of panic and doubt to remember anything else.

"And nothing Edgar or Dickinson. You've been too consumed by them, and I cannot hear another from either," Oliver says, smiling, a jest over shared nights of reading.

His face lights the poem up for me, their melody on my lips before I can think better of it.

"*I do not love you as if you were salt-rose, or topaz, or the arrow of carnations the fire shoots off. I love you as certain dark things are to be loved, in secret, between the shadow and the soul.*"

I know the moment the words leave my mouth that they're a mistake. Everyone is looking at me, the lapping water the only sound. My single reprieve is that Ally is busy at the picnic area. Still, June will tell her. My face heats into a fever, eyes dancing anywhere but to Oliver's. June giggles. Then his voice breaks in.

"*I love you as the plant that never blooms but carries in itself the light of hidden flowers; thanks to your love, a certain solid fragrance, risen from the earth, lives darkly in my body,*" Paxton recites. "Neruda, right? Isn't that the book you were squeaking about not getting wet before we tossed you in?"

Pax has saved me, taken the embarrassment and made it evaporate in a magic trick I'll never learn. I nod my head, trying to hide the appreciation I feel, before running into a cannon ball jump, landing smack in the middle of them in the water. I burst from the depths, spitting droplets. I want to tell Paxton how much I love him in this moment with the way he's staring at me, like he's happy to hide all my secrets.

"You all know how to make a guy feel forgotten," a boy calls out as feet pound the dock boards into a rattle.

"Tyler!" June squeals in a pitch that rivals any birds.

She swims to the ladder, scurrying up to flop herself into a big wet hug on Tyler's still dressed chest. He laughs, squeezing her tight until he's almost as soaked as she is.

Tyler Manetti is beautiful. Between the honey streaks that flow between his chestnut hair and his matching hazel eyes and skin, I have trouble looking away anytime he's in a room. The best part is he's a scholarship kid, kind of like me. His middle-class family lives four neighborhoods away, and he doesn't flash brand names like it's his job. If there is any boy, I could have a crush on, and act on it, it is Tyler. With the caveat that everyone loved him, and I was merely tolerated.

It was nice that when girls at school played MASH or asked who my secret crush was, I could say Tyler, and no one would gawk. They didn't roll their eyes or taunt me, saying it was impossible. Not like they would with Oliver. Tyler was obtainable, *and* a catch. Occasionally, I even thought he might like me, too.

His roving gaze lands on me, and I feel my cheeks flush.

"Hey, Eve," he says with a tiny wave that I return.

Water douses me as someone slaps it in my face. Paxton laughs and by the time I wipe it away, everyone is climbing out, up and onto the dock to join Tyler and June. I haul myself over and out just in time to watch as they set off toward the picnic area, June pulling Tyler behind her. His feet shuffle in obstinance as he looks back, throwing me an apologetic smile. I sigh and follow along, tracking Oliver's backside as he slows his pace to allow me to catch up.

Ally sits in her low-slung lawn chair while a short top table is filled with snacks and drinks in front of her. Five other chairs surround it, leaving who the odd man out is glaringly obvious. My brow furrows in frustration while everyone else takes a seat. Paxton is the first to notice I'm still standing.

"Hey Ally," he says, "we got another chair for Eve here?"

Ally looks distraught as she replies, "Oh no! I only brought six. I wasn't sure if Tyler was going to show or not. Sorry, Eve!"

She is completely, utterly, *not* sorry.

"It's fine. I can stand. Or sit on a towel."

I'm used to being left out. Even though Paxton and Oliver's presence at school has all but stopped the bullying, they didn't win me any friends. I have a few people I can talk to, who will eat lunch with me or be partners in class, but that is where it ends. Every interaction was just enough to fulfill the social contract the boys demanded. And everyone knew that if I wasn't invited, they wouldn't show either. But that didn't mean they wouldn't take every opportunity to make sure I knew I wasn't welcome.

"Nah, this is my fault for not responding to the texts. Eve, you can take my chair," Tyler says.

I shrug him off with a smile. "Thanks, but I'm ok! Really."

"Hmm. What if we... share it? You can sit with me. If you want to?" His voice still holds a polite, playful edge. Friendly. But I can see the pink lighting his cheeks and the nerves making him run his fingers through his hair in an act to keep them busy. *He wants you to say yes.* Butterflies steal through me, their wings not stopping even after seeing the death glare June is giving me.

My head is nodding. "Ok."

I'm walking towards him, round the table, past both boys. Before I can make it to Tyler, an arm swings around my waist and pulls me down into someone's lap. My stumble into the chair is not graceful and I'm pretty sure I slap a shoulder against my elbow trying to gain balance. At first, I'm not sure if my fall is an accident or intentional, until I hear the voice rumble through my back.

"Eve can share with me. I mean, we share a house and books and chairs, all the time. No need to make you uncomfortable, Tyler."

"*Oliver,* you're being ridiculous," I scold, wiggling a bit to show my dislike of his bossiness, but not enough to break myself free.

Oliver's arm squeezes at my hips, then stays firmly locked, making it impossible for me to escape. Time feels like it's slowing down. Gravity shoves on all of my organs and I'm positive I weigh a thousand pounds. A million. Oliver and I have always been close, but as age and hormones have caught up with us, things changed. Touches were more careful. Casual affection less public. After too many teases of 'liking' each other, and death glares from Madeline, we became more restrained.

But this... this was something new. It felt like a claiming. For Tyler. For me. While part of me is outraged that he would even dare try to control me, another newer part of me craves it. Makes me want to stare down everyone here and show them I'm more than just a tagalong. By the looks of it, they might already know. Both girls are staring daggers, and a chill sweeps down my spine at the look Ally has in her eyes. I look around to see Tyler's face fall, if only for a moment, before he shoots us a dashing grin again.

"Alright man," he says, clapping his hands together. "What else do you have on the agenda for today's outing, Ally Cat?"

She doesn't take her eyes off Oliver's hand at my waist as she replies.

"Well, I thought we'd do some truth or dare. Except for every truth or dare you refuse to do, you lose a piece of clothing. *Strip* truth or dare. To keep us all honest."

Her canines look feral in the sun. I look down and realize all I have on is my bikini and a pair of shorts. Three articles of clothing, while everyone else has put on a few layers. *I'm in trouble.*

"I'll go first," Ally continues. "Eve, truth or dare?"

I know no matter what I pick, her request will be brutal. I glance between the faces all staring at me now, Oliver's warm hand light around my middle, an anchor trapping me here.

"Dare," I say.

She smirks. "I dare you to kiss one person in this circle right now."

My palms sweat as my neck bursts into flames. She has me. There's no one here I can choose without consequence. If I kiss Paxton or Oliver, I'll never hear the end of it at school for the rest of the year. Not to mention the backlash I'd get at home from the two of them. Especially if they thought it *meant* something. Matt is firmly off limits. If Oliver would piss off Ally, Matt would cause her to put a hit on me, damn what either of the boys said.

I can't kiss either of the girls, even as a saving grace for not wanting to choose between the boys. I can only imagine the rumors they'd spread. Locker rooms before gym would never be the same. And Tyler. Sweet, beautiful, crush-worthy Tyler. Oliver's fisting fingers, that lightly graze my hips as he places them on the arms of his chair, are enough of a reason. Even if we can be nothing more than friends, it's obvious from this little show that he doesn't want me to have a crush on Tyler, either. Not to mention how June will feel about the boy she likes locking lips with me.

But what other choice do I have?

"OK. If it *has* to be someone here, I pick... Tyler," I say quietly.

Oliver's whole body stiffens. I do my best to ignore him and the fact that he's no longer trying to hold me back. I smile shyly up at Tyler, who is looking straight at me as I stand up from Oliver's lap and lean over the table towards him. He mirrors my every move, long limbs missing the cheese plate as his hands bend with him to keep his shoulders steady as he puts his face level with mine.

This is it. The moment I get my first kiss. I wanted this to be different, to be special. A hidden moment between me and a boy who loves me. Or at the very least, I knew liked me. Instead, I get this pieced together, fabricated one where the girl who hates me most has put me between the ones I care about. She's forged everything about this and even as my heart picks up as I lean down, my excitement stays buried underneath the humility.

My lips barely touch his before I'm pulling away. A peck, no more than what I've given my mother as a child. Hardly a graze of skin on skin where I didn't even take away the wetness of his mouth. Tyler is smiling, staring, still leaning toward me, almost as if he's asking me for more. I'm embarrassed and feeling like a prude. This is nothing like the stories. No poetry or waxing of beauty and lust. But the crowd of teens around me *oh* and *ah* anyway at my lousy attempt. All except Oliver. I sit firmly back on his lap. *To hell with the mockery.*

"Ok! My turn," I coo, eyes staring daggers at Ally.

I know I can hurt her, make her squirm, and embarrass her in front of both Matt and Oliver. I could ask about her parents' messy affairs. How she feels about her father falling in love with the maid and the children he's paid her off for. I could dare her to jump, fully clothed in the lake. Watch her perfect hair and makeup swirl into a puddle and take a photo before she can laugh it off. There are a million ways to highlight her insecurities. But I don't.

"Paxton," I say, clear and full of humor. "Time to pay the piper, golden boy! Truth or dare?"

He smiles, ready for me, hands folding and stretching to crack out his knuckles.

"Dare!"

Of course, he would choose the thrill.

"I dare you to climb this tree," I say.

I don't have time to add anymore before the others are groaning.

"Eve, that isn't even a dare! He can do that in his sleep," Matt says.

I roll my eyes at them, hating what they've reduced me to, but knowing I have to play along.

"*Naked,*" I retort.

Matt snorts on a laugh. "That's more like it!"

Everyone chuckles, and by the wink and big smile on Paxton's face, he's happy as a clam to oblige.

"Excuse me, ladies. Don't want to be improper around young impressionable women," he says as he strolls behind the enormous trunk, flashing us his swim shorts and tee shirt from the side as they come off.

"While he's busy, I'll go again," Ally busts in. "Eve, truth or dare?"

"Eve's already gone. Pick someone else," Oliver grumbles.

"No. My game, my rules. Eve, *truth or dare?*"

I sigh. "Truth."

She smiles like she's caught me, "Ok, it's a two part-er. First, who is this love note from that I found in your towels? And second, why do they call you Puddin'?"

She's laughing, each vowel catching on a *ha* as she tries to get the questions out. She's waving the letter in the wind, unfolded and unsuspecting. If she's read it, she knows it isn't a love note. Not really. It's the letter from my dad that Paxton stuffed in my book bag two days ago after he found it in the trash that he begged me to write back to.

One day, Eve, you're going to wish you weren't so full of this hate and fear. You've got to forgive him for you, or it'll always haunt you, Paxton had pleaded, refusing to let me leave without it.

I'd listened, and was mulling over what he said, keeping the note as a bookmark until I'd made my decision. It was full of apologies. Of misspelled words and memories, things he thought might make me remember more than just our last time together. Things to prove he was, at one time, my dad, and that with time, he could change. That he wanted to.

He started calling me Puddin' when I was two. Said I loved the stuff. Demanded it. After my first words of momma and dada came Puddin'. So, it just fit. Who I was to him. Who I'd always be. But right now, with Ally McVie smirking in my face, that nickname chortling out of her mouth, it was so far from who I wanted to be.

I stood up, body rigid with anger, tears of frustration imminent. I stomp over to where she sits, the letter still held out, and snatch it from her hands. I crumple it into nothing in my fist.

"The letter is from my father," I say deadpan.

Then I remove my shorts, throwing them down in front of her. It may be a game, but I'll be damned if this wretched girl is going to know a single thing more about this letter—or me. I give her one more solid look before reeling away in just my bikini to make the long walk home.

"Not cool, Al," I hear Oliver say before he runs up next to me, wrapping a towel around my shoulders. "Need some company?"

I nod. I couldn't imagine ever not needing Oliver's loyalty in the face of so much pain.

DEEP ECHOES

Thursday, Present

M Y BLOOD RUNS COLD, my pinky twitching beneath the paper. I'm still stretched against the wall, holding it as if it can hold me up. Instead, it tears under the weight of my arms that drop in shock. Flight mode kicks in the second my feet touch the hard concrete of the floor. I don't even lift my eyes to confirm who's standing in front of me. I don't need to.

"Oliver, I'm leaving," I say loudly, unsure of where he could be and terrified to look around.

I can only hope he realizes I don't just mean from this room.

Head still bent down, I shuffle my feet, only to find a scruffy pair of work boots appearing in front of them. The left toe is so dry, the leather is cracking. My heart jumps into my throat as I shift to go around them. They move with me, blocking my path forward. Thin, fragile hands I don't remember hold out, pumping up and down as if I am a wild thing in need of soothing. I throw my head back with breakneck speed, glaring as hard as I'm able to stare down the man responsible for my failed escape.

Except, he isn't the same man I remember. His face is sallow and pale. Yellow skin stretches under his eyes and down his neck in between the bright purple of bruises. His hair has been shocked white from root to tip and there's more missing teeth than one's left in his head. If it weren't for his eyes, the same color as mine, I would believe him a stranger.

"Now, *Eve*, normally, I think I'd let you leave," my dad says sternly, almost as if he's been a parent all along. "I know you ain't got a lot of love for me no more, and while I wish you did, I can't say I don't understand why not. But... this may very well be the last time I ever see you. So, I'm hoping you'll have some pity on an old man and have a chat with me." His arms are stretched and moving with each other, a maestro trying to lull me into a credenza of his making.

Somehow, it works. I can't move. I'm rooted in this nightmare, paralyzed by his words and the look on his face. Damn my curiosity and every need I have to know *why*. He takes my stillness as his chance to pull the trap that'll leave me no choice but to stay.

"I'm dying, Puddin'." His eyes are sorrowful, the look of a man on the edge of being consumed by his regrets. We breathe it in for a second. Two. Before he continues, voice just above a whisper. "Your friend said you would stay. That you would hear me out. So, this is it. What are you gonna do, girl?"

Dying. The word vibrates through my ears into my teeth, tasting of metal. I search for words, for a decision, that I can make. *He doesn't have long,* is all that greets me. Either way I go, I lose, and I hate that he's put this guilt and regret in my path of retreat.

I step back and sink my weight into the chair, the only consent I can give for him to continue his story. *Let him say what he has to say, and then you can go, Eve. That'll assuage your morals **and** your curiosity. Find what Paxton left, then go. As for him? You owe him nothing.* The voice in my head is my mother's and an odd determination returns. I can get through this.

My father moves to the benched side, scooting in, more delicate than I've ever seen him. Gone are the hard plops on the vinyl and banging elbows to the table. It's replaced with ginger knees and shaky hands I can't believe I was ever afraid of.

He's old. Much older than I realized. And he's sick. If I were to guess, cancer, since I've seen it before. But I doubt even now he'd tell me what's wrong. That's not why he's trapped me here.

I hear the scrape of metal on the concrete floor as Oliver pulls up another chair beside me. Dark brows scrunch and meet over weary eyes. He doesn't want to do this anymore than I do. But he will. For Paxton. *For me,* a voice in the back of my head whispers. He grabs my hand, twining his fingers with mine under the table.

"You've got us here. Now what is it you have to say?" Oliver asks, pointed and sharp.

Dad eyes him. "I never liked you. Or your brother, for that matter. Didn't care for you taking away my girls. Pretending they were yours when they belonged back home. But as long as Isabel had the Poes behind her, I didn't stand a chance of changing her mind. Or Eve's, I'd guess. You all just couldn't leave well enough alone."

He looks over at me and sighs. The weight of it brings his head down, hands cupping in front of him, defeated. *It wasn't them that kept us away,* I think, but don't say.

"It don't matter now though. You won. I hardly recognize the girl anymore," he waves toward me, still addressing only Oliver. "Hell, I knew that years ago. I knew I messed up, but I did everything I could to bring her back. When nothing worked, I had to admit defeat."

My heart feels swollen remembering the letters. The pleas. So many times, I had written back, but I could never bring myself to send them. What good could it possibly do to repair our bond? What could possibly be said that would ever make me feel whole again?

His eyes stay focused on Oliver, as his hands continue to rub at the table in fits and starts. "But then, a boy I thought I might recognize came stumbling in here looking for me. Asked around, found out I played cards most days in the backroom. He wanted to know if I remembered him and if I was ready to make amends with my daughter."

He looks at me, eyes glassy with what I imagine is excitement. *Paxton.* He has to be the boy my dad is talking about. I squeeze on Oliver's hand with everything I've got, but he's frozen, his fingers staying solid but unmoving in mine.

"He had no right to offer that to you," I say, the familiar irritation at Paxton's meddling rushing to the surface, even if it's not polite to be angry with a dead man.

"And yet, you're here. He said you would be. Told me that if I showed up, eventually you would too. I'm just glad you weren't too late. I started getting worried I wouldn't make it much longer. Looks like he knows ya better than you give him credit for, Puddin'."

I release Oliver and put both my fists on top of the table, wanting to scream that *he* doesn't know me at all. That just because I showed, doesn't mean I'll forgive. Just because we share blood doesn't mean we're family. Not anymore. But Oliver beats me to the punch before I can say anything.

"When? When did Paxton make you this deal?" Oliver asks.

Dad reaches into his pocket, pulling out what looks to be a photo. He stares at it while he answers.

"Oh, probably a little over three months back. Him and some friends. We sat, and they drank. I've been sober now going on three years. We chatted. I told him all the things I wanted to say to you. Told him about my diagnosis and that it ain't looking good or long for me. He paid. Left me a few extra bills too, *to help with the medical stuff,* he'd said. Then he asked me to take this picture with the promise that I'd give it to you when you showed, along with a message."

He holds out the photo between us, eyes only for me. I gingerly place my fingertips on it and try to draw it towards me. It doesn't budge.

"Now, wait just a minute. I want to tell you somethin' before I give you this. Puddin'."

I feel the anger of his ultimatum deep in my toes. He may have changed, but no one can splice every part of themselves. And my dad was nothing if not an opportunist. I let the irritation show in my eyes, but he doesn't waver.

"Evangeline Owen Pierce. I love ya more than anything else in the world. I messed up. A lot. And there is enough I've got to atone for in the end. I know that. I've never been any good for ya, but it wasn't because I didn't love you. No." He is on the edge of tears, voice drowning in the wet, snotty suck of them. I feel my rage dissipate, a dam breaking in the face of remorse and empathy that's trying to overwhelm me.

"I didn't know how to be a dad or a husband or even a good man. And I hated that. *Hate* that. It's made me miss so damn much. And now, there's no more time. But I need you to know that I loved you in all the best ways I knew how. And that these boys, this family, loves you. And I'm grateful for that, *I am*, but please don't let it overshadow that I do, too."

The sound of his voice is like a noose around my neck. It's tying me to the man he should've been, the one he wanted to be, and threatening to pull the floor out from who he was. He's broken, crumbling, hands fiddling with the air, as if he could manifest a drink where there isn't one. But his eyes bore into me, driving home the sincerity of his words.

I don't forgive him. I can't. My fingers flex as I try to shake out the nerves of it all. My body wants to recoil, to take flight from this mess. But I know that if I don't do something different, right here, right now, this moment will replay on loop for the rest of my life.

He may not deserve my forgiveness or my friendship or my time, but in this moment, I *have to* show him my love. All of it. Show him the letters I always wanted to send. The hope I always held that he would come back, be better, and allow me to be his little girl again.

I've been carrying the weight of it for so long that I'm not sure how to let it go. It's as if my soul has frozen, the shape of it molded in. But I need to try.

I let go of the picture. He must not have been holding on tight, because it drifts unbidden to the table. I get up, chair squealing as I shove it back, my hand gripping the top of it for strength and balance. I must look as uncertain as I feel. Both men jump up, too. Oliver's hands are already waiting as if to snatch me up and carry me away from here.

"Eve, wait, I'm sor—" My dad starts.

But he doesn't get to finish. I round the booth and slide my arms around him, tears fresh on my skin. They burn with pain and injustice. In 'what could have been' and 'what never was'. They scorch the reminder that the only reason it hurts so much is *because* I love him. I've always loved him, even when I didn't want to.

"I love you, Daddy," I whisper to him, angry but true.

The rest doesn't matter. Right here, in the dark recesses of a dingy old bar room, I let it all go. Just for this moment, I'm not searching for peace. I've found it. One memory in the vault of a few worth keeping. And somehow, I know it's enough.

His body feels thin in my arms, the bones jutting in places they shouldn't be. I hold him, careful not to squeeze. He doesn't have the same worries I do. He envelopes me. The tobacco I remember, even if I'm unsure how, swirls into my lungs as his clothing releases any last wisps of air between us. I know I'm crying. I'm pretty sure he might be too. It doesn't matter. The entire bar could be staring at us, the sky falling down around our feet, and I'm not sure we would notice. Who cares enough about an old man's tears?

A throat clears. Music turns on. Someone comes through the door hollering for the bartender to pour him something cold. My dad steps back and just like that, it's over. He's wiping the sweat and snot and salt away, looking for all the world as if life didn't just shift on its axis. He laughs. Thick and phlegmy, a cough sticking to his lungs at the end.

"I am so glad you came, Puddin'. You have no idea how much this means to an ol' dog like me."

And he's right, I don't. But I know what it means to me. My chest is already feeling lighter, even if my head is throbbing and my nose is plugged. I needed this too, and I don't think I could tell anyone how grateful I feel to be given the chance before he was gone. The only person who knew has already left us.

My eyes drift over to the table, but the photo is gone. I can only guess Oliver pocketed it while we were busy saying goodbye. I step back, letting the last of my dad's hold on me drop. Oliver stands there, waiting for my cue.

"Well, Dad. We've got to be heading out. We have a plane to catch and the rest of a funeral to attend..." I say.

This will probably be the last time we ever see each other and I'm not sure how to say that kind of goodbye to a man I both hardly know and have known my whole life. He must feel it, too, with the way his hand cups the back of his head, scratching out the scruff. But he doesn't let it sour his mood.

"Always jetting off. That's the life these boys'll give ya. No judgments. We were just always destined for different things, I guess." He takes another step away from me and toward the bar. "We'll be seeing you around, Puddin'. You tell your momma I love her, too. And not to blame herself for none of it. And Oliver... take care of her, will ya?"

The stillness stretches. Oliver gives in and nods.

"Bye, Daddy," I manage to get out around the knot in my throat.

He turns away and waves behind him. He doesn't glance back. His steps don't falter. He knocks twice on a door behind the bar and then disappears through its hazy brown wood. I'm stuck in time, staring into an ever-fraying space. My eyes blur from the strain of trying to hold on. Thankfully, Oliver pulls me out of it with his palms on my cheeks. He tilts my face toward him. We share three breaths before either of us can speak.

"You ready to get out of here?" he asks.

He doesn't need to say it twice. I'm already gone.

DISCARDED STONES

"**D**ID YOU GET IT?" I ask.

We don't even make it to the car before I need to know about the picture, the real reason we're even here. Paxton was clever. I'll give him that. Making me face my father in perhaps the only scenario I would have. And if I'd known the clue would've led me here? I'm not sure I would have come. A small voice inside whispers, *yes you would*. I suppose I found it odd that he'd picked the beach memory as a clue and dragged us down only miles from where my family was finally and truly broken.

He always was one to wrap plans inside plans. Why not have us chasing down his murderer and make us face the things we always refused him when he was alive? It was just like Paxton to need to be right and I guess death didn't change that. Slivers of irritation open in my chest at the thought. Momma always says not to be angry at the dead, but I think this might be the exception.

I'm pulled from my thoughts by Oliver's wicked smile. He slips a small rectangle from his coat pocket and holds it out so I can just see the silhouettes of the group over the roof of the car before hiding it back, away from view. My sigh contains an irritated growl, coming out as more of a struggle than an intimidation as it's meant to.

"Well? Are you going to share with the class?" I ask sarcastically.

He rolls his eyes. "*A watch's minute hand moves more quickly than did mine.* Patience," he whispers before ducking into the car.

"Do *not* quote Edgar to me!" I squeal as I scramble in, too. "And really, you're going to bring *The Tell-Tale Heart* into this? Are you trying to tell me you killed him?"

The joke is supposed to land, a needling to rile, instead of an actual accusation. Especially since I'm now unsure if I'm convinced he was murdered to begin with. But it doesn't. It drops into the canyon between us with an echoing thud. Oliver's mouth hanging before his glare rips me open.

"Regardless of what you think, *regardless* of how our relationship seemed in the end, Eve, I loved my brother more than any other person on this planet. In the history of loving other people. Not even you could change that, even after you tore us all apart."

His chest heaves and I know I need to dig the splinter out of us now before it goes any deeper.

"Oliver, I—I didn't mean it. I was trying to be funny. Of course, I don't think you killed Pax. But I didn't either. We must stop blaming—"

"*We.* WE? You mean *you* need to stop blaming *me.* You think I didn't recognize that pullout the moment we got here? That I didn't know exactly where this clue was leading us? Darkness, this was the first time we started breaking. All of us." He rakes his hands through his hair, eyes wide with the confession. "From the minute you got back on that plane home, I felt like I'd lost a piece of you. That you'd left it here. Pax felt it, too. But we both knew you blamed me for it. And now, seeing you... forgive *him* and still be yelling at me? I get that he's your dad, but after everything he put you through. Sobriety doesn't erase the abuse he doled when he was drunk, and yet you just accepted it."

He's visibly shaking with anger until he looks at me and takes a deep breath before continuing, "For once, I feel like I don't know you."

The glass I've placed around my patience, the one labeled '*break only in case of emergency*', explodes. The way Oliver sounds is as if he doesn't know what happened, what he did, or what he said. As if *I* was the only one who came back different. As if it was only me who decided nothing could be the same again.

"Are you serious?" I shout. "*You* were the one who made sure I knew my roots grew here. That the bond between you and Paxton was just that...

between you two. You were family, after all, and I was just the stupid little girl that fell into your laps. Dirty and full of wasted potential. The trip here only made you see exactly how far below your stature I was. And in the car, all you wanted to do was leave me behind. Forget this place existed. That I existed. *You broke us, Oliver.* You."

I'm stabbing my fingers into his chest, our positions in the car making my words echo with each punctuation I make. He shifts towards me, bewildered and wild.

"What are you talking about? I remember that day clearly. It stands out in only the handful of truly bad days we've had together, and I didn't do any of those things. Eve, I tried to remind you that Paxton and I were *your* family. That you needed to leave *him* behind. That there was nothing for you here. Everything you would ever need was back at Dellbrook. With us. That you were better than anything this place could give you. You deserved *more*. But you wouldn't hear it. Couldn't let go. For some reason, you rejected me. Even though they abused your love. Even though they wanted to drag you back into an unhappy abyss. I've loved your loyalty from the start, that stubbornness that made me beg my mother to give yours the job, but I never thought it'd be used against me. Not like this."

My mind reels, thrown back into a decade of memories. I replay every word I can remember, every look. Paxton's interruptions and sad eyes. Oliver's desperation for me to see him. Every part of me wants to reject what he's saying now, to settle into the comfort of what I've been sure has always been. But the plea and anger in this car, exuding from him, doesn't allow me to. His chest is heaving, taking up all the oxygen I need to think clearly, to remember why we don't talk about the past and why I shouldn't find reasons to love him again.

"Oliver, my loyalty has always been yours. I *don't* forgive him. There's still such a big part of me that is so angry with my dad. I don't want to be his daughter, but I can't change it. I can't remove every piece of me that he gave. And I can't erase the pull my cells have to be whole again, in a way that only letting go will allow." I push the desperation into my eyes for Oliver to see me, to understand.

"Back then, I thought I needed them to want me, to see me, and while I was begging to find that, you were telling me I didn't belong. That I've never belonged." Oliver opens his mouth, wanting to interrupt. I don't allow him. "No, it's true. I may have been wrong about your intentions, but that's what

I *felt*. And back then, I needed something different. Now, I just need to let myself rest in the fact that I love them despite whether or not they deserve it. I have to forgive *myself*."

My voice is cracking. Fresh waves of tears stream out with every syllable. I know one day I'll read a poem in a book with a name I know as well as my own, and see this moment reflected in every word. The determined focus of his gaze and trembling bend of his brow tells me he's cataloging it all. Storing it away. But I can't stop giving him the ink to spill. So many pieces of me still want to be his muse. He breaks away from me, looking at his hands on the wheel.

"Your loyalty is still mine..." He says it like a prayer, a quiet whisper I'm not meant to hear. "Eve, I... I wish we could go back to those kids and tell them what we can only see now. I never meant for you to feel that way. You have always belonged with us, no matter the promises made. Nothing, and no one, can change that."

His hand drops to cup mine and the heady feeling of its weight in my palm ground me in only a way Oliver can. *We can get through this, the dragging up of the past, together,* it tells me. I close my eyes and let myself rest in that feeling for a few seconds before reality sweeps in. We'll get through it, but I'm a fool if I believe we'll be healed. Nothing can fix what's been broken. All we can hope for is to be able to finally let go. Just like I needed to do with my dad.

I remove my hand from Oliver's, stretching out my fingers against my legs. "Thank you, Oliver. But I'm done living in this memory. Let's move on. Tell me about the picture."

Oliver takes longer to remove his hand and look up at me, but he does, frustration back to curling his lips. He passes me the photo before starting the car and peeling out of the lot, gravel flying out of our tires as we reach the paved street. I want to ask where we're headed, but all my attention has been sucked into the smiling faces staring up at me.

"Notice any old friends?" Oliver asks. But it isn't the well-known faces from childhood, or the suspicious one to Paxton's left, that have me in thrall.

A scruffy blonde beard and pale blue eyes demand my attention. His arm is wrapped around Paxton's shoulder, gripping it in a friendly pull. He's got on his NYU swimming tank from senior year, showing off the broad line of his shoulders and toned arms. The only tell I have that he's nervous in the photo is the way his free hand fists into the hem of his shirt. Roger has stretched out every workout top he owns, from that same gesture, *an irritation knot*, he calls it.

Why is Ro in this picture? How does he know Paxton? He lied to you. The thoughts reverberate in my skull to the thumping of my heart. I swallow the beats, forcing myself to look at the other people in the photo. Besides Roger and Paxton, there is Isaac unsmiling, his arm wrapped around the waist of none other than Ally McVie. Beside Ally is her long-time accomplice in all things horrid, June. The five of them look like college friends out for a drink after work. Each dressed down in beachwear, soft olive tans from days in the sun adorning all but Isaac.

I've got to go to Carolina. A close family friend needs some help, and you know how I feel about going when called. That's what he'd told me months ago. I thought nothing of it then. We both had friends all up and down the east coast. Friendships didn't just die when someone moved for a job or for their family. But now staring at the photo in my hands I had to wonder, was Paxton the close family friend he'd mentioned?

"Looks like we have three more possible suspects. Although, I'm not sure why Catz is even there. He and Isaac hate each other." Oliver keeps looking from the road to me in quick succession, waiting for me to respond.

"Catz?" I ask, unsure of who he's referring to.

Oliver stabs his finger right into Roger's face.

"Roger Thompson. He shared an apartment with Pax freshman year of uni."

"Why… why do you call him Catz? Were they friends?" I ask, desperate now.

"He picked up the nickname Tom Cat, which just eventually became Catz," he shrugs. "As far as I know, they stayed friends, but he transferred junior year to NYU and then moved around a bit. He and Isaac got into it a few times at a couple of different parties. Catz said he couldn't stand being on a team with him anymore, and he needed the swimming scholarship to afford school, so he left."

My mind spins. Why wouldn't Roger tell me he knew the Poes? I couldn't believe anything, including this being a coincidence.

"You ok, Darkness? You're looking pale," Oliver says.

The nickname slips out with the tinge of concern, a habit that the years cannot even break. I can't tell him—the thought of exposing my relationship as the lie that it is too embarrassing. I can only imagine the smug smirk he'd give, the 'I told you so' burning his lips. No, I couldn't tell Oliver anything. I nod my head, hair swishing against the back of the seat.

"I'm fine. Just surprised. Why do you think they were all together, here, in Folly Beach, of all places? What does this mean, Oliver?"

"Flip it over," he mumbles.

I do. On the back in faded blue ink, Paxton's looping letters can be found.

`Is all that we see or seem, but a dream within a dream? October 17—calmer.`

The Edgar quote swirls like smoke in my mind as I try to connect it or the date to any memory I have, but nothing comes. I scrunch my nose in frustration.

"I... I don't know what this means. I know the poem, but it had no significance that I'm aware of. I don't even recall Paxton ever reciting it before now. And I'm not sure what the date has to do with it."

Oliver maneuvers us into park and I look up to see we're already back in front of the hotel. He hesitates, fingers grasping and tightening on the wheel, threatening to strangle it before releasing it again. I wait in silence, letting him find whatever words he needs to say. Finally, he sighs before turning away and throwing open his door.

"That's because this one isn't for you..." He steps a foot out before turning back to me. "We'll be on the first flight home in the morning."

INFINITE WORLDS

FALL, 12 YEARS BEFORE

M Y BONES RATTLE FROM my toes to my teeth, some pop song thrumming wildly through the floorboards of the summer cabin. Teenagers stream around me, some walking into the safety of the structure, others out to the bonfire in the woods. The soda I'm sipping has gone flat, and I can't help but ask myself for the millionth time why I even came tonight. A hand wraps around my shoulder, guiding me out the door and away from the music.

"Let's get cozy by the fire. It looks so *cozy*," he coos.

Oh yeah, this is why. Paxton's breath is sharp with liquor, his words as airy as a balloon accidentally let go to the sky. I'm here to babysit him while he chugs drinks he isn't old enough to have. I let him pull me toward the flickering heat. Oliver should arrive soon. His tutoring session ended 20 minutes ago, to take over the Paxton Patrol Watch. Paxton, when drunk, is happy, but careless. The last party he went to, Alexander had to pick him up after he was found taking a bath, suds and all, in the community fountain.

The clouds are becoming bruised, nighttime ready to descend and bring with it the chill my sunburnt shoulders need. Fall is already in full swing, but none of us are quite apt to let the ache of summer go. That's why we're here, at the Let the Light Shine Bash, a right of way for every St. Botolph student and the boys insisted I needed to experience my youth.

"There's our log! Hurry Eve, before someone snatches it!" Paxton says conspiratorially.

He releases my shoulder then sloppily jogs over to the space just vacated by a couple, now making out against another tree. He reaches his hand for mine and pulls me down next to him. I stumble into place, a sharp edge of bark digging into my thigh, making me yelp and throw my weight over to Paxton to get away from the pain. Paxton wraps a hand around my backside to protect me, even if he isn't sure what from.

"Whoa! Easy! What happened?" he asks.

He's so close I can see the orange of the flames reflected in his silvery blue eyes. Flashes of moon and tide play with every dance the light does. He smells of lemon and vodka and honeysuckle soap. The tiniest bit of stubble beginning to peek through on his jaw and cheeks. *He's handsome.* The thought slips between the space of reality into objectiveness that I dash away. Still, the burn of them brightens my cheeks, anyway.

"Well, don't the two of you look... comfortable."

The words are curt, and my blood overheats at the sound of them. I hurry to slide my legs off Paxton and away from his hand, which has now ended up resting on my ass. I'm barely breathing when I look up to find Oliver's mouth pulled flat, his wild curls tossed everywhere, hiding what can only be the deep set of his brow. Irritation spills out from his features. Before I can ask what's wrong, Paxton barrels toward his brother, arms flung out to wrap him in a bear hug.

"Brother! You've missed so much. Matt and Ally had a spectacular blow out! She's been asking about where you've been. And then, Eve here, had an ouch, but I helped her," he says, words slurred and hiccupped.

Oliver stares at me before patting his brother twice on the back, turning his full attention to him. He sees the red plastic cup in his hand and takes it, looking in and sniffing at the contents.

"It's water. I had him switch right before we came out here," I say, happy to have some sober company.

Pax has had more than enough, and he may be unhappy with me taking away his drinks now, but he'll thank me in the morning. To punctuate my point, Paxton frowns.

"She was *so* mean to me, Oli. I even quoted Tennyson to her, and she *still* forced me to dump out my drink," he pouts.

"Tennyson? That's impressive given the fact you are saying things like *had an ouch...*" Oliver smiles. It's small but I hurry to return it.

"The Lotos-Eaters. He actually didn't do half bad," I laugh. "Had most of the words right. Even if he started to go into quoting The Odyssey by the end."

Paxton's drunken, lopsided grin is hard to be mad at, and Oliver releases the rest of the tension in his face. Whatever happened today that upset him melts from his shoulders. Oliver hands Paxton back the water and takes the seat he vacated next to me. I feel the warmth of him through my shorts as his black jeans brush against my bare skin, causing gooseflesh. He always feels like a furnace.

"HEY! JASON! Wait up, man!" Paxton yells as he skips into the crowd.

I move to follow, but Oliver's hand on my knee stops me. I raise my brow, wondering why we're not preventing the drunken mess from doing anything stupid, since that's why we're here.

"Let him go for now. We'll find him in a bit," Oliver says softly.

He's staring into the fire; lost in thoughts I desperately need to know, eyes turned down and vacant. All I've ever wanted is to crack open the mind of Oliver Poe and let the poetry leak from it. To swim through the waters of his consciousness and let it sweep me out to sea. I can't, so I settle for asking, his words never quite leaving me satisfied enough. But they'll have to do.

"How was today? You look a little shallow, like your darkness is going to run aground at any moment," I ramble.

I always try to keep up with the boys. With their eloquence. With their polite society raising and entitlement to the soul. Their quick wit always seems to outpace me. This time, though, Oliver smiles, allowing me to relax my shoulders. I must be saying something right. With Paxton, it's easy. He doesn't carry the weight of his ancestry as much as Oliver. He'll forgive the small talk or gossip. But Oliver has never been anything other than bone deep.

"It's only ever you that sees that part of me. Or at least, decipher it from the rest. Most just assume I'm lost in some story I'm telling myself. I don't even think Paxton notices the truth. Maybe pieces of me just come to the surface when you're around. Like calling to like. What if... What if you're the darkness and I'm only opening to you?"

He still isn't looking at me, and I cannot thank the stars enough because I'm positive the blush in my cheeks is lighting me up brighter than the bonfire ever could. I don't know whether to feel ashamed or delighted. If anyone else had said I reminded them of darkness, it would be an insult. Something to make me crawl deeper into myself and throw on a cheerful face. But this was *Oliver*, and to him, darkness was revered. A *reflection*. Surely, he didn't mean to attach such a thing to me.

"Does that mean we're damaged, then? Since we don't shine like Paxton? Do you wish that you could hide it?" I ask.

What I really want to know is if he wishes he could hide it from *me*. That he wasn't around me and didn't have to be reminded of shadows and questions. Of asking more from the world at sixteen than who he'd take to prom in May. Did he want to shed the parts of him that made him so entirely Poe, the eye for poetry in the mundane? Parts that I secretly loved about him. Parts that I wanted so deeply to see in myself and who longed to live a romantic life, too.

He turns to me, his moss eyes looking like a meadow at midnight. "Not at all. It's... comforting. To know that I'm not alone. That we're connected. Sometimes I worry that the loneliness will swallow me whole until you remind me that you're with me in the shadows."

His hands fist and stretch, making them look as if they're inching closer to me. I watch as his eyes focus on Paxton, who is laughing with a group of our classmates.

"Madeline says the Poes were made for darkness, that our best selves wait only past the edges of the light. But Paxton doesn't. His personality shines in the spotlight of the world. He was meant to stand at the precipice and lead. But I'm not like that. I scribble away truths most people want to forget, just so they can't. I yearn for what could be and bleed it into what is. No one follows me into the black recesses of existence," he says on a sigh before his words turn to me. "So, you, you must be the keeper of my best self. The only other one I see when I feel at my best. My own personal darkness," he finishes.

The shouts and laughter have faded away and all I can see is Oliver's soft smirk leaning towards me. My heart is sitting somewhere beneath my toes as I scramble for what to say. I want to wrap him in the inky black galaxies of my arms and transport us away to the stars. I want to sink the boat that is this party into the depth of a quiet ocean just meant for us, smiling while we drown. Even so, no words come out.

He's everything when he says things like this, when he looks at me as he does now. I forget we're just friends. Forget our vows of found family. I forget my crush on Tyler. Forget my mother's voice telling me I don't fit in. Forget Ally's threats and Paxton's frowns. I forget everything that tells me loving Oliver Poe is a mistake. All I know in moments like these is that he is air, and without him, I cannot breathe.

"OLLLLIVVEERRRR!"

The distinct pitch of Ally McVie shatters the moment as she calls Oliver's name from across the fire. She's walking toward us, two cups in her hand, straight blonde hair dancing around her shoulders. Right behind her, I can see the broad shoulders of Tyler, following. She skips from foot to foot, kicking rocks and sand from between her flip-flops, as Tyler laughs. I wish she'd catch a sharp one in her toes to bring her down.

I never feel as violent as I do when she waltzes into the picture, ruining things.

If he's irritated by the interruption, you would never know. Oliver greets them effortlessly, like the moment was just waiting for their presence to take shape. His body remains curled toward mine, but his face tilts just enough to meet her call.

"Hey Tyler. Al. Heard you've had a rough night," he doesn't ask, just states it as fact.

Ally's eyes shine in the flickering orange. Her makeup is light, clearly worn off and cleaned up again. Her cheeks are redder than normal, and by the tiny hiccups she is having trouble swallowing, probably already drunk. She nods, causing her hair to stick against the gloss of her mouth.

"I was hoping we could talk. I really need a friend right now," she pouts.

Tyler moves around her and settles on the other side of me.

"Hey Eve," he hums, sounding more sober than Ally by far.

"Hey Ty." I tilt my chin to my shoulder and smile.

I catch the frown that pulls on Oliver's mouth even though he doesn't move, his hands planted on the rough scraps of wood we're sitting on. He sighs, barely audible enough for me to hear. I know this hesitation. It's the same one he uses when Madeline asks him to perform some work he's written in front of her admirers. He doesn't want to be rude—doesn't want to embarrass Ally, but he also despises the task. He'd rather fade into the background of this night, another faint outline in her memory, instead of the standout event she's trying to make him. As if she knows him too, she holds out one of the plastic cups she's gripping in her hand.

"I even brought you a drink! A gift for... being such a great listener."

She's pleading and I hate the way her mouth trembles. Hate the way Oliver misses nothing. His eyes dart from Tyler to me before he lifts his hand, takes the drink, and sniffs. It looks to be the Spootie—a disgusting mixture of fruit that's been drowned in whatever bottom barrel liquor high schoolers can get their hands on. I cannot take another moment of this polite disaster.

"Sorry, *Al*. Oliver doesn't drink," my voice takes on a righteousness I seldom use.

It's one of the few reasons I agreed to come tonight. Oliver and I both don't drink. We've known and seen too much to dabble like the others. And not being the odd one out at a party full of drunks is comforting. Special. Something I wouldn't be able to handle Ally taking away from me. Before she can respond, Paxton stumbles up, hurling his arm around Ally's shoulders, throwing her arm off balance and sloshing part of her drink into the dirt.

"Al! You found him! All is back to rights in your world again, sweet peach! Hey, Ty!" He sings.

I'm pretty sure he's had at least another drink in his absence, but if Oliver is going to let it go, who am I to interfere? Ally glares at Paxton.

"Actually, it's not. I brought your brother a gift and apparently, he's lost all sense of his manners." She smiles sweetly back at Oliver. "Come on, Oli, just a sip! I made that one myself."

She's petulant. A child in a store with a toy that isn't yet hers. She thinks if she gets him to drink, if she convinces him once that she's worth loving, he'll cave. I've never been worried I'd lose Oliver to Ally. Someone like her could never truly understand him. But he's staring at her longer now, staying silent when he should be politely declining.

Tyler brushes my hip, trying to get my attention. I turn to him as he points out someone stumbling into the bushes, demanding to sleep amongst the pines. *Idiots.* When I turn back, Oliver is staring at Tyler's hand, resting, touching me. He shoots his now folded brows back to the drink. Paxton laughs, seeing the indecision in his brother.

"C'mon, brother! It won't bite. One night will not kill you. Promise," he says.

Paxton wants Oliver to let loose. To let go of the tragedy he carries. I just want to help him shoulder the burden. I plead, every thought in my head screaming for him not to take that drink. But he doesn't hear the silent screams. *Or doesn't want to.* He tips the cup into his lips and downs the entire thing in one long swallow.

The universe stills as I lose another piece of Oliver Poe.

UNINVITED GUESTS

DELLBROOK FLOATS AMONGST A bevy of cars. We've arrived in time for the expansion, a tradition long held by the Poes and their ilk, to elongate the festivities of mourning. It would be a shame to let a good death go by so quickly, after all. So many expectations to manage, oddities to fall into, that not for the first time I wonder how they've been able to keep this up for so many generations, especially with the advancements of the world.

The secrets of the Poes are more like whispered myths the public pushes them to hold. Alexander is more than happy to oblige, like every Poe son before him. So, the parties, that for normal society, would be better placed for celebration rather than sorrow, continue. There will be blood red tablecloths and dark gashes of tar-soaked skulls adorning tonight's expansion. Talks of illness, how it would rot the skin if taken hold, and how we're all lucky Paxton didn't have to suffer that fate. A hint placed, to those close enough, that they should consider death themselves, and that there may be a grave or two available in the Poe's private cemetery—for the right price. All of it only to prove to the gatherers they do not fear the sadness of losing their son.

A few photographers mill at the bottom back gate, knowing better than to sneak onto the property, but unwilling to abandon the perfect shot completely. They snap a few of our rental as it slides by, but the flashes do very little through the tinted windows. Oliver has been a statue since we started the trek back home. My body, familiar with the years of tension from him, lulls me into believing it's a companionable silence, even if we're anything but.

For the first time since South Carolina, I consider my phone, about the missed calls and how I'm going to explain to my mother, *and Roger*, why I've been remiss. She'll worry I've fallen back into old habits of letting Oliver consume my every thought, easily pushing aside my life at his whims. I'm not sure how to tell her I haven't when the lie sits fat on my tongue.

I cannot begin to try to wrap my head around what I'm going to say to Ro. Do I just ask him outright or is this a secret better snooped through? The knot in my neck creeps into my forehead, trailing a tight pain through the inner workings of my skull. I work at it, my fingertips spiraling like the mess I am, on each temple.

"Here," Oliver says.

I lift my eyes to see him motioning for me to turn my back to him, his lithe fingers already reaching for my nape, as if it's nothing. I'm reluctant to let him provide relief, worried I've crossed enough boundaries already. But the headache is more violent than my guilt or my common sense. So, I do as he's asked, unbuckling the belt as we ascend the drive. My skin lights up with involuntary shivers at his touch. He smooths his fingertips down the curve, from chin to shoulder, pressing and pushing against the tension. He doesn't give in to it. Instead, he demands it relax beneath his will. My eyes close and a soft whimper of gratitude escapes me.

"I miss this," the traitorous words escape my heart's cage in a whisper.

My rage pounds at the door. *How stupid you sound, Evangeline.* But I can't take them back, can't hide their existence in the space between his breath and mine. They're alive, grounding us into this moment. All I can do is lean in. I push my neck into his hands, trying to say with my body all the surface things I want him to believe. *I miss the touch. Miss the massages. Miss your fingertips and their familiarity with my curves.* I'd rather he believe it purely lust than what it really is. What it has always been. What I cannot admit again.

All he husks out is, "Me too."

I'm undone because I don't know what he means. The car has stopped and now the driver is clearing his throat, obviously ready to be rid of us and whatever is about to happen. The brush of Oliver's hand on my shoulder, his lips leaning down to tell me *something* in my ear. Warmth and the hum of his words. I'm too distracted by the new throbbing, and the ghost of his kiss to my neck, to catch them. Then he opens the door and I know the moment is over. I follow him.

The days have blurred what I remember and what actually is. I'm having the sneaking suspicion that Paxton, for all his games, knew it might do this. Or maybe he didn't, and that's the brilliance of who he was. Oliver grabs my bag along with his and we make our way to the kitchen door. The only thing I want to do is shower the Carolina coast from my skin and sink into the next part of Paxton's letter.

Assuming Oliver is going to share it with me.

I've been asking for it only to be met with silence. His idle hands and far off look tell me he's thinking, lost in the past, some memory they shared. It only makes sense that part two is for him, since the beginning was mine. But what it could be, I cannot even begin to fathom. The years between us feel longer when I think of all the signs I could've missed, all the clues he could've chosen.

The picture itself is proof of how much I do not know about their lives, if not their person. I've missed so much. I have no choice but to trust that Oliver knows he needs me if he has any hope of finding answers. I decide to try one last time before we part ways in the house.

"Oliver, I—"

I stop before I've even stepped through, the door still being held behind me. Oliver's frustrated *tsk* sounds over my shoulder as he pushes into my stilled body. Here, in the kitchen where my whole life changed when I was seven, where I grew up and played and ate after midnight huddled next to two mischievous boys as we shared secrets, now stands Roger.

He's holding two wine glasses above the sink, surprise at seeing me come through the door, frozen in his cheeks. Time stops. I can't put together the two worlds I've lived in colliding at this moment. A brain freeze without the delicious ice of a summer treat. I work the rock of shame that's lodged in my throat as I feel Oliver's hands on my lower back, pressing me in. I worry how I can face him, when my feelings for this place are so raw and unfair to us both.

Then I remember the photo and it stirs me forward. Stirs my curiosity, and more importantly, my anger. *You don't get to be surprised. You're in **my** childhood home,* I internally scold him.

I don't get the chance to say anything before Oliver pushes around me to see what's caught my attention. He looks between us, knowing he's stepped into something, but unsure what it is. Instead of questioning though, he puts down the bags and moves around the island to Roger, cuffing his back and pulling him into a side hug.

"Hey, Catz! Funny seeing you here. We were *just* talking about you."

His words are friendly, but suspicious. He knows nothing is a coincidence, and from the look on Oliver's face, Catz was not an intended guest this evening.

"Hey, Ol. I know, I know. I wasn't on the guest list, but I didn't come for Pax. Not that... well, you have my condolences, but it's not *just* for Pax." His fingers run over his hair, pushing back the strands until they're mussed.

He keeps glancing over, shrugging, looking guilty as if he has an apology at the ready. I wait, hoping my own nerves will settle instead of being spurred along with his. He doesn't want to tell Oliver the real reason he's come, and he's expecting me to jump in at any moment. To scream and spill our secret. A secret I didn't even know I was keeping, one that he has made me an accomplice of.

And I want to. I want to lay it bare, cause a scene. But I can't. Because this is an expansion. Because Oliver is here. Because I cannot stand to be this raw, out here in the open like this. I wish I knew what to do to stop this train wreck from happening. But if we're going to crash, he's going to be the one responsible.

Oliver removes his hand from Roger. "Alright. Then why are you here?"

Roger stares at me, stilling his wandering hands and anxious movements. I nod my head, just enough to let him know I'll be of no help. I'm waiting for answers, too.

"Uh. I'm here for her. Eve... When she," he changes directions and talks only to me. "When you didn't answer your phone and your mother hadn't heard from you, I knew I had to come out. You've never been one to just go silent. I thought maybe something happened."

Oliver's shoulders have been climbing up to his ears as he's thrust into realizing this isn't what it seems. His voice lowers and storm clouds gather around his entire demeanor.

"How do you know Eve? Better yet, why is Isabel contacting *you* about her whereabouts?" he asks through gritted teeth.

He's violence and threats. Protectiveness and confusion. Oliver wears his anger like a shield, keeping the truths he makes for himself about who we are, and the lives we may have without each other safely behind them. I know he's catching on to the only reason we might know each other. Nevertheless, he fights it.

"Ro," I say, interrupting their stare down and bringing Oliver's glare full force to me. "You shouldn't have come. Especially because it seems you have a lot of explanations to give, which believe me, I am *dying* to hear, but this isn't the place for this. *For you.* You should leave."

"Eve..."

"Now, wait—"

Roger steps towards me, my name on his lips, while Oliver's hands are reaching out to still anyone who might try to escape. That is until he realizes Roger is only moving closer to me. He roughly moves between us, his back to me, breaking any eye contact I had. I take a deep breath, knowing shit is about to hit the fan.

"Explain. Now," Oliver rumbles to Roger.

Gone is the softness of my poet. The understanding, bleeding heart I've known. In his place stands the temper of a monsoon, more often glimpsed on the face of Paxton, and my blood pounds seeing how alike they are in this moment. To know Oliver will forever need to be both the shelter and the storm now that his actions are no longer in tandem with another, forces my breath to shallow in pain.

"Whoa!" Roger says, hands fisting, just as stunned at Oliver's aggressive transition. "Oliver, I'm not going to *hurt* Eve. She's... my girlfriend."

"She's..." Oliver starts before I interrupt, anger making my tongue lash out when I shouldn't.

"Actually, Roger, or should I say *Catz*, I was your girlfriend," I lower my voice, realizing someone could overhear, and the last thing I needed was Alexander and Madeline learning of this fiasco at their son's memorial. "Now is not the time or the place. You really need to leave. We can talk about this back home."

Tears threaten, from anger, from confusion and sadness. From the realization that I never knew the man in front of me, even if I thought for a second, I could. He was supposed to be my new beginning, the easy honesty of a future, and instead, the realization of this moment is that he's only dragging me back to my past.

Oliver spins to me. "This is Ro? *The Ro*? The picture..."

I watch as pieces click in Oliver's eyes, lines being traced and followed to create pictures only he and Paxton could see, and I'm left wandering in the dark again. No one moves, as I'm sure he plays through conversations and timelines in his head. I'm tired of always playing catch up, especially when it's my life that's left me behind. Furiously, I move around both men, making it to the inner doorway that'll lead me to the hall before either has the inkling to stop me.

"Fine. If you don't want to go, I will," I growl.

I don't wait for a response, hoping they'll take a hint, but knowing it'll never be that easy. My head is spinning. I've lost someone I thought a friend, someone who had held me. Who had loved my body even when my soul refused him. And I lost him to a life that had already broken me. I didn't want to stand humiliated in the house I promised I would never need again.

Deep vibrations and harsh sounding words echo behind me as I make my escape. *If I can just make it to a locked door*, I pray. But there is no such thing as luck in Dellbrook. Only destiny and hard truths and the weight of your name.

"Eve, wait!"

I pick up my pace, the stairs giving protest at being used when they know I know better. I don't make it—two steps from the top, there's a brush on my elbow, a hand at my neck, pulling me to the landing and into a chest of fine lines and hot flesh. The buttons of his rumpled dress shirt have come undone and my nose rests in the hollow of a throat that is bobbing with words.

"Oliver, let me go," I sigh.

I refuse to let the trails of his skin call forth my tears. A sudden wash of relief hits me as a thought occurs. *I'm so glad I never told him I loved him.* It's followed by rage at the man who's holding me. For knowing that I hadn't opened up. For being right. For causing *all* of this. I push my fists into him, but he holds tight.

"Eve, I'm sorry. I didn't know. I would've never... I cannot explain... We'll get answers. I am so, so sorry." He's muttering and clamoring for words that'll make me stop fighting.

But right now, I'm not thinking of Roger. I'm too focused on the sharp reminder that Oliver Poe has ruined everything.

"You should be," I spit. "This is all your fault. It's always your fault. When are you going to stop causing chaos? When will you give up haunting me?"

I give a final push and he lets me go enough to stare into my face. I'm positive I look feral, like the wild thing he met in the kitchen decades ago. He must see me sinking into the ferocity of my mother, to the depths of stubbornness where I can no longer hear anything but the ocean of my rage floating through me. His teeth worry his bottom lip and I know he doesn't want to let me go, even though we both realize he should.

And then he does the last thing I expect him to. He leans in, rough around his edges, demanding, and kisses me. His mouth moves into mine, pressing, begging, to be let in. My thoughts only know torture, so I push back, rake my hands into his hair, nails gliding down into the small curls that drift along his nape. Somehow, my legs wrap around his hips and he's sweeping me back into the wall.

I should back down. Away. Tell him never to touch me again. I should be livid, and I am, but the lines are so thin between passion and rage that I'm not sure which is driving me anymore. By the scattered heartbeat in Oliver's throat, I'd guess he isn't sure either. We might regret this when we're through, but the heat of his tongue dancing around mine tastes of inevitability.

A picture drops to the floor, the sound of a cracked frame like a whip to our frenzy. I need more. He's taken so much from me, so I'll take this, leave him worshiping at my fury. I trail my mouth along his cheek, his chin, landing in the soft spot just under his jaw where the thrum of his need is felt best. This is not undying love or promises. I'm not a teenager asking him to stay. This is revenge of a woman scorned by loss. Bloodshed of our bond. A rupture of our future. This is the final straw, and I'll be damned if I let him stand a champion in the end.

My lips and teeth are unyielding, yet he matches me with ease. I've lost track of our movements until a doorknob is resting at the base of my spine. My lungs are burning from too much shared air and the taste of maple trying to overwhelm my anger. Memories of Oliver pulling me close, brushing my hair from my face, telling me I belong with him, overtake the moment, and I'm lost in the past.

I slow my hands, then my mouth, before drawing back and sliding down from his hold. He's reluctant to relent, shaking from the nerves of the calm energy taking over me. I reach back, finding the knob to open my door. He's panting, eyes wide and pleading. *Don't,* they whisper. He must know what's coming. I lean with the inswing of the frame, placing the door to be shut between us.

"I should have never come back here," I seethe before slamming the wood in his face.

Only when I hear the soft scuff of his feet retreating do, I let the tears go.

SCATTERED PINES

THE FORMAL DINING ROOM is packed with caterers and guests, which leaves me confident no one will notice one less among them. Everything is drabbed in red, black, and morally grey, including the staff. Most guests are muted in their dresses and ties, all trying to wring the last drops of their own style into the very strict dress code by deviating from the boldness of the hues. They whisper and stare at the ones unlucky enough to realize what deathly casual meant, showing up in staggering purple or green, and easily plucked from the pack for judgment.

The room is hot with the number of bodies toasting to the dead. I can feel the soft prickle of the first dabs of sweat on my neck. I'm on my second stiff drink, still working to erase the still-building heat of my memory and my instant regret with the ever-turning wheels of my curiosity. The distinct feel of hands in my hair and soft gasps at my ear has me forcing the tide of want and depression back, choosing instead to focus on Pax.

I know Oliver has more of the letter hidden somewhere, and that he is reluctant to share with me how the clue we found in Carolina fits into the next part. He stands now, startling in his dark black suit and midnight blue shirt, drink in hand, smiling with June and Matt. The pull of our youth is strong as I see them in a variation of a place I've seen them in a thousand times. Back then, I would've joined in, walked to stand next to Oliver just a little too close, and laughed too, even when it wasn't funny. Now, I only see the opportunity to slip further away from them all.

I've made it to the edge of the room before a man steps in, blocking my exit. I look up into crystal blue eyes, dark blonde stubble trimmed, and lips set in a crease that is made for apologies. I know I can't run from Roger all night and if I stay here and argue with him in the open, I'll lose the only chance I'll have to find Paxton's letter. I grab his hand and tug him along.

"Eve, I think—" he starts.

I spin, teeth bared, and grit out as quietly as I can, "Shut up."

I don't know who's listening and I can't afford to cause a scene. The humiliation of this group of people learning of Roger's betrayal is enough to make anyone's stomach turn. Not to mention what'll play out once Oliver spots us together. I can't take the chance for the gossips to catch on. Thankfully, Roger takes my words to heart and continues to follow me silently the rest of the way out of the room.

Once we cross the threshold of guests into the belly of the house, where I only see workers bussing from the kitchen and back again, I release my hold on him and continue walking toward the front of Dellbrook. He follows without prompting, eager to try our conversation again.

"We should talk," he says.

I sigh, rolling my eyes. The enormity of his explanation too big and too obvious for such words.

"We do," I give. "Just not here. Come on."

I lead him through the hall and into the foyer, where a grand staircase waits. The stairs are trimmed in black, railing ingrained in gold. Soft wooden wings fly up and away, the details worn but impressive still. This is the part of Dellbrook even I do not know well. Where I feel most out of place. The kitchens and the servant stairwells feel like home. But this? This is the reminder of why it isn't.

Still, this is the fastest way to the room I need to be in. I climb the stairs, Roger, hesitantly, following. These stairs don't creak or bend as we move, and we reach the landing as if transported. The ceiling glistens from black to dark grey and back, letting the light play tricks with the dimensions. The hall here is wide and long, nooks for windows and seating found every few doors. A small bookshelf always within reach when you find yourself wandering with nothing else to do. Luxuries provided for a wealthy family whose lives are wrapped up in words.

No one is up here now. No one would dare. The only ones welcome here are Poes. I pray, again, we're not caught.

I come to the door I need, and hesitate for only a single breath before I grasp the knob and push. The first inhale is filled with citrus and cedar, a remnant of his favorite cologne, and I smile a watery smile. I forgot how much I missed that smell, one I would forever pair with Paxton's tanned skin, shining from the lake, breaking out into a grin that lit his face. It's the invitation I need to fully step inside.

His room is how I imagined he left it—clean and tidy. Nothing out of place. Everything folded, and the bed made. His awards and trophies perfectly lined up in his glass bookcase. The cleaners have been here making sure not a single speck of dust mars the effect of his just left room. The walls are still painted bright royal blue, a harsh clash to the black, grey, and red of Dellbrook. Exactly how he wanted it.

I walk farther, dragging my hand against every surface absently. I catch the paper sitting on his desk and rush over, hoping but not believing it could be that easy. When I see that the paper is blank, I huff a laugh. I would've been disappointed if it had been anything else. Still, I see it is only a single sheet, so I gently fold it up and put it in the pocket of my dress. Just in case Oliver overlooked it.

Next to the paper is a book, twilight purple and etched with gold. The flaking swirls and dips, mimicking clouds, as it writes out the word, *dream*. My blood pounds in my ears as my heart picks up speed at the word, remembering the clue. I hurry to open it, fingers catching on a hollow spot in its pages. When I flip it open, I see the perfect cut out for a key tucked in close to its spine. *Empty*. I sigh out in defeat, knowing Oliver has already beaten me here.

"Eve?" Roger says a question in his voice.

I'd almost forgotten him. The book shuts with a *thump* that rings with finality. I turn to see he's leaning in the doorframe, keeping himself outside the room I'm now encased in.

"Yeah... we can talk now."

I don't know what else to say. There are a million questions, but I'm too locked up in fear to ask any of them. *What if I ask the wrong one? What if he can spin his way out?* One of the greatest things adulthood has taught me is that if you're looking for answers from a liar, you let them hang their own rope. So, that's what I do. Let Roger tell me what he thinks I need to know first.

"Here?" he asks, arms splayed wide like I've lost my mind. Like it is sacrilegious to talk about secrets and breakups in the room of a man who just died with them in abundance.

I shrug. "It seems fitting. He would've loved it." *And even if he wouldn't, he deserves to bear witness,* I think.

Roger's laugh startles me. "Yeah. Yeah. He would have." His words are a confirmation and a slap all in one. *He knew Paxton.*

"He always said you were going to rip me to pieces one day, and that when you did, I needed to remember it was my own fault. I could never blame you. That was a promise I made. To him." He points around the room as if I've forgotten what *him* we're talking about. "One of them, anyway. We were friends. I thought the world of Pax. He was the only thing I was sad about leaving behind when I went to NYU. So, naturally, when he asked me for a favor, I didn't even think twice. Of course, I'd help him."

I wrap my arms around myself, telling my heart to stay still. *You wanted answers. You could've gotten on a plane and been home by now. You needed to stay,* I scold myself. I try to picture a younger Roger looking at Pax like he hung the moon. It isn't hard. He always had that effect on people.

"He said, '*Catz, there's a girl, she's like family, but we've had a falling out. She's at NYU too. Would you watch out for her?*' And I thought, sure, why not? I'd be there, anyway. He wasn't asking anything crazy. He just wanted to make sure you were alright. I could understand that. But then I *met* you. And I couldn't mind my own business. When I started asking questions, he just laughed, like he knew I'd be sucked right in."

"You were sent to hook up with me?" I ask, mortified. This is so much worse than I imagined. I thought he just lied to me, that maybe he didn't know in the beginning, but once he did, he kept it from me. But if Paxton had orchestrated this whole thing... If he wasn't already dead, I'd kill him.

"NO!" Roger shouts. "The opposite. He told me to leave you be, said you'd been hurt enough. He never told me what happened, but I could guess. And after seeing that you left with Oliver... I have a pretty good idea. Though, I liked you. I wanted to hang around and I think when he realized I had actual feelings for you, he let it go. He stopped asking so many questions, only sticking to one."

"And? What did he *have* to know?" My heart pounds wondering what he could want to be kept apprised of. *Did he know all the times Roger and I slept together? All the times I hooked up with other people, desperate to forget my past? How many times I cried and cursed being alone, while Roger tried in vain to tell me he was there for me?*

"He always asked if you were happy," he says with a soft sadness.

Of course he did. Never mind that he didn't call and ask me himself. Or visit. Or text. I know I said I wanted to be left alone, but he knew better than to think I could mean it. Not for this long. He had to know I still talked to Madeline and Alexander on the rare occasions they'd call Isabel and I'd pick up the phone. He had to know that my stubborn heart made sure I never hit dial, no matter how many times I pulled up his or Oliver's number on my phone. But maybe if *he* had tried again, I could've forgiven him. Maybe we could have moved on. Instead, he put Roger in my path. Set me on a course to be here, in the mess of being a pawn.

"What did you tell him?" I ask, unable to stop the morbid need to know from escaping my lips.

He looks at me, head tilted in thought. "Most of the time, I told him you were happy enough. Other times, I said *not yet, but she will be.*"

Tears prick at my eyes. No longer able to stand in this room as its walls close in around me and the pain I thought I'd done so well to hide surfaces. I hurry to escape, frustrated that I can't look around more. I want to open drawers and roll his things between my fingertips. I want to smell his last days here and feel them soak into my bones. But not at the expense of seeing them tarnished with this confined grip around my throat. Not with knowing he tipped over the domino that's cascaded into the first man I could have almost loved since leaving here, being a liar and a con. A man who knew I was never whole, no matter how I tried to conceal it.

I skirt around Roger, done with his explanations. They're enough. If he's a suspect for killing Paxton, if there's more to the picture than a happy getaway for him, I, for once, do not want to know. Let Oliver untangle that mess. I need to pretend he doesn't exist in this place, which is impossible when I can hear his feet pounding behind me as I walk deeper into the hall. I spin on him.

"Ro, that's enough! I don't want to hear anymore. I don't want to talk to you or see you. I can't be around you," I gasp.

He nods, eyes stricken, lip pouting.

"I know, Eve. I do. But I just need to tell you one more thing and then I'll go," he sighs out, looking behind him in solace. "There was one other thing Paxton made me promise. It made little sense to me then, and it still doesn't. But if I were a betting man, I'd guess you know exactly what it means. A few months ago, he begged me to take a trip with him. I hadn't seen him in ages, and I didn't want to lie to you, but he was obstinate. So, I went."

The trip to Carolina. Even if I don't want to know, he's going to tell me. I wait for the car to wreck right into me.

"We got drunk, and he kept saying how much he missed you. Missed how things were before. Then he pulled me close and forced me to promise that if anything ever happened to him, I would get you to come here, to Dellbrook. That I would tell you everything. He sounded worried but convinced I could help him. That I needed to. He kept mumbling that you needed to find the letter, and I needed to make sure you were here so you could."

My mind is stuck on *letter* and it repeats in my head. *It wasn't only for Oliver to find, this was for me, too.* An elation in my soul floats up through disappointment, a constant golden light from my youth of following the boys around. Of being included in their games. I choose to snatch it up and sharpen my focus on finding it instead of on the tattered mess of my life lying before me.

I practically run deeper into the house, to the next door I need in the hallway. I fly past the oil portraits, floor to ceiling windows and reading nooks, and then hesitate outside its solid ornate oak. Roger has fled with me, standing only paces away, staring, waiting.

"I... There's something I need to do. Alone. And I can't talk about us or this. At least not now."

He nods. "Oh. OK. A few guys from college are here, so I'll be around for the night at least. And for what it's worth, I *am* sorry. I never wanted to lie to you. If you believe anything, please let it be that." He gives a sad, lonely wave. "Whenever you're ready to talk, and I do mean whenever, I'll be here."

For all his resiliency, I always liked how Roger knew when not to push. He never made me crazy. Never left me reeling. Even now, when I can see in his eyes that he wants me to ask him to stay, that he needs me to tell him it isn't over, he won't try to overwhelm me. He won't fight that I want to be alone. He trusts I know best for myself, even though it's the biggest lie I've ever told. If this trip back to Dellbrook has taught me anything, it's that I know nothing.

"I'll... let you know," I grit out.

It's the best I can offer him. He leaves back the way we came, and I breathe out a lungful of relief. I try the door and unsurprisingly find it locked, which is expected. The good news is that I know the trick. I've understood the Poe boys for years. I know how they move, how they tick, and I know where they hide their keys.

My hand grazes around the door frame, looking to catch my fingernail on an unsuspecting seam. A tiny sliver of wood drags out from it, three-quarters of the way to the top, just past the third hinge, and I hurry to dig my nail in and pull. A small, finely made block of wood releases itself from the rest of the oak and I smile to myself.

The core of the un-lodged block is delicately carved, a tiny raven stamped at its end. I walk to the short bookshelf, directly across from my prized door, and scour its contents until I find one that reads *Edgar's Greatest Works*. I pluck the soft leather binding out, flipping it over until I see the metal lock on its front with the smallest indent that, to others, may be an undetermined blob. To those who know, however, it is a single, solitary bird who has carried the Poe name far and wide for centuries.

The lock clicks out of hold, and tucked inside the paper with a bolded title of ***Ligeia*** is a key. I run my fingers along the story the metal was once holding and down the carefully scribbled notes in the margins. Blue and black ink run wild, a long-held conversation between brothers, until I hit an odd dash of purple at the bottom, messily scrolled, reading, '*you're both wrong, Ligeia was the embodiment of freedom, unfit for the burden of marriage. Death becomes her*'. I laugh at my audacity, even years later.

Hurry, Eve! You have little time to find the letter. I rush back to Oliver's door, knowing it is true. Once Roger returns to the party, it's only a matter of time before Oliver wonders where I've gone and comes looking. I click the key into place in the lock and shoulder in the door, holding my breath.

The sound of waves greets me, lulling and quiet, from a tiny speaker tucked into the headboard of his massive black bed. I roll my eyes at his predictability—the last time I'd been here, it had, at least, been midnight blue. Now, everything has turned to ash and smoke. Tar and tobacco. Towering stacks of tilting books line the floor, blooming open as my eyes reach the top. There are notes and highlights, post-its and receipts marking miscellaneous pages. Each I know is carefully placed. A chaotic organization of words. Just like his mind.

A small shelf sits just above his desk, filled with scattered notebooks whose bindings can barely hold their overused pages. I move to it, knowing somewhere within one of them must be what I'm looking for. What I *need*.

I start gingerly at first, sorting through the pages. A few framed photos catch my eyes, a few of young Oliver and Paxton, happy and carefree. There's one of the three of us, a candid Madeline caught, where we're all reading underneath the leaning tree. Then I see a newer one, certainly within the last few years, of Oliver and Ally. They're dressed to the nines. Oliver's eyes are soft, his grin a ghost, but she's smiling hard enough for the both of them. I scoff and pull my eyes away from the photo. I force myself to sort the pages faster. I move through them, loose reams falling to the floor unbidden. I pick one up to find a poem that is both flushing and embarrassing to read;

The song I want to make love to is
The sound your hips make rubbing against mine,
Your breath rasping into the hollow of my neck
Soft moans against the underside of my ribs
And curse words that sound like gospel
Your body is ink
Spilling onto the page
Of our white bed sheets

I see Ally's smiling face in my peripheral and the piece of paper rips beneath my nails. I follow the sound apart with my sanity. I pick up and read another.

An item on his leger.
A word in his poem.
A moment to be smiled on, reminisced, and then promptly
forgotten
only to be picked up again when reality became too cruel to bear.
Unlike the other women, he wrote into his body.
Just like the one he wrote into his heart.
The one who still resides
His tattoo, his scar.

With each one that describes a curve of a breast or a smile like the stars or a passionate love he cannot let go, I become more frantic, until finally something feral rises in me. I slash poem after useless poem, thought after reckless thought. Large slits of notes lay at my feet, but I still haven't found one that resembles the handwriting I long for.

Only the one inflicts pain.

I hadn't planned on this. I wanted to come and go like the ghost I was in his life. To take what I wanted and flee. The crunch of paper on my toes and the mess laid out around me shows there's no chance of that now. He'll know. He'll see my envy cleaving through eight years of his loving someone else. *Many someones, by the looks of it.* He'll feel the rough edges of my heart, soaking the pages in gasoline. He'll smell the sulfur of my fury in the torn words. The hurt I could no longer push down deep inside. And I'll be left with nowhere to hide.

I suppose this is the least consequence of shattering a heart, so I'll hold my head high. At least, I can hope. Who knows who'll I'll be when he turns his hollow eyes on me after this. Oliver puts words above all, and I've silenced a decade of his voice in mere minutes. *He'll never forgive me.* In the madness that's taken hold, I'm not sure if I mind. I didn't want to risk my heart again. Two birds, one stone.

Just as I'm about to give up, a single sheaf falls to the floor. Its thick paper is folded up and appears more yellow than the other scraps around it. I bend down and grab it up, unfolding it by the edges as carefully as I can. There I find a scrawl I know. I scan the first few lines.

> Oliver, I need you to know what hap-
> pened to me, **if** it happens, which looks
> inevitable at this point. But *first,*
> there's something you must do if you
> want to know the truth.

Below is my name along with Paxton's bible verse telling Oliver to include me. I'm burning to read the whole thing, to dissect every ink stain, but I don't want to be caught here amongst the rubble before I've even copied it. Like lightning, I push it into my pocket and waltz out, mindful to lock back up as I go. Oliver will know it was me, and destroying his work is bad enough.

I don't want to allow a random guest open access to the one place he keeps under lock and key, too. Even my impulsiveness has its limits.

I cannot stop the urge to jog down the hall and stairs, from the foyer into the main hall that leads me into the formal dining room where everyone is still sipping drinks after eating dinner. I pant, less from the exertion and more from the nerves of what I've left behind and what I've found. In only a few days at Dellbrook, I've become ruination. Shame paints my cheeks. I don't have to worry about the girl I was because every action since I walked in has proved she's no longer in control. It cuts another piece off my already tattered heart.

It's fine. Once I'm home, I can go back. Be different. I can finally be kind and healed and happy. It's a placation Roger would give me. One I would despise for its falsity. My brain stutters as I realize it's a sad reminder he'll no longer be a wall I can hide behind. *Don't think about it. Only the letter.* The letter that is pushing me to believe something sinister happened, and that I need to look more closely at Oliver's suspects. I imagine its thick edges in my pocket waiting to be read. *Soon*, I tell it as I pat where it sits.

My whole body feels like it's vibrating on nerves as caterers' stream by me. I'm almost to the thrown open doors where the world can calm down and I can pretend to be normal again. I square my shoulders and lift my head, ready to take on what's left of this evening, even if I'm not ready to face Oliver after what I've done. Tiny cuts bleed out my confidence, but I don't let it show. Not until the second I cross the threshold and lock eyes with him from across the room.

He's smirking, glass held loosely by his side, an arm snaked around his middle. I follow that arm until I reach the face of a woman who has tucked her lips so far into his neck she practically kisses him as she laughs. Her poppy red gown gleams in the lighting, somehow sticking out amongst the others. Memory plays tricks on me as I swear I can hear the high-pitched tinkle of it from here, even through the crowds of mindless chatter and gossip. My blood runs cold as it hits me.

Ally McVie is in Dellbrook.

CURSED GOLD

SPRING, 10 YEARS BEFORE

"**H**OW DO I LOOK?" I ask the room.

Madeline turns toward me before my mother can and a grin splits her face wide. I've never seen her smile at me like this before and my whole body warms at her brightness. My hands fidget from the attention, drawing her eyes down, bringing her lips with them. I immediately stop, but the moment is over.

"Oh, Evangeline. You're beautiful," Mother coos as she sets down the other dress in her hands and walks toward me.

Homecoming wasn't planned for me this year. Both boys already had dates and Mother didn't want me going alone. *Sixteen-year-old girls shouldn't be running around aimlessly in fancy dresses,* she'd said. Then along came Tyler, like a knight carrying a hand painted posterboard, asking me to the dance. I couldn't say no. It would be rude and even Mother had to relent.

While we never went without, we still didn't have enough money to spend on luxuries like this. Not if Mother ever wanted to retire or if I ever wanted to go to college. Madeline was kind enough to let me raid her closet to find the perfect dress, even though she was leaner and taller than I was. There was no shortage of options to try.

I was on dress number four and by the looks of both women, I'd found it. It was a slim, black cocktail dress trimmed in gold meant to drape down a slim body, so on my curvier parts, it clung, defining them. Delicate tendrils of velvet curled around my hips and breasts, each adorned with only the faintest shine when I walked. It reminded me of the darkest hour of night, just before it bloomed into morning. I loved it.

Madeline pushes a pair of gold block heels into my hands.

"These are a half size too big but won't look it. And you'll be able to dance in them just fine," she says.

I think, not for the first time, about the look of want in her eyes. I know she loves her boys in the odd way she can, but I also know she mourns never having a daughter. I see it in fragile moments like this when, even if it's only for a second, she can pretend. I never hesitate to follow along because I want these memories with her. Even if I can never live up to her harshness, I can live in her yearning. After all, I've been playing Poe for years.

I slip the shoes on and I'm ready to go. My hair has been curled and teased, left down because Mother insists it's too beautiful to pin. My makeup is painted on, not too heavy per Mother's request, by Madeline's delicate hand. All that's left is to meet my date. *My date.* I roll the words around in my brain and try not to radiate my excitement too much as to raise questions from the women in the room.

"Thank you both! I think I'm ready," I say nervously as I stand to walk out the door.

Madeline's hand juts out onto my shoulder, stopping me. "Eve. Ladies do not simply *run* into a room looking like you do. We make an entrance." She grins, walking to the door, then slyly adds over her shoulder, "Wait for me to call for you at the stairs."

Once she leaves, Mother laughs. "That woman is remarkable. I will never hold a raindrop to the ocean of confidence she has."

I giggle with her. If there's one trait Madeline is rich in, it's confidence.

"Now, Eve," Mother starts, "I know you know this, but what kind of mother would I be if I didn't say it? Don't let those boys, or **any** boys, talk you into getting into trouble. I know dances have a lot of expectations, but don't be stupid. Not like me. Not like your daddy. You've been given an opportunity with this family. A future. Don't throw it away for a pretty smile or some nonsense words. You hear?"

The south is sprinkling into her voice, and I know she's aching to beat the fear of disobeying into me. I nod my head, knowing she needs my affirmations as much as I need her silence.

"Yes, Momma," I say to appease. "Tyler is a good guy. He won't pressure me to do anything, and I'm not ungrateful. I know who I am and what I need to do."

She stills her hands in my hair and stares me down. I feel her eyes on my soul and want to wiggle away until she stops searching for secrets I keep hidden. Time feels unfathomable as we sit, locked in this second.

"And what about Oliver?" she asks, deadpan.

My heart picks up full speed, thundering into my vocal cords to strangle them.

"What?" I squeak. "Mom, Oliver and I are *friends.*"

I know she doesn't buy it; her mouth keeps tilting down and her eyes darken into a deeper brown.

"Eve... you cannot lie to me. I see it. You and Oliver..."

The sound of a bell interrupts her, followed by my formal introduction by Max, the driver. My feet cannot move fast enough. I stand up and my mother's hands fall to her sides and I turn to grab them in my own, kissing each before looking at her.

"I love you, Momma. And I know you're worried. But it's ok. I'm sixteen and not a child anymore," I say, trying to make her see me instead of the past she still runs from.

Her eyes water, but she just nods her head and lets me go. I race down the hall, but slow as I come to the stairs remembering what Madeline said. I take a deep breath at the top and realize I'm about to have my staircase movie moment. The one all girls dream about. The dramatics and romance of this family never cease and for once, I'm thankful for it. I place my hand on the railing and, as gracefully as I can, I begin my walk down to those waiting.

The first person who comes into view is Alexander. His arm is wrapped around Madeline, who's watching him as he sees me for the first time. He already has tears in his eyes, and I can't help the giggle that bubbles up when I hear his gasp at the sight of me. The pride I feel at their attention is filling my lungs, making it hard to breathe.

On the other side stands Paxton and Tyler. Both their jaws are open, eyes widened in surprise, and I don't know whether to be flattered or offended. They're dressed up in their sleek black and white tuxes, plucked straight from a novel, matching perfectly as the gentlemen they want to be. I turn my body toward them, smiling like a loon, choosing flattery.

And then Oliver walks into the foyer.

His suit is pitch black, with midnight blue velvet running down the lines. Tiny flecks of gold are inlaid throughout the buttons and stitching, unconsciously matching the ones in mine. He's forgone a tie of any type and instead leaves the top three buttons undone. His hair is wild, curling over ears and cheekbones, dark as his jacket and damp at their edges. He's fixing a sleeve cuff, head tilted down and away from me, but when he looks up, the world shifts and he is the only North I know.

I force myself to inhale and then exhale until my body remembers how to be alive again. *I wish Oliver was taking me to the dance.* The thought comes unbidden, and I wipe it away with finality. Wishing for impossible things is a waste when what I have is enough. I demand my body to stop in front of Tyler, instead of continuing to where Oliver's eyes haven't left me. It does as I ask, but I can still feel the pull of him.

"Hey," I say to Tyler, nervous. "You look great!" My hands are shaking, but he's all warmth and calm.

"You look beautiful, Eve." He takes my hand and places a blood red rose corsage on my wrist and shrugs. "I didn't know what you'd be wearing, but figured red goes with anything in the Poe house."

He isn't wrong, as many of the luxuries behind any door here will tell you, but the words jar me from my dreamland. *I'm not a Poe,* I think. It's a glass of cold water to my fire, but I fight to not let it show. *Would he even have asked me if I didn't live in this house? If this family did not take me in?* The questions are irrelevant. Of course, he wouldn't. Without the Poes, I wouldn't be *me* either. Following that line of thought only unravels threads to a very delicate make up that is my life, leaving me naked in a body I don't remember. It's better to let the loose ends go.

I huff what I hope sounds enough like a laugh, to hide my heart. "You're right! Besides, anything goes with black, so I guess we both got lucky." I turn my attention to Paxton, stepping toward him and grabbing his bowtie to straighten it.

"Hey there, stud! Are the girls hiding somewhere?" I ask.

He laughs, big and boisterous. "Naw, they haven't arrived yet. You know how girls can be." He rolls his eyes, then steps back, gaze brushing against every part of me. "But YOU. You look amazing. Who knew the girl who climbs trees and beats boys would become this stunning woman in front of me? Tyler, I may have to steal your date..."

"Paxton. Behave. Tell Isabel you're only joking, she looks like she's about to wring your neck, and I've a mind to let her," Madeline interrupts.

I spin to see the mock horror on my mom's face, concealing the actual concern only someone who shares her blood can see. Still, Dellbrook feels the lightest it ever has with all of us in its entrance. There's a laughing gas effect to our joy that fills it with a sense of hope and inevitability. As if nothing can happen to us. As if we can live forever in this suspension outside of reality.

I forget the desperate pull of want for only an instant, but it's enough to shake my foundation when I'm suddenly in front of Oliver. I stare into the transience moss of his eyes, lost to their ever-changing wilderness. Thankfully, he breaks the silence, since I'm not sure I can.

"She walks in beauty, like the night, of cloudless climes and starry skies; And all that's best of dark and bright, meet in her aspect and her eyes..." He whispers just loud enough for me to hear.

My eyes well up. "Lord Byron tonight, Oli? You must be in a mood."

I want to keep my tone lifted, so he doesn't see how affected I am by his words. They curl and settle into my veins, telling his secrets. I'm not even sure he knows he's doing it, speaking in riddles, but I should know better than to hold them this close to my heart. It isn't me causing him to wax and wane. This is just who Oliver is. Lyrical in his existence.

His lip quirks. "I suppose, but it doesn't change the truth of things. You look stunning, Darkness. Will you... will you save me a dance tonight?"

I know he's being kind, including me in his life as he always has, but my heart does flips in my chest that is too tight to allow such things. The use of my nickname feeling like an oath between us, unbreakable in its intimacy, making it so I could never refuse him.

"Sure," I say.

"Hey, what about me!" Paxton asks, changing the mood and allowing me to sigh in relief.

"You?" I feign surprise. "I couldn't dare be seen with the likes of you." I give my best Audrey Hepburn impression, my vowels elongating and my hands whisking to my forehead in distress. Paxton plays along, slipping into a roguish brute, grabbing at my arms.

"But you must, my dear! You must dance with me, or I'll die!" he yells. Alexander is gleeful in his appraisal of our mock battle, easily joining in.

"It's just one dance, sweet girl. If you dance with one son, you must dance with both. Give an old dying man his wish," he pleas, stepping towards me, but not so far as to release Madeline from his arms.

I break character and laugh, full and loud, the weight of love lifting into an easy hug that carries me this time. For tonight I belong. In this dress, with these boys. I am everything I could be at sixteen. Even as I see my mother's worry trying to tether me to her, I cannot be caught up. Clipped is the ribbon from my balloon of possibility. *Just for tonight.*

The front door to Dellbrook, which is only used by guests, opens, and in walks the needle to pop whatever magic had been spun. Ally strolls in, a deep red dress with a slit clean up to her thigh and heels that have been made to break ankles, giving her a regality I thought impossible. She and Matt were in their 'off-again' status, and she jumped at the chance to guilt Oliver into taking her to the dance.

"Hey, handsome," she says as she sashays over to him.

She delicately, and without touching skin so as not to ruin her make-up, kisses the air next to each of his cheeks. I fume. I tear my attention away and instead focus on the second guest who walks in behind her.

May is quiet, her nerves being worn more vividly than the dusty pink dress she's got on. Her hair is pinned back tight into coils that fall beautifully out of her bun. She's beautiful in the way someone who reads a book they love is; understated and honest. She doesn't demand you give her attention. She's simply happy to exist in a world with her favorite things. And right now, that favorite is Paxton.

Paxton doesn't wait for her to come to him. He slides in front of her, kissing her hand as he places the matching corsage on her wrist. They're an odd couple, one that Madeline would never approve of, given the poor disheveled state of her family and weak backbone. But seeing the way he carefully places her under his shoulder brings my heart back to a slower rhythm. He deserves someone who will look at him as if he's the sun and May has that in spades.

"You all look wonderful," my mother says, breaking the quiet greetings and anticipatory silences. "Should we take some pictures?"

Madeline rushes to grab her camera, a skill that Alexander loves telling anyone who will listen that made him fall madly in love with her. She places us all throughout Dellbrook's space, the stairs, both inside and out, the Nest, and lastly, in front of the stretch limo. She pairs us up and pulls us apart, getting pictures of all the different couples she wants to remember.

"Alright, if you kids don't mind, I'd like one of just mine now." She commands.

Everyone moves away from Paxton and Oliver. I scoot far out of the shot, looking at the boys with their arms linked over their shoulders, smiles bigger than any photo before. She snaps a few before looking my way.

"Eve, if you would please. The middle. Yes, I'd like all of mine, thank you."

My heart swells at the open endearment as I let her direct me. The boys envelope me at the waist, neither surprised nor uncomfortable. As if this is how it was always meant to be. When she finishes, Paxton peels away, eager to join Tyler in taking selfies with the driver. Oliver's hand, however, stays firmly on my hip and I turn into him, hand dropping to his lapel as I look up into his face.

"You ready for tonight?" he asks, voice heady with the depth of becoming a man.

"Are you?" I throw back.

We both know plans have been made. An after party arranged. Drinking and other youth debauchery to attend to. We know that Madeline and Isabel have extended our curfew, even if we hardly pay attention to them anymore, knowing they'll all be fast asleep or preoccupied well before 2 am. Tyler has hinted for the last few weeks that he isn't content being just friends, and as much as I want to hold on to the innocence of loving only the Poe boys, I know I have to grow up.

The serenity of this darkened Peter Pan house has lost its glimmer.

The distinct sound of a shutter disrupts our intense stare down and we look to see Madeline, the camera pressed to her face as she snaps away.

"Sorry, my loves. You just looked too perfect to pass up," she coos. "Now, you better be off before it gets too late! Have a great night. Behave yourselves enough not to get caught, but not enough to not have a few good stories to tell."

She waves us off and we all pile into the limo, sailing our way down the interstate to the dance. When we pull up to The Bradley Estate, in all its glorious lights and outdoor dance floors, I am in thrall. The others, so used to opulence or at the very least pretending to be, shrug off its beauty and head straight into the venue, looking for friends to gush over. Tyler hangs back with me, allowing me to take it all in as he takes my hand in his. We wander into the tent where tables line the walls, each laden with small bites and punches.

"Would you like something to drink?" he asks. I smile and nod, untwining our hands so he can go.

"Eve, come here. There's something I want to show you."

His voice over my shoulder startles me. I didn't realize he hadn't gone in with the others, wasn't hanging off Ally's arm. But Oliver stands just steps behind me, holding his palm out for mine. I take it without thought, letting him lead me into a side door and through the interior that doesn't look like it's part of the event at all.

"We have our dances here every year, and you know how I hate a crowd," he says, shrugging, as if that is all the explanation that is necessary. By the trill in my heart and my willingness to go, I suppose it is.

He continues pulling me through the house until we reach a backdoor and then we are back outside, under the starlight, standing in front of a fountain lit with faint floating candles in its waters. No one else is to be seen, and the party can only faintly be heard in the distance. A band plays a melody that fades into the night. To anyone else, it may feel haunting, but to us, that isn't a bad thing. We stop at the fountain's edge and Oliver grabs my other hand in his.

"I wanted you to know this was here in case you needed a break. And you *did* promise me a dance. Might as well be your first," he says, playful.

He pulls me in close, hip to hip. His chin leaning lightly on my shoulder, his breath unsteady against my pulse. He holds me like that, swaying to a beat we can't really hear. But oh, we can *feel*. And for the first time, this feels like a true confession of the want we've been hiding for years.

In an explosion of movement, he pushes me back just enough to catch my face in his fingers, rubbing the pads of them along my chin. He looks startled. By himself. By me. Then he whispers words I'm not sure if I'm hearing or dreaming, bringing life to something we've both kept veiled.

"Here, when it's just us, I can admit things. Family and burdens and promises mean nothing compared to this. You are my darkness and I... I want to be your first kiss. I know it makes little sense, that it isn't fair. But I won't make it through tonight unless I am." His breath comes in pants, his fingers never stilling on my skin. Everything is electric. "You deserve someone who knows you, who loves you, to give you that. And even if we can't be more, I know I can at least be this."

The confession is nothing. *Everything*. I can't breathe. I don't want to. I want to drown in his sound and shatter on the rocks of never again. I don't tell him that Tyler was my first kiss at the lake after reciting a love poem meant only for Oliver. I don't try to force the whys and why nots of us being together or suffocate him with how much I *want*. If he needs to give me this moment, I won't ruin it because the truth is, I need it, too. And Oliver Poe is nothing if not this.

I nod my head and he smiles that soft, sweet, innocent tilt. He rubs his thumbs along my lips, testing them out before he leans in. The smell of fresh maple and coffee tingles my nose, new from his quest to give up adding sugar to his drinks. I feel the press of flesh on flesh, soft, but insistent to be remembered. He doesn't push for more, but I'm a hungry little thing.

I wrap my arms around his neck and force the weight of my body onto him, pulling him down. He catches me, wrapping me up and meeting me, eager kiss for eager kiss. I don't know what I'm doing. Tyler had given me the briefest peck, nothing like the entanglement I'm in now. But Oliver doesn't seem to mind. He leads me into a slower pace before gliding across the seam of my lips with his tongue. I don't hesitate to let him in, to taste the velvet of his expression.

I now know why Edgar always feared he was death to his loved ones. This kiss alone steals my breath and my heart, trapping me in the peaceful march toward the underworld. Happily, I go. I will follow wherever Oliver leads. It is no surprise I don't hear the footsteps coming up behind us.

"Oliver! Eve! Where are you two?"

Paxton is yelling from inside the house. He sounds suspicious, as if he knows what we're up to, and the fear of being caught jolts us apart. By the time Pax barrels through the door to us, Oliver and I are on opposite sides of the fountain, looking guilty and out of place. Thankfully, he's alone, so I don't have to share this embarrassment in front of a crowd.

He looks between us, his dastardly smirk making me want to scream. Oliver's lips look swollen and pinched, his hair mussed despite the hands combing it back into some semblance of calm. I'd bet my whole life savings we're a matching pair. I can only imagine the blush of my cheeks and the thick reddening of my lips. My hands shoot to my own strands, praying all the waves are not undone and frizzy already.

"You two look as if you have a confession to make. Are we having a Tell-Tale Heart moment perhaps?" he hums, dark jealous laughter on the tips of his words.

I go to open my mouth, unsure of whether the truth or a clever lie will spill out, but he doesn't allow for either. His pointer finger pops up in a 'one moment' gesture and I seal back up my lips.

"No. I don't want to know. If Madeline asks me anything about tonight, I cannot keep whatever lie you are spinning or the truth you are leaking from her. Leave me out of your schemes. I only came to find you because your *dates* have been looking. They want to get a few dances in before we call it a night here and go to the actual party."

He pushes his hands in his pocket, spinning on his heel to head back to the door. Before he reaches the threshold, he calls back to us.

"Coming?"

He doesn't trust you to follow. It's for good reason because if the choice were between heading back to the dance or to Oliver's arms, I know what I would choose. Oliver is staring at me, but at his brother's call, he sighs and breaks his statue hold. He mimics Paxton's casual stroll and follows, leaving me in the moonlight, alone.

I look around. One last glance at a night I know will change everything inside of me, even if it can change nothing between us. I will remember, and that'll be enough. *More than I could hope for.* I hurry to catch up with the boys and make our way towards our dates and the dance floor.

CHIPPED STONE

I SWING A HARD left to the bartender instead of weaving my way over to my high school friends. I can't face Oliver with Ally draped over his arm. Not after the rumors and the eight years of silence between us. Not after what I've left in my wake. She'll curl under the mosaic of my calm and split it into the pieces it truly is, and I can't crack now.

Even though I know a drink isn't what I need, it's all I can want. The jittery nature of this night is more than I can handle alone. I hear Oliver's harsh whispers in my head calling me a hypocrite as I order, the past too vivid to allow for the growth of our years to dissolve the argument from a decade ago. Another wound not quite healed. Another brick in the wall between us.

"Now, why is the prized-would-be-daughter hiding out at the bar?"

A hand waves the bartender down next to me, asking for a refill. The bright gold of his thumb ring shaped like a chain, catching my eye. Isaac's face comes into view as he leans against the counter next to me. His suit tonight is ill fitting, as if he's done so on purpose. It folds off his body with the slouch of his shoulders, leaving no sign of his trimmed arms. The pale black of it washes his skin out, making him appear sick, but his eyes shine bright as ever.

"I'm not a Poe. Death does little to inspire me," I snap.

My edges are rougher than I can afford them to be, and I know I need to wrangle them in by the cruel number of teeth he's showing. *Where the fuck is my drink?*

"That's fair. I'm not one to party over it, either. Us Langley's tend to just move on when someone dies. After all, it's just another day at work. Still, I can't help but admire the opulence the Poes show. How much fervor is given to the black sheep of this family. It's a bit... much, don't you think? Even for them." Our drinks are placed down in front of us, and Isaac brushes the rim with his finger before continuing. "Almost as if they're looking for something in the show. Or hiding it, I suppose. Perhaps if they had a body, this wouldn't feel so *performative.*"

His smile is sick and cunning as he takes a drink. *Who doesn't have a body?* I did find it odd that Paxton was cremated, since, as I'd learned as a child, none of his ancestors were, but I never thought it was because they didn't have a choice in the matter. Alarm bells blast from every direction inside my body. They tell me to run, to ask point blank what he means, to cave to the pressure of whatever it is he thinks I know. He's too close to me, and all I can picture is Oliver's eyes as he proclaimed death was not the end before leading me to monsters who wish it to be. *This could be Paxton's murderer.*

I let out a breathy laugh. "You think so? Tell me, what is the conspiracy here? Why the pomp and circumstance? Are you telling me the people here would feel more comfortable having a dead person in their presence during the days of mourning? Would that change how he will be missed? No... I don't believe you're speaking from logic. Only from your obvious envy for who you'll never be and what you'll never have."

His thick fingers grab roughly at my arm, squeezing only enough to frighten. There's an instinct as a woman, a primal fear that some men initiate, telling us to tread light. To obey. I fight it now, so I can think straight so as not to get pulled into the past. For Paxton. *For myself.*

"You think you know things because you've been their favorite pet, but I am their equal, little bird. We were partners. And even then, they were snakes. Take it from me. There's no loyalty among the elite. Even when their entire existence is built on being cast out. It's all a very delicate lie. You'd be better off spilling their secrets to the highest bidder than protecting them, Evangeline." His voice is direct, seething underneath the thinly veiled threat.

"Isaac," a female voice lilts beside him. "Uncle is looking for you by the weeping angel."

Emily is encased in dark purple, the silk of her matching suit creased from too many hours of wear. Her hair is piled on top of her head, giving her a needed inch to her height. Something fierce flashes in the lines of her cheeks, seeming to say that Isaac should take heed. Thankfully, he does, slowly releasing my arm and nodding at her.

"Thank you, cousin." He says as he goes to move past me, stopping only briefly at my ear to whisper, "Remember what I said. Time to sing, little bird."

And then he's gone, off to find his father in the far reaches of the room, no doubt plotting horrible things on the way. I'm shocked to find Emily has not broken the pinch of her plum colored lips, now directed at me. She orders a drink and leans into the space her cousin just left. I'm not sure why she stepped in to break up Isaac and mine's conversation, and I pry with little regard for stealth.

"Thanks," I say. "He was creeping me out." I know the words are blunt. I can tell there's some fondness she has for him, and he is her family.

"Isaac can be... impatient. He's always been one to tip his hand before the game has even begun. He's all bark and no bite. Mostly," Emily says, her words soft and yet, with an undercurrent of rage.

"Game? I don't think grabbing a woman in public is a game," I intone. She rolls her eyes so far into the back of her head I wonder if her features will ever recover.

"Please, Eve. Don't be so dense and pretend me so stupid. *Everything* with the Poe family is a game. We all show up, and *we all play*. Whether we want to or not. The allure of their riddles, of their intrigue, calls to us all and even when we're hurt, we come back for more. It's their curse and they are so good at weaponizing it that others can believe it isn't true. But you're not that naïve. You know as well as I do there's more going on here. Everyone has an agenda, and somehow, you've ended up on Isaac's, which means you've also ended up on mine."

It's the most I've heard the woman say and I can see why Paxton liked her, even if he couldn't love her. Her unequivocal way of ripping down the masks of those around her would have delighted him to no end. Her boldness to stand out when everyone else is determined to fit in. I could see him bringing her to parties just to irritate Madeline. The thought makes me like her a little too, even if I don't trust her.

I cut the façade and match her bluntness. "Fine. It's all a game. So, why am I on your agenda? Why step in at all? I thought you loved Paxton." *And hated me.* The words go unsaid, but their implications are obvious.

She laughs. "You tell me your plans and I'll tell you mine."

Her tone is playful, eyebrow quirking up, daring me to spill. My face freezes. Ripping Oliver's work to shreds is one thing, as unforgiveable as it is, but giving this secret to someone who could hide the answers we need to solve it? That would be an act of war. Emily seems to know this because she continues her laugh.

"Didn't think so. And as I said, Isaac has a knack for ruining things. I wanted to make sure he kept all the necessary pieces on the board. Liking you has nothing to do with it. Not all of us have the luxury of being run by emotions. Pragmatism is my sharpest tool, Ms. Pierce, and I intend to use it to my full advantage."

With that, she takes her drink and saunters off, more than likely to talk to her cousin and remind him of whatever rules they need to play by. At this point, I have more questions than answers. I'm practically drowning in them. I need to talk to Oliver, tell him what happened, and hope that we can figure out what's missing. *Before he won't speak to you again.*

Swallowing my pride and my shame, I search for him, hoping I can catch him before the party ends, and he sees what I have done. I scan the room, picking out Ally's grating glow from here. She's still surrounded by Matt and June, but Oliver is nowhere to be seen. I choke down the knowledge of what I need to do next and head towards them.

"Hey guys," I interrupt, trying to sound happy enough to see them.

They all quiet. If looks could kill, June would be murdering me right this instant. The three of them and I never talked outside of Oliver, Paxton, and Tyler. If they weren't present, we might as well be strangers. Matt looks shocked I'd even have the gull to address them. I ignore them both. Neither is who I've come for. My attention focuses solely on Ally.

Her cheeks are pink with youth that cling to her despite the years. She's studying me, face neutral. The hate and jealousy I'm used to, wiped clean. As if she has nothing to worry about with me anymore. The sinking of the stones in my gut pushes bile into my throat.

"You guys haven't seen Oliver around, have you?" I ask, casually as I can.

My question is pointed directly to the blonde in front of me, and she knows it. A smirk lights her lips and I see triumph blossoming.

"Actually, he was just here. He had to step out for a bit. Said it was something important to take care of but that he'd be back. You might be able to find him in the drive. He went that direction," she responds, being far too helpful. I tip my head in thanks, not wanting to push my luck as I move to leave, but she hasn't let loose the arrow yet.

"Oh, and Eve. I hope everything between us is alright. I mean, it's been so long, and he assured me you'd moved on as well. I just want you to know there's no hard feelings. I would never let a boy get between us girls." Her words drip satisfaction that she doesn't even try to hide.

So, the rumors are true. Oliver and Ally. The flash flood of questions overtakes me, and I forget what I've come to do. *How long? When did it start? Why would he choose her? Are they still? Does he love her?* Then the shock of the one pervasive thought I cannot control leaks in and skewers the last remaining piece of my heart. *The poems were about her.*

I can't breathe. I think I nod or tell her *no hard feelings,* but I can't be sure. I don't know where I'm going, but the walls and art and flooring are all blurring away from me and before I know it, I'm out the front door into the drive. I pace down the stairs and back, unsure of what to do next, knowing I need to calm down and think.

Pragmatism is my sharpest tool. I hear Emily's words shoot through me. They soothe something deeper in me than I'd like to admit. Right now, the emotional typhoon raging within me must make way for reason. *Focus on the letter. Find Oliver. Find Paxton's murderer.* Each syllable becomes a prayer, a mantra, to pull me off the precipice of more bad decisions.

I pull the letter from my pocket, terrified that when I open it, there'll be no going back on this night, a silly intuition since, from the moment I walked into Dellbrook, everything was changed. I thumb it open and force myself to read.

> There's a night we've always fought
> about, and now, I'd like to have the
> last word. Some hard truths you need
> to face, baby brother, but it's time.

Dances are supposed to be fun
But you went ahead and ruined this one
The girl in the dress
That you went and kissed
Then sharply broke the three of us up.
You know the place where the companion to noon laid claim
To what was and rhymed with grave
Where no key could unlock it,
Without the story, our girl was mocked for
But you got in without her, anyway.


```
Go there, Oliver, and find what you
lost.
```


The lines are that of a child, loopier and sloppy, written in a rush. Unlike Paxton's first clue to me. But there is no doubt this is him. I read through the lines again, this time slower, trying to make out the riddle to lead me where I need to go. The most obvious one, regarding me, is the second to last line of the riddle—the story I was mocked for has to be referring to the raven heads I had brought for show and tell, and the poem Edgar was known for.

The next part that slides into place is the first line—noon's companion must be midnight. The rest of the riddle escapes me. I reach to all ends of my brain, replay the dances we've been to, but know that homecoming is the only one Paxton could be referring to. I run through all the words I can think of that rhyme with grave, *brave, rave, crave, save, Dave...* None of them makes sense to me. I need Oliver.

As if by magic, a figure down the drive catches my eye. It's dark and they're dressed completely in black, except for what I'd bet is a midnight blue shirt. All that I can make out is their height and the sharp slide of their shoulders, but I know without a doubt, when they start walking, that it's Oliver. He's pacing erratically, as if he's on the clock, when a car pulls up. A valet rounds the vehicle and hands him the keys. He peels out, making his way to the exit.

I panic. He's going to the clue without me. It's the only explanation for his quiet and quick departure. *I don't think so,* I mutter determinedly under my breath. My steps pick up as I look for a valet or any car with the keys still inside. I'm not above a minor crime if it means solving a bigger one. With every car I pass with no luck, my nerves jump higher into my throat. *What if I can't find him?* That's unacceptable.

"You look like you need a ride," a husky voice calls from the driver's side of a lifted truck just up ahead.

My heart stutters and I smile in relief.

"You couldn't have more perfect timing," I say, racing toward the passenger side before jumping in. "Follow the beamer that just left!"

Tyler laughs as he presses the gas pedal down, eager to obey.

"You haven't changed a bit, Evangeline Pierce. Not one bit."

I look him up and down, appreciative of the handsome man next to me and his ability to show up just when I need him.

"Neither have you, Tyler." *Neither have you.*

DESOLATE INTENTIONS

Friday, Present

"**Y**OU KNOW I LOVE a good adventure, Eve, but are you going to tell me *why* we're following Oliver around town this late at night?" Tyler asks.

His voice is easy, inviting. Exactly as it always has been. I can feel the years between us melting away. The awkward last semester before graduation. The breakup when he realized I could never love him the way I loved them. And he deserved to be loved that way. He hadn't been mad. He had just hugged me and told me how lucky they were. Only I know that luck isn't always a good thing.

"What do you remember about homecoming?" I ask instead of answering him. He doesn't force his question, instead he moves along with my own, giving it genuine thought.

"I remember showing up, being excited to get to take you out, seeing how absolutely breathtaking you looked, ready to make *us* official." He smiles at me. "We got to the venue, danced a bit, then left early to go to the party. I remember you being upset, unwilling to talk to me about it, begging to go home, and us dropping you off. It gets a bit vague from there."

Of course, it does. I remember all that, too. I also remember the party, where Oliver's entire demeanor changed as he demanded me to leave. I had cried to Tyler, begging him to call the car for me, needing to sit in my sorrow alone rather than spend my night holding back tears at Oliver's judgmental stares.

"Yeah. You'd had a few drinks by the time I left, but if you can remember anything after, you would really help me out," I plead.

He switches between the road and my face, head bobbing back and forth, before he finally responds.

"How about you tell me what you're looking for, exactly? As much as I love playing 20 questions with you, if you want my help, you're going to have to let me in. You know how this works," he says, the last part on a swallow.

We both understand the implication of his words. Remembering that the last time we really talked, he told me the same thing. Instead of opening up then, I slammed the door in his face. I could never share my heart with him when I'd already given it away. Yet, tonight, it wasn't me he needed to see, and this wasn't some selfish crush I was trying to use to forget everything else. I needed him for Paxton. For Oliver. I inhale deeply.

"*You know the place where the companion to noon laid claim. To what was and rhymed with grave. Where no key could unlock it. Without the story, our girl was mocked for. But you got in without her, anyway.*"

Tyler slams to a stop at a yellow light and we watch the car we've been following three cars behind slide into a free right and disappear. My stomach sinks, praying for the light to turn green and with every second it doesn't, hope slips further away.

"Tyler, we're losing him!" I shriek, his tone on the edge of panic.

He doesn't move. Doesn't flinch. His face tilts toward me, staring. The light flashes green and I my hands flail at it.

"Tyler! It's green! Let's go!"

After what feels like eternity, he does, but not at the breakneck speed my anxiety is demanding. Instead, he crawls through the streets, missing the right turn Oliver took. I'm about to lose my mind when he finally joins the conversation again.

"What the hell was that you quoted, Eve?" he asks.

I stare at him agape, "Really? That's the important question right now? *You* wanted to know what I was looking for."

He shrugs. "Yeah, it's important! Especially, the fact that I helped write it. Although some lines have been changed."

"Excuse me?" I say, surprised. My whole body vibrates with the coincidence.

"A couple months ago. Paxton said he wanted to add a touch of Poe to his high school reunion. He wanted to get us all together again, even though we were in different grades, and asked if I could help with creating a riddle for just our group about his senior homecoming. Apparently, he wanted to be surprised, too. I did, and now you have it."

Paxton gave you a way back in. Without Oliver. He knew that there was a good chance Oliver might leave me behind. That he would try to keep this from me, so Paxton put in a failsafe—a way I could find the answers even if Oliver refused to give them to me. *Do all the clues have one?* I mentally slap myself back into the present. Trails of thoughts like that would keep me spinning for days. Months. Right now, the only one that matters is this one.

Paxton played this on a very sharp edge. He had to have thought about the possibility of how his mourning would play out, and the faith that Tyler would show when I needed him. *Or that you would call him if you did.* Paxton's intelligence has always awed me, but now it is his conviction in it that has me floored. He had to have contingencies upon contingencies. He had to have believed so completely in knowing us and himself to make this happen.

And so far, he's been right.

"He really did plan for everything, didn't he?" I hear Tyler ask, breaking my thoughts.

I stare, his words circling my mind.

"What do you mean?" I ask, still puzzling it all out.

"The reunion. He must have passed it along to you and Oliver in case something happened to him, right? That's why we're following him?" he says, looking at me like I've lost my mind.

I need to steer the conversation back to finding where Oliver went, but I'm still reeling with other questions. Mostly about why, if Paxton plans for everything, he did not have a will in place. It hadn't occurred to me before to ask. I was so wrapped up in him being gone, seeing Oliver again, and then finding out he was murdered to really think about it. But the reading of the will had not been called. Or I had been left out of it. Neither seemed plausible. *He didn't plan for everything.* With every clue, murder was looking more and more likely.

"Yeah… You're right. He did. Can you help me solve it? I wasn't there, so I'm having trouble."

I try to fold the unanswered questions away for later. I need to talk to Madeline. If she knew nothing else, I would bet my life that she'll know about the state of his affairs. And that means she would know who sent the letters upon his death. Right now, though, I need to focus on having Tyler help me find where Oliver's gone and why.

Tyler smiles over at me. "Of course, I'll help." He turns on his blinker and blows through a yellow to make the turn, giving me the urgency I've been wanting.

"Where are we headed?" I ask, elated to be on the chase.

"To the place that rhymes with grave… If we want in, we'll have to get there by midnight."

Neon red blurs and drips from the nightclub's sign that hangs on the outside of its brick exterior. *Chadwick Lead Works* is etched permanently above it, a history that cannot be erased, even for the likes of the upper echelon revelers of Boston. In a building that should hold multiple offices or warehouse spaces, there is only one.

"Password," the bulky man in front of me grunts.

It's the only thing he's said since Tyler drug me into this back alley to him.

"Like I said, my friend, we don't have tonight's password. But I can guarantee you want us in there. This lovely lady next to me happens to be Boston royalty…"

I'm not, but I'd let Tyler say anything if it got us inside. *Did Oliver have any trouble?* No. Why would he? He actually *was* royalty. Tyler steps away from the man, corralling me to the side to let the others in line have a shot. We watch them fail before he leans into me.

"Sorry, Eve. I thought we could get in. I'll make a call, but by the time she can help, it'll probably be too late. You'd think the Poe name would carry more weight," he scoffs, apologetic.

I'm only half listening, but it's enough to catch his comparison of me to them. *It might,* I think, *if I were a Poe.* But no one outside of the family, close friends, and absolute fanatics would know about me. I mentally flip through the lines of the riddle, searching for any clue for what will get us inside. Tyler starts the walk back to the truck, his fingers texting furiously. *Where no key could unlock it. Without the story, our girl was mocked for.* That's it.

"Tyler. Wait!" I take a few quick steps and grab his arm, pulling him back to the door.

"Look, if you don't have the password, I can't let you in…" The guard is gruff and irritated, no longer entertained by us.

"Nevermore," I interrupt him.

He goes silent. His eyes feel like they pierce into me, see the darkness I'm hiding. The pain. I'm sure he thinks it's a trick, but he undoes the velvet red rope and steps aside.

"Welcome to Crave, Miss Poe," he says, as Tyler and I rush by, not allowing him to change his mind and keep us locked out.

We barely get up the narrowed staircase before Tyler's arm wraps around my shoulder.

"Wow! I am taking you to all the exclusive clubs I can never seem to get into. How did you know the password?" he asks, awed.

"It was in the riddle. *Without the story, our girl was mocked for.* When I was young, before we went to school together, I brought a few raven skulls for show and tell. The kids were ruthless. It's why Paxton and Oliver transferred from their all-boys' school. Why they stayed with me through junior high and high school. The story had to be Nevermore."

The question I had now was *why*. The bullying was a bad memory, sure, but the night the boys fought to protect me? I had always thought it was the start of our bond. Maybe Paxton saw it as the beginning of our breaking. *Or theirs.* Tyler wraps his fingers around my shoulder and forces me to stop, eyes full of concern.

"I'm sorry that happened to you, and I'm sorry Pax changed the line and brought it back up. But you know them, there's got to be a reason. So, what do we do now?"

He sees me drifting into the past and is pulling me back in like a lifeline. He's always been practical and easy. Unburdened in a way the boys could never be—were never allowed to be. I grab the hand on my shoulder and give it a squeeze. Something to tell him I'm grateful he's here. That I care about him, too.

"We find Oliver. I'm not sure what he did here or what he lost, so I have nowhere to look. Unless you know of something?" It's a long shot, but I ask anyway.

Tyler shakes his head. "I don't. Once we got here, I went from being a little tipsy to wasted. He could have lost the car, and I would have had no idea."

I nod. "OK, then plan A. Find Oliver."

We enter the main level to a smoky, open floor plan bathed in red lights. There's a round bar smack in the middle of it with an additional level where the DJ is bobbing to the beat at its center. People are milling about, but it's a lot less crowded than the line outside would have you believe.

"They're private events mostly," Tyler tells me without prompting. "They only have public events every few weeks. Other than that, it's exclusive access only. The draw being the lack of a crowd. No fans, no fanfare. But every now and again, they let in someone who doesn't belong."

He looks pointedly at me. Tonight, we're those people. Thankfully, we're dressed nicely enough in black attire from the expanse not to cause too much of a scene. If it were any other night, though, I would be thrown out of here on principal.

"Let's split up and meet at the bar in ten," I tell Tyler.

He answers by slipping his arm off me and disappearing into the sidelines of the dance floor. He's confident and casual, lingering into shadowed booths and peeking around dancing women. Even though he didn't have the password, he fits in here. He morphs before me into one of them and I wonder if I do that, too. If living with the Poes as long as I have has garnered me the same ability to hide my true status among the wealth.

I walk my perimeter looking for the raven hair of a man I could name only by his breathing. I sway my hips and arms to the pounding bass, bumping into any dark suited man who has his back to me, just to see his face. None are Oliver, although by the way a few of them look at me, I know they wish they were. *How easy would it be if I could just embrace them instead of this desperate chase my heart refuses to give up.*

I reach the bar before Tyler does. I ponder over whether to get us both a drink, knowing I shouldn't, but feeling the awful sting of defeat pushing against my better judgment. Once Oliver goes home and sees what I've done, he may never share the next clue with me. Hell, he might never speak to me again. He'll be determined to figure it out alone, Paxton be damned. And as punishment, I'll never know the truth of what happened. I'll never stop wondering what could've been. It'll be the ultimate, and final, slash Oliver Poe can give to my heart.

Then I see him. He's removed his jacket and button down and instead stands in a rumpled dark grey tee shirt and black slacks. He's got one foot kicked out behind him and is leaning against the coat check desk, waiting. His fingers graze circles on its surface, the anatomical heart tattooed on his forearm pumping with the motion. I don't hesitate as I spring from my seat, eager to have him close before I lose him again.

"Funny seeing you here," I say, not hiding my irritation at being left behind.

He doesn't immediately turn to me, but I watch as my presence comes to him in waves. First his shoulders sink, his foot connecting to the ground. Then his hands grip the edge, and his chest deflates on a breath. I can almost hear the argument he's having with himself right now in his head; *she shouldn't be here, you left her behind. This is what you get for trying to hide things.* I've heard him enough times to know the turmoil he feels between what he thinks needs to be done and honesty.

"Eve," he says. "You made it. I was wondering when you might show."

"Bullshit. You *knew* without you I didn't have a chance of finding this place. How could I? We both know the after party was when you sent me home. I didn't make it this far 10 years ago and I shouldn't have made it this far now."

His reply is cutoff at the tip of his tongue when a scantily clad girl comes to the window.

"I can take your ticket if you have one, but I don't remember you dropping anything off," she says to Oliver, looking him up and down. "And I would remember."

His lips twitch up. "You're right. I didn't. I was looking for your lost and found. Should be under Oliver Poe."

Her eyes widen as she nods. "I'll be right back with that, Mr. Poe."

"*Mr. Poe,*" I mock. "Since when did you take the reins from Alexander?" I want to needle him, but it does the opposite. He laughs, a real one.

"Please, we both know Alexander never held them in the first place. Madeline has always worn the pants, Poe by blood be damned. Besides, I've gotten used to it. Job hazard and all that."

Often, I forget Oliver is renowned for more than just his name. He's always been Oliver Poe to me, and Oliver has always written poetry. One never existed without the other, so it is easy for me to forget that the world didn't always know it, too. With book tours and readings, he's shared a vital piece of himself that I had always thought of as just ours. The family's. Something he shared with only those he loved. And that made it hurt too much to remember.

"I guess it would be," I mumble. The coat check girl doesn't take long. She slips a piece of paper towards Oliver.

"If you'll just sign right here saying you've received your item. You can leave your number, too, if you'd like," she says as she leans towards him along with the pen she's holding out.

Oliver takes and signs it without hesitation, leaving only the scribbles of his name. He doesn't admire her or flirt. For all I know, he hasn't even looked at her. A minor slip of satisfaction races through me as she drags back the paper, rejected, but unfazed. With no fanfare, she hands him a book, well-worn and read. Some pages slightly water warped.

"Why do you have my book? And why is it in the lost and found of this disgusting hell den?" I ask, shocked and on the verge of violence.

He holds the first edition Neruda tenderly in his hands, thumbs holding onto the binding while his index fingers skim through its pages. Every single one is painstakingly rewritten by him in the margins, of favorite English versions he's found or ones he's taken the liberty of translating himself. It was a gift from him for my twelfth birthday. It had stuffed away just after the incident at the lake, too terrified I'd quote another love poem, to continue losing myself in its pages.

"I... I don't know. I'd thought I'd lost it. I don't even remember bringing it here," he whispers.

"Well, you did. My question is, why did you have it in the first place? You gave it to me. If you wanted it back, you could have asked," I say accusingly.

He looks struck, unsure. The broken shards of my anger sharpen, ready to be let loose.

"And you O my soul where you stand, surrounded, detached, in measureless oceans of space, ceaselessly musing, venturing, throwing, seeking the spheres to connect them."

He quotes Whitman as if he cannot breathe without his words, eyes unfocused on where we are, lost instead in the pages, before he continues and answers me. "It doesn't matter anymore. It's here, and Paxton knew. A little devious to leave it until now to tell me, but how can I be mad at the dead? Since you're here, are you going to help me look for the next clue, or are you going to pick a fight? Because if it's the latter, you can leave. We'll fight when I'm home."

There's no bite to his words, just resignation. A man unsure of the path that lay before him. He may have known where to go from Paxton's clue, but he didn't expect what he'd found. As much as I want to know why my book is here and why he'd taken it from me, and the pure irritation at how it may have been handled, I can't leave him here alone when it's obvious he needs me. *For Paxton*, I remind myself.

"We'll find the anchor, Oliver. Just as Whitman said. Do you see anything out of place in the pages?" I ask.

He shakes his head. "No. Nothing."

"Do you remember anything from homecoming night when you were here? Anything that Paxton said, or that you did that might give us another clue that connects this place to that book?"

"There you are!" Tyler calls to me.

I watch as Oliver's face tightens, his chest losing the ease of it being just us. Tyler is making his way from behind us, back where I was supposed to meet him at the bar, a pretty brunette clasping to his arm. My eyes focus in, a question on who he is escorting our way, but he either doesn't see or ignores it. Instead, he notices Oliver almost immediately. His smile doesn't waver, but I can see the light dim from his eyes enough to know it still stings for us to all to be together.

"You found him," Tyler says as he holds out a hand, which Oliver takes in a firm shake. I eye the woman with him, waiting for him to explain. Both Oliver and Tyler don't bat an eye and continue on as if it is just the three of us.

"She did. I didn't realize she had a partner in her search, though. Or did you just happen to be at the club tonight and you both ran into each other?" Oliver asks.

He eyes Tyler, unsure of why I would bring someone else into the puzzle only we should be solving. He doesn't know Paxton has contingencies. I straighten my spine. He was the one who tried to leave me behind. I have nothing to be sorry for.

"Actually, we ran into each other in the driveway of Dellbrook. Tyler was just arriving when you tried to sneak off without me." I do not waver from my locked stare on Oliver. "Good thing too, since he's the one who originally wrote the riddle for Paxton. Otherwise, I may have never found you. And it looks like while I was searching, Tyler found someone of his own. Are you going to introduce us?"

Oliver's eyebrows raise, skeptical as I of Tyler's involvement and the high pitch of my question.

"Sorry! I forget not everyone has met. Eve, this is Rose. Rose, this is Eve. And you already know Oliver," he says, squeezing her across the waist.

Rose leans towards me, hand sticking out. "It is so nice to finally meet you, Eve! I've heard so much about you. Tyler texted to see if I could help get you in, but it looks like you didn't need it after all."

Her smile is soft and understanding, like she knows all the secrets the three of us hold. My throat is squeezing with trepidation, but I land my palm in hers anyway and give it a small but firm shake. "It's nice to meet you, too!" I squeak out.

Thankfully, Oliver saves me as he chuckles and claps Tyler on the back.

"For all Paxton was, no one could ever claim he was careless. Riddles upon riddles, huh my friend?" he says.

Tyler warms in the glow of Oliver's companionship. Of acknowledging their shared history, of their fondness for each other outside my company. Before I'd become more in both of their eyes, we were all genuine friends. No matter how long ago that was, I can still see the yearning for it in Tyler's eyes. Oliver's face goes serious too quickly, and he mumbles something below the volume neither Tyler nor I can hear.

"What's that, Oli?" Tyler asks.

"Riddles upon riddles..." Oliver looks to me before grabbing both of Tyler's shoulders shaking his arms loose from Rose.

"Tyler, this is *very* important. Do you remember anything from this club on homecoming night? Do you remember this book?" Oliver holds the book to Tyler's nose.

My hopes fall. If Oliver is relying on Tyler, he's going to be disappointed, and we'll be back at square one. Tyler already told me he was good and drunk before he got here, and that he doesn't remember much.

"Is that... Actually, I do remember saber that book!" Tyler exclaims, clamoring to hold it in his hands.

My gut clenches with uncertainty. With fear and anticipation. Tyler is flipping through the book, hands steady even in the face of his obvious excitement. With every crisp turn of paper, his eyes skim through the writing, growing antsy and wild. He's tossing smiles to Rose that say, *are you watching? Look how they need me!* It fills me with sadness that he needs this validation and ache when I see Rose nodding, giving it to him.

"When I met up with Pax about creating this riddle, he had this book. I didn't think much of it. You guys always had some book in your lap or bags or whatever. But he kept looking at the pages, pen in hand, but never wrote anything in the margins like normal. So, I noted it and teased him a bit. Asked if he'd lost his God-given talents, and if I'd have to take away his Poe card. He laughed, turned to a page and wrote something. Then he told me that, sometimes, the truth takes time to reveal itself."

Oliver wants to ask more. It's on the tip of his tongue when suddenly, Tyler is shoving the book's cracked spine into Oliver's face, smiling like a madman.

"You tell me what the odds are that he would have that exact same book, on the exact same day, I wrote the riddle you are currently trying to solve? Doesn't your family always say that coincidence is just another word for fate?"

HEAVENLY FLAMES

GRADUATION IS THE DEATH of my childhood.

At seventeen, I feel the itch of maturity and long to shed the confinement of adolescent rules, just like all my peers. The thrill of university, of decisions that are solely my own, and the ability to live without parental rule, is appealing to us all. Unlike my classmates, though, I don't want to say goodbye.

This is the last year I can call this place home. Where, even if the boys were off at college or traveling during their gap year, they were always destined to come back to during summer or holiday. But after this, I'll be gone, and my free days will be spent in the boroughs of New York, in my mother's new home. I will be entering adulthood, leaving parts of myself in the greying halls of Dellbrook.

"Evangeline Pierce! Where is your mind today? You've got to get dressed, child."

Mother is losing patience with my procrastination. While she doesn't want me to run off on my own in the city for college, she's ravenous for the opportunity to finally leave Boston. Since the boys and I have grown out of needing her guidance, she's had to stay on as a personal assistant of sorts for Alexander and Madeline. A kindness they gave to show we were more than just the help. We were part of their lives. While the money is good, Mother is ready for a life of her own. *At least one of us is.* I snort at my melancholy.

"What's so funny? Perhaps you wouldn't mind saving your internal monologue for later. We're going to be late!" Mother cries.

"Isabel, calm down," I say, knowing her name on my lips digs into her skin like a shovel to the Earth. "The only thing I'm missing is my cap and gown. Once I find where *you* put those, I'll be ready to go." She eyes me, wanting to pick a fight but knowing that if she does, it'll only prolong our departure.

"One of these days, Evangeline, you're going to regret how you talk to me. Once I'm dead, anytime you hear the wind howling, just know that's me saying I told you so," she says.

Mother likes to think the Poes haven't changed her, that she's been immune to their darkness, but in truth she's embraced Madeline's sharp standards and ability to talk of morbidity as if it is mundane. Her accent has softened, her posture more poised. She's taken and wrapped the Poe armor around her heart gladly. It makes me satisfied to know that there are pieces she'll carry with her, too. Changes that even her beloved New York can't fix. She's been talking about the city in reverence, as if it is the answer instead of the problem separating us from home.

"Knock, knock," Alexander says from the open door to my room.

He's holding in his hand the silken crimson gown and square hat in question. I wave him in, giving him my best smile.

"Come on in, Mr. Poe. You've got the last piece we've been looking for and then we'll be ready to head out," my mother says in greeting, but Alexander doesn't seem to hear her.

His focus is on me, emotion already forming in his features. I'm positive he'll have a dozen new poems about this moment in the morning, ones that he'll slip over to Madeline at breakfast, who will no doubt pick her favorite to frame as a gift for my mother and me. His writing and emotional nature, something he's passed down to Oliver.

"You're such a beautiful young lady, Eve. I am so overwhelmed by my luck at being able to watch you grow into who you are now, and I cannot wait to see who you become," Alexander says. Tears prick at the corners of my eyes, but I will not melt down. Not here. Not now.

"Thank you, Mr. Poe," I say with as much reverence and gratitude as I can.

For all the conflict I feel for the boys when it comes to their family name, I don't blame Alexander, or even Madeline. Both have been good to me in their own ways, and I can never repay them for it. Thankfully, Alexander pops out of his nostalgic daze, clapping his hands together to jolt the rest of us with him into the present.

"Tad is downstairs with the car, ready to go. We must hurry if we don't want to be late or hear the wrath of Madeline for making her wait any longer." He gestures out the door and we both scurry through, the frigid chill of Madeline's displeasure enough to make me forget any hope of lingering.

My heart stills as I walk through the main doors onto the front drive and see two handsome figures waiting. Oliver has both hands tucked into ash grey slacks. His hair has grown longer than I remember, the ends curling every which way like the leaning tree in the yard. He's lounging on Tad's freshly washed Cadillac as if he has all the time and none of the care of the world. Paxton is his opposite, arms crossed, legs at command, waiting to be called to move. His limbs have grown sharper, the athletic build he's always been known for now stretching at his shirt with its bulk. They're chatting as if they were always meant to be right where they are.

But they're not. I got the call from each saying they had been held up, Paxton by school and Oliver by a rogue plane cancellation from France. Neither could make it. Apologies were given and the tears I'd cried were nothing short of an ocean. To see them in the drive, at ease, *at home*, makes me boil with the embarrassment of wanting them to be real and the deceit my sorrow feels at their unexpected presence.

Alexander clears his throat, and both boys turn to attention, catching me in smiles that I don't return.

"Surprise!" Paxton hollers, stepping toward me, enveloping me in a hug.

He doesn't realize or doesn't care that I'm not returning it, both trains of thought in line with who Paxton is. Oliver is standing back, waiting his turn, while soaking in every overflow of energy from my mood. Every hair on my body stands, waving toward him as if he is the wind. World travel hasn't changed the electricity he brings to me, something that both ignites and shatters my will to stay angry.

I absorb the warmth of Paxton's arms and, without thought, sink into them a little more. *I missed this.* Tension I didn't even realize I was holding drifts off with the safety of him being home. My days cannot be so bad with my protectors in reach. *They don't know about New York. They don't know about the breakup with Tyler, and the falling out with Liz, or the acceptance letters that have been burning holes in my underwear drawer since I got them.* They don't know that today is the beginning of the end.

Paxton finally lets go, and I have to stop myself from holding on. He steps back and Oliver fills the space. His arms don't entangle me just yet. He stands, breath to breath, and chucks me under the chin once before pushing his chest against mine and nuzzling his face into my hair. The special blend of maple and espresso dissolves any chance I have at keeping my irritation, filling me with a different emotion entirely. I'm immediately wrapped up in him, and the rest of the world stops existing as he lifts me into his arms.

Even after miles and days of distance, being with Oliver is like this. He's the first warm sip of the darkest chocolate on a snowy winter morning. The soothing rumble of thunder over sweeping hills of rain before the lightning ever shows its face. And just like every happiness I've ever known, even if I can never grasp him and make him mine always, it doesn't stop me from basking in the joy of this moment.

"I've missed you," he hums in my ear, sending waves of excitement through me.

"I know," I reply.

I can't give him the satisfaction of knowing that I missed him too, not when it's so clearly painted in the way my body clings to his. The phone calls and texts, while frequent between the three of us, have been brief and lacking the vibrancy their presence fills. My heart fractures as I remember that this feeling cannot last. Soon enough we'll be displaced again, apart for longer than we'll ever be together. It stings of impending pain, just like the last time I left a place I thought might be home. I step back, releasing Oliver and taking them both in.

"I thought you couldn't come," I say, the words fragile in a way that hope always is when leaning over the edge of oblivion.

Paxton smiles, reminding me of the day he last left Dellbrook, when he assured me he'd always come back. *I would never leave you behind, Eve. We can't be Poe without you.* It'd become their oath to me, a fact of life rather than a baseless truth. And he always punctuated his promises with golden smiles, making them feel weighted with worth.

"It's called a surprise. Although, if you ask me, not much of one. You really thought we'd miss your graduation? The last day of confinement before you joined us in freedom?" Paxton says.

He says this because he doesn't know I won't be joining them at Harvard. Not yet.

Oliver stares at me. I can't tell if he wants me to be surprised, or if he'll be offended if I say I am. Thankfully, Paxton's ask is rhetorical. He doesn't even wait for a response before he jumps in between us, weaving an arm around my shoulder, pulling me into his chest as he guides me towards the waiting car.

"Your chariot, my lady," he says before turning to my mother, who waits by the open door. "Is it alright with you, Isabel, if the three of us take this car and the parents ride separately? It's been too long since we've been together and, as you can imagine, we have many stories to tell."

He's earnest in a way with my mother that he isn't with Madeline. As if he feels like she should be treated like a mother, instead of simply a queen. Mother scratches her thumb nail against her pointer's cuticles, although unless you knew to look for it, you'd never know. She's told me it's a habit she picked up when she was very young. Her own mother was always quick to slap her hands away screaming about the state her fingers were in, making her learn to shield the small anxious movement.

"I was really hoping to talk about her future some more, but I guess that can wait. If Madeline says it's fine, I'll agree," she says, voice stretched with dismay. My chest releases one of the many knots it's been tied into at the thought of a half an hour without her hovering.

"Mads?" Paxton asks, and I cringe, sure that she'll say no at the nickname.

Over Christmas, something big had happened privately between Paxton and Madeline, and they had reached a level their fighting never had before: silence. Neither spoke to the other, only casting occasional dirty looks or worse, indifference. They pretended the fight had not existed, and with it, the others' existence altogether. Amongst the holiday cheer, or what could be considered as close to it as the Poes came, there was tautness. Paxton was never one to be quiet. Passionate and angry? Absolutely. You could expect that. Deal with it. But when he went still, everything sat coiled, waiting for the strike of his piercing teeth to come.

As far as I knew now, that still hadn't happened. What *had* happened was Paxton now referred only to his mother as 'Mads', which spurned Madeline to her core. The more she flinched from it though, the further he dug in his heels. Thankfully, she was in a good enough mood to ignore the misnomer, at least for today.

"That's fine, dear. You all have fun. We'll see you at the venue. Come now Isabel, I have a special bottle, 1858 Croizet, waiting for us." Madeline loops her arms through my mother's, showing she both understands her hesitancy and is insisting she move.

"Oh no, Madeline, I couldn't..." I can hear Mother whisper, but she lets Madeline whisk her further down the drive to wait for their car, Alexander close at their heels.

I wait until they're a little further down before I round on Paxton. "Why do you insist on needling her? Today of all days!" Paxton's face draws back, redness filling his cheeks. He looks as if he'll crumble in an apology that is so unlike him, but Oliver steps in, cutting between us.

"Madeline is enough of a force. She doesn't need you to come to her defense." His eyes are narrowed, daring me to continue before they sweep over to his brother. They share a look of understanding and connection I will never know.

You'll never be one of them. Paxton must have told Oliver about the fight. Told him his reasons and showed him his heart. *They're family, of course he did.* My heart pumps thickly with the thought, bile rising again into my throat. It seems that's become a constant as I fight with what my future holds. I just never realized the same reaction could come from my past, my history, with the boys. Since they've been gone, I've idealized what we've had. And that I've been stupid not to know what it would always be.

"I'm leaving," I blurt out.

It isn't the time or the place, I know that, but there's no shoving the words, or the tears that are now forming, back in. Paxton is quick to shoulder Oliver out of place and grab my hand.

"It's ok, Eve. We're all going. Oliver's sorry. You can defend Madeline, and I'm sorry I said it. I shouldn't have. Not today. Today is about you," he coos.

He's so wonderful when I cry, giving me the warmth I need to stop the tears. But Oliver knows. He knows me. He knows heartbreak. And he knows that if you don't let it hurt now, the pain will only intensify. So, like any unwanted infection, he demands that I bleed.

"That isn't what she's saying, Pax. I think Eve is trying to tell us she's leaving Dellbrook. Boston. That she's leaving *us*," he spits the word.

Paxton's face morphs into one that matches his brothers. Now both Poe boys are narrow eyed and angry, looking down at me from their larger-than-life frames, demanding that I explain away Oliver's accusations. Instead, I nod my head.

"Two weeks. My mom already found a place in New York. We leave in two weeks." My breath is rushed and straining, feeling like I've run a hundred miles to get to these words. The car beeps twice, our driver letting us know our parents are at the gate waiting, and that if we don't get moving, we're going to be late. I step back to the open door, readying to get in, but a hand on my elbow hauls me to a stop.

"Paxton, get in. Have Tad drive you to the gate, let our parents know Eve forgot something, then drive around to the backdoor to grab us. We'll be ready when you get there," Oliver instructs. To my surprise, Paxton just nods, then slides into the car. Oliver twists his fingers in mine and tugs me back into the foyer.

"Oliver, where are we... I didn't forget anything," I protest, but don't drop his hand.

He doesn't stop. We sweep through the hall, past all the stairs, and head straight for the kitchen. As soon as the picture window from the breakfast nook is in sight, Oliver spins me around, palms grabbing onto my elbows to keep gravity from tearing us apart. The force of Oliver's hands alone brings us together; first hips in fingertips, then chests breathing as one, and finally, his lips are catching mine.

Gravity is nothing compared to this.

Before I can enjoy or even question what is happening, he steps back, our breaths still mingling as his palms circle my face, thumbs pressing in as if I'm slipping away.

"*The moon is distant from the sea, and yet with amber hands she leads him, docile as a boy, along appointed sands,*" he whispers into my mouth, lips catching on every syllable, begging me to understand.

But it's been so long since I've lost myself in Emily Dickinson's pages and I've wished for something like this too many times to misunderstand.

"Oliver..." I sigh, wrapping my palms to his knuckles, ready to push them away.

It's unfair of him to do this, to give me hope in the face of a future that's already set. We both know whatever this is between us, reality will never allow it. *Hasn't* allowed it. A few stolen kisses don't change a thing. Madeline expects the boys to marry well, to carry on the name and the legacy, and she wouldn't tolerate teenage crushes that grew into love in adulthood. That's why, until now, we've never even pretended to try.

"Shh, Eve. Listen." He looks at me with those heavy green eyes that contain every hue of love I will ever know. "Convince Isabel to give you one more summer at Dellbrook. *I've missed you.* More than you know. More than *I* knew. I'll call off the rest of my trip and we'll stay here. Together."

His words grow more frantic with every one that comes out. I've never been on the receiving end of Oliver's desperation. It is intoxicating, and I know that if I hear one more plea, I will give him anything he asks. Even when I know I'm only delaying the heartbreak.

"Tad is coming up the drive. We've got to go…" I say, scooting even farther away.

But those hands… there's no stopping them and he stills me with the invisible weight tied to his fleeting touch.

"Eve, *stay with me,*" he whispers against my ear, but I can hear the panic. I can hear every word he isn't saying.

You can't leave. I need you. You belong with me. Here. Stay. I love you.

I don't know if they're really his, but the hope inside me at the possibility that they are blinds me into an overwhelming sense of fearlessness.

"Stay?" I ask and he smiles.

"One more summer… together. You and me."

And he knows I'm his. He always has.

LACERATED THREAD

FRIDAY, PRESENT

Oliver and I lean into the page Tyler is pushing towards us. I feel dizzy from the strain of squinting to read the words in the darkened light of the club. Try as I might, I cannot figure out which poem I've landed on. But I don't need to. There, in bright liquid blue cursive, is Paxton's writing. It stands out glaringly from the black and white of the rest of the text and further still from Oliver's elaborate hand. It's messy, as if jotted, and I'm not sure many could interpret it into actual words. But we can.

You knew your angels loved you
but you also knew they would leave
someone they could not save.

```
First, you must bleed before you can
be healed. You must drop before you
can land. And you must know the right
question to ask before you can get an
answer.
```

For that, I'm sorry. To all of you.
This will be the last time you find
answers at the bottom of a bottle,
Oliver.
Enjoy.

I read it three times before looking over at Oliver's glowering face. Storm clouds gather around him, and a panic rushes through me that I might lose him to the darkness altogether. Before that can happen, instinct has me reaching out to grab his hand, forcing him to acknowledge me. To take me with him. His eyes shift to mine, never losing the brim of distaste.

"Oliver, did Paxton... Did he really write a Philip Schultz poem in my first edition, Neruda? Isn't that... illegal to mar a poet's work with another poet's words? Does he know no mercy?" I gasp.

I'm horrified by the complete lack of propriety, but that isn't the full truth of why I say it. I want to shift his eyes away from distrust, back to wonder, and I expect my outrage to, at the very least, elicit a smirk. Something that shows the camaraderie and agreement that even in death, Paxton has finally gone too far this time. Yet Oliver's mood does not change, his face as stagnant in disgust as ever. Apparently, Paxton went too far, just not in the way I've assumed.

"What's wrong? What does it mean?" I ask, desperate to know what I'm missing.

His jaw clenches, nose furling like he's smelled something rotten. I take a tiny sniff to make sure it's the mood that's setting off his senses and not something more tangible in the air. The sweat of dancing bodies and boozy rich alcohol fill my lungs, rooting me back to this place, but it's nothing unexpected or extraordinarily foul. And yet, Oliver continues to stare and brood. It's only Rose's voice that snaps us both out of our frozen bubble.

"Tyler... do you know what this means?" She asks. He swings his arm back around her, kissing her cheek, before turning to us.

"Well, I might've been drunk that night, but the one thing I do remember is where we threw them all back. My guess is Paxton planted the next clue there," he says.

Oliver's glower deepens. Resigned, he sighs and nods towards an upper floor, turning to lead the way. I look between Tyler's joyful face at being regarded, Rose's pride for him, and Oliver's hunched shoulders drawing a defining line down his back, feeling as if this is another trap. Just like the one Paxton had set with my father. I tug on Oliver's hand, still encased in mine, begging him to stop and look at me. Surprisingly, he does, with no more incentive than the pull of the string tied between us.

I hurry, worried he'll break this tentative bond, and sink my face towards his shoulder, whispering to him as I do, "We don't have to do this. Whatever is waiting for you up there... if it's anything like what was waiting for me... We don't have to. Or if you want to go alone, I understand."

My eyes plead with him to believe me. We may be broken, but this? This isn't what I want. It's one thing for us to tear each other apart. It's something entirely different to watch someone else do it.

A vile spider of darkness crawls up my throat at the thought. My father was a wound I didn't want healed, and it shreds me that I was forced to face it, but at least he was blood. Family, if only the bare ends of what that can be considered. Still, I could understand that. *Forgive* that. However, Paxton's game or not, I won't play something that allows an outsider the upper hand on Oliver's heart. Not to mention Rose and Tyler bearing witness to his turmoil.

Oliver's lip twitches and his angry mask slips just enough to see the hurt beneath. I can only imagine how much he doesn't want to do this. That he selfishly wants to take me up on my offer to leave him be and let him face whatever's to come, alone. But to my surprise, he doesn't let go of my hand. Instead, he squeezes it tighter, as if it is a lifeline tethering him to the future, as his past tries to swallow him whole.

"No. We do this together and we do this *now*. For Paxton," he says, re-signed.

He leans down and presses the barest kiss on my palm before gently tugging on my hand, urging me to follow. I turn, remembering Tyler, cheeks dusting pink, knowing he witnessed Oliver's and mine's intimate moment. I wish I hadn't. Tyler's eyes are downcast. He's still sporting a smirk that creases the dimple in his cheek into view, but it's smaller, sadder than it was before. Even with Rose on his arm, I know old embers can still burn and it's the last thing I want either of them to see.

A wave of déjà vu slams into me so hard I can barely breathe. *It's the same look he gave when you smashed his heart into pieces at graduation as Oliver pulled you away from him for the last time.* Or what I had assumed would be the last time. Hurting him was supposed to remain a memory. Not for the first time do I hate the webs I'm tangled up in. If only I could be satisfied with not knowing. If only I could accept things and move on.

Rose must see all the things I do, or at least the shadows of them, as she wraps Tyler closer to her body and kisses him deeply. When they pull apart, a small smile forms back on his lips and he nods forward, signaling me to follow Oliver. I want to reach out and grab Tyler, terrified he'll disappear the moment he leaves my focus, but I know it's a promise I can do nothing more with than break. *He doesn't need you now. He has Rose.* And I'm grateful. So, I tell myself it's unwelcome, that he'd reject the inclusion anyway, even when I know deep down the way his hope would bloom in my hand. Karma, should she exist, is branding my name into her memory for later.

Just another notch on my tombstone.

We find the stairs tucked back behind a leathery black couch set, visible only to those who already know where to find them. *A secret within a secret.* Just like Paxton. Just like a Poe. My aching black heels stumble and click, unfamiliar with the curves of each step or the distances between them. I use my free hand to glide up the handrail for support. Unsurprisingly, Oliver doesn't seem to need the balance. He rises up them, floating, as if haunting the place.

When we reach the landing, small, soft yellow and red glows of lights give hope of finding footing, only for me to realize they're scattered down at least a dozen hallways. A sign shines above, laying claim to the space, *The Labyrinth.* Its brightness reflects down below onto a black-light chalk board, bolded with cursive words reading, *Rules: Must Read.* Unease swims in my stomach while curiosity pumps through my blood. I step forward, ahead of Oliver, to read.

ALL WHO FOLLOW WILL BE LOST. ENTER AT YOUR OWN RISK.

I don't get to read farther as Oliver grabs my arm and hauls me down a hallway.

"Hey! Oliver, wait. I was reading that. Shouldn't we—" I protest.

"No. I just want to get this over with. Besides, those are all nonsense, anyway. Trust me, Darkness, I am more than capable of being our guide. A regular Ariadne."

His comparison feels foreboding, the words thick tipped and weighted, but he leaves them at the entrance, forcing us all forward. My feet still stagger, needing more of an explanation from him, until I feel Tyler's warm palm at the small of my back, pushing me forward.

"It's ok, Eve. We've got you," Rose says loud enough for Oliver to hear.

Oliver's shoulders stiffen, though his stride doesn't falter. I'm overwhelmed by the understanding this woman is showing not only Tyler, but me, too. It makes me wonder what all she knows, what Tyler could have said to make this woman give me so much grace. Grace that I wasn't capable of even giving myself.

I lose myself in the thoughts and give in to the blindness of being led into the unknown, not feeling satiated, but still safe enough to follow. Ruby red and piss yellow lights float by, plastered above doors and outside of tiny nooks.

We stop and turn to one such door, but the light above is purple and the door itself black beneath it. A crooked letter 'P' hangs in the middle. Oliver pulls out a small, ornate key, brass and laced with curves. The one he must have taken from Paxton's dream journal I had found too late. He shoves it into the door, and it pops open, revealing a den of velvet.

Inside, the lights are turned up to at least a jazz club level, enough to see each piece adorning the space but not enough to pick out the stains from whatever revelry has happened here. The walls, chairs, and couches are all purple and black crushed velvet. There's a tiny stage that connects to a small round bar alongside a flimsy poker table.

I can just imagine the boys here a decade ago, lounging around as kings. This room purchased indefinitely for the Poes to enjoy at their leisure, and the boys taking full advantage of their status. Ally draped along Oliver's lap in a drunken haze. Paxton boisterous behind the bar, pouring drinks while Tyler tries to talk some poor soul into playing a round of cards for money they'd undoubtedly lose. Pain punches me in the gut and regret boils up.

These memories could have been mine. If only I hadn't let Oliver dig into my skin. If I had not let insecurity burrow over and take away my ability to be included. Instead, I'd left and cried until Oliver had called drunk, coaxing me outside to spend the early morning hours underneath the slide, in the cold and dirt, apologizing. *If I would've stayed, that night might've been so much more.* And yet, I know, it wouldn't have mattered in the end. Only another moment to torture myself with.

Tyler releases Rose at the door and spins around the room, a smile lighting his face.

"This brings it all back. Man, they haven't changed *a thing*. I can almost feel 16 again," he says.

Oliver stills, eyes closed, as his chest heaves at the thought. I can't help but wonder if he feels it, too. If he wants to. *If you could go back, Oliver Poe, and change everything, would you?* I want to ask the words hot in my mouth, but I know he wouldn't answer. Not with Tyler and Rose listening in and the hurt of whatever Paxton has left for him here. Still, I try to read his body, try to gleam the answer, anyway. *No. I don't think you would.* It tears at me, but I know it's the truth.

Released from whatever memory was trapping his lids, Oliver finally opens them and steps into the bar, searching. He picks up a dozen bottles, sipping at only a few. He pushes the rest aside after looking into their contents and deciding against them until he hefts up an inky, ornate one. It clanks against the bar top as he sets it down to unscrew its lid. He peers in and huffs, turning it over to spill the contents out.

Liquid streams across the bar and down onto the carpet in dark puddles. The spicy scent of alcohol and barley makes my nose itch with its warmth. Tyler and I look at Oliver as if he's gone mad, watching as he shakes it uncontrollably.

"I think you've got it—" I try to say, but Oliver isn't listening.

He grows tired of shaking the bottle and instead smashes it onto the counter. Tyler and I sit stunned as glass pieces shatter around him. Rose moves forward, into the room, gasping, ready to help anyone who may have been cut. Tyler darts his eyes to her, putting his hands up to still her momentum.

"Hey, man! What are you doing?" Tyler yells, shocked and tinged with anger.

But then we see it, the tiny waterproof baggie sitting on the counter, glittering in amber bottle shards. Oliver pays little attention to the glass and grabs it, removing its contents in one movement. A small USB dongle is being held up, pinched between his fingers. He sighs, then moves to the large screen TV on the wall behind me.

My brain is entrenched with nonsensical actions. Nothing since coming here has made sense. Has felt normal. And yet, in its complete lack of propriety and uncommon twists has it settled in my heart as right. I never feel more alive than when I'm chasing down mysteries with Oliver, and that alone terrifies me. Has me asking, if after all this, I'll ever be whole again.

"Figures he'd hide it in the Hennesy," Oliver mumbles as he passes Tyler.

Tyler just laughs manically. "You are crazy! You know, you just dumped out hundreds of dollars of expensive liquor *and* did a bunch of damage. Not to mention your hand. Lookslike you got cut! Management here is going to be pissed."

Rose tsks.

"Here, let me help..." she says, trying again to come to the rescue, but Oliver just shrugs.

Why would he care about the cost of breaking things and a few drops of blood? When you have a legacy that's praised for your oddity. For your destruction. One to hold you above mere mortals. There is nothing you cannot do. Nothing you cannot destroy. *That* is the real gift Edgar left his family.

Rose folds her arms across her chest, unhappy with being helpless as we all watch as Oliver hesitates to plug in his prize to the port. I worry that he'll take me up on my earlier offer and ask us to leave. *Ask me to leave.* I wish I never would've offered because I'm not sure I could walk away. Not now, after I've seen the way he worries it in his palms.

Thankfully, he doesn't. He finds the courage to let it click into place and the flatscreen comes to life. The boy's drunken faces, flushed and glistening with the night, lights the screen. Their arms are wrapped around each other's shoulders, bodies hunched, while standing in this room. A white play button holds them in place, waiting to let the memory take us back.

"Oh! Look at that! I *swore* we had photos and videos of homecoming night, but I could never find them. And when I asked Paxton, well, he never gave me a straight answer. I guess now I know why..." Tyler says.

Oliver just stares at the photo, all color draining from his face. He turns to me, holding my eyes in dread.

"Eve... This... It's your last chance to leave. I don't know if you'll want to see what's on here, but I'll leave the choice to you," he stutters.

It's so unlike him to want to hide from me like this. My curiosity stutters with him, and the better parts of me ask if I want to know. If I can take being pulled any further down these memories. Like the pieces of the bottle Oliver broke, I know I'll be shattered, too. But just like a rollercoaster, I am here, locked in tight, and along for the ride. Whether I think it's a good idea or not, I'm in too deep to be saved now.

"I'm not going anywhere," I say, the determined words hammering my feet into the wood below.

Rose hesitantly steps up to me, then grabs my hand and holds tight. I doubt she knows what's coming either, but the warmth of this stranger's hand in mine, with no expectations or wanted outcomes, gives me strength.

It's ok little heart, you can make it through this too, my courage tells my fear. My mind snaps to memories all my own, to words whispered lovingly in dark corners, then ripped away in shouts. The last-ditch effort my soul can make, begging me not to do this. But my stance has been locked, my proverbial envelope sealed. And my hand locked tight against the need to run.

Tyler must not remember what could be so bad to warrant the energy Oliver and I are putting off. He's looking between us and the screen, probably chalking it all up to the two of us being dramatic. But he doesn't pull Rose away, and she doesn't leave, so we must be giving enough off for them to know it's serious enough. Oliver, for all his hesitation, sighs and presses play. Laughter fills the speakers, but none of us smiles.

Tyler's drunken face, swollen and red in the lens, slurs into the camera, *we're here at the famous Crave! And it's Homecoming night, wooooo! Say hello Paxton. Wait, you have to meet Pax. Pax!* He twists the camera to pan over to Paxton behind the bar, pouring drinks. He's smiling, golden even in the sickly back lighting of this dark room. Tyler's voice squeaks back in, *tell the people who you are and what you're doing, man.*

Paxton, ever the participant in whatever party game is being played, easily does as he's asked, and I almost cry as his voice comes over the speaker. *Well, my friend, I'm Paxton Poe of the illustrious Poe dynasty. And right now, I'm pouring all of your sorry asses a drink because it doesn't appear that anyone is sober enough to do the job right except me. I am far too sober to be doing this.* He continues to pour into three glasses, mixing things I would guess by the murky color of the liquid, shouldn't be mixed. We watch as Tyler's hand greedily grabs for one.

My heart is squeezing so hard, I fear all the love is being wrung dry. Tears prick at the corners of my eyes, and for the first time since arriving here, the grief of Paxton's death comes over me. Hearing his voice and seeing his face, even younger and drunk as it is, only reminds me I'll never have it under my fingertips again. I'll never feel the warmth of his hugs or the crushing tightness of his arms. He's really, truly gone.

Hey, where's Oliver? Ollliiiiivvveeerrrrr! Sixteen-year-old Tyler's voice calls through the room. Paxton's smile dims as his eyes search for his brother. I know the moment he spots him by the flare of his nostrils and the furrow of his brow. Young Tyler doesn't notice as the camera bounces in his hands, looking. *I'll find him. Hand it over, Sullivan.*

We watch as Paxton's hand covers the lens, then we're moving with him, into a dark corner where two people sit, limbs tangled together on the couch. I take a quick peek over at Oliver. He's not watching the video. Instead, all his attention is focused on me. My skin pills and my hair stand on end. Anxiety grips the pit of my stomach, my body knowing what's coming well before I do. I grip Rose's hand even tighter.

Paxton zooms the camera in enough for us to see Oliver brushing his thumb across Ally's cheek. She giggles, leaning ever closer to him. Oliver pushes the lip of a glass between them, taking the liquid into his mouth and swallowing. Ally grabs onto it, her teeth clanking against the rim. Oliver frowns, pulling it away before she can take a drink.

Tssssk. Tsssk. That's my drink, Al. You'll have to get one of your own, he slurs still oblivious to Paxton or the camera that is pointed at them. *C'mon Oli. I just want a taste.* Ally desperately grabs on to him, pressing herself into his space. He dashes empty, drink-soaked kisses onto her face, never quite meeting her eager lips.

How about you give her that one brother and we'll get you a new one after we have a word, Paxton cuts in, his voice sounding cold stone sober, no longer playful as before. Oliver must hear the warning in his voice as he concedes the drink to Ally, then lightly pushes her legs from his lap. But Ally must be too drunk to understand. Or she is too drunk to care. Because she gets up from her seat to follow, unwilling to let the younger Poe out of her sight now that she's finally got his attention.

Oliver turns back, irritation bending his features, and stares at her. She shrinks back, the glare of him enough to still her intoxicated movements. Paxton steps gently in, out of character for his usually fierce demeanor, to smooth over her stricken fears of being left behind. *I only need to borrow him for a bit. It's a brother thing.* He tilts just the edge of his lips to her, and she settles, head nodding at his first word. *Alright. I'll be here when you're done, Ol.*

The camera shakes and pans as Paxton grabs the collar of Oliver, moving him outside of the room. I can make out the fuzzy corners of the labyrinth just beyond the crescent of Paxton's finger in the lens. It's jarring, the similarities I feel standing in the place I'm watching on the screen. An odd sense of déjà vu hits me for a memory that has never been mine before tonight. I look over at Tyler, wondering if he feels the same. He may have been here before, but by his accounts, he doesn't remember much. *Does this bring it all back*, I wonder.

Are you going to put that down or is this some sort of home video to show the kids one day? On screen, Oliver asks as he barks out a laugh and shakes Paxton free. The snide defeat in his comment shoots quick slips of pain to my chest that I bat away to focus. *Right,* Paxton responds. The camera twists and flips through moody lights before landing in complete darkness. The crinkle of a pocket can be heard, but it doesn't cover the voices, still clear as before.

Alright, Pax. You got me out here, now what is it you want, Oliver asks. The slur is still evident, but I can tell he's trying to be more sober, more on-guard, for whatever it is his brother is trying to throw his way.

What are you doing, Ol? I know you're mad at me, but that'll pass. You smiled, really smiled, for the first time in too long at the dance, and then we got to the house party, and you were swallowed back up into your shell. What you're doing right now, though, that might haunt you.

The house party I know. I remember. I can feel the fluster of it on my cheeks all these years later. Oliver's hand on my back as he guided me up the house steps, Tyler in front of me, Ally behind him. We were sandwiched between our real lives and expectations, but we had each other. At least, it had felt that way. That was until Tyler surprised me with a kiss in the kitchen and a shy request to be his girlfriend, as I waited for Oliver, who had asked to talk to me.

After that, Oliver was inconsolable. A volcano of pain ready to erupt. We fought, the worst one ever at that point. And I went home early. Crying and waiting in the hollow of the tree in the backyard because I couldn't imagine going inside until curfew without the boys and explaining why I was alone.

But none of that had to do with Paxton, and that he thought it did, even so many years ago, breaks my heart a little more. Paxton was always taking the burden of our suffering on his shoulders, even when his load was more than enough to carry.

*Mad. How could I be **mad**?* He gloats sarcastically. We hear a distinct thump and rustle, as if Paxton has been pushed. *You were just reminding me who I am. Who **we** are. You don't deserve the blame for that,* past Oliver sighs theatrically. Another thump. Then a wrestling noise crackles through.

Are they fighting? Confusion pulls my eyes away from my feet and up to Oliver's eyes, that are still stuck on me from across the room. He's waiting like a bomb that is about to go off, all nerves and unbridled energy. He knows what's coming and I latch onto the support his pain is giving me so I can stay grounded in the present instead of drowning in our past.

I'm sorry, Paxton says, voice strangled and winded, *I don't want to be the one to remind you. But we made promises. To ourselves. To each other.*

Past Oliver huffs on a laugh that makes the hair on my arms prickle. He's closer to wherever the camera is pocketed, his pants loud. Paxton ignores him, and I strain to hear him continuing.

And those can't be broken. Not even for Eve. You can't openly love her, Oliver. Oliver's breathing gets further away as Paxton's voice booms. *We won't settle. Won't marry. There is no family for us. This burden has broken us... everyone before us. And we agreed. It stops here. She deserves more than that... more than the Poe name, and I know that deep down, you don't want to curse her with it like it's cursed us. But what you're doing with Ally and the drinking ...* Paxton doesn't get to finish before past Oliver is cutting in with fire and the Oliver five feet from me flinches, causing my heart to triple its speed in my chest.

*There's no need to worry, brother. Ally knows what this is. What it'll always be. She doesn't care. It isn't really me she wants, anyway. It's the allure of our **reputation**. There will be a thousand Ally's in a thousand cities, so I might as well start now.* We hear the shuffle of clothing, as if a shoulder has aggressively brushed by, before young Oliver's voice comes back in, louder now. *And as for Eve, she and I are **nothing**. Like I told you at the party, kissing her was a mistake. She will **never** be a Poe. Not in name. She will break before I'd allow it. I can keep that promise at least.*

For the first time since the video started, Oliver isn't looking at me. I bore my eyes into the side of his down-turned face and still he refuses to lift it. The room spins and I feel Rose trying to wrap her arms around mine. Tyler leaning in close to pull us both into his embrace. Because he knows what this will do to me. He *knows.*

The video must still be playing by the mumble of *fuck* I hear from a young Paxton, but can't focus on. All the attention feels sucked into my body, making me the center of the universe. The only living thing in this room. In the world.

His drunken words that early morning, of how sorry he was for everything, of his insistence that I follow my crush on Tyler. How all he would do was ruin it, and he couldn't do that to me, comes roaring back. It clicks into place, and I feel hollowed out. He'd tried to tell me, warn me, that I didn't belong with him, and I was stupid. Naïve.

A drip hits my chest from my chin. I wipe at the silent tears I didn't even know to hold back, wanting the room to animate again. To live outside the feelings and memories and pain that are consuming me from within. I want the sympathy to stop suffocating me from all the eyes that I know are watching. I beg my heart to harden, to become stone in my chest. To remember, we don't want this anymore. Still, the traitor just thumps furiously as Oliver steps towards me.

"Eve..." he says, soft as a love song.

I should stay and listen. Figure out the next clue. Finish the video and hear what else might be lying in wait. But I can't. All the strength I thought I had coming back here is nothing in the face of what I've found. I would never be healed of the mark this family has left. That *he's* left.

So instead of facing the truth of our past, I run.

BRUISED FRUIT

FRIDAY, PRESENT

F AINTLY, I CAN HEAR my name being called behind me as the door to the room slams shut. I don't turn back. Instead, I follow the curves of the darkened walls and let the flash of dim lights carry me as fast and as far away from Oliver as these heels will allow.

Numbers and letters and symbols adorn every door I pass, some so obscure I slow long enough to consider opening them. *Maybe I'll walk into another dimension and leave this one behind.* My imagination runs with the story I could unfold in a novel if I wanted to. Only this isn't fiction, and I know behind each oddity all I'll find is drunken club goers trying to forget the drowning emptiness of their lives, too.

But we made promises. To ourselves. To each other. And those can't be broken. Not even for Eve.

My senses start coming back to me as I pass another black hole hall, this one with doors labeled by gargoyles and midnight-colored angels splattered in red. Their greedy little faces, desperate for a pound of flesh, set panic into my limbs. I can see them stretching toward me, ready to consume my sorrow.

I need to escape this place, to see the sky in its endlessness, and remember that there's more to the world than the debauchery this place elicits. I need peace and air and a bedroom, I remember. I need New York and its eccentricities instead of the madness only Boston brings.

I knew getting on that flight was a mistake. That coming back here only held answers to questions I've never dared ask. I would hide my head in the sand and let the sea of guilt try to endlessly wash it away for the rest of my life rather than face the truth of this solitude.

Rather than accept I meant nothing to those I gave everything for.

Paxton wanted me here. He crafted everything with such care. He knew the venom that Oliver's words would infect me with. That *his* words would infect me with. Knew there would be no cure, that I would live on with my greatest fear recognized. The man I had thought a friend, *family* even, had thrown me to the wolves. This had nothing to do with murder, but everything to do with pain.

She will never be a Poe. Never was. Never will be. A promise they made together. A promise Oliver, no matter the consequence to anyone, has kept. And a lie they fed me with, baiting me to hope that one day I would be accepted when, in truth, I was always meant to be an outsider. Madeline would be so proud.

The violent stab of those words throbbing through my head causes my lungs to crack and wheeze. I struggle for breath; the panic morphing into what I fear might be a heart attack, my vision swaying and spinning the lights into a tunnel with no end.

She will break before I'd allow it. I thought the worst had happened between Oliver and me the last time I was here, but I was wrong. This felt just as soul crushing. More so, even. Before was about *us* and the devastation of being star-crossed. But this? This was only about me. About how I would never measure up. Never be good enough, no matter what I did. And it was woven together by someone I loved to make sure I heard it all. *Why would Paxton do this to me?*

My arm swings out, hoping to catch onto a wall as I slow, needing to find center again before I fall, or worse, pass out. Only it doesn't. Instead, my fingers grip soft fabric between them. I hold on to it for dear life as my weight gives way into something more solid than my legs. Hands wrap around my biceps, crushing my shoulders into my neck to hold me up and away.

"Easy there, little bird," the figure says.

My ears prick with familiarity, but all my senses are so thrown off by the panic attack that no singular thought can click into place. Nothing makes sense except my body's need to escape reality. Another wave of breath-lessness and dizziness hits me.

"Whoa! This way," they say, and I feel myself being tugged under a doorframe.

My proclivity to weariness wails at me to stop, to breathe, to not let this stranger drag me further into the maze, his fingers sinking deeper into my skin. But everything is wrong. And when everything's wrong, nothing is. How can you seek one string of pain when everything hurts so damn much? So, I let myself be led and focus instead on getting air into my lungs and for the floor to stop spinning.

I flop onto a seat, cool leather seeping through my dress, and before I can do anything more, my head is pushed between my legs.

"Breathe!" the voice demands.

And I obey. I suck it down greedily in loud whistles through my nose. I gasp, sputter, and try again and again until eventually the oxygen goes down easily. I count through my box breaths, *one, two, three...* Stare at the pointed velvet toe of my heel as it taps along with my progress. See the slight skip of nude, in what is sure to be a run tomorrow, in the toe of my panty hose. The world becomes just me, and everything encased by my inner calves, flexing hello to each other.

"Better, now?"

My back tenses and the hand rubbing circles I hadn't even noticed on it, stops. Touch by touch, he removes it, but I do not relax. I begin to take notice of where I am without lifting my head to look, panic morphing into something more - survival. There's a black shag rug on the floor, dusted with glitter. Several other shoes stand at the edge of my vision. Heart-rattling music pumps out of the speakers that must be placed in every corner, the bass pulsing the couch beneath me and into my thighs. *At least you're not in here alone with one strange man.*

Instead, I could be trapped here with many.

I fight to stay present, to not be catapulted into chaos again. Bullies I can handle. I've had to struggle my way through enough situations to know I can make it through this, too. *If Oliver were here, you wouldn't have to.* My heart betrays me with thoughts of him. I can't help the scoff I let out, knowing I can never rely on a Poe again to save me. I'm not sure I really ever could. Especially not now.

"Man, is she alright?" A voice bellows from the other side of the room. "She can't be here if she's sick."

They're worried I'm too high or drunk. That I'll ruin their good time with my misfortune. I slowly lift my head as the man beside me answers.

"She's fine. Just a bit out of breath. We'll be out of here in a minute."

His voice is scratchy, prickling my memories with remembrance. It has the faintest hint of the accent of this city that's hidden behind prim words. Someone desperate to hide who they are in favor of who they wished they could be. A feeling I know intimately.

I turn to face him, taking in as many details of the room as I can on the way. *Two guys, one female. Startled, wide eyed. Two couches. A black door. Dance floor. Disco lights. Bar.* Similar to the room I left, although much cheaper and run down.

My stare finally meets the man who pulled me here, and ice hardens my bones as I catch on one blue and one brown eye looking back over the dark fabric of a mask. *Issac.* The man with violence in his gaze. The family Oliver believed to have motive, opportunity, and wherewithal to kill. His mouth flattens before I can school the shock on my face. He reaches for my arm, but I step away.

"OK. She's up. Seriously. You guys need to go," one guy says in a nervous tone.

I search the room for help, for one of the three, to understand what's going on. To see the fear and step up. But none do. I only see it reflected right back at me, along with the accusatory stare that I have somehow put them here. *Cowards.*

I have a better chance of getting away if I choose to leave than if I let Issac get his hands on me and drag me out. I have to hope that the maze itself will help me, that I'll be able to lose him in its halls. With one final look to the others, only one stares back at me. Sympathy fills her gaze, but she makes no moves to interfere.

We both have a sense of self-preservation, it seems.

I nod once, saying *I understand without words*, then high tail it to the door. I'm desperate to get into the hall enough steps ahead that I'll be able to run, even if it is aimless, once I'm back in the labyrinth. The doorknob rustles uselessly before finally caving in and clicking open. I get the fifteen steps to the end of the corridor and then, just like Orpheus, I make the mistake of looking back.

Issac doesn't look like he'd outrun me, but somehow his strides have eclipsed mine in a blink. He isn't frantic or frustrated that I've taken off. He just ropes his thick forearm around my waist and yanks me back to him with an unexpected tug that takes the wind from my lungs with it. Instinct kicks in and I stab my heels into his clunky boots over and over, stomping frantically, before trying to use any available limb to punch him in the groin.

But his boots protect his delicate toes from being severed from his body, and in these heels he's shorter than me, so I miss him by a mile. It is the first time in the history of humankind a man has been grateful to be shorter than a woman, I'm sure. That leaves me to do the only other thing I can think of. I scream.

"GET AWAY FROM ME!" I put as much energy into my voice to get it to carry past walls and doors and drunken stupors as I can.

"Shhh. Stop. There's no need to shout," Issac is saying through my screams as his hand wraps around my lips.

I bite down on a fat little sausage finger as hard as I can the minute it grazes my mouth. I can feel the dirt of unwashed skin between my teeth, and then the delicate rip of tissue. He squeals out in pain as he shakes it away. I continue to scream as I try to wrestle out of his arms, but he's got a vise grip on me. The harder I try to pull away, the harder it becomes to breathe, until my voice is struggling to carry out my pleas at all.

"Have you used up all your songs, my little bird? Huh?" he gloats, squeezing that much tighter on my stomach in punctuation.

I grunt a cry of frustration. Cold sweat pools in the vertebrae of my back, only dropping the next wrung as I squirm. I'm positive he can feel the wet on the thick drab of his belly. All that bulk and there's still a soft pudge even the gym can't beat out of him. *The world may label you a Poe yet, if you're murdered in this nightmarish den of morbid posterity and puzzles.*

I can't help the mad laugh that escapes me, which only makes me laugh harder at the Edgar like insanity I must be presenting. Even in danger, I'm searching for their approval. Tears prick my eyes and fall down my cheeks.

"There, there," Issac mutters. "I'm not going to hurt you. I just need to talk. No need to be frightened."

He tries to calm me down. To quiet the hoarse whine I'm taking on between the screams and laughter.

"*I am no bird; and no net ensnares me!* I'm not scared, you putz! I'm angry. And resigned. And honestly, I thought my end would be so much better than... *you*," I spit the words.

Of course, I'm terrified, in truth. I don't want to die. Not here. Not like this. If I'm being honest with only myself, not anytime soon. I have a heart that's drowning and a curiosity that has peaked, and I cannot move on from this world with either tied round my neck. And I would be damned if I became a ghost because of *this* man.

But I can't tell him those things. I can't snivel and grovel and hope. For all he knows, I'm a member of the Poe family, and some things are easier to kill than the liquid steel they have injected into my veins since I was a child. Poe or not, I would not fear tragedy. Even the greatest stories eventually ended. And I would embrace mine with ferocity.

"You're a fiery little bitch, aren't ya? Might not be so tough when put under actual pressure, though." He squeezes his arms so tight I think a bone might snap before releasing again. "I *was* trying to find Oliver. But my gut says you're just as good. Better even. The weakest link, since that slimy little shit hasn't given us anything," he spits Oliver's name, and his disgust sends gooseflesh down into my hands. "Now, I have a question for you. Answer me, and I'll let you go free to fly away."

"And if I don't, I'm assuming that's when the real *pressure* begins, right?" I snort the slight hiccup of air I must suck in to do so, ruining its effect almost entirely.

He swivels me around to face him, slackening so his embrace is less like a lover and more as if we're playing a child's game of red rover, hand clasped bruisingly around my wrist and making the bones shift under skin. I fear the sound they'll make if I try to break away.

"Nah. Don't and I just snap a bone until you do. If you make it through that, *then* we'll talk about next steps, OK?" The mask ruffles as if he's smiling.

I want to call his bluff, the swirling in my gut making me irrational and wild. A wingless bird begging for flight. Then I hear the small whispers of Oliver, words he's never said, but that rattle in my brain, anyway. *Be careful. He's killed before, he can do it again.* Then, poetic as ever, Edgar jumps in, a voice I've never heard and yet know with every fragment of my soul. *Words have no power to impress the mind without the exquisite horror of their reality.*

These deep cashmere reminders echoing through my skull keep me silent and nodding along to Issac's request.

"Good girl. Now, tell me, where is the contract?" he leans in as he asks, sickly sweet cigar breath threaded with grape hitting my cheeks, inflicting acid into my throat.

My mouth slackens and the flush rises through my collarbone. Whatever I expected him to say, it wasn't that. I'm dumbfounded, surprise making me stupid and weak.

"The contract?" I ask, confused.

The crack of his knuckles on my jaw throws my head back so hard tears immediately stream down my face. My nose turning on like a faucet from the pain. I cannot even fully comprehend he's hit me before I'm righted again, staring into his contrasting gaze, only it is now spun into a single murky color with my dizziness.

"*That* felt good. You can continue not to answer, makes no difference to me. It might to your little boyfriend though if you come back bruised and beaten."

He gloats his courage like salt in a wound. He wants me to know that there is no one who can save me. No one, not even a Poe, that can stop this injustice. And while I can recognize his intent, the only words of his that stick are *if you come back.* Right now, I feel no guarantees for my future.

"I am going to need an answer. Where. Is. It? Paxton had to have left it somewhere and since you were the one he was in love with, you must know." He's snide when he says love as if he's never believed in the word. As if Paxton, just like him, could never be capable of it.

I don't argue with his implied emotions. Don't try to convince him of the man Paxton was, and that he was built to withstand the shattering of his heart without flinching. That even in the face of the impossible, he loved fiercely, like every Poe before him. Even with the painful sting of his betrayal, I know it wasn't in the absence of love but driven by it. Even if that love wasn't mine.

Instead, I try to think around the spots I'm seeing and the disassociation my mind is skirting into, to remember anything I can about the mention of any contract they might want. Moments with Emily spring forth, of players and games, but none are helpful. None of it is what Issac wants.

My mind spins.

Issac ticks his chin back and forth, shoulder to shoulder, until it cracks. He's posturing, showing me he's ready to do what he must. And I ready myself to accept it as my mouth hinges open to speak, knowing he won't be happy with the only thing I can say.

"I don't know. No one has told me about a contract, including Paxton. If you want the will…" I sigh, resigned, trying to give him anything he might want.

He grimaces as if he's the one in pain and, like any good sadist, he's enjoying it.

"Wrong answer," he says as he pulls hard on my wrist, causing it to pop and I shriek at the shock of it.

"EVANGELINE!"

The scream of my name is close and panicked. My hand is released. Issac chucks me under the chin as he whispers *next time* through the throbbing that's taken over my ears. It stings the bruise that I'm sure is already blossoming. My brain demands I move, but my body screams at me in pain. I'm unsure which to give in to until the air around me floods into the vacuum that Issac's body has left as he books it down the hall, turning back only to wave. Agony bowls through me, replacing my name with the noun itself.

I stare at the open hallway Issac has run down and step backward to create as much distance between where he might be and where I am now, stumbling into something. Hands catch onto my shoulders, causing a loud cry to escape me.

"Eve! It's me! Are you ok?" Tyler asks as he withdraws his hands, unsure of where I'm hurt.

I'm shaking, the adrenaline running down at the instance of my nerves. But I take a deep breath, focusing on the fact that Tyler is here, instead of despairing in the echoing cavern Oliver's vacancy has left. My subconscious brain cannot worry for him and with fear riding at the front of my features, I cannot control looking beyond what I have in front of me for him. Tyler would be a fool not to notice. Thankfully, his concern has always been for the better of me.

"He ran after the guy. But he'll be here soon. He didn't leave you, Eve," the last few words slip from him as soft petals being plucked from a rose.

I don't deserve the gentleness. He doesn't deserve the hurt. But here we are, pulling and breaking from our nature toward each other, anyway.

"Rose! I found her. She's over here!" Tyler calls.

Rose. I had forgotten about her. She jogs around the corner to meet us, stopping in front of me. She's panting and worried, studying Tyler's face before turning to me. Her soft grey eyes look into mine, dark freckles I hadn't noticed dusting underneath them, and I can't help but wish neither of them were here to witness this, even though I am so grateful they are.

"Eve," she asks, tearing me from the distraction of my emotional pain from the very real physical one that's currently happening. "Who was that? What happened to you?"

I can't take the vulnerability Rose is pushing on me, so I focus instead on Tyler. He's eyeing my chin that I'm sure is a pinched blueberry by now, which somehow, I've tilted perfectly into the light. His hand is left dangling in the air, far enough away not to touch me, but close enough that I know he wants to. I want to gather into him and cry. To tell him everything that I know. To feel like this isn't happening and my world can be safe again. Or at the very least, not at the attention of a murderer.

But Tyler's arms aren't mine to sacrifice my pain and fall into.

I look at Rose again. *Not anymore.* I suck down the hazy labyrinth air. Fold every word and action of the last hour into tiny letters to be opened only by their addressed reader and pretend.

"I... Rose... I don't know what's happening." And it's true. I don't. "Can you get me out of here, please?" I plead.

I meld the worry I feel into the words. Beg her for grace. To listen, if only just once. And without fault, she does.

"Oh yeah, of course. Let's get you somewhere safe," she says soothingly. Tyler steps in, pushing Rose back a step to get next to me.

"Can you walk? I don't want to touch you to help until I know what's hurt," he says, looking me over.

"I can walk. It's my arm and my wrist. My face, too."

I try to gesture to the side of the cheek Issac hit but wince when my right wrist demands not to be moved. I can already feel the thickness of it, the swelling making it impossible to flex. Tyler's mouth grinds down and I imagine his teeth sound like crunching gravel. Thankfully, he doesn't dawdle. Doesn't demand answers like Paxton would or wait to coax the truth from my lips like Oliver. Tyler just follows my lead, nudging me in the direction I want to go. My heart pushes the sludge of gratitude through the thick concrete wall fear has left.

"Thank you," I whisper.

I say it repeatedly to them both, unsure if it's out loud or just in my head. I'm saying thank you for this, but also thank you for everything that came before. My nerves are live wires without an outlet, sparking emotions that have no direction or filter. I'm going mad from the sorrow and worry and angst.

We only get out of the labyrinth and to the top of the stairs before my world shifts again. There, walking up toward me, the wild of Oliver's curls piled on top of his head. Both hands are in his pockets, eyes downcast, watching the party still going on below as if he's looking for someone, until something brings his attention to me.

For a fraction of a second, the safe warm bubble of Oliver wraps around me. The sounds of the club, of Tyler and Rose, of the throbbing my blood is doing, stop. We lock onto one another and if my face didn't hurt so damn bad, I'd smile. I think he wants to, too. Until the reminder of the night floats in between us, dousing water on any fire that used to glow.

"Tell me what happened."

RUSTED BRAKES

"There you are!" Oliver yells as he jogs over to me in the yard.

I'm standing in the sliver of a dying sunbeam that's somehow found its way through the leaves of the trees, book tucked to my chest, reading. He's closer, or faster, than I realize because before I'm finished with my sentence, he has me two feet off the ground, the book casually tossed to the side. I laugh at the breathlessness of floating. I spread my arms out as if I'm taking flight.

He smiles, wide enough to see the one crooked tooth he can be self-conscious about, but refuses to get fixed. Wide enough that it could suck the air from the skies and leave us all gasping in its wake. He gives into my whimsy and twirls me around. The loose ponytail I haphazardly had thrown up falls out immediately. I laugh again as hair flings into my mouth.

"Ok! OK! Put me down," I squeal.

It feels good. Normal. Happy. The weight we usually have between us has been suspended in time. With Paxton gone on a summer trip with his fraternity brothers, and my mother in New York, there's been very little to remind us that what we're doing is foolish. In lieu of living in the world we've known; we've created a new one.

"Not on your life, Darkness," he says, the words pulled deep and thick from his chest.

He lowers me just enough that our lips are even before devouring them. He floats between nipping and sucking, pulling me further into his mouth and into the abyss. Which is why I take too long to remember that we're standing in the middle of the yard, where anyone can come upon us, and come to my senses. I pull back and wrap my arms around him in an embrace that could be mistaken for any of the ones we've shared our whole lives.

"Oliver, we have to be more careful," I whisper in his ear.

A small shiver runs through him, and he squeezes tighter. "Why?"

I huff at the nonsense. He knows why. We may have created our own reality to live in for the summer, but Alexander and Madeline have *not*. I don't know what kind of chaos it would bring if they saw us together, but I know Madeline would put a stop to it any way that she needed to.

"Your parents..." I mutter.

He laughs as if I'm silly. A worrier in no need of worry. But we both know I'm right. I wiggle, trying to make him put me down, losing the helium of joy that had been lifting me up. But his arms are steel.

"They're gone. Alexander has whisked Madeline away for the weekend on a romantic end of season jaunt. For the next few days, it's just the two of us in this big ol' house."

His smile is still wide and my impulsive traitor of a heart mirrors him instantly. His cheeks gloat in triumph before he tilts me back into another round of kisses. These are less sweet. Less carefree. And more *hungry*. Our tongues are anticipating the night to come, leaving our bodies no choice but to be desperate for the dark. They're filled with promises and oaths and reassurances that everything is falling into place.

"Hey—" a voice calls in greeting before fading away into a cough.

My blood freezes. I push at Oliver, but he either doesn't hear the person who's walked up to us, or he doesn't care. I turn my face to catch Paxton's disapproving wince.

"Hey Paxton." I struggle to get down, ready to have my feet firmly back on dirt before having this conversation. "Oliver, put me down."

He does as I ask, but his arm doesn't move from around my waist. I try to sidestep him, but he moves with me, like water clinging to my skin. I'm frustrated that he's decided this is the time to take a stand and embarrassed to be caught red-handed.

The boys just stare, the blissful quiet of a beautiful day turning into a long stretch of awkward breathing. I look from one to the other, unsure if I should be the one to break when neither is aware I exist right now. Thankfully, Oliver turns to me before I say something that will only make whatever is happening worse. He brushes my hair away from my face, gliding the pads of his fingers across my cheek, currently heating from knowing Paxton is watching.

"Would you be okay to go inside and wait for me? I think the conversation my brother has for me right now is best given privately," Oliver says before he leans down and whispers just for me to hear, "and I don't want the perfect bubble we're in to pop just yet."

He kisses my ear as he stands back up and I'm left reeling, divided by want and distress. There's nothing I am more desperate to have than one more day, one more hour, of our love story. To enjoy the little time we have left in it. I want the last real secret we've kept from each other to be shared tonight. I want that fated moment we've been promised since the second I walked up Dellbrook's path.

But I also want the look on Paxton's face to vanish. I want the next time he sees me not to be in disappointment like it is now. I want him to know that nothing needs change between us. That I can love him as I always have. That we're family, regardless of what happens with Oliver and me. Yet, no matter how much I want this encounter to be wiped from our ledgers, I know that it's here, and that somehow, nothing will ever be the same.

So, instead of begging for his forgiveness, which already feels lost, I kiss Oliver full on the mouth and make my way to the house. I don't see them again until I'm well hidden inside, looking out the second-story window where I can catch the corner of the spot they're standing in. The hall I'm in is murky, the descending sun already well past this part of the house. A place I'm sure they cannot look up and see me spying.

There's exasperation in Paxton's gestures. He's solid and unflinching in the face of Oliver's neglect for his words, but taunts him with points and shoulder shoves. Oliver does not move. Does not react. He says few words, but his glare is stone, punctuated with a determination I know so well. *I will not relent*, it says. For Paxton is the fury born in a wildfire, but Oliver, Oliver is the ember.

They do not yell and still I know their words are not kindness. My heart bleeds for them being at odds over me. The disapproval threatens to engulf my happiness and drag me back to the truth of my situation. *It isn't forever,*

Paxton. Soon it'll be over, and everything will end anyway. I want to scream it at him. The only thing that stops me is knowing that the second those words leave my lips, they become true. They ruin whatever time I have left.

I stay at the window and watch them as minutes tick by. Finally, Oliver puts his hands up, mouth moving in finality before he walks back toward the house. My feet yearn to meet him, to ask what's happened, or just to forget it did, for a little while longer. But my heart tells me to stay.

Paxton watches Oliver's retreat before his head slices up to the window I'm staring out of. My guilt leaps into my throat, making me choke on being caught *again*, but I stay still. *He cannot see you,* I say to myself, trying to calm the nerves. His eyes narrow as if he's heard me and finds me as ridiculous as a child. I've seen that look a hundred times and never has it cut this deep.

"He'll come around." Oliver's voice is deep, unsure, but solid, taking my attention from his brother.

He wants to believe it. Even if we all feel that the ground beneath our feet has shifted irrevocably. I look back to where I saw Paxton last, but he's gone. My hand lifts to the window, a small wave goodbye that only we can see instead of the person it's meant for. I leave my hand there and flutter my eyes back to Oliver.

"Is that what he said?" I ask. I know it isn't. He knows, I know it isn't. Still, he nods.

"In not so many words. *To while away forbidden things! My heart would feel to be a crime,*" he says, each syllable lulling me back into our dream-world.

"Oliver August Poe. Are you trying to seduce me with your great-great-how many greats-grandfather's words?" I laugh. He takes several steps towards me until we're sharing every breath.

"Maybe. Is it working?" he asks, head tilted down to allow him space to nibble at my neck. At the feel of his lips on my skin, I forget Paxton. I forget the cliff we're running a million miles toward. I forget myself and instead lean into whoever this boy in front of me needs me to be.

"Mmm," I hum, already losing the words in anticipation of his hands. He kisses me one last time in the hollow of my throat, the soft *pop* of it lingering between us, before grabbing my hand and pulling me further into the house.

"Come. There's something I want to show you," he says in trepidation.

As if I might not follow. My curiosity spikes, and I'm pushing him forward, eager to see what he might have hidden. Every time I think I know the

Poes, there's always a new mystery to solve. It's my favorite thing about loving them.

He stops at the door to his room, looking over at me shyly through dark lashes. I haven't been inside since puberty hit us and made things like closed doors and dark rooms less than honorable. Instead, we hung out in dens and libraries, or occasionally, my room in the house staff's quarters, where being alone for too long was impossible. Even now, we hadn't dared grace this hall where Paxton and his parents' rooms were also located.

"It's locked," he tells me.

"So, get the key," I urge in ambition. He chuckles, head shaking at the bounce of my heels.

"You don't even know if what I'm going to show you is good. What if it's something weird or terrible?"

He's earnest, nervous, which forces me to calm. I know there is nothing that'll change tonight. If Paxton showing up didn't force us to give up our hearts early, cutting this off before the end of summer as planned, nothing will. I am desperate for Oliver to know the truth of how I feel and wipe the nerves from his features. I take his hands in mine.

"When we were eight, you showed me the taxidermy. At nine, you pulled me into the catacombs of your family's graveyard and urged me to bring your skull collection to school. At thirteen you forced me to listen to your first horror story, in the dead of night, causing me to dream about murderous brambles and weapon wielding ghosts. And at seventeen, you read me a love poem that likened rotting flowers to desire. There is nothing your morbid little heart can hold that I would shy away from. And weird? Do you know where the word derives from?"

I expect his 'no'. I feel it in my bones and as soon as his head confirms it, the electricity between us intensifies. Every second up until now, I've always felt one step behind. But standing in front of this midnight hued door, Oliver Poe's hands wrapped in mine and his attention on my every word, I am the most powerful I will ever be.

"It comes from the Old English noun, wyrd, which means fate." I pause, letting it sink in, knowing he's thinking about Edgar and our first moment like this almost ten years ago. "Now, if you opening that door shows me our fate, I promise I will not run."

Oliver once told me that his famous ancestor believed fate did not have to be begged for. That it would just be. And Oliver said we have to embrace every ending, to accept our next beginning. Remembering that now emboldens me to stay perfectly still. To allow Oliver the chance to take everything I'm giving and open that door, or to run from it. I will not beg or barter or steal his choice.

Making when he grabs me and crushes our limbs together in a breathless kiss, even more satisfying. Fate, it seems, has found us. Together.

He pulls back, now just as excited as I am, to get it open. His hands work the keys and riddles to get in, going slowly so I can remember. *He wants you to come back here.* I try not to let my inner thoughts cloud what's happening in case I'm wrong.

The door finally opens, and I am encased in the deepest part of the ocean. Dark blue walls and furniture only delineated by gold greet us. It's my favorite color. My favorite element. My favorite time of night. He's encapsulated everything I aspire to be with a color. It catches my breath, and I cannot remember if this is who I've always been, or who I adapted to be, because it's who Oliver is. I can feel him watching me wander around, eyes wide.

"It's a... lot, I know. It is your favorite color, though," he says offhandedly.

As if his words don't rip at pieces of me. Don't try to pull down the illusion we've been weaving and tell me what's happening is real. It's too close to the truth of us. And I can't take the blurred edges of our double existences right now.

"What is this on your shelves?" I ask, ignoring his words and walking over to the safe space of books instead. "Austen and Dickenson stories mixed in with your Edgar poetry? Oliver! Madeline would have a stroke," I say, my hand fluttering to my heart to accentuate my shock.

He comes up behind me, happy to leave whatever I need to, to rest, and wraps his arms around my waist, swaying me with the movement.

"You know, I'm a writer. A poet. And I say that anything can be a poem." His voice is husky and confident. Exactly how it should be. How it's always been.

"Is that so?" I ask right back.

"Mmm. Yes. *Anything* can be a poem when tasted on the lips of a poet," he drags out the word anything, then punctuates his proclamation with a kiss on my ear, the thick echo of it making me laugh in a completely unhumorous way.

I don't let him distract me further, though. We came in here for more than flesh, and I'm determined to get answers before we get lost in it.

"Show me," I whisper.

I know he wants to believe, I mean the other, that I'm playing a game we're both bound to lose. I squeeze his arms to pull him out of the lust the moment has run in to, so he knows I mean something profoundly less flirtatious.

"Right," he sighs, resigned.

He lets me go. I turn to watch him shuffle through some papers and journals stacked around his desk. There are dozens, along with scrap papers littered in every spare spot on the wall and floor. Old quill pens and ink pots are placed around the room. Pens and pencils strewn, always within reaching distance. Typewriters stacked haphazardly. So that if, at any time, Oliver had a thought, he had a place to jot it down.

"You know, they have computers and recorders and phones to put your notes in, right?" I ask good humoredly. I already know what he'll say, but I can't help but needle him.

"You can't write, *really write,* on any of those. You know that, Eve. And that you think technology can help with any emotional endeavor, one that really captures the heart... I would swear you didn't grow up in this house, same as me."

He's joking. It's an old game we have. With every new gadget or evolution the world sees, Oliver's dislike grows. To that end, the entire Poe family has a dismissal towards technology. At least in using it in creative spaces. Or social media. But his words open something up in me. A memory, or just the memory of a feeling. *I didn't grow up in this house, same as you. I was an outsider.*

I don't say it out loud. I find every strength I have to keep it from showing on my face. Later, I can remember this part. Can use it as a reminder of why I'm in New York and why he hasn't called and why I'll never be a Poe. Later it can all crash down.

Thankfully, he doesn't see or feel anything off. He finds what he must be looking for and gestures for us to sit on the bed as he brings the sheet over with us. He waits for me to get settled before handing it over, a large sigh escaping as he does.

It's a yellow dyed piece of parchment. Expensive and creamy. The writing is in navy blue cursive, pristine, and carefully placed. Every word plucked out of Oliver's mind. Delicately scrawled. I scrunch my nose in confusion.

"Just... read it," he says.

"Okay," I croak.

And I do.

Darkness in Truth
They say that darkness causes your senses to sharpen
like when I see the prism of your golden eyes dilate
as they travel down the plains of
my chest as we swim.
Or, how I imagine the taste of your salt will sting my tongue
leaving me parched for you
as my teeth bite down on the softness
where your throat and collarbone meet.
We collide in the burnt embers between shadows
unable to pull apart where I end and you begin
our senses so heightened as to know this is more than just lust.
You are the thread tying together
our two dying stars,
alone and in love
infinitely with darkness.

I don't know what to say, unsure of what this means. When you ask a poet about love or destiny, you forget any opinion you had on it before you'd heard their voice. And I'm not sure I'm ready to let go of the dream just yet.

"Oliver?" I ask, too scared to want an answer.

"What if... what if we didn't just have the summer? Maybe we don't end in August. What if I could give you September?" he breathes.

"Oliver." I interrupt, knowing I cannot let him give me this much hope.

"And your birthday. Christmas. We must see December like this, Darkness. And January... I bet January with you would be even better." He's pleading and I can feel the tears pricking my eyes at what I have to do.

"What about Madeline? And Paxton? What about our lives? You know this will never work." I beg him to understand, but he doesn't relent.

"No, Eve. What I _know_ is that all the books on my desk are filled with poems just like this. All about you. What I KNOW is that I have loved you all my life. I could come to New York. We can figure everything out as we go," he says, picking up confidence with every word. The idea grows. _Maybe we can figure it out._ He cups my face and looks at me as if our future is fathomless.

"My whole being craves the night, begs me for it. Even during the day, the sunlight cannot persuade it. And you are the only thing that has ever satisfied that want. The single piece of the dream I'm allowed to have. The one cure to being Poe. You are the beautiful inky darkness my soul needs, Eve." He prays to me as if I am an altar for his sins. And that I alone can absolve him.

"Oliver..." I start, standing on the cusp of the tallest branch on the tree, unsure if I'm going to fall or fly. "From the moment I met you, my heart shattered. I knew how much I loved you then and how devastating it would be when I lost you." I suck in a breath and pause, unsure of what I know I'll say next. "Still, I could never stop the inevitable. You have me for as many days as you'll give," I whisper back, unwilling to shatter the glass of our future with words louder than a heartbeat.

"Every day. Always," he breathes, fanning kisses over my cheeks, as he rolls us both back into his bed. "I love you, Evangeline Pierce."

"I love you, Oliver Poe." I say, gasping at the tender joy I feel.

This time, the words are a foundation instead of a folly. A truth we've made in the face of a lie. And I cannot be beholden to the page when the poet finally makes me a poem.

GOSSAMER SHEETS

The night doesn't feel real. Everything that happened at Crave, at Dellbrook... everything after I got on the plane at JFK feels like a dream. Or a nightmare. I'm having trouble putting the pieces into place within my reality. Paxton dying. *Being murdered*. Roger outed as a fraud. Oliver being so close. A man wanting to kill me. The past continuing to haunt me in the eyes of a boy who'd rather I break. It was a practical joke of devilish proportions.

Poe did always write like he was at war with the heavens. That death was God's weapon against him and love was the only shield he could wield in defense. He loved recklessly and without pride or shame. For no mortal could be his true enemy. Not when his being alive proved there was hope of loving again. Only fitting that death and love would go hand in hand. Fate always had a way of finding you.

"And then he died," Oliver intones.

I didn't realize I had been speaking out loud. A habit, no doubt. Knowing the boys always loved my musings on Edgar and other literary masters. We'd spend hours just gossiping and assuming and riffing on their lives. Their whims. It was only natural I would do so now. Old hat, as they say. Even so, it doesn't make me feel any saner.

"Sorry. I must sound moronic. I... I didn't know I was thinking out loud," I try to explain.

We both know I don't have to. Oliver lends me the grace not to answer. He simply twines his fingers deeper into mine. He hasn't released my good hand since he found me on the stairs and I'm unsure of why I let him. Fear over fury seems to be the only equation right now, and while Oliver has hurt me, at least he wants me alive.

Weary glances keep going to the wrist I have coddled against me, threaded in his shirt like a sling, and the cheek, I'm sure, resembles a plum right about now. My gaze lingers between his bare chest peeking out of his jacket and his frown. His phone vibrates for the third time in the console, and I peek over, too nosy for my own good, only to see Ally's smirking face.

"You should pick that up. Might be important," I say, flatly.

He shakes his head. "No."

He doesn't elaborate or pay any mind to his phone at all. He's too despondent. Worried. He'd lost Issac somewhere in the maze. Had tried to beat him to the door, with no luck. He wanted to insist we go to the hospital or police, Tyler ever eager to back him up. Until I explained to both the media show that might cause. That while I know who did it, he was masked. That it would be my word against his. All while trying to find who we were now sure killed Paxton.

It'll do no one any good, I explained. *Call the family doctor and have her meet us at home.* The word for Dellbrook had tasted dirty in my mouth, but I refused to replace it. I needed Oliver to agree, to believe me on his side, at least for now. Which, reluctantly, he did. Tyler, on the other hand, left more furious than I can ever remember him being.

That's it, Poe. We're through. I've dealt with this bullshit long enough. Eve is hurt and you still only care about you and your reputation. Rose had tugged him close, choosing a side we were not on despite the sadness rolling on her face. With her hand tight in his grip, he'd stormed off, curses and curse words flying.

I watched as each one hit Oliver like a punch, and by the end, he was as beat up as I was. *He'll come around,* is all he said before he marched me to the waiting car. The silence stretched between us, the words threatening to throw me back to another time Oliver had promised that same resolution to me, until my brain couldn't take it and started mumbling on about Edgar.

Thankfully, the drive is short. We barely have the car parked in back by the kitchen entrance before Oliver hustles me into Dellbrook, motioning me up to the family rooms. Before we make it to the stairs, Ally, in her tight-fitting dress and glistening hair, rushes to cut us off.

"Oliver! Where have you been? I've been calling you," she scolds.

"Not now, Ally," he says, skirting her entirely without slowing or even taking her in.

"Where are you going? Oliver!" She's pleading now, anger making her sound desperate.

"I said, *not now*! I will talk to you later. *Goodnight*!" Oliver calls over his shoulder.

He's cold and removed, not even glancing back. But I do. Ally's face is scrunched in hatred as she watches me head up the stairs, towards his rooms. As much as I'd like to gloat, I'm so numb that all I can do is face back forward and ignore her presence, too.

Just inside his room, in the small sitting area, the family doctor waits, poised and ready to take whatever had called her to Dellbrook in the middle of the night. Panic settles into my stomach as I see the shredded papers in the dim lighting strewn from his bed to his desk. Luckily, Oliver is too distracted to notice.

"Oliver, are you alright?" she asks, looking him over from the distance between us. She spares me only a glance, a single nod *hello*, already morphing into someone well adept at taking care of trauma.

"Dr. Sheryl, I'm fine, I'm fine. It's Eve," Oliver says, putting me in front of her, his back to the rest of the room. Finally, she takes me in. Seeing my face, puffy through the lips, and the hand I'm holding carefully in front of me, wrapped in a makeshift sling of Oliver's undershirt.

"Oh. OH! Come here, let me look at you closer." She gestures towards the only bright light where, once I step into it, nothing can hide.

"May I?" she asks, pointing to Oliver's shirt tied around my neck.

I nod, unable to speak. She loosens the sleeves and removes its support from my arm, handing it back to Oliver once she's done.

"I believe this belongs to you," she says, looking pointedly at the bare skin of his neck, smirking as she does.

As if his playboy ways have caught up to him. As if this might just have been a rollick gone wrong. She's known the Poes since the boys were young, and her father had known them before that. Her family was as tied to them as mine, more so throughout the generations. Of course, she wouldn't blame Oliver. Wouldn't assume the worst.

A small sliver of pleasure jolts through me when she asks, anyway.

"So, are either of you going to tell me what happened?"

She gently tilts my head from side to side. Prods at my bones, my jaw, and my wrist, all the way up into my shoulder. I hold in the whimpers. Tell myself the bruising looks worse than it is. That pain doesn't exist. Not anymore. The words echo through the caverns of my internal screams. I cannot make truths out of lies.

Still, I try.

We are silent. I don't know what to tell her that would suffice.

"Eve... got into a fight." Oliver provides.

The doctor tilts her head in understanding. "Ah. Did a fan get too overzealous again? It's ok, Eve. I get it. First loves die hard."

If looks could kill, I would be on trial for murder after tonight. She laughs, as Oliver rubs at his neck as if he will play into her innocent assumptions. My pride blisters at the thought that everyone here thinks I've just been waiting for an opportunity to lay my claim. That I would physically force my way into his life again.

"But they do always die," I retort, sure to enunciate clearly so as not to be misunderstood.

That silences them both. Dr. Sheryl finishes her work, then looks at Oliver when she's done with me, unsure of how to deal with me this way.

"It looks like she's just got a terrible sprain. I'll need her to come in. Here's the appointment card, to make sure, but she should be fine. It'll need to be wrapped and stay in the sling for a bit. Make sure she's in my office on Monday, got it? Ice and NSAIDs should do the trick until then."

Neither one of us tells her I'll be long gone by then. What's the point? I make a mental note to make an appointment with my doctor back home first thing.

"Have Oliver wrap this tonight, and then ice in the morning," she emphasizes to me, her medical training outweighing her awkwardness.

Oliver nods when I can only glare in response, and that's enough of a confirmation for her to pack up her things and take off, closing the door behind her. I'm at a loss as I watch her go, feeling Oliver watching me.

He picks up the wrap she left and closes the distance between us, unafraid of my wrath. He's gentle as he lifts my arm and begins rolling it around and around my wrist and hand, dedicated to his pursuit. The brush of his fingertips over delicate skin has me swallowing more than necessary. My attention bleeds into him. I need a distraction and I focus on the unfairness of it all instead.

"She won't even question it. That's the power you have, Oliver. A person can walk in here, see the worst and be told it's grand and never think any different. It didn't even matter what happened to me. Not really. Everyone dangles on the cliffs of your words, on your family's words, and just does as they're asked. Doesn't that bother you?" I ask him, wondering if his answer has changed.

"You know it does," he scoffs. "But what am I to do, Eve? Just let you not get checked? Not use all of my resources to take care of you? We're not children anymore. I can't just *relinquish* my name. It would just make me more of what they expect, anyway. I cannot escape my nature any more than you."

I know he's right, but I'm still angry about it. And being angry is better than the guilt I have at the scattered pages, just out of reach of the pooling light, that I'll have to explain to Oliver soon enough. Or the pain as his words hollow me out, a damn near reflection of how I felt coming here to begin with. I hear the poison in each sentence and the promises he made to Paxton reflecting in his voice. He knew he'd never marry. He'd promised not to have a life with me. And even though we're not together, something in me snaps as I realize he's *still* keeping his oath. That it's the thief that's stolen over eight years between us.

Before I can do anything, the soft melancholy of Oliver's voice stills me.

"Is it true?" he asks, pining his finished ends together, fingers still pouring heat through to my skin. The question is a needle in a haystack that, once dropped, is impossible to find.

"Is what true?" I ask, cruelly.

"That our love died. That there is nothing left at all?"

He's so still. An animal at warning. Even in the graves of his vows, his worry is still only that I love him. *It's all he can hope for when keeping promises like he does.* I try not to breathe. It's the hush on a field decorated for battle, right before the war begins. *What will the death toll be this time?* I wonder. I mirror his statued face with one of my own, only moving my lips to answer.

"For years, I've hoped so. I want it to be," I sigh, releasing the tight grip I have, realizing that I have no more control on this moment than I have had on any in the last eight years. I'm too tired tonight to hold fast to hostility. It has done nothing but drive the wounds deeper, anyway. I drop the façade and give him my pain. "But try as I might, I cannot escape you."

It's an accusation. A demand of repentance. Fire, to leave burns on his soul just like his touch has left heat on my skin.

"I figured you wanted clean cuts to our ties. I've left you be…" he says, but I don't let him finish. I don't give him the forgiveness of excuses.

"Oliver. *You* wanted clean cuts. You couldn't keep your promises to Paxton if every day you had to look at me. You made me… you left me believing it was *my fault*," I say.

"I didn't have a choice… I had to let you go," he whispers.

A callus laugh escapes me. "Let me go? LET ME GO? Don't you know you're everywhere? The wisp of your black curls as I swear you disappear down an alley just ahead but are gone before I can get there. I hear the squeak of those damn shoes you refused to throw away because you'd loved them so much, claiming they held your memories, even after they'd broken. The smell of maple syrup and coffee, from the time you wanted to quit refined sugar and ended up loving it so much you never looked back." The tears are now thick in my throat, making the words scorching, telling me to turn back. That this is too much, too raw, too close to things we shouldn't say. Feelings I don't want to be true. But it's too late.

"You're everywhere. In all of my senses. And I'm not okay, but the world thinks I am. Because normal people don't like it when you live in graves. Only in the dead of night, when the rest of the world sleeps, am I able to crawl into my casket. Only then can I miss and hope and wither without you. Then, again, in the morning I pretend I don't hear your laugh or smell your kiss or see your skin in my peripheral. I'm forced to remember that *we* don't exist anymore. *That* is where you've let me go."

My breathing is ragged. I feel wild. Alive and fragile and new. It calls Oliver to answer. And even shattered, he cannot resist his heart.

"Darkness. We have always existed. *Will* always exist. And there is nothing more I want than to lead you back home." Oliver's eyes are blown out, and he's matching me, inhale for inhale. The pain seems to lessen in the cascade of our words, something feral finding home.

He closes the gap between us, careful of my battered body, and gently lays a kiss on my mouth before leaning away. I don't let him. There's too much pain. Too much want. I'm too caught up in the fear that tonight could have been my last. That a few weeks ago, for Paxton, it *was*. I'm angry and frustrated and sliced to pieces. But most of all, I've been in love with a ghost, who for tonight has become corporal, and I cannot let that go so easily.

I grab for him, a woman possessed, kissing him harder than my wilted face allows. The pain blooms, pricking and needle thin, only spurring me on. Reminding me I need it. That I can feel more than emptiness.

He meets me in stride, hoisting me up, easing the strain of my lips on his enough to not scrape like gravel, without losing the momentum of our kiss. His fingers dig into my thighs, pulsing fiery circles against them. His body wraps tightly to mine, letting me feel every ridge and dip. His heartbeat pounds a rhythm between us. The pressure in my chest lifts at being wanted. At openly wanting. I forget all the regrets that could follow and instead allow him to carry me towards the open bed.

One more night I can be his muse. Give him something worthy of blank pages and fanfare. Give us both a memory worth keeping before we destroy our future.

I feel his foot slip on a loose piece of paper. He kicks it out of the way, easy to cast it off as a misguided outcast from the rest. But then there's another. And another. His feet are slipping through a slurry of words. And the encumbrance of it all comes back, slapping my gut full force. I wiggle down from his grasp, needing to be on the ground for what comes next, which he allows both out of confusion and concern at not hurting me.

"What the—hold on, Eve. I've just got to turn on this light," he tells me as he disappears into the dark towards his desk.

The warm yellow glow flickers on and with it, any chance I have of forgetting. Oliver's face falls, his heart bobbing in his throat as he swallows and then swallows again. His fist pumps at his side. He doesn't know what's happened. I watch as he tries to put together the pieces. For a split second, I consider letting him come to his own conclusions. Allowing whoever else to take the blame.

"Oliver... I can explain," I say instead. His eyes shoot to me as if I'm a traitor.

I feel like a traitor.

"I only came in here to get the rest of the letter. I didn't intend on any of this happening. But then I saw the poems. And I had heard about Ally. Knew there were other women. Something in me snapped."

I'm ashamed that the doctor was partly right, after all. That I couldn't control myself. That I'm not the woman I pretend, only the girl I'd hoped to leave behind. But I don't apologize like I intend to. Sorry doesn't feel adequate, anyway. His laugh is hollow. He stoops to pick up some of the ripped pages, along with others that somehow remained intact. He's calm, deliberate with his movements, the disbelief at what I've done, not allowing the veracity of it to kick in just yet. He startles me when he speaks, a cold sweat dampening my skin from the chill of his tone.

"A huge part of myself had been ripped away when you left. When everything *happened*. Even though it was my fault. And for a while, I thought, maybe I should move on. Heal old wounds. I was so angry at the world. But the truth was that I didn't want to heal. Healing meant accepting that that piece was gone for good. I couldn't allow it. Didn't want to live without the dream of it. I still had hope. For me. For you. *For us*. So, every day, I got drunk enough to forget the pain, long enough to breathe, but not enough to forget you."

His eyes are glassy and red, making my veins feel on the precipice of bursting. I want to go to him, but I know I'm unwelcome. His confession is turbulent, a piece of his soul I'm not meant to see, and it makes me hot with embarrassment at being a witness to it. Unable to do anything else, I stand and take what he has left to say in the absence of comfort.

"Then, about a year ago, I was in New York and stumbled into some university's library, drunk and miserable, to sign a few books. It wasn't planned. I was on a layover for another tour. And when I looked over, there you were, stunning as ever. I couldn't remember why you weren't next to me. Why we weren't together.

"Then some guy came up and kissed you, which I expected since I wanted to do the same. What surprised me was that you kissed him back. Really kissed him, and when you pulled away, a soft smile I hadn't seen in years lit your face. One that I didn't think still would when everything to me felt so royally fucked. That's when I realized I was the only one broken enough to want to live in pain with the memory of you, rather than in the joy of a life where you no longer existed."

He runs his hands down his face, wiping the evidence of distress onto his sleeves. My entire world is crumbling at his confession. At the realization that we've cursed each other to this. I do not know what to say. What to do. Leaving me nothing but to stand like the shadow I am. He paces, picks up another poem, then decides he's not quite done with me yet.

"This, *these poems*," he waves it in my face. "Were about *you*. Not fucking Ally. Not some other woman. All of them are about *you*." He whispers the last part, a splintered record trying not to skip over the melody. "Get out."

The words aren't shouted. They're swallowed and sullen. Poison hidden in their demureness. I can feel them killing me as I take careful steps out of his room, unable even to look back at the man I've crushed.

I don't even try to argue, too stunned and ashamed to do anymore damage. I'm not sure how I manage to drag the door shut. My body feels leaden, sunken with guilt and the unmistakable weight of shame. I can't say I never wanted to hurt Oliver. I did. I wanted him to feel my pain. To remember, I existed once before. But I never wanted him tortured. Destroyed. Left in the desolation of the past, alone.

Thousands of poems, all for you.

I know our past wasn't easy and that he made mistakes, too. Justice still cries out that I be angry at what he did to us and let him simmer in the silence of these memories. Animosity still settles as I hear his voice on video telling Paxton I'll never be a Poe. Nineteen-year-old Eve wants everything to burn. She wants to dance in the war our love has created.

But eight years without him, and one week back, has taught me that mercy is the companion of passion, and I cannot be whole without either. And while my heart is punishing a younger Oliver, what I just did in there cannot be blamed on the past. I should have known better. *I should have been better*. Somehow, Oliver and I will need to find peace in the turbulence of our pain. Or we're both conscripted to continue our lives fighting ghosts.

I find the will to move, knowing for tonight at least we're finished. No amount of revelations I'll have darkening his doorway will allow me back inside. I'm not sure I could even face him now if it did. All I can hope at this point is that we haven't gone so far as to not be able to find North again.

The hall through the bedrooms is haunting, deep shadows blending with each other to create pools of ether. The air is heavy, leaving me to feel as if I'm swimming through it, trying to catch my breath underwater. I pick up my pace, only to still at the distinctive creak of a door. All the nerves I'd thought fried fire up in recognition before I know what I should be afraid of. I tiptoe towards the open cavern where a door should be, realizing I'm heading into Paxton's room.

The place has been ransacked. The moon spilling through a broken window, allowing the light to glow on the complete mess that's been left. None of the pristine placements are to be found. His room robbed of when he last stepped foot in it. I know I should back away, but curiosity kills everything it touches, for it is the hand and I am Midas, so instead I move forward.

The remains of books and pictures lay smashed and shattered. Glass glitters in the inky edges of the light. My mind sees no pattern, no reason, but I look for one, anyway. Something that sticks out of place in the heaps of out-of-place things. Until finally, I think I've found it. A torn envelope, ripped right down the middle, whose contents have been taken. The sender's address, still intact in the corner, is one I don't recognize. All except the name. *This is a clue to follow, an address of importance.* I pocket it before making my way back to Oliver's room.

I hesitate far longer than I should to knock. *I don't want to do this. To look in his eyes with our hearts still dripping from our sleeves.* But I have to. He's the only one who can decide what to do, if he wants to report the robbery or hide it before Madeline sees. I owe him that much.

He doesn't answer the door, so I open it, thankful it's still unlocked. He's sitting at his desk, torn papers still fluttering around him, head bent down, and pen in hand. A bottle sits nestled within reach, liquid already dribbling down to pool at the edges of his words. As if this is how he's always been meant to be.

"Oliver," I start, but he interrupts.

"Leave me be," he croaks, vocal cords thrumming like a bass string that's just been plucked. I sigh, hating to have to do this, but knowing it can't wait.

"It's Paxton."

He turns, eyes sunk, and hair battered from anxious fingers running through. The blackness of his room swells to him as if he's calling it forth. He closes his eyes and when he opens them, Oliver, in sorrow, in love, is gone. In his place is the shell of a person whose only need is answers.

"What happened?"

SCORCHED PATHWAYS

THE GOLDEN NUMBERS FLOATING in front of me become a chant inside my head. *8-3-1.* I want them to mean something more than just a marking for a door. I rattle them around in my brain, moving and turning them like the missing piece of a puzzle I've gone into blind. But if they have anything more to give, their secrets are well kept.

Not for the first time since arriving do I stick my good hand out and rest it on the handle. *Still locked.* I sigh at the wasted minutes I'm stuck in this hall and pray the nosey bell girl from downstairs doesn't wander up to find me here. The pain in my jaw and wrist have been dulled by the pain relievers, but the thrum of them can be felt all the same. I curse Oliver again for being late.

We drove separately. Him, still angry with me. Me, still bruised and battered by more than just the physical altercation. Last night couldn't be considered one of our better days. The lingering sound of his voice telling me I'm not a Poe melds and morphs between Issac's cold calculation, and then Oliver's distraught plea at finding his work destroyed by the one he made it for, had kept me up, spinning emotional blankets to be suffocated with.

Only the tiny rip of paper tucked into my pocket and the prickling sensation that I was getting close to something forced me to get dressed and drive over here. It is the only thing fueling me forward and moving toward whatever waits for me behind door 831 instead of hopping on the next flight home. Though my guilt is what led me to confess my plans to Oliver.

The rustle of someone behind me has me twirling, only to find Oliver strutting up. He gets a few feet from me, and I can already smell the booze. His smile is casually cruel, as if last night it wasn't passionately pursuing mine. As if we are nothing at all. He looks from me to the door expectantly.

"It's locked," I say, even though the way he's looking at me now makes me feel foolish for it.

His eyebrows arch as he sits back on his heels, a condescending acknowledgement that makes my nails bite into my palms at my side. He stands there for a moment longer, locked onto my face, before he reaches into his pocket, producing a key.

"You have a key?" I ask dumbly. I shouldn't be surprised. Oliver has never been kept out of anywhere, even when I am.

He scoffs, "Of course," like it is his God given right.

And maybe it is. I'm unfamiliar with the way his entitlement feels when used so blatantly against me, making me want to believe any way his mouth tilts. He holds the door open, motioning me inside. I put the smell of whiskey, and the odd tension coiling in my stomach when my arm accidentally brushes Oliver's to the back of my mind. I'm here to find one thing, and I won't find it in the man behind me.

Inside, everything is a blinding white. Windows adorn the living space at the end of the entrance, allowing even the murky meddling's of light from the overcast day to illuminate the furnishings. Small ornate busts sit on top of stacked coffee table books. Colorful abstract paintings are nestled between each window's frame. Fiery red trim bleeds into maroon, giving the space the only amount of color to be seen consistently throughout. It reminds me of blood.

"Paxton *lived* here," I say aloud.

I'm not really asking, the statement one of disbelief more than argument. The longer I look, the more I find pieces of him, pieces he wasn't allowed at Dellbrook. You can see his exuberance in the accruements that are delicately placed. The bright colors of someone who wants to be seen. It felt lighter, conforming to beauty instead of being beautiful despite it.

"Hardly," Oliver responds, disgust evident. "He stayed here. A place to piss off Madeline, no doubt. Dellbrook was home. You know that."

But when I look at Oliver, I see the shell breaking against the shore. He's becoming more unsure of himself with each new item he picks up and puts back. Paxton and Oliver always shared distaste for what was expected of them, of the confines of their name. Oliver was under no assumption that Paxton ever fit within them to begin with, but the distance between them was growing wider in this room. He's seeing firsthand the consequence of time lost and probably feeling a little like I am. Like maybe in the end, we didn't know him enough.

I can't take how much we're losing for the sake of getting answers anymore. I'm a gambler on my last hand, and if I don't move past the way Oliver's eyes are downcast right now, I'm not sure I'll be able to play the game. The survival parts of me take hold. The ones that lack empathy, that drive me forward when all is lost. They convince my legs to take me to the door that's tucked just past the kitchen and open it.

And then they tell me to panic.

There, shuffling through the bedside drawers, is Roger. He freezes at my intrusion before lunging into action.

"Eve, wait," he says, desperate, reaching for me.

But I don't. I'm already scrambling down the hall to where Oliver waits, unwilling to be caught twice alone with a man who has no business being where he is. The thrum of my jaw and the wrap of my wrist are a good reminder of that. Once Oliver is in sight, I round to confront him.

"Roger, what are you doing here?" I spit.

"Eve, are you okay? Your arm..." Roger says.

He tries to take another step towards me, and I feel the brush of Oliver at my back. He stops dead in his tracks, forehead condensing when he sees Oliver. His face steels as he must realize this isn't a friendly finding and decides to answer.

"I was invited. Paxton left something for me. Told me it was here, along with a key," he says. Though it isn't to me. His eyes are solely focused on Oliver.

"Liar. Get out," Oliver snarls. He snakes an arm around me, a man possessed by alcohol and crushed sensibilities. We may be hurting each other, but the outside world will never be given the privilege. It's the Poe way.

But I am not a Poe.

The thought slams into me over and over, pummeling the safety Oliver brings. I step out of Oliver's arm, and I know it's the wrong move based on the smile Roger gives.

"I was *invited,* and I'm not going anywhere. My key is on the table behind you if you'd like to verify," Roger says.

The snotty tone of triumph makes me want to step back into Oliver, but by the dead air I feel behind me, I'm sure that ship has sailed. Besides, I'm teaching us all a lesson we need to learn.

"Don't sound too smug, Roger. I don't believe you, even with the key. What could Paxton possibly give you? You told me yourself that you hadn't heard from him since the trip, and you had one job. Well, you did it. I thought you'd be on a plane home by now."

I'm direct and callous. Unwilling to let him see the rift between Oliver and me, as if it puts me with him. This time, I'm taking my own side in the war.

"I want to see the letter," Oliver chimes in. Roger stands defiantly until I hold out my hand expectantly. He looks at my palm and sighs.

"Fine," he walks past me, pulling a folded envelope from his jean pocket, and puts it in Oliver's hand, without letting go. "But I need your word that this stays between us. Paxton didn't want it getting out."

He looks at me, and my ears burn. Oliver just nods and the letter is released. His eyes scan the page and I try to decipher the words by the escalation of his eye's movements, to no avail. I cannot fathom what Paxton would need to say to Roger that Oliver could know, but not me. I am famished by the need to find out. Oliver finishes reading and looks up, the letter still perched for reading in his hands.

"And you think it's you?" he asks Roger.

"I do," Roger responds.

Minutes of silence tick by, making me want to scream. Oliver looks between the note and Roger again and again. I look between all three. And Roger just stands, patient and proud, without worrying about what might come. The silence I've worked to master as a weapon is being used against me, and I can hardly take it for another second.

"I don't agree, but I can't deny what's written here. Not that it's Paxton's choice or that I think you're right. I can help you look, but you'll leave the key with me and after today, whether you find it or not, we're done. Got it?" Oliver demands.

He's still holding tight to his mask, letting nothing slip in the tick of his jaw or the taste of his words. A man I could read better than any language has changed alphabets, and I'm left scattered, looking for translations.

Roger is all but happy to agree. "Of course."

Both men spread out, Roger moving back toward the room and Oliver to the bookshelf, as if I have ceased to exist.

"Excuse me," I say, voice pitching higher the more words I get out. "Are either of you going to tell me what's going on?"

"No," they both chorus back.

I'm astonished. Furious. Needy with the want to know. But even my curiosity has its limits, and I am unwilling to bend for either Oliver or Roger right here, right now, so I succumb to their nonsense. I know that nothing I do would bring me closer to answers anyway and only embarrass me further in each of their eyes.

"Okay. Well, will you at least tell me what we're looking for so I can help?" I ask.

"NO!" they respond.

I like it far less when they're on the same page than when they're at each other's throats.

"Fine. Then both of you can rot," I yell. "I'm leaving."

Everything else be damned. I'm tired and sore and bruised. I won't be led through the shadows anymore. Not for Roger. Not for Oliver. Not even for Paxton. I move to the door, intent on leaving, but feel the soft heat of a hand gripping my good arm. Oliver turns me to him, leaning down that only I can hear, and I startle at his closeness. His anger at me still burns bright, but he sets it aside for the task at hand.

"Eve, you cannot leave alone." He eyes over toward Roger, begging me to see the bigger picture. *If Roger is here, who knows who else could be lurking?*

He may not want me to stay to help, but he doesn't want me to leave. He doesn't trust what happened last night won't happen again and, at the very least, he still cares enough not to want that. Chills take over my arms as I think about the possibilities. I nod in understanding. As much as I hate it, I know he's right. He releases me, going back to his search, satisfied I'll listen.

I decide to do a search of my own. After all, I came here to find something, anything, that might lead to the next clue. Careful to keep in Oliver's eyesight, while still weary of Roger and his part in all of this, I start to snoop on the other end of the bookshelf. While Oliver is focused on the assortment of art pieces, boxes, and potential hidden nooks, I set my sights on the books.

I brush my fingers along their spines, reading each before selecting one off the shelf to thumb through, using my bandaged wrist as a hold for their covers. Most of these are newer volumes, the classics and antiques kept at Dellbrook. Still, I'm able to find old favorites, even if they are reprints. *The Scarlet Letter. Leaves of Grass. Mark, the Match Boy.* I smile at them all, remembering his quotes from each that he'd try to use to play into Oliver's and mine's games.

Then, out of the memories, tucked at the end of a shelf, a smaller hard back spine sits. I don't know how or why it catches my eye; all I know is that once it does, a firm block of certainty sits in the bowl of my stomach, pinning me to the present. I float the pad of my pointer down each word, careful not to trigger the mirage. *Walden; or Life in the Woods.*

Thoreau was a favorite of Paxton's, someone who was forced upon me from the moment he finished anything of his. He admired his quiet peacefulness, whose spine still stood straight in the face of injustice. A man whose memory was built on simple living. *How nice it would be, to be descended from a man who expected nothing*, Paxton would say. However, once Madeline saw the notes and markings in his copy of *Walden*, the book and its author had been banned from Dellbrook altogether.

I pull the book down, delicate in my opening of its cover, knowing the pains Paxton must have gone through to keep this single copy of his youth. There, on the title page, ten-year-old Paxton's name is carefully written, so unlike the scratch he would come to use. The scrape of memories threatens to tear at my throat, making the bobbing of my swallows painful. *Just a little more,* I ask my heart.

And as if Paxton himself has rewarded me, a fragment of paper slips from the binding toward the middle. I turn to the page and pull it out completely. The papers are folded, stapled together, making a thin packet. Each is adorned with letterhead from what I would assume to be a lawyer's office. I open it up further, scanning the printed-out pages for anything that's familiar, only to see my name highlighted several times. I scurry to read, to gain a better understanding of what I'm seeing when another familiar name pops up.

"Did you find something, Eve?" I hear Oliver ask behind me.

I hurry to fold the paper back up, cursing my clumsy left hand, my gut telling me to keep this to myself for now. I try to hide it in my pocket and produce *Walden* to Oliver instead.

"Walden. It looks like Paxton had been disobeying Madeline for quite a long time," I say with a smile, wanting to tie Oliver back to me with the reminder of a wonderful memory.

It doesn't work. The frown he's showing only deepens further as he looks at the pocket I'm sure is being charred from the inside out by its secrets.

"What about you?" I ask, staring at the small box in his hands.

He looks at me a moment longer before pocketing the box and sliding his palms down his slacks.

"Nope. Nothing," he says flat-faced.

Liar, I want to scream just as he did to Roger. I want to tell him I don't remember him ever being such a hypocrite. But then again, neither was I. I decide to let it go. For now. The choice feels sticky, even in my mind. Used gum long stuck to the bottom of a desk.

We continue to search the place for another hour, all of us coming up empty, besides the secrets in Oliver and I's pockets. I don't allow any of the attempts Roger is making to corner me to talk. I don't answer his questions about my bruises and arm. Even with the hell that's vacationing between Oliver and me, I still prefer it to the unanswered pleas and feelings of forgery with Roger. The less he knows, the safer I feel.

"I can't believe it's not here. He said it would be here," Roger says as we all end up back in the living area.

"What can I say? My brother was an enigma," Oliver responds, pulling the flask from his pocket and taking a swig.

He's back to leaning, like the first night in Dellbrook, but this time it doesn't feel romantic. It feels contrived. Too easy for all that's happened. My guess is that the show isn't for me though. It's for Roger, whose unease of the youngest Poe is palpable.

"We must have missed it. We should keep looking..." Roger says, turning to start back at the beginning.

Oliver jolts to attention, his hand clamping down on Roger's shoulder with purpose.

"I don't think so. I've humored you. Let you rummage through my dead brother's things like you were at a garage sale. But now I'm done, and so are you." Oliver's tone is laced with smoke, making alarm bells in my head ring.

Roger is well built, but Oliver is several inches taller and in just as good of shape, if not better trained. Madeline made sure both boys were well versed in combat sports, always requiring they take at least one as an extracurricular. Not to mention the determination that is now propelling him forward.

He's pushing Roger toward the door with a fight that's always been reserved for Paxton alone. Roger at first resists, but when he looks to me for help, I can only shake my head. *Stop. Just go.* I plead with my eyes. Oliver is a fraction of the man he was only days ago and with the threads of his existence unraveling, I don't want to witness what happens when they fray.

Roger must see there's no winning the hand he's been dealt because he stops and lets Oliver herd him to the door with little more than gruff words and huffs. I don't mind Roger's frustration. *Good. I hope you feel helpless, too,* I think. They make it all the way out into the hall before Oliver turns back to find me still inside.

"Coming?" he asks.

The word feels like an olive branch he's lending me, one to pull me back into the comfort of us. So many parts of me are desperate to grab hold. To suffer together, instead of being tortured apart. But there's history and words and secrets that keep my feet planted. Accusations and healing that my mind can't make itself up on. I know that if I lose my ground now, we may never find our way, and my heart just can't let that hope die here in repetitive cycles.

But, God, how it breaks when I shake my head no and see Oliver's betrayal marked in the lines of his face.

"Fine. Stay. *I will not doubt the love untold, which not my worth nor want has bought, which wooed me young, and woos me old, and to this evening hath me brought.*" Oliver spits the Thoreau quote like a curse.

The pain of yesterday comes flooding through me, morphing into rage.

"*There are chords in the hearts of the most reckless which cannot be touched without emotion, even by the utterly lost, to whom life and death are equally jests, there are matters of which no jest can be made.*" I say in return.

The Poe quote slips from my lips as if I've turned my very breath into a hurricane. I want him to remember this isn't my doing. I didn't ask to be here. Didn't want this pain. For him or for me. He can blame me, curse me, use the entirety of the past to shoot at me like bullets, but it changes nothing. And I cannot sit any longer in the carnage of our war.

Apparently, neither can he. At the last of my words, he's hauling Roger off down the hall, even at his protests.

"Hey—Wait a minute. I need to talk to her…" Roger is saying, but Oliver has checked out.

"You can talk to her later. Right now, we're leaving. Both of us," I can hear Oliver growl. "Ten minutes. Keep your phone on," Oliver spits to me before they're gone down the stairs.

"Go," I call out to them both. "I won't be much longer."

It's a consolation left without knowing if they heard. All I can hope is that they won't kill each other in the parking lot by leaving them alone.

I walk back into Paxton's apartment, poking around aimlessly, until the overwhelming sense of wrongness of it all hits me. None of these things feel like the Paxton I knew. They hold a certain air of who I assume he wanted to be, but nothing is quite right. It makes me want to grab and smash and destroy. Erase this era of silence between us so I can help him furnish a place that was *him*.

I imagine us visiting this renovated historic building together. How it overlooked what used to be a church but has been turned into a hipster community center. Something so sacrilegious and mainstream that we would have instantly been in love. I picture picking out this apartment and talking about paint colors and decorations. I imagine him showing me *Walden* with a look of pride that would make me bark out in laughter.

And then my daydream betrays me, allowing Oliver through the door, dead flowers in an ornate vase that he adjusts on the kitchen island saying, *a piece of Dellbrook for you, brother,* before marching over and kissing me full on the mouth. The thought of it all crushes my lungs and sends me into a spiral where I cannot catch air. I hurry to escape, needing to leave more than the confines of the four walls of this home.

I dash out, hearing the faint click of the automatic door locking behind me, before I'm running to catch the stairs, too panicked to want to sit in an elevator for even a flight. At the end of the hall, on the right side opposite the staircase, a door opens. Ally walks out in a skintight black dress, sky high pumps, and a blazer that costs more than my car.

She glances once to me, smirking, but does nothing more. As if we are strangers. I watch her say a few parting words to someone in the doorframe before skipping down the steps. I toss up my hand, unsure if I even want her attention right now, but knowing I don't want her to catch Oliver downstairs. I prepare to call out, but my voice stops at the base of my throat as a small, unmovable woman pops out from the door.

She looks at me, throws her arms across her chest, gesturing me inside with a nod, and waits like I'm an expected guest. I school the shock of seeing Ally coming out of her home, dripping in expense. I let go of the fact that her apartment is mere feet from Paxton's. Squelch the fear that quite possibly I am facing a murderer. Instead, I square my shoulders and continue walking toward her. One way or another, this ends now.

"Emily, we need to talk," I say, tone more confident than I feel.

She sighs, humor and relief clear.

"Come in."

VOLCANIC ASH

SUMMER, 8 YEARS BEFORE

THE SINGLE LITTLE PINK line makes me giggle in relief. I've never felt so fortunate while still holding onto the sting of lost possibility. *We're too young,* I remind myself again. It isn't like this has ever been in the plans. At eighteen, especially.

As a matter of fact, I had thought little of children before. They've always felt distant, and I have always been careful. The families I've seen were never ones I wanted to live up to. Rather, they were sordid tales of what I never could do. Of who I never wanted to be as a parent. But Oliver had a way of making me forget my own expectations. He allowed me to see the messy parts of life as special. Coveted. He made me want to see the joy of hardship. Even in something like this. Making the mixture of melancholy and reprieve clustering in my clavicle, disorienting.

I'd worried about whether I should tell Oliver for days, and now I knew this would be mine alone. I couldn't take either possibility of his reaction when I was so conflicted with my own. I toss the white plastic into the trash, making a mental note to take it out first thing in the morning so no one sees, before flopping back onto my bed.

I don't even get comfortable before the softest tapping comes through my door, quickly followed by soft whispers.

"Eve, it's me. Let me in."

I lunge off the mattress as if it's on fire, flinging my door open enough so he can crowd inside before quietly closing it again. It's just past eleven, too late in the evening for him to be visiting me with my mother, asleep in the room next door. By the dancing of his eyes, he doesn't seem worried, though. He looks me up and down ravenously until his smile flattens at my faded leggings.

"You're not ready," Oliver says.

I scour for a modicum of what he's talking about, but my mind goes blank. I know he can see it in my face and thankfully, he prompts me to remember.

"The party..." He smiles encouragingly, his fingers playing with a piece of hair that's come loose from my ponytail. His closeness is distracting, but even without it, I still wouldn't know what he's talking about.

"Party?" I ask, confused. He sighs, letting the hair fall back to my neck.

"Paxton didn't tell you," he says, and I shake my head in confirmation. "Figures. Matt is having his end of summer bash. I thought we'd go. One last hurrah and all." His smile is soft and knowing, and I imagine he's picturing us in front of a different skyline two weeks from now.

"Did you get the apartment?" Excitement soars through me like lightning at the thought. He nods and I fling myself into his arms, almost taking us both down with the force.

"I can't believe it. You actually got the apartment in the city. And I'll be at NYU. We can do this," I ramble, breathless with the need to get out all the words.

The actualization of us being real clicks into place. There'll be questions from our family to dodge, but without the careful eyes of Madeline or Isabel or even Paxton, we can have normal days. Easy days. Together. He laughs, a deep huff, as he pulls me in closer.

"We can *actually* do this," he confirms. He pushes me away from him, arms holding us apart, a serious look taking over. "But first, you need to get ready so we can go! Paxton already has the car waiting."

"Right," I say as I hurry to my closet to grab a coat. It's not my best party outfit, black leggings and a faded black t-shirt that's boxy and cropped, but it'll do. And I know Oliver really doesn't mind with the way he peruses my backside as I bend down to throw on my shoes. I start for the door, head already living in the future where we won't have to sneak through closed doors and hallways anymore, when I realize my phone is still on my bedside.

"Oh!" I say as I turn to grab it, running smack into Oliver's chest. "I need my phone." He turns back to the room instead of letting me pass.

"I'll get it. Where is it?" he asks.

"On the nightstand," I say before I realize what else is by the nightstand and my whole heart bottoms out.

I watch as he grabs for my phone and the little white plastic catches his eye. All the air is sucked from the room. I imagine this is what outer space must feel like—my organs cloying for oxygen while my brain becomes fuzzy, looking for a way out. But the damage has already been done. He doesn't look at me. Doesn't move.

"Are you..." he begins.

"No," I say, without letting him finish the question.

I watch his shoulders stiffen and release, the sag of his coat creasing even with the softness of his movements. He finally grabs my phone and comes back to me, but won't look me in the eye, causing shame to boil in my belly. He hands me the leaden brick that I want to throw, cursing myself for thinking I needed it, then twines our fingers into loops. He kisses the back of my hand before dragging me to the kitchen door and out of the house to Paxton's waiting form.

The drive to the lake house is reticent, our voices hanging in the balance of a verdict not yet read. I know something's off, but am at a profound loss on what to say or do. Especially with the presence of another settling in between Oliver and me.

Paxton may not know what's wrong, but he feels it just the same. He shifts his legs in his seat, desperate to find comfort between us. *I know how you feel.* When we arrive, both boys take off like a shot. Neither one can be persuaded to slow. I'm not sure Oliver even waits for the car to be stopped. Paxton is quick on his heels all the way through the front door.

I sit and watch from my seat, unsure of which path to take before me; the concrete walkway that stretches out in front of me or back the way we came, to a home that lies in wait. I sigh and get out of the car, thanking the driver before I do. The car saunters off and I feel my comfort and safety slip away with it.

I release the knot of worry that is sitting on my chest like a troll, taunting me with the things I fear hearing, and walk into the house to a chorus of greetings. I tip my chin in acknowledgement. Force casual smiles to say hello. *They don't know anything's different.* But I do.

I spend two songs and a non-alcoholic drink making small talk with classmates I don't long to remember. It's only been months, but it wouldn't matter to me if our time apart vanished into years. There are only two here I care to pursue. Only two I have ever seen in visions of my future. And neither can be found.

By the third melodic beat and Denison's second *'keg stand'* cry, I've had enough. I begin my search for the brothers in earnest. I move from room to room until I find, through the slit in an off-limits door, two brooding figures squaring off. They're talking in hushed, brutal whispers that from this distance I cannot hear. Oliver already has an empty shot glass in one hand and a three-quarter empty tumbler in the other. The shock of him drinking after spending the summer sober is my first confirmation that something is very, very wrong. I scoot a little closer so I can eavesdrop better.

"Oliver..." I hear Paxton rumble, a threat in the name.

"Enough. What's done is done. There's no changing anything now. All I can do is the right thing moving forward," Oliver replies.

He isn't happy, but he throws an arm up to Paxton's shoulder in camaraderie, anyway. Both boys look drawn, but an understanding has been met that by the hopscotch rhythm of my heart says it might very well have to do with me. *Maybe Oliver has told Paxton of New York.* Flutters burst through the panic at the thought. If Oliver told Paxton, that would make it tangible. And it could, quite possibly, ruin everything before it even begins.

My thoughts have taken me from the room, and I've missed whatever else they've just said. Thankfully, I catch myself in time to see Oliver barreling for the door, and I move deeper into a group of people I don't really know enough to join. They look at me with unease, confusion flittering by, like signs on a highway, in their drunken state. The ease of the party wins over judgment as they decide to make me one of their own.

"Wooooo!" one girl, who I think is named Lizzy, yells.

She wants me to echo her, but nowhere in my DNA would that be allowed. I stay silent, and I can feel the group turning on me with each Woo-less second. I'm just about to excuse myself when Oliver catches my elbow, pulling me away without time for explanations.

I swivel my head to see where we're going and catch on to Paxton's angry eyes following us as I'm led deeper into the house. Oliver doesn't stop to explain. Doesn't lay secret kisses into my hair or sneak *I love yous* onto unspeakable lips. He just moves as if the stars are in reach. Purposeful and destined. Before he finally finds an empty, quiet room to pull me into.

I see the evergreen tartan sheets stretched across a well-made bed and the snake that's been coiling my muscles releases. *This* I can handle. Enjoy. Being with Oliver, in the solitude of each other, is easy. *He just wanted you to himself,* I realize. I let the softness take back my face and twist him around to see it.

He isn't relaxed, but I won't let the fight with Paxton hold him for long. I wrap my arms around his neck, stretching my body so my cider-soaked lips can inundate his. He fights it at only the briefest whisper of my skin, but by the time my mouth parts, he's mine. That's when I make my first mistake, and I smile.

I don't know if it is the sharpness of my exposed teeth or the biting wisps of air that are relieving the warmed fog of our tongues, but Oliver abruptly stops. He's heaving air, fighting whatever instincts tell him to continue.

"Oliver, breathe," I try, reaching out to calm him.

Only it steals him from me. Panic races through his eyes, but I watch him transform into the cold Poe I know. The one before secret rendezvous and midnight trysts. To the boy who locked secrets, and himself, away.

"Eve, we need to talk." He's business and detached, and I want to scream for him to stop.

"*Okay,*" is all I can say, the word being pulled from my throat as if I'm choking on it.

"This. This was a mistake. We never should have taken it this far. I don't know what I was thinking."

Every word is a puncture to my heart. A nail through my limbs.

"Oliver. What happened? What are you doing?" I demand.

He can't mean what he's saying because if he means this, the lie would be the last three months. If a few sentences are the facts we must live by, then my whole life unravels into fiction. He can't take back what's already been.

"*We* happened. I knew it was wrong. *You knew it was wrong.* We are giving into silly childhood crushes. And we can't pretend this can or will be anything. We can't destroy our families for... for a summer fling," he spits the words in malice.

I want to believe he's lying. To me and to himself. But if Oliver is anything, it's a maker of words. He's careful and consumed by them. Lives in a world controlled by emotional linguistics and passionate honesty. He's never been one to hide behind silence, always quick to throw to the wind exactly what he means, regardless of who it inflicts upon. I just never thought he'd be so careless with me. That his feelings would be so fickle. The shaking of devastation floods my veins, coming to the realization of these truths.

"*Our families?* Your family, you mean. You can't bear Madeline's disappointment and your disgrace at being with the help. At *loving* me. I was good enough to be a guest at your home, but never at the head of it. Is that the reminder you found in hushed words with Paxton, and the possibility of accidentally making a family with me?"

My words are the raining of hail when the worst of the storm is yet to come. I feel my bones like tectonic plates rupturing against one another in a plea to break free the skin and sink all that's laid before it. My tears want to flood the home of our kisses and wipe the slate clean from the filth he's succumbed us to. For when the hurricane comes, there's no time for anguish.

"Fine. *Yes.* Madeline will never approve. You've known that. I'm only saying what we've *both* understood. I admit, I was foolish to give you hope for New York. The minute I transferred to Columbia, she would have known. She would have come for me. One way or another, I would have been made to come home, Eve. You know this. And being reminded that we've been careless with our feelings, and our futures, showed me just how fragile it all is. I'm only doing what needs to be done now. Before it's too late."

He's resigned in his justification. A villain in his origin story. He knows this will change us. Will change everything. He'll become the martyr of our love story, ingraining his status as a Poe for the rest of his life. The legacy he's always dreaded and yet, could never escape.

"Coward," I seethe.

My voice is deep, hardly recognizable. I don't yell or cry it, but Oliver flinches at the utterance, anyway. He feels the ground splitting us apart with the word. Sees that his opportunity to turn back is fading. And I cannot do anything but hope he'll take it.

So, when he turns and walks out of the room like he was never here at all, I become ruin.

I don't know if it's minutes or hours that pass. Somehow, I've found myself on the bed, stricken from my body and the confines of time. Nothing seems to make sense. *You're not good enough. You've never been good enough.* The words sing on a constant loop and I can't find the pursuit to leave or remember why I'd want to. I have nowhere to go that won't try to make this slow death more painful. The door to the bedroom opens and I have enough sense to look up. Paxton takes one look at me before wrapping me in his arms.

"Oh, Eve. I'm sorry," he says as my wet cheeks dampen his shoulder.

His apology is soaked in regret as if he was the one who couldn't love me enough. As if he made me inferior. It splits a splinter of my grief into guilt that my pain is spreading like a plague. I try to rein in my tears, my questions, for Paxton's sake, but control has escaped my abilities when I pull back to face him.

"Why, Paxton? Why would he do this? *Choose this.* I can be better. I can prove I'm enough if he just gives us a chance," I mumble. His hands layout to hold my cheeks between them, letting the salt flow through his fingers.

"This isn't your fault, Eve. You've done nothing wrong," he says, and I scoff. He pinches my cheeks with enough force to stop the tears. "Hey, look at me."

I do as he asks, eyebrows bowed in frustration.

"This is about him. *Us.* You know the family. You know our souls better than anyone. Don't let our burdens crush you. Don't let us snuff out your light. You're better than we can ever be, Eve. *You are everything.*"

I close my eyes and lean into his palms, feeling the warmth of his body as well as his words. They burn with the reminder that I'm the other, but somehow Paxton makes that feel special. As if I am beyond their reach and not the other way around. Still, it's threaded with the fact that I'm losing them both.

It's disorienting the way Oliver consumes every part of me, cocooning me in the opacity of love, while Paxton digs away at the shadows to exhume me from hopeless futures. Where Oliver made me feel less, Paxton could only revel me as more. It makes me drunk on emotion and reckless with my words.

"It would have been easier loving you," I whisper, only enough to be heard, leaning into him just the same. "You don't hide behind your expectation. You do exactly what you mean to and life others up to be equals. You're a *gift* among them, Paxton Poe."

I open my eyes to see jolts of shock and pain flutter beneath his skin. His lips and brows pulled in anguish. My words have ripped open wounds I didn't know existed, and I fear can never be hidden again. But I can't force the words back in or create the distance between us. We're both alone in this family and I know what I want from Paxton isn't real, that he isn't the Poe, I want to hold me right now. Still, it doesn't change that I'll take him just the same. He must see the realization dawn on me, the urgency to do something we'll both regret that makes his face flatten and be replaced with steel. He feels all of us slipping apart, too.

"You were never meant to love me. I know right now, the whole world is turning on its axis, but I need you to know that I was always meant to love you. *We* were always meant to love you. And you don't want to do this, not really." His last words are choked, the last gasp before drowning.

Before he can protest, I lean in, tenderly asking him to give me one last breath. To capture a single moment of a different life. Because without them, I have nothing left to lose. The salt from my eyes is briny between my teeth as I pull my lips into them. I know this is a mistake, even before I make it, but like sand between my fingers, I feel as if the entirety of myself is slipping, gliding away in the trail of the Poe's tide. I'm desperate to hold on to whatever I can, making Paxton's mouth an anchor I'm desperate to use.

I've barely felt the pressure of him against me when my nightmares are let loose.

"Get. Off. Her," Oliver growls like a guard dog at the end of his chain.

He's feral in a way I didn't think his reservation allowed. The tender, patient poet turned into a monster like a Grimm tale. Paxton, for all his honor, releases our closeness immediately. His movements are stricken and confused, as if unsure how we all got here. Oliver, on the other hand, is not.

"Was this your intent? All your reminders? Your *insistence*. Just to end up here?" Oliver steams, pacing toward us. Paxton jumps up to stop him short, unrelenting in letting the fight come toward me.

"No. Oliver. This... it isn't what it looks like," Paxton pleads.

I want to scream at Oliver to listen. That this is what heartbreak breeds. That we're torn and messy and there's nothing real if it isn't with him. But I know better than to step between the brothers when words aren't what they're looking for.

"It's exactly what it looks like," Oliver says. "Madeline warned me you loved her. I just didn't think you would be so bold after everything."

Paxton's shoulders square at the mention of their mother, the gentle apology of his manners dissipating. He snorts with derision.

"Me? *Me.* You're really going to call me bold. YOU were the one who went against everything, Oliver. **You**. I'm just here cleaning up your messes. Just like always."

Oliver takes a step forward and I fear the fight might come to more than just a verbal altercation, so I shield Paxton with my body and look Oliver square in the eyes.

"It was me. *I* kissed Paxton. If you want someone to blame, I'm the one. *A wrong is unredressed when retribution overtakes its redresser.*" I say, broken yet bold.

The Poe quote slips out like a knife from its sheath, slicing my throat to pieces but deadly to them all the same. I know I've marked myself eternally, that I've played into the course of history, and any chance of a fairytale ending has been murdered in this room. But I cannot let Oliver and Paxton destroy each other. Each needs their brother, more than they will admit, and if I cannot be the solace in their lives after tonight, at least I can grant them this.

Oliver's face crumbles, but his backbone never bows.

"I never want to see either of you again," he intones like a curse before stalking out of the room.

We're encased in silence until Paxton is in motion, quick to be on his heels.

"I'll fix this," he tells me.

But I know my world has been smashed to pieces and there's no chance it'll ever be whole again.

CHURNING GROUND

SATURDAY, PRESENT

"**C**OFFEE? TEA? WATER?" HER voice is polite, but nothing more.

"No, thanks," I say, too convinced that she would give me poison just as easily as cream.

Emily sets to making herself a cup, undisturbed by my rejection. Her apartment is similar to Paxton's, in that it's bright and open. But her personal touches are more pronounced. Opinionated. The thick red candle, the size of an arm, that's in the shape of a naked woman's body. The black casket, meant for a child, where someone painted a setting sky into its bed, hanging on her wall. I catalog all the pieces of her personality and feel the strangling vines of jealousy wrap around my thoughts at the surety she's found in herself.

I'm only starting to learn how simple things can be when you are the one to put the value on your own worth.

She allows my eyes to wander, the silence languid and stretched with every *tick... tick... tick* of her nails against the mug. She doesn't rush my perusal, nor demand that I get to the point of my visit, lending my curious gazes to turn to the woman herself.

At the Nest where I first met her, I thought her confidence merely produced by her thick-bodied cousin and a family name she could wield. Now I see it is fissured into the bones of her ribs. She isn't graceful or entitled with it, like Madeline. Nor is she demanding and brood, like Issac. She's sincere, bound to the fact that she is who she is and can be no other. That no matter how the world asks her to bend, she remains like a stone, incapable.

With each assessment I make, my admiration for her grows, if for no other reason than I can see a fraction of what Paxton must have. Still, it doesn't change the circumstances. And I'm not foolish enough to believe that I know the person standing across from me. I have seen firsthand the destruction great minds create.

"Should we sit? You look like your body needs a rest," she says, gesturing first to my arm, then to the pale grey couch that looks out onto the court-yard.

I move without answering, unwilling to explain myself, sitting on the furthest edge from where Emily is standing. She floats down, crossing her legs at the knee, leaning over them toward me.

"It's ok, Evangeline. You can ask. I know it's on your mind, and I don't think we'll be able to have the rest of this conversation until you get it off your chest," she says.

I take a deep breath in, letting the scent of vanilla fill the nausea in my stomach. I want to know so many things. *Why was Ally here? What contract did Issac want? Where do you fit into all of this?* But there's only one that really matters. Only one that dragged me here to begin with.

"Did you kill Paxton?" My words are low. Calm. My eyes are focused on her fingers enclosed around each other, sandwiched between her knees and her breasts. Waiting for any movement that tells me to run.

"No," she whispers. "Evangeline, look at me."

Her body hasn't moved, not even a twitch in discomfort, so I do.

"I didn't kill Paxton. My cousin, for all his stupidity, didn't either. Though, I would be happy to let him get framed for it if you'd like," she says.

"Why should I believe you?" I ask, worry etching my words with more excitement than they should. I work to pull back my heart from being so exposed, so raw, in the face of this stranger. I'm grateful when hers begins to surface as well when she scoffs.

"How can you even ask that? You received the letter. You *know* I'm telling the truth," she answers. My face goes blank. *She knows about the letter?* My heart pounds at what that could mean, at what game Paxton was playing. I don't confirm or deny deciding instead to play dumb. She looks at me, exasperated. "*The letter.* Paxton left you a letter telling you to find me. At least, something to that effect. And he told me in my letter to expect you," Emily prompts.

My mind reels. I never received a letter. Oliver did. And nothing in it said to find Emily. Nothing pointed us here but an envelope where the contents were stolen. That and a bit of intuition and luck. *The letter from the envelope was yours.* The thought is too much. Knowing someone has stolen the last piece of him from me causes my veins to tighten and heat to rush into my limbs demanding action. I push it all behind concrete walls in my mind, unwilling to shed tears or regrets here.

"I never received a letter," I tell her. "Show me yours, and then I can believe you." If what Emily says is true, she has proof, and I want to see it. She laughs, breathy and condescending.

"Not on your life," she says as she stands. "Well, it was great seeing you again, but without the letter, I'm afraid you and I have nothing to talk about."

Panic races through me, the legal papers in my pocket burning a hole into my thigh. I cannot leave without answers.

"Sit. Down," I command.

I'm not even sure where the forcefulness in my voice takes shape, or why she raises her eyebrow in interest before plopping herself back into her seat. I know I should be cordial. Should catch the fly in this room with honeyed words and carefully woven webs, but between Oliver and Paxton, all the barriers between *should* and *want* are being burned down, leaving me with only the malice of *need*.

"I found something. And I'm not leaving until I get answers. I'm tired and beaten and ready for this game to be over so I can go back to a life that makes sense. Letter or not, you know I'm supposed to be here. You know what you're supposed to give me when I arrived." I stare her down, ready for any fight she might bring when I ask her the question that's unraveling us at both ends. "Do you know who killed Paxton Poe?"

She eyes me in appreciation, smiling between her maroon stained lips.

"You're asking the right question, just to the wrong person," she answers, and it's then that I know.

She knows who did it. Exhilaration and fear vibrate through my teeth, sparking off an energy that has no outlet but to rattle through the rest of my body. *She knows. She knows. She knows.* The words chant through me. I desperately try to telepath to Oliver, shocked that I've come this far, and he's off pouting.

"Let me see what you found," Emily says, leaning forward again, reaching out toward me.

"Tell me who did it," I answer in taunt.

She sighs. "You know that isn't how this works. If there was something I could tell you about it, I would. I can guarantee you it wasn't me. And it wasn't Issac. Other than that, I have nothing more to give on the matter."

Each of her words is even. There are no hitches or loss of eye contact. Her breathing doesn't change, and her eyebrows do not rise or fall. As much as it kills me to, I believe her. And I know I won't unseal her lips for the secrets she's been told to keep.

"Fine. Who am I supposed to ask?" I try instead, hoping to hit a loophole.

She smiles. "He always said you were bright. That you had an ease at unraveling even the toughest knots. Determined and obsessive when it came to something you wanted. Things he loved and admired about you."

Her words slap me, the sting of her familiarity like hot coals to Paxton's memory. I work to recompose myself out of the illusion she is leading me to create.

"Don't pretend you know him. Or me," I sneer.

"Ah, but I did. Very well. Paxton and I were... close. In many, many ways. At the end, I would argue that I knew him best. I know he liked to take his tea out to the fifth bench in the park at dusk just to watch the sun settle. I know he snored softly when he slept the deepest, and that those nights were rare. And I know he loved you and Oliver more than anyone else in the universe. More than me, and more than himself," she says, her sadness sweeping the indignation away like wind from the sails.

She waits for me to contradict her. To spit angry accusations and violent half-truths. She wants me to break down, but I wouldn't give her the satisfaction, even if her words are tearing me apart inside. Instead, I lean in, trusting the crumbs Paxton has left. I pull out the now crumpled papers from my pocket, holding them out for her to take.

"He left me these, tucked safely in an item from our past. I don't understand what they mean since I haven't had time to read them. All I know is that they are on a lawyer's stationery and that you and I are both named in them," I tell her, frustrated that I'm giving her the upper hand, but seeing no other choice.

She takes them from me, scanning before her brow breaks, and she laughs.

"Clever, clever, boy," she mumbles before directing her attention back to me. "This is how you and I protect each other. How Paxton protected us, in the end."

I look at her, confused. "You're going to need to explain."

"I know you're probably curious about Ally being here. And from what I've heard about what happened at Crave the other night, what Issac wants from you. This tiny packet of papers you found answers them both." She readjusts to lean back, leg tucking under her, as the room's energy shifts. "Before everything happened, Paxton was in the middle of a deal with my cousin. I won't bore you with the gritty details, but there were several patents being filed on ideas Paxton had to break into, and ultimately change, the death industry. And the Langley's wanted in."

I nod, remembering the conversation Oliver and I had the night of Paxton's wake, feeling like a lifetime ago.

"Right, something about environmentally friendly and affordable burials," I inject into her story.

She nods. "Yes. But that is just the tip of the iceberg. Overall, Paxton filed 72 patents in total. All of which he held under his sole proprietorship, *The House of Poe.* My uncle prompted Isaac to work out whatever deal he had to, to get access to those patents."

I jump in, "And then Paxton died. Without a will. But you're telling me Issac didn't do it."

A sad smile splits for only a second before she takes her teeth to her lip. "They had a contract. Or at least, he thought they did. Giving them total access to everything. A partnership with Paxton was more than my uncle could dream. The Poe name gave credibility, *notoriety,* to the Langley's. Where once my family was a big fish in a small pond, now the oceans would open for the taking. The patents were only the goal because he never believed a partnership was possible."

I let her words sink in, trying to find the fox in the hen house. But nothing sticks. I'm confused and reeling and unsure why I have anything to do with Paxton's secret life that I never knew about.

"I... I don't understand what the problem is then, or what Tyler had to do with it," I say.

"With Paxton gone, that whole plan falls to pieces. There's no way Madeline will honor the deal or the partnership. She hates the Langley name as much as any predecessor ever did. Not to mention that Paxton's company, The House of Poe, is not listed under his trust. It wasn't part of the Poe family assets, making it inaccessible to Madeline unless she petitions the court unopposed by the beneficiary. And the contract Isaac was promised for the patents doesn't seem to exist. Leaving my family, no matter who controls the company, empty-handed without it," she explains.

"And Ally?" I question.

"Didn't you read the name of the law firm on these papers?" she asks. I shake my head and she sighs. "Ally is a newly partnered lawyer with a hotshot reputation. She's the one who set this all up for Paxton."

Realizing how deep Ally could be in all this has my breath hitching in my throat. I push the questions and distrust of her aside, filing it away for later, so I can focus on what's important right now.

"What does this have to do with me?" I ask. At this she laughs, elation at the secret she's keeping.

"Haven't figured it out yet? He would be so disappointed."

Her jest bites, prompting me to immerse myself in what I know and put away how I feel. The riddles Paxton's left. The venom Issac feels. I think about the slim packet of papers and *The House of Poe* name. The intentional deviation from Madeline and Alexander. From his family. I imagine the safety of Paxton's presence and how, no matter what, he would always take care of things. No ends would ever be left undone. And then it hits me.

"He signed it over to me," I say, stunned. Her smile slices across her face, comradery thick in the air.

"To *us*," she corrects. "The House of Poe shares were put in our names months ago. The patents, the business, all of it is ours. All of it separate from Paxton's assets and thus, out of Madeline's reach. You've been listed as a silent partner, with absolute power to revoke my institution in the company entirely."

The shock I wear on my face is enough to light a city.

"Why are you telling me this? Why not just continue to run the business without my knowledge?" I ask, incredulous.

"Because I need you, Evangeline," she says, resigned. "We need each other. Not only would you be informed of your position eventually, but your signature is the only thing that provides me with leverage to convince my uncle to make me his heir. I can bring him the Poe partnership he craves; I just need you to confirm that I'm the only one you'll work with."

"Why would I do that, Emily? After everything. How can I trust you? How can I work with your family?" I ask in disbelief.

I think of the way Issac's hands on my skin had cascaded through me like an avalanche of pain. How his threats of retribution reverberated through the walls of my veins. And how I still believed he may have killed Paxton, regardless of what Emily claims.

"Because you need me, too. We both know that you can go to the police for what was done to you." She gestures to my damaged arm and bruised face, disgust lacing her words, "but we also know he'll only get a slap on the wrist, if that. It's your word against his. Those with a family name and money don't abide by average rule. Only the powerful can punish the powerful. Our partnership, and my deal with my uncle, will guarantee your safety and their retribution. I promise you; they will pay."

She stands up to circle the couch, the delicate tension of our tenuous bond too much for her calmer sensibilities. She picks up a trinket, a black stone carving, from a shelf. It's hidden too far in her palm for me to see what it's of.

"As for trusting me... Paxton did. He thought that would be enough for us not to destroy each other, too. He told me I'd like you, and as much as I hate to admit it, I do. Whatever more Isaac has planned; I can tell you it's vile. But I can stop it. They would never go against my uncle and my uncle will never take the chance of losing all this back to Madeline. Of always knowing his greatest accomplishment is just out of reach."

She hands me the item in her hand and all I can do is stare. It's heavy, an onyx raven, cut from the rock into hard angles. A rough scratched *P* on its chest. Tears grow quick in my throat as I think about another scratched *P* I know. I stop them before they can make their way up into my eyes. I think about what she's saying. The opportunity and security of what Paxton has done will afford me. *Or cost me.* I dash the thought away. Paxton always knew that no matter what I said, our lives would be inextricably linked forever. And yet, he'd left me a way out of the labyrinth, anyway.

"There's one more thing I need to tell you about the business... Paxton has ensured that someone with the Poe name can never run the House of Poe. Madeline would've had to put it in a trust with unrelated advisors should she have contested and you didn't show. It would've been passed to someone else eventually, regardless. No one knows this but Ally, me, and now *you*."

Her voice emphasizes the secrecy of this information, and I'm not sure why. Paxton's meaning is perfectly clear—Oliver and I will never marry. Even though I know the promises made now, it still scrapes at me to see how deep they went. If only he knew he has nothing to worry about anymore.

"Ok," I say, tracing the rock as I do. "I'll sign whatever it is you need me to sign."

Emily closes her eyes, lips moving as if in prayer.

"But..." I interrupt. "I need to know what you're supposed to tell me from the letter, before I do." If I'm holding all the cards, I need to start acting like it.

She doesn't fight like I expect, our time together dialing down. Instead, she reaches for the raven, which I reluctantly hand over, and answers.

"Paxton and I shared secrets, you know. Ones from now and the past. From our adolescence. You were in some of them. I knew he kept a lot locked away from me, but I also know, especially now, that there was a part of himself meant only *for me*, too." Tears form but do not fall, and it makes me like her more.

"His letter didn't tell me everything. When it comes to you, it left me with two directives: tell you about the House of Poe, and to give you your next clue."

She hands me a small, folded note, tucked inside the raven. The note reads:

```
His decease will leave me the last of
the ancient race of the Poe.
```

It's a play on Roderick's quote from *The Fall of the House of Usher*. A story of deceit and greed and family. Realizing where I need to go has me jumping from the couch, livid and ready to put this to an end. Before I can get to the door, Emily calls out to me.

"I realize your roots with Paxton run deep. That you understand him in a way very few do. But I can promise you, there was a whole life that you never knew, and probably never will." She takes a deep breath, as if weighing what she's about to say next. Still, she continues, "That man held multitudes and if anyone can live multiple lifetimes, it's him."

SUNKEN FIELDS

"**W**HERE HAVE YOU BEEN?**"** Oliver screeches at me before I even make it to the car.

"Is Roger still here?" I ask, instead of answering him.

He glowers at the name. "No. He decided it was in everyone's best interest that he left."

I have the distinct impression that *Oliver* decided, but I don't prod.

"Good," I punctuate. "Get in."

I'm done playing follower. Done letting the Poe family walk all over me, cracking my spine, and leaving me to lie in mud. I can no longer be smart, compassionate, or even curious. All I have left is to be angry.

Oliver's cheek twitches with the command. Unhappy with the pull on his leash. But he does as I say anyway, grumpily climbing into the passenger seat of the car I borrowed from Alexander, leaving his driver to make his way back, alone. If my emotions were any less eclipsed, it might make me smile.

I start the trek back into the suburbs toward Dellbrook, unsure of what I'll do once I'm there. I try to formulate what I need to say to Oliver, but the ease of language doesn't come with righteousness like the old books proclaim. I shed away the poetry and purple prose in lieu of direct confrontation.

"Did you do it?" I ask.

Oliver stays looking out the window, fingers drumming on the door frame. He doesn't catch on to my meaning, or more than likely he doesn't want to. I repeat it.

"Oliver. Did. You. Do. It?" I say a little louder.

Finally, he turns his head to look at me, unfazed. "Did I do what? If you're going to be on a tirade, at least be clear in it."

The thread my sanity is hanging onto snaps.

"Did you kill Paxton? Did you kill your own brother?" I scream. He freezes, becoming an iceberg floating in calm waters. A wolf poised as a lamb.

"Did I..." He can't even finish the words.

I keep driving, terrified to look over and yet unable to stop. He's stricken, eyes glued to mine, hand already turning purple from crushing the door handle. His neck and cheeks are slack, even while the rest of him is coiled, ready to spring, making me feel like prey. My nerves dance like wildlings while I wait for the suspense in time to drop.

"How can you even ask me that?" Oliver says, tone flat and concealed.

"Paxton left..." I don't even get it out before his whole-body folds, losing its fight with gravity entirely.

"Paxton?" he asks, strangled.

His question isn't furious or guilty or calculating. Instead, it is the embodiment of despair. He knows what I'm going to tell him, that there was a clue. He watched me pocket it at the apartment. Saw the book I'd found. He may not know the entirety of what happened, but he knows enough to tie strings to my conclusion.

"You're saying that Paxton is framing me?" he asks sincerely.

But that isn't what I'm saying. I realize the pain in Oliver's eyes and remind myself of who he is. *He didn't do this.* Oliver could be a lot of things, but someone who would kill his own brother, someone he loves, wasn't one of them.

Still, that left a clue that didn't make sense. Paxton wouldn't frame Oliver as much as Oliver wouldn't kill Paxton.

"I... I don't know what I'm saying. The clue clearly points to you. Here," I fish out the note from my pocket and hand it over to him to read.

I watch as he takes it in, nose scrunching in concentration, and then his head tilts back in understanding. He pulls out his phone, blowing up a picture from a letter I have yet to see.

"I can't read that. I'm driving," I say.

He sighs and reads it out loud, "*The flush of anger'd shame, O'erflows thy calmer glances, And o'er black brows drops down, A sudden-curved frown.* I wasn't sure what it meant, I found half the words in the letter and the other half in the clues—*shame, calmer, drops,* and today I found *frown.* I hadn't heard the quote before, but after looking it up and seeing your clue, I know where we need to go."

"It's from Tennyson. A poem entitled *Madeline*," I mumble, dreading what this means. "What does my clue have to do with yours?"

Indignation fills Oliver's words. "The quote he pulled was originally written about Madeline, Roderick's sister. He's pointing us to the same place."

We find the matriarch of Poe in the Nest. She's stretched along a bookshelf, returning a tome to its home. Our presence doesn't alarm her nor cause her to rush her delicate handling of the matter at hand. *She doesn't find it odd we're here,* I think. But she should. She knows what we've been whispering about. *Or maybe she's delusional enough to think you obeyed her, that Oliver and I are reconciling instead of solving.* It wouldn't be out of Madeline's narcissistic bravado.

I'm so focused on the curve of her wrist as she pushes the book into place, imagining something so pristine being marred by something as dirty as this, that I miss Alexander in the wingback chair, until he speaks.

"Oliver. Eve. Good to see you running around again. I bet you both miss this old house more than you thought!"

His cheeks are flushed from the fireplace and the deep burgundy glass sitting next to him. He has one book laid open on the table while his own notebook and pen are poised in his lap. I can make up tiny sketches of what look to be the lines of a woman, no doubt inspired by the one we're here to see.

Oliver and I both looked at each other in silent conversation, knowing it was never the house we missed. The soft click of Madeline's heels touching wood breaks our hold and we remember why we're here.

"Madeline," Oliver starts. "I think we need to talk."

His words give nothing away, sounding as dull and formal as every other conversation I've heard held between mother and son. Her breath releases, eyes closed, before she moves to Alexander. She stands behind him, lightly brushing his shoulders.

"Perhaps later. We are in the middle of our afternoon drinks," she says, not looking at either of us.

Oliver's voice breaks character to reveal a glimpse of the monster he hides. "No, Mother. We should talk *now*. It's about Paxton."

It's very rare I hear him call her mother, and the name makes Madeline's neck snap back in surprise. If she didn't know something was wrong before, she knows now, all pretenses laid to waste.

"My love, can I meet you in the theater to finish our afternoon? It appears I am being summoned to speak," she asks Alexander.

Her words sound lovely, more tender than they are for any other. They're a grueling reminder of the woman she can be, that she chose *not* to be, for her children, making the furor of my accusations hard to hold in.

Alexander nods, pulling her hand to his lips and kissing it softly. He stands to leave, stopping only between Oliver and me.

"Whatever it is, go easy on her," he whispers, then leans over louder to me. "Please come find me before you leave. Both of you. I'd like to say our goodbyes if I cannot persuade you to stay."

I nod, only because of the love I have for who he was and who he could have been if not for his devotion. *Did you know?* My heart breaks at the thought. He's barely out of the room before Oliver turns on Madeline like a viper that's been disturbed.

"You did it," he accuses, stepping closer.

Madeline, for all her faults, is nothing but grace. She rounds on the chair Alexander vacated and sits, poised and proper. As if this is a meeting she's called. As if she isn't being accused of murder.

"Oliver. Eve. Sit. We're nothing if we are not civil," her words as cold and dominating as ever, the master in a ring of lions.

The southern grip of my mother tells me to follow. To be respectable. But the wild, tormented heart that beats in my chest tells me to howl. To spit in her face. To meet violence with violence. With my curiosity satiated enough to take a back seat, all that's left is retribution.

But Oliver's cooler head prevails as he sits. He must be allowing reason to take hold of emotion, letting it remind him we don't have enough to make anyone believe us. We have no course of action, no punishment to dole. The years of dealing with Madeline must be replaying in his mind, showing him how to make things just so.

Emily's words shock through the murk of my intensity. *Those with a family name and money don't abide by average rule. Only the powerful can punish the powerful.* I follow Oliver's lead, not Madeline's words, and sit.

"There. Now, what am I being accused of?" Madeline asks, taking a sip of her wine.

"Paxton. You killed him," I say, no longer able to stay silent.

Madeline scoffs, head tossed to the side. "Hardly."

"What the hell does that mean?" Oliver grills, indignant.

"It means, *son*, that I cannot take sole credit in your allegation," Madeline says.

"But you did have something to do with it?" I ask, unable to believe that she would confess so easily.

"Darling, we *all* had something to do with it." Her laugh is brittle, cracking with disbelief.

Oliver moves to the edge of his seat, menacing in the strength of his control.

"Madeline, you need to start making sense. Now." His threat is clear, fists curling into the crushed red velvet of his chair.

Madeline finally sees the danger in the room, her defenses falling enough to see the true age of her under the careful illusion she's used to hiding. She may not be breaking, but she knows she holds a losing hand.

"My, how the love between you boys grew. You'd be willing to watch your mother, the woman who gave you life, suffer on his behalf. Because of a few silly letters. It's my fault, I know. Forcing you to make promises to each other. To keep them," she sighs, knowing the house of control she's built is crumbling around her.

"I didn't take Paxton's life. That's what you're asking, isn't it? I merely picked up a phone call that told me it had already been done. That my son," she chokes on the word before composing herself again, "that my son had chosen this. Had taken his life in his own hands. And that I wasn't allowed to know any more than that. That I wasn't allowed to recover the body. All I could have from him was the leavings of his trust, the power of his belongings outside of his business, and a letter. That *that* is what Paxton wanted."

She spits each syllable, furious at telling us what she knows. Appalled that it even exists in the first place.

"I... I don't understand," I say, unable to believe it, too.

"No. There's more you're not telling us. Who called? What happened to him? It had to be a murder! How could he do this? He *wouldn't* do this. I don't believe you," Oliver says thickly.

The fight in him is waning, deflation making his arms sag on his knees and his head hangs in his hands. They pull and thread through his curls on instinct and even though I'm lost in what's happening, I want to do the same. To bring him whatever comfort I have left.

"Does it matter how he died? Will it quell the tide of grief and guilt that the two of you have been harboring? I tried to save you, but neither of you would let me. You can call this a murder all you'd like, but it isn't one that can be wrapped up tightly into who drew the final breath from his body. It's a killing of the soul that led us all here. There's no smoking gun, no hanging rope, no plugged-in hair dryer to point to. Paxton died by the knives we named words and distance. By the bloodletting of expectations. He died wanting us all to ponder *why*, giving me exactly what I'd wanted. What I'd asked for."

"And what's that?" Oliver asks, repulsed.

"To feel more like Edgar. And he won. He did it. So, I've mourned him as the son I made instead of the one I bore. I've given him in death what I couldn't in life and all I can hope, all any of us can hope, is that it'll be enough to live with in our next days. Because fire has molted our bones and survived the River Styx. Regret cannot take us. That is the gift of being Poe. Death does not break us against its rocks, it only forms us into mountains."

She clasps to the words, more a desperate plea than a vote of confidence. Truths she makes because without them, how would she survive? Silent tears roll down my face. I'm unsure where to go from here. What to do now that the mystery is solved and yet there is no solution? *Paxton took his own life.* The words scorch the forests of my thoughts barren.

Oliver stands, unsteady and disheveled, but Oliver all the same.

"The only thing being Poe *gave* us, *Mother*, is despair."

And he leaves the room, taking all the remains of my heart with him.

DANGEROUS SCAFFOLDS

"**M**OMMA, TELL ME YOU didn't," I whine, begging this to be a joke.

"I did. You need to finish getting ready. They'll be here soon!" She says, shooing me away, back into my room to get changed.

"Why... why would you do this?" I ask, incredulous at her audacity.

She knows we're not speaking, that we haven't for years, even if I've never told her why. She knows we don't talk about Dellbrook, or Boston, or especially the Poe boys. So why, on the day of my 21st birthday, would she invite them here?

"Because Evangeline," she sighs, fed up with my tantrum. "They are your oldest friends. This is a milestone for you and besides your birth, they have been at every big marker of your life. It seems only fair to, at the very least, invite them to this one as well."

Her words are too calculated, and I know that underneath them she's hiding something.

"Liar!" I exclaim, knowing the distaste she feels at the word. "You are not that sentimental, and I am not that stupid. Why did you really invite them?" I beg.

Her mouth is straight as an arrow, but surprisingly, she answers.

"Don't talk to me like that. I am your mother. Show me a modicum of respect." She releases the last breath of resistance she's been holding. "I didn't. Paxton has been calling me for months, hinting and then downright begging that they be included in tonight's festivities. Who am I to tell him no?"

Paxton wants to be here. Oliver wants to be here. My stomach turns in excitement and dread. It feels like a betrayal to the delicacy of my survival to allow them back in, but my heart has always been a traitor. Bubbles lift me onto my toes as I kiss Momma's cheek, letting the excitement spill out and away from the fear.

"You're right. I need to get ready." I dash into the bedroom before she can respond. As I close my door, I see the flit of disappointment she has at my eagerness. I know I should be disappointed in myself and maybe, after tonight, I will be. But right now, the stubborn rock of hope is lodged too deep.

I take longer than I should primping myself. I don't want to admit it's all a show, a blatant sign that screams *look how good I'm doing* and *don't you wish I was yours?* The curled hair and dark kohl are there to hide the emptiness I've felt in the middle of the night when I'm replaying what went wrong again for the millionth time. Thick mascara and ruby red lips distract from the fact that I haven't let myself love anyone else because that would mean there was less of my heart to give to them. I wrap myself in all the ways I'm better, now.

I want Oliver to burn with regret at his silence and have him beg me to forgive.

I only know they're here by the exclamation of Paxton's name from Momma's startled cry. I'm smiling timidly, catching the shadow of Paxton picking her up in a hug and spinning her around from my open door. It's unkempt and playful in a way that I'm sure Momma doesn't expect from a Poe. I try not to race down the hall and into the living room where they're standing.

Paxton dwarfs my mother, making her look frail and far past the age she is. My head swivels around him to peek out to the apartment hallway, unable to hide my interest in who else may be darkening it. The light in me dims when I find it closed and no one else in sight. Paxton must notice, too.

"Oliver isn't here. Yet. I told him to meet us at the bar. Now come here so I can get a look at you!" He says, turning the full of his attention on me.

Oliver will be here soon. I can't help but throw up my arms in a 'ta-da' stance to Paxton, as if I am a prize on display, easily slipping back into who we used to be. He laughs as I hoped he would, time melting between us, as if it never existed at all. *Will it be like this with him, too?* I know it won't, that Oliver's a different beast and it will take feeling every second missed to come around. But there's a beauty and an excitement in that, too.

Paxton whistles in appreciation.

"You look happy, Eve," he says.

And I am. Tattered edges that have been ripping since the summer I lost them are ready to heal. I can feel the new pages already binding in, allowing for the world to begin again.

I take Paxton in for the first time in years. He doesn't feel as much of a stranger as I imagined. Probably because we've had a few letters and telephone calls. I've seen him on social, the few times he's posted, even if he never knew the abstract account was me. But to see him in the flesh feels electric and I cannot look away, even if I wanted to.

He's broad, with the dark, handsome face the family is known for. While he looks as familiar as always, he feels different. Confidence has taken over where expectation used to rule. I would bet he's found a stylist outside of the Poe name, by the way he's dressed to the nines in bright purple button down and black and purple pinstriped pants that are so incredibly *him*.

His presence is still conflicted, on the edge of aggressive, as he's known, but there's a new anxiousness to him too. He plays with his watch, like it's new, and he's reached for his phone three times even though he leaves it in his pocket. I decide to leave it be.

"You do, too," I say, and he smiles.

We sit in the moment, just staring, where I can see nine-year-old Paxton Poe making a startling jump from a tree, taunting me with this same smile. He claps his hands together, startling me back into the living room with my mother.

"I'm sorry to do this, Isabel, but I've got to steal her away now or we're going to be late!"

He hugs Momma one more time and whisks me out into the streets of the city. The sidewalks are lively with the decorations of December, and there's a chill in the wind causing me to tug my coat tight to my chest. Paxton doesn't seem to be affected in the slightest.

"How have you been? How is school? You're still going to school, right?" he asks.

"Yeah, I'm still going. I'll be going for the rest of my life at this point. I'm applying for graduate school next year at NYU," I tell him.

"You're actually going to do it, aren't you?" he asks. "Wow. I don't think we've ever had a librarian in the family. Which you'd think, given our history, someone would have." My chest coils at the word *family*, squeezing tight against the old hopes, pains, and fears I've kept locked away. I laugh instead, needing to ward off the drag of sadness that's creeping ever closer.

"Yeah. I'm going to do it." I stop, turning to the building we're about to walk by. "Isn't this the place?" But Paxton keeps walking, oblivious to my frozen form. I hurry to catch up before he crosses the street without me.

"Pax wait up!" I yell, but he keeps up his pace.

By the time I catch up to him, he's standing in front of a door, to what looks to be a very busy restaurant, looking at his phone. He's frowning down at it when I push into his shoulder.

"Hey! What was that?" I ask, frustrated by his odd behavior.

"Sorry! I know we're meeting your friends for your big bash, but I wanted to get a drink alone with you before that. We haven't seen each other in so long. I just need you to myself for a little while." I look at him, eyeing his bashful expression with suspicion.

"One drink?" I ask.

"Just one. Promise." He grabs my hand before I can answer, hauling me past the hostess.

The inside is split in two. On one side, the tables are dispersed around a stage and the other is set up as a speak-easy. Paxton pulls me to the lounge, passing us by the couches and beelining it for a black silk laced booth in the back marked *reserved*. He lets go of me so that I can slide in.

"Well, this is very on brand," I say, picking at the parts of him I know are loose. I'm going for the teases of our past, but it comes out too trying, almost harsh. I can't take back the words now, so I lean into them and let the silence hold their weight instead.

He eyes me. "It's tradition. Besides, it's one of the only places that serves even a decent drink."

I groan. Anyone else would rage at his words, especially in New York. You can throw a rock and hit a bar all the way down each borough, each special in their own way. But he isn't talking about just any drink.

"Paxton, no," I plead, as a waitress sets down two sickly yellow glasses in front of us.

"It's *tradition*," he emphasizes, pushing one glass toward me while taking a sip of the other.

"But I hate eggnog and I highly doubt that's going to change just because you've added alcohol to it." He looks at me sternly, tapping the glass in finality.

"You know, this was Edgar's favorite. We all have had to drink this on our 21st year. You will not be an exception in the face of generations of compliance. Can you imagine the embolism Alexander would have?"

I sigh, knowing there's no way I'll get out of this. The liquid swirls as I pick it up and take a quiet sip, letting the thickness run over my tongue. I work to ignore the eggnog and instead focus on the vanilla and the sweet burn of cognac. My lips wrap around the rim to take another drink just to appease Paxton and the spirits of his bloodline.

He smirks. "See? Not that bad."

I set the glass back down, ready to address the missing black hole between us.

"Will Oliver be having one too? Or was he smart enough to insist on meeting us at the party?" I try to keep the desperation out of my voice, but know that I fail. Paxton loses his good humor, the dimple of his left cheek expanding back into creaseless skin.

"Actually, Eve, he isn't coming." He's looking at his fingers that haven't stopped turning his watch.

"Oh." It's all I can say. *Of course, he isn't. I was a fool to believe he would.* I knew better than to think a few years and hundreds of miles between us could bring him back. I have been naïve to keep my life on hold for the insignificant possibility that he still loved me. That we could be star crossed and not die alone in the end.

"I tried. I did. I thought he was going to agree, that he'd show up morose and gloomy and *Oliver.* I guess I was wrong," he says, dejected.

"It's okay. I should've known better. Honestly, it's my fault for getting my hopes up," I tell him, struggling not to cry.

Paxton grabs my hands in his. They're warm and large, feeling of safety and home.

"No. It isn't your fault. He's being stubborn. You know him. You know *us.* And he's stewed on this long enough. He's written his poems and his stories. Locked himself away from the world. Now it's time we all sit down and face this, so things can be how they're meant to be. How they were always meant to be," he says.

His words are a march. A call to action. A rally to the troops. And if I had been even a year younger, I might have answered it. Might have schemed and plotted and allowed him to create the riddles that needed solving so I could run his mazes back to Oliver. Back to Dellbrook. But today has reminded me of the cost of time and I'm unwilling to rot in the poverty of my future for the Poes.

"No. Paxton. I can't do this anymore. I've spent all my life running after you boys, dreaming and wishing and wanting to be something I'm not sure that I am. Or can be. Oliver has accepted that, moved on from it, and I think it's time you do, too. That we both do."

"Eve, he hasn't, though! If you only saw—" he tries, frantic. I cut him off.

"I've seen enough!" My voice raises to a level unbecoming of public, so I bring it down before continuing. "It's enough, Paxton. I've given enough. It's time I learned to live with this open wound. And now there's a group of people who have constructed what little of a life I've allowed them to, waiting for me. I owe them the courtesy of showing up."

I slide out, pausing to stand in front of Paxton Poe for what feels like the last time. I let my love and pain and all the emotion I've trapped go just long enough for him to see that I mean what I say. Then I bend down and hug him close, hoping he knows how much I love him.

He grabs me back tightly, then whispers into my hair, "I promise I'm going to fix this. I swear it. On my life, Evangeline Pierce. I'm going to fix it."

I straighten, determined to not let his parting oath affect me, even as it chips off another piece of my heart. Before I can take anything back or change my mind, I turn my back, one last time, on the Poes, and the life we had.

TATTERED ENDS

SUNDAY, PRESENT

I DON'T SEE OLIVER again, and in the morning, the day I'm scheduled to fly back home, I decide to seek him out. My insides are so scrambled, empty and numb and destroyed, that I don't know whose screaming is louder, my reason or my heart. I decide to ignore them both. I embrace the truth that I'm simply an accompaniment for misery, and there's no one I'd rather sit with through this than Oliver.

Besides that, I was leaving. Come hell or high water, I would be walking out of Dellbrook today, and although I knew better than to say it would be my last, I wasn't naïve enough to believe I would be coming back for anything less than tragedy. I owed us all the goodbye we never got. After seeing what happens when you let infection set in firsthand, I owed myself the opportunity to heal. Something I've never done.

Before I can make it to Oliver's room, I'm stopped by Alexander, beckoning me into his office. He sits at his desk, papers strewn and the pale-yellow glow from his lamp lighting just the center of his face as he rests his cheek in his hand, staring at the picture before him. His eyes flutter up to catch me.

"Eve, thank you for coming in to say goodbye," he says. I don't remind him he called me in here or tell him I was seeking out his son. Instead, I just nod.

"Of course. I know you wanted to say goodbye," I say.

It's hard to keep my voice even. I don't want to blame Alexander, but a part of me can't help it. If he and Madeline had only been more open and kinder to their firstborn, everything could have been different. I suck down my thoughts, knowing I could never say them and see Alexander's face crumble at my words. Especially when I knew I was just passing blame.

"That I did," he says, smiling. "I know this week has been difficult. On all of us. But on you most of all. Love is never easy, and I'm sad to say that it's made even more difficult by loving one of us." He takes a sharp inhale through his nose before continuing. "Eve, I want you to know you're always welcome here. This is your home. You've stayed away and I understand why, but now I think it's time we heal. As a family."

My gut clenches at the word. I know I should just smile and nod. Tell him the things he wants to hear so that I can leave and never look back. After everything, though, I know I can't. I cannot allow myself to hide anymore.

"I'm sorry Alexander. But we're not family. I love you all, but I think it's time I stop hoping to be a Poe." The words twist and shred my guts and my heart. They take with them the final courage I've had at living a life I've always dreamed of. Telling Alexander Poe this simple fact makes it bleed into my skin like a stain. But it also makes way for something new. *Something real.*

I look up to find him pensive, a look of worry as if he's about to tell a child Santa isn't real.

"Evangeline. Just because you are not a Poe doesn't mean you are not family," he says. His voice is solid, with little room for contradiction. Still, I cannot stop it.

"You know that isn't true," I whisper. "Madeline has made sure..."

"Madeline?" he sighs, coming around the desk to stand beside me, looking down as he does. His arm reaches out to rest on my shoulder. "Madeline loves you like a daughter. She has dreamed of your wedding, bragged about your accomplishments at NYU, and hung your portrait among the boys in our parlor. She is tough, like a thorn sometimes, but she has always thought of you as ours."

The confession sets off a thousand bees through my veins, stinging and flapping their papery wings beneath my skin. But it still doesn't change what I know.

"Alexander, I know you love her, but she made sure I wasn't part of this family." I say with finality. He has to see the wreckage she caused. With the boys. With me.

Instead, he grabs a stack of books sitting on top of a stool in the corner and sets them to the floor. He drags it over to me and sits so we're at eye level.

"Did you know that the first day you got here, Madeline told me fate had gifted us our own Helen of Troy? I had laughed it off, told her it was nonsense that the boys were young. You were young. But she swore to me they would both come to love you, and I'll be damned if she wasn't right."

He taps the arm of my chair as the silence bubbles with expectation. I'm trapped by the story he's weaving, entranced by a tale I didn't realize I was part of.

"You were her greatest fear. And her biggest blessing. You see, Madeline isn't a Poe by blood. She was given the name, and she knows firsthand the sacrifice and burden it is to carry. All she could see was the boys ripping each other apart, and, in turn, ripping you apart. And that was unacceptable. Losing *any* of you was unacceptable."

I roll his words in my head, finding the cracks and excuses for behaviors and words that don't feel like love. Still, while prodding, I find empathy and understanding, too. In the end, all I'm left with is the harsh reality.

"But we did anyway," I say, holding Alexander's gaze.

He nods. "No one is saying her plans worked. Obviously, nothing went the way she expected. You see, Madeline loves consumingly. If she thinks someone she cares about is sinking, she jumps in the deep end. Even if that means they'll both drown. She doesn't believe in sidelines or guidance or regrets. Only action. Only intention. And sometimes, she loves so hard it feels like a punishment."

"I wish she would love less," I say, both in all earnestness and to chase away the clouds that are taking over our goodbye. I don't want the last conversation I have with Alexander to be all about Madeline.

He cracks the thinnest smile. "That's why I'm stepping in. I've already lost one son because he didn't feel like he belonged. I'm unwilling to lose anyone else. You, Evangeline Owen Pierce, belong with us. You don't have to be a Poe, or live at Dellbrook, or be in a relationship with my son. As far as I'm concerned, you're ours and we're yours, infinitely. Regardless of your blood or name. Neither of those is a choice, so how could they ever hold such weight?"

His words spin hope where only pain has been living, and I feel more certain than I ever have with his proclamation. I lean over and squeeze him tight, a few tears leaking out. He returns my hug, its warm comfort causing my head to spin. I slowly extract myself from his arms, knowing time is slipping away and there's one last goodbye on my list.

"Thank you. For everything," I tell him.

"I should have told you sooner," he says, nodding. He watches me go from his stool, eyes misty in the dim light. When I reach the door, I hear him stand.

"Eve," he says, and I turn. "All is not lost."

I make my way to Oliver's room, and with every step, the somberness of what's occurred takes over any love I feel at Alexander's words. The revelation of Paxton's death, his *suicide,* eats away at my core again, leaving me raw and replaying all my choices to get here. What if Madeline was right, and we all had a part to play? Regardless of her intention, Paxton is still dead. The repetition of fault terrorizes my dreams and now leaves me, heavy as stone, at Oliver's door.

Déjà vu breaks in, reminding me of the last time I did this. Instead of going in, I fled to New York. Never called him. Never wrote. Of course, I had the occasional internet stalking, but very little was ever to be found besides some poorly taken pap photo or a professional headshot in an article about his next book. It was never enough, and yet I did not bend. Alexander's words float back to me. *It's time to heal as a family.*

But today, today I would break.

I decide not to knock and instead just try the door. Astonishingly, it's unlocked. Oliver must believe his presence enough to keep unwanted guests out. *Or he wants to let you in.* I dash the thought away. None of it matters. Not now.

Inside is dim. The fire burnt down to embers, and a few lamps turned on. His bed is unmade, the scattering of papers still left on the floor amongst the kicked over books and torn pages. Oliver is hunched over his desk, staring at a blank canvas pen in his hand.

"Oliver," I whisper, not wanting to startle him if he hasn't already registered that I'm here.

When he doesn't answer, I move further in, shutting the door behind me. I dance my way around the mess until I'm directly behind his shoulders. My hand reaches to his back and I struggle not to feel my own pain at touching him and the memories it evokes.

"I wanted to say goodbye," I try.

Oliver sighs deep, leaning into my hand. I move it up to his nape so as not to get crushed in his chair and rub small circles unwittingly.

"And into this bizarrerie, as into all his others, I quietly fell; giving myself up to his wild whims with a perfect abandon," Oliver chokes out the Edgar quote. "Eve, he knew. He knew I would follow the path, that I would put each piece back in the puzzle. No matter the cost. He pulled up every painful moment in our life, every single one that has caused me to feel unruly, and, at times, insane. Things I have buried for years, I dug up. For him."

His words are kinetic, nerves ticking up with the pitch of his voice. He's struggling to hold it all together under the weight of his resolve. I turn his chair so he's facing me, shove my palms to his cheeks.

"You know what he left us?" he asks me. I shake my head, tears lining my eyes just from the shock of emotional chaos I see in Oliver's.

"Each other," he laughs, melodic in its sadness. "And a promise I made to him when I wasn't even old enough to understand what it meant. What am I supposed to do, Eve? What do I do?"

I look at Oliver, see the conflict amongst the devastation. He's unsteadied and unsure. I want to curl him into my arms, give him comfort and my own promises. Tell him that Paxton loved him. That I love him. The Eve from our past wouldn't hesitate. She would shield him from everything she could. She would take the broken pieces that were left and try to make them whole.

But I'm not the same girl I was when I left. Nor the one from the first day I returned. It took every day I've been here to find a path forward, and it wasn't because Oliver led me there. So, I know I can't lead him now. He has to find his own way forward.

"The only thing we can do. Live. Remember. *Heal.* Find help for the things we cannot shoulder alone. Try not to regret or make any more of our lives regrettable," I say to myself as much as to Oliver.

"Regrettable," he scoffs. "What you're asking is impossible. No matter what I do, I lose. If I keep my word, I'm right back here, trying to forget. If I don't..."

He eyes me, longing breaking through the despair. We both know where that road leads. The ghost of Paxton will haunt every moment we're togeth-er as long as Oliver holds each of us apart. I know I need to take away the option, to let his heart settle so he can find home again. Even if that means he feels alone.

"Oliver, I'm not ready to forgive," I say, forcing the words. My heart is in my throat, knowing that I'm putting everything at risk.

"I know. And... I don't think I'm ready to be forgiven," he responds, sinking lower into himself. He closes his eyes, then lazily kisses my palms, before removing my hands from him entirely.

"Are you going to be okay?" I ask.

"Someday. But for now, I'm going to accept that I'm not. And I think... I think it's time I got myself together."

Worry laces his tone for all the things he isn't saying. *Like Paxton never did for himself, but always wanted for me.* I know Oliver is punishing his nature and questioning every road he did not take. Asking himself, *would he still be alive if it were all different?* Nothing I can say will ease that guilt. Not when I'm fighting so much of my own.

Oliver turns and jots down something on paper. He then folds and stuffs it in my hand.

"Darkness, I want you to have this. No matter what happens, this was always my gift to you. I was just too stubborn to give it. Everything will be set up when you arrive. Just tell the doorman your name. And tell Isabel that I'm sorry." The ghost of a smile graces his lips as he says this, making me itch to see what he's written.

I fight the urge and instead pocket the note for later, knowing whatever it is, I don't need to quarrel with him on it now. There's an ease to this goodbye that I never thought I'd feel. Of course, it's doused in sadness, in the realization of our faults. And yet, it's the most truthful I've felt in so long. The most solid my feet have been on the path laid before me. It doesn't feel like the world is collapsing in this room, but that something tender is in bloom.

I'm not worrying that I'll never be a Poe, or if Oliver believes I'm worthy or not. I feel grounded in the fact that I am a Pierce. That I am a woman who has loved and lost. That I have stretched my heart across galaxies and found myself loved by the dark and the stars. I am broken and scattered and tormented, which is why I think this goodbye doesn't feel like the end.

The mournful romance of this moment has me leaning into Oliver, leaving the briefest kiss upon his mouth. My heart pounds at the softness. At the possibility, with or without him. That there's even a choice. He opens his eyes to stare into me, and I replay the Edgar quote that has felt inevitable since the moment Paxton used it.

"Even in the grave, all is not lost," I say out loud, readying us both for the next chapter of our lives.

And what a glorious story it will be.

EPILOGUE: FINAL THREAD

I LET OUT A string of curse words as the pot boils over. I want Annabel, my therapist, who suggested that I cook tonight, dead. There is never a good enough reason for me to be making more than a microwave dinner. *If only she wasn't doing so much good for my soul.*

The days are finally turning from soggy spring into the warming heat of summer in the city. While I dread the peak season that is fast approaching, where tourists will crowd the already crowded streets, right now I am happy with the long holiday weekend that is often found absent of New York's daily bustle.

The library, while normally my haven, has left me feeling cooped and confined this week. Never have I been so eager to leave its doors behind for several days before, making me question my sanity altogether.

What would Paxton say to see you like this?

The thought comes unbidden but not unwelcome. I have been learning to let him in, to unlock the chains holding the steel door of the crypt to my heart more open where the light could trickle through. Just as everything could change at dusk, so too could they alter in the dawn. I didn't have to suffer through one. I could love both, in their own ways. I wasn't great at it, but I was trying.

The sound of footsteps on the stairs outside my door causes me to hurdle across my kitchen to open it.

"Mom—" I start, but the word fades, turning to dust in my mouth.

Oliver stands just on the other side, his expensive black slacks cuffed messily at his boots. Just how he likes it. He's stripped down to a black tee that's rolled up his arms from the pull of his jacket, which is now slung along his bag. His dark head of curls is bent, making him a shadow among men. Then he looks up and catches me staring, the ghost of an apologetic smile on his lips.

"Not quite," his voice quips.

He's languid and cruel and honest with just his looks. A poet on the precipice of greatness. His presence alone makes me question morality and the things I would do if only to have one more chance to make everything right again. I feel the thick sludge of blood in my veins, my heart trying desperately to keep the rest of me going, but my brain is trying to shut it down. It knows I cannot survive another heartbreak.

"Darkness," he says in recognition. "You look good. Different, but good."

My hands bury themselves in my freshly cut hair, the flush in my neck the punishment for my embarrassment. I don't know what to say, stunned into silence and mind running blank. I'm stuck on a forked road with no logical destination.

"You can't stay silent forever. Are you going to at least invite me in?" he asks.

I move aside so he can step through the door. I couldn't legally keep him out if I wanted to. It was his home, after all. Well, *our* home. The one he'd bought for us, the summer when everything changed. The familiar scent of espresso and maple fills me as he passes, but the distinct wisp of whisky is gone. I look at him closely and notice there is no trace of glassy eyes or rosy cheeks to be found. Oliver Poe is sober. That fact alone causes me to scramble to find words.

"Oliver? I wasn't expecting you," I say, trying to be diplomatic and friendly, unsure of why he's come.

He ignores the subtle question in my voice, noting instead, "I like what you've done with the place. Very you. Very *us*."

He rolls the word *us* around like candy. A sweet delight he'd like to use again and again. I feel his flirty nature through my body, landing at my toes, daring me to curl them into my slippers. I resist, but just barely.

"Oliver," I say, void of the pleasantries. "Why are you here?"

The sight of him is not unwelcome, just surprising. Still, I'm not interested in games. Not anymore. He tosses his bag down before stretching out his frame, taking all the time to adjust his body just right so I can see the curves of a man who's put in the work. He sees me staring and prowls towards me, all moody grey and shadows in the falling sunlight. When he finally gets to me, his movements slow, so as not to spook, his thumb coming up to brush at my bottom lip.

"I came here for two reasons," he says like a secret. "One is for salvation. For redemption. I came here because *you* are here, Darkness. And I am done living in a time that can only be looked back on in reflection as a nightmare. I am ready for the dream."

My heart races, as if the finish line is happiness from this journey of challenging existence. I fear having hope from anything he's said. Fear wanting what he's offering, only to have it stripped away as it has before. As it will undoubtedly again. I cannot free fall into the chaos of loving Oliver Poe in the whisper of a moment. I cannot yet take a splintered boat to sea. We're still working on who we need to be.

My lip trembles at his touch and I do the only thing I can.

"And the other thing?" My words are choked and rotten. As if I could care about anything else. As if I should. But I need more time, more space, before I can answer.

Thankfully, Oliver gives it. He steps back on a knowing sigh, not at all deflated by my deflection. Each delicate suck of air goes down a little easier with every step he takes away. I watch as he reaches into the pocket of his jacket to produce an envelope.

"We cleaned everything out, Alexander, Madeline and me. Went through all his things. Put up the stuff we wanted to keep around, dispersed the rest." He thumbs the folds of the paper before continuing, "I found this. It only felt right to deliver it in person."

The pressure in my body sinks as Oliver walks back to hand it to me. I carefully unfold what he's given and see the familiar scratch of my name on the front. I flip it over and notice the dark gold wax seal holding it together, one name on its stamp. *Poe.*

"Oliver..." I say, tentative, unsure if I should open the pandemonium again. If I'm even ready to.

"It's ok, Eve. Madeline told me we all got one. My counselor thinks the letters were his goodbye." He rubs at the back of his neck. "You don't have to open it now. Or ever. But I thought you should have it."

I see the curiosity in his eyes, the hope that maybe my letter is different, even if he doesn't really believe it is. I feel the familiar pull of knowing, of chasing Paxton's riddles. *Come play with us, Paxton!* We'd scream. *Only if you solve the clues first,* he always responded. The memory is both haunting and healing.

"Thank you. I want to open it. I think... I think I need to," I say to him.

To his credit, he doesn't pester as I take my time tearing the top of it, woeful to break the actual seal. I want every piece he might have touched to stay as intact as possible. Oliver stays impossibly still, holding dominance over his desperation even as I pull out the paper inside where he cannot see. The first fold flops out and Paxton's signature assaults me. I can't help but read the end of the letter first.

```
Forgive him. Because regardless of the
truths we make of our lives, the univer-
sal one is that we're all broken. Messy.
Morbidly self-conscious and self-sabo-
taging. But there is so much love. To
give. To get. To hold. Even in the
obscurity of our connections. Even in
the midst of our reflections. And if
we don't take even a single moment to
recognize that life is going to pass us
by in the blink of an eye, and somehow,
we'll miss all of it. I had to learn
that the hard way. We all do. But at
least this way you'll be together. Like

you were always meant to be.
I am nothing if not a man of my promis-
es.
Forever yours,
Paxton Poe
```

"The boundaries which divide Life from Death are at best shadowy and vague. Who shall say where the one ends, and where the other begins?"—Edgar Allan Poe
P.S.
Riddles upon riddles. Lives upon lives.
We can live in multitudes, Eve.
December 13th—New York

My breath catches in my throat as I choke on the knot.

"Eve?" Oliver asks, eyes wide and pleading. "What does it say?"

I can't move, can't speak, wanting to deny the haunting curiosity inside me that's waking up. *In other words, I believed, and still do believe, that truth, is frequently of its own essence, superficial, and that, in many cases, the depth lies more in the abysses where we seek her, than in the actual situations wherein she may be found.* Edgar's quote floats through my head in a cloud of whimsy and suppressed hope that this isn't the end. Fate has found me once again.

My smile is timid, knowing I have to tell Oliver something and if there's anything I've learned since Paxton left us that first letter, it's that I cannot lie. Not to Oliver and, least of all, not to myself. I give myself three breaths before I steady my heart once again.

"How about we get a drink? I know a place."

The End.

QUOTE SOURCES, FUN FACTS, & FURTHER READING FOR THE TRUTHS WE MAKE

Author's note: I tried to include all the quotes and a few fun facts from this novel so you could continue your reading of these pieces in order of appearance. There are many additional Easter eggs that are not included in this list. Most of these are all in the public domain and predate the 1900s. The ones that are not, permissions are given, or they have fallen under fair use standards.

Austen, Jane, 1775-1817. Pride and Prejudice: a Novel. In Three Volumes: By the Author of "Sense and Sensibility". Chapter 31. London: Printed for T. Egerton, Military Library, Whitehall, 1813.

[S:1 - WORKS, 1850] - Edgar Allan Poe Society of Baltimore - Works - Poems - To —— [I heed not ...] (reprint)

Edgar Allan Poe. The Pit and the Pendulum (Short Story, 1842, 15 pages)

Giles, Ella A., Forgiveness, 1890, Local and National Poets of America

Neruda, Pablo, 1904-1973, One Hundred Love Sonnets, Sonnet XVII

Poe, Edgar Allan. "The Tell-Tale Heart." The Norton Anthology of American Literature, edited by Nina Baym, W.W. Norton & Company, 2016, pp. 287-291

Poe, Edgar Allan. (1903). The Works of Edgar Allan Poe, The Raven Edition, Volume 5. New York: P. F. Collier and Son.

Poetry Foundation. (n.d.). The Lotos-Eaters by Alfred, Lord Tennyson | Poetry Foundation.

*Fun fact (page 123) – Tennyson was inspired by the Odyssey when writing The Lotos-eaters. ()

Homer., & Fitzgerald, R. (1961). The Odyssey. Garden City, N.Y., Doubleday.

Poetry Foundation. (n.d.-a). She Walks in Beauty by Lord Byron (George Gordon) | Poetry Foundation.

Poetry Foundation. (n.d.-a). A Noiseless Patient Spider by Walt Whitman | Poetry Foundation.

Poetry Foundation. (1999). The Moon is distant from the Sea – (387) by Emily Dickenson | Poetry Foundation.

Academy of American Poets. (2014). The silence. Poets.org.

*Fun Fact (page 199) – Ariadne is the savior of Theseus in Greek Mythologies Labyrinth story. She was the daughter of King Minos and was believed to be betrayed by her love, Theseus, after helping him. ()

Charlotte Bronte. Jane Eyre. Chapter 23.

Edgar Allan Poe Society of Baltimore - Works - Poems - Romance (Text-05b). (n.d.).

Henry David Thoreau. | The Walden Woods Project. (2024, January 19). The Walden Woods Project.

The Project Gutenberg eBook of the Masque of the Red Death, by Edgar Allan Poe. (n.d.).

The cask of Amontillado. (2021, July 3).

The Early Poems of Alfred Lord Tennyson by Lord Alfred Tennyson: Madeline. (n.d.).

Tracey, L. (2023). "The Murders in the Rue Morgue" by Edgar Allan Poe: annotated. JSTOR Daily.

Giordano, R. (n.d.). The Premature Burial by Edgar Allan Poe. PoeStories.com.

Poe, E. (1903). The Unparalleled Adventures of One Hans Pfaal. The Works of Edgar Allan Poe (Lit2Go Edition). Retrieved July 22, 2024, from https://etc.usf.edu/lit2go/147/the-works-of-edgar-allan-poe/5257/the-unparalleled-adventures-of-one-hans-pfaal/

CONTENT WARNINGS LIST

Alcoholism
Abuse (child & adult/physical & mental)
Sexual assault
Death
Grief
Cancer
Murder
Suicide
Familial violence
Torture
Strong language

ACKNOWLEDGEMENTS

Everyone claims writing is a solitary act, though, in my experience, that has hardly been the case. Sure, there are moments of complete isolation and loneliness. But without the care, guidance, community, and service of so many other people, this book would not exist. And although I'm terrified (and because of Murphy's Law, sure) that I'll forget someone, I am determined to do my best to wrangle up my thank you's.

To my mother, who will never get to read this book but whose existence shaped so many of its pages.

To my first draft readers, Kayla Hill, Kylie Niedermeyer, and Casey Provost-St. John (who has read almost every reiteration of this book). You all gave me the tools to shape this story into more than I thought it could be. I cannot thank you enough for your time and grace.

To my beta readers, the support you have shown this book is unmatched. Thank you for all the screaming comments and teary DMs. For showing up and reviewing and sharing and posting about this book. You know who you are and know that this story would not be the same without you.

To Jess Robling, who became my person all because of this book (and her determination that it is an entire personality). You have championed me every step of the way and I am beyond lucky to call you my friend. Thank you for flying across states to meet a stranger and traipse through Boston with me all for the sake of this story.

To my indie publishing heroes: Rose Bentley, Rachel Bellamy, Sarah Richhelm, JP sina, Lizzie Brown, Thea Verdone, Jamye Smith and Emily Rath. You have all let me pepper you with questions, send obnoxious voice notes, sat on facetimes with me, and just been the best cheerleaders for this journey that a girl could ask for. Without your guidance and friendships, all the trials of this journey may have beaten me.

To Kaitlyn Mitchell, who over the last four years has pulled me from the edge of quitting more than I'd like to admit. For every time I said, *I'm done,* she insisted, *just one more book.*

To the writing communities I have been a part of and all the writers I've met through them, I am so grateful to know you. There are too many to list but your kindnesses have not been overlooked. Whether it was one interaction or a million, you changed the courses of my days.

To Sapir Frozenfar, who never misses a call or text (even when she's in a meeting) and is always the first to make my emotional distress an emergency. I don't want to imagine a world without your friendship.

To all the readers who clamored for this book, you are the best. Without you, this story would be aimless.

And finally, to my husband, who believes in me without exception. Who will sit for hours in the car, parked outside of our house, just so we can curate the perfect playlist. Who listened to me read chapters aloud, let me sit in complete silence so I could think, and told me it's ok to change my mind to make sure I'm happy. You're the reason love stories exist. Thank you.

9 7 9 8 9 9 9 1 0 1 1 8 0 8